NETHERFORD HALL

ALSO BY NATANIA BARRON

Queens of Fate
Queen of None
Queen of Fury
Queen of Mercy

Love in Netherford
Netherford Hall
The Viscount St. Albans
The Game of Hearts

The Godlings Saga
Pilgrim of the Sky
Gods of Londinium

These Marvelous Beasts
Frost & Filigree
Masks & Malevolence
Time & Temper

Rock Revival

ℕETHERFORD ℋALL

LOVE IN NETHERFORD VOLUME I

NATANIA BARRON

SOLARIS

First published 2024 by Solaris
an imprint of Rebellion Publishing Ltd,
Riverside House, Osney Mead,
Oxford, OX2 0ES, UK

www.solarisbooks.com

ISBN: 978-1-83786-334-1

A CIP catalogue record for this book is available
from the British Library.

Designed & typeset by Rebellion Publishing

*For every queer heart
who wished for their Darcy.*

CHAPTER ONE
ꟼETHERFORD

THE GENTLEWITCH HAD at last returned to Netherford, and Poppy Brightwell was unmoved. All week long carts had come from London, laden with housewares, furniture, flowers, and trunks—and the entire town was in an uproar. There had been hardly time to prepare, after all, for though they had heard word of the tragic fire claiming the lives of nearly all the Rookwood witches a year ago, there had been no indication they would be returning to their ancestral country home. Especially given its lacklustre state.

Yet here she was: Liege Edith Rookwood herself.

Poppy's elder sister, Viola, peered out of the front parlour windows of Harrow House and let out an appreciative sigh. The Brightwells, like no one else in town, would have the closest proximity to the gentlewitch, as they were her tenants. Their parents had rented Harrow House from the Rookwoods for the last fifteen years, after relocating from Northamptonshire.

"Poppy, you should see the size of the coach!" Viola said, turning to her sister. As always, the eldest Brightwell daughter dressed neat as a pin, even in her simple day dress of creamy white muslin. Her thick, dense curls were braided and twisted back with precision away from her slender neck. "I've never seen such a thing."

"You must beg Mama to get out more," said Poppy,

sticking her needle in at the wrong angle, and briefly considering giving up altogether. "There are plenty of good, sturdy carriages in Netherford on any given day."

"*You* should know, you spent all last spring poised at the window waiting for Captain Evans to visit," said Viola. "Such a shame you didn't take pity and marry him."

Captain Evans was a very nice man, and for a time Poppy had thought she might be the sort of person to make him happy. But, like so many things in her life, their love had been just a season.

"If you like him so much, *you* should have pursued him," said Poppy. "You do go on about him."

"Oh, shoo, Poppy. I jest. But truly—this coach is a work of art," said Viola. She pulled herself from the window, her dark amber eyes kindled with mischief. "And there's an entire cart full of flowers behind it."

Poppy sighed, resigned to her curiosity at last. "If you're lying about the flowers, I shall be quite cross."

Casting her embroidery—an interlacing bluebell design she had been fussing over for a week—to the sofa, Poppy joined her sister at the large windows. She could see all the way up the slope to Netherford Hall, the great, sprawling Tudor mansion owned by the Rookwood witches and left derelict for more than a century, barring necessary repairs. Despite its state, Poppy loved the house with her whole heart, and harboured a great deal of envy for its new owners.

"How they can get peonies, I have no idea," said Viola, gesturing to the laden cart. "I suppose it's a coven secret."

"Or a good greenhouse and a clever gardener," said Poppy.

"Truly, Poppy, I would have thought you'd be beside yourself with joy, given your preoccupation with the Hall."

Preoccupation, indeed! Poppy's clandestine visits to Netherford Hall had begun when she was but a child. And that was at an end, now. Not even Viola knew.

Before Poppy could say anything more, however, a figure disembarked from the largest carriage, eschewing help from the footman and hopping down on a pair of impeccably shiny black boots.

Even at this distance, Poppy could make out the figure's bright red hair, cut in a masculine fashion, and the strong nose. Well, no mistake, that had to be the gentlewitch. She wore an impeccably tailored waistcoat-and-pantaloon combination, with a feathered hat, and a long, black velvet cape about her shoulders, trimmed in black fur.

For a moment, the gentlewitch turned her gaze away from the high towers of Netherford Hall and its myriad diamond-shaped glass windows and down the slope toward where the young women sat peeking. Poppy could swear they locked eyes.

But then Viola squealed and drew the curtains back, laughing. "Oh, I know what we must do! We must go to town. For surely there will be news and we can hear all the gossip. Besides, you need a new ribbon for your hat."

Poppy knew better than to argue with her sister, but then again never took much convincing to go to Miss Rawlings-Vijay's delightful shop. And if she had to look at the new gentlewitch out that window for one more second, she might actually go mad with envy.

IT IS A truth universally acknowledged that a young gentlewitch, in possession of great magical acumen and significant landholdings, is rarely in want of a wife. Yet that was not so for Edith Rookwood, Gentlewitch of Netherford Hall.

Liege Edith Rookwood, her young cousin Henry, and their uncle, Auden Garcliffe, were all that remained of the Rookwood coven, famed across the Empire as necromancers and advisors. A coven, especially one of the High Houses, typically held dozens of witches, relations, attendants and servants. The gentlewitch employed a majordomo, an ancient position typically held by a non-magical male relation, who assisted in her extensive affairs. She would rely on her extended family and social connections to rise through the ranks, work for the good of England, potentially sit on the Coven Council at Parliament, and occasionally perform acts of arcane power.

But Edith Rookwood had never been expected to rise to such a rank, and nor had her uncle, her majordomo, been intended for his position. Theirs was truly a coven of one— for want of issue, for many years, and most recently by dint of tragedy.

Were they a superstitious sort of folk, they might have ascribed this ill-fortune as a curse. But neither Liege Rookwood nor Mr Garcliffe saw the world in such a way: the Rookwood coven was known far and wide for a staunch kind of practicality. Difficult times were not ascribed any significance, for they were merely the result of living in the oft-chaotic mortal world. Gentlewitches were not immortal, but they were preternatural, their power stemming from an ages-old pact between the now-vanished fae and their legendary progenitor, Navia the First.

It had only started to feel personal about a year earlier, with the tragic fire at Hatchney House, the Rookwoods' primary residence in London. Lady Edith's mother, Georgina, and Georgina's sister Cassandra, were lost, along with the servants—and the majority of the family's belongings, including a sizable wardrobe and, most heartbreakingly, the entirety of their beloved library.

Little Henry, at ten years old, was the only soul left alive, found beneath some rubble by what had once been the pantry. Though coven-born, he was without the craft. He was simply a little boy with a keen mind who liked to collect butterflies and climb trees. It had fallen to Cassandra to continue the line, and they had all hoped she might foster a more powerful daughter before long. Alas, there was no hope in Henry; even should he once father a child, the gift could not be conveyed through a son. Yes, adoption was always a possibility, to inherit the property—but magic, alas, was conveyed by blood.

And although Liege Edith had passed the Harrowing, proving her arcane powers, she had shown no exceptional merit. She was a witch, the council concluded, but not a particularly talented one. In most things she resembled typical London gentry: well-educated, well-dressed, and entirely in control of her emotions. Perhaps a little too in control of her emotions, given the circumstances.

A year had passed since the tragic fire, and the initial shock was over, though the loss still lingered on the edge of every conversation between Edith and her uncle Auden.

Netherford Hall was the Rookwood country residence, frequently referred to as 'that Tudor monstrosity,' for it was little changed since its initial construction. A century or so of wilful neglect in favour of London's modern amenities made it even less appealing, what with the mildew, the encroaching vegetation, and considerable animal life. To say nothing of the thousands of leaded glass windows peppered across the entire house, all in need of a rigorous cleaning that no simple charm could manage.

Yet there was no choice. They simply could not subsist in London as matters stood.

"I am planning to go to town tomorrow morning with Henry," announced Uncle Auden on yet another grey autumn afternoon, just as they were settling in to the house.

"Very well," said Edith, unbothered.

Edith stood at the large, honeycomb windows overlooking the green rolling hills of Netherford, standing perfectly still, as she had a habit doing. In her suit of deepest azure, adorned only with the silver and gold chains of her rank, along with her chatelaine.

"You could come with us," said Uncle Auden. Though her uncle, he was only seven years Edith's senior, at thirty-five. Unlike Edith, and many of the Rookwoods, Auden was possessed of a cheery disposition and sunny countenance that seemed at odds with Netherford Hall.

No, he and Edith could not have contrasted more with one another, in either their interior or exterior existences; and yet Auden had spent a good deal of his youth caring for Edith directly. She doubted anyone else knew her as well as he did. And they nurtured a fierce affection for one another.

Auden's sweet countenance, however, belied his once rakish life, living life to its fullest among London's most fashionable and notorious elite. No one had expected he'd inherit the title of majordomo to the gentlewitch, least of all him, and he'd sucked the very marrow out of his youth.

Now Edith saw the burden of it heavy on his shoulders, and it made her heart ache.

"That would require being in the presence of other human beings, and frankly, overseeing the cleaning out of the old larder already turned my stomach enough," Edith replied.

"Oh, Edith, they would love to see you," said Uncle Auden. "And we should do everything possible to get to know the folk here." His voice echoed in the cavernous great hall, once the jewel of the house. Now it was two steps away from a barn—and that was *after* they had spent almost two weeks trying to remove the bats to better locations; there were still piles of guano in the corners that had proved impossible to remove either by hand or spell.

Not that the spells even worked that well. Ancestral home or not, Edith was not yet attuned to Netherford, and until she was...

"Who did you say the family was at Harrow House? Our tenants?" Edith changed the topic, as was her wont when the conversation displeased her.

"The Brightwells," said Auden.

"You say that with such mild inflection I cannot tell if you approve of them."

Uncle Auden cleared his throat, a sure sign of discomfiture. "If you recall from their letters, they are somewhat a diminished family. Though certainly not below our acquaintance. What with their children, and Mr. Brightwell's illnesses, they are considered by some rather desperate. As of yet, payment has always been prompt."

"Ah," said Edith. "Four children, if I recall."

"That is correct," said Auden. "Minor gentry through the mother's side, but a blended family on the father's— Mr. Brightwell's mother was descendent of the Chief of Merchants himself, Mulla Abdul Ghafur. Or so our records indicate. Though they have some connection to the Dowager Viscountess St. Albans."

"I see," said Edith. "Though clearly, despite that pedigree, they have fallen on more challenging times. Am I right in remembering that Mr. Brightwell is quite ill?"

She raised a gloved hand to smooth away some of the moisture building upon the glass. In a few weeks, it would be cold enough to freeze over, and she couldn't imagine that being good for the house.

If she looked hard enough, Edith could just spot the chimneys of Harrow House, where the Brightwells lived, across one of the tributaries of the River Rothley. Smoke trailed high into the milky white sky, and there was a good deal of moss on what she could see of the roof. For a brief moment earlier, she had thought she'd spied one of the young women peering through the windows at her, a lovely oval face with a riot of black curls.

"Sadly, yes. Should I invite them for tea?" said Auden. He sounded a little impatient, and what the with mound of work he had to tackle—sorting through deeds, matching old sums, arranging for their furniture and deliveries—Edith could not blame him. Not to mention *staffing* this place. But that was a process, even out here in the country, and it required speaking to locals. *Who*, exactly, Edith hadn't the faintest idea. In London there were firms for everything: Warder guilds, first and foremost, as well as registries for ash-touched families who could work safely alongside a gentlewitch.

"Not today, but perhaps next week," Edith said at last. "For now, you are quite right. We must look to staff the house with what funds we have, visit the farms, take stock of what is left and try and move forward."

DESPITE THE WET weather, Netherford itself was significantly less dreary than the mansion, and Auden Garcliffe found himself almost enjoying the bustle of carts, farmers, merchants, and school children. Little Henry, for his part, kept quiet and out of the way, which he did not always do, while Auden tried to navigate the stone-faced houses to the main crossroads.

As all good gentlewitch-blessed towns went, Netherford boasted a hexafoil-carved stone in its very centre. This massive monument stood taller than some of the houses and, to Auden's surprise given the state of Netherford Hall, was quite pristine. Though the gentlewitches no longer collected harvest tithes, preferring bargains and promises and spiritual tithes, there were still baskets of bread, berries, and wreaths strewn about the base of the monument. There was even a little beaded bracelet that Henry tried to grab.

"No, no," said Auden, gently replacing the bracelet. "This is not for us."

"It is for cousin Edith, so I will take it to her," Henry said, hope in his big, brown eyes. "I will be very responsible."

Auden smiled at Henry's childish logic—they had oft discussed the concept of responsibility of late. "Yes, that is quite gallant of you. But it's been quite some time since the gentlewitch herself was in town, and were we to take everything here, it might raise some questions."

"No one's come to the house at all, though. And there are so many people here," said Henry, staring at a passing gaggle of school children in matching green cloaks and straw hats. "Is that strange?"

"Not in the least. There are many rules around gentlewitches in the country, and I am afraid even I am unaware of most of them," said Uncle Auden.

"But they came 'round all the time back home. People, I mean. So many ringing bells."

"It's true, we did have lots of visitors when we lived in London." Uncle Auden swallowed back on a suddenly thick throat as Henry nodded in agreement. Grief came to him in unexpected gales, it seemed, even as the year had come and gone.

It was not easy to explain to Henry the nuances of what a gentlewitch must do to secure her land and her home and her people. If he was honest with himself—which, to his credit, he most often was—he didn't even know the half of it. His sister Cassandra, the more gregarious of his siblings, had given him some training, but the most she required was that he function as a loving, supporting figure for his nephew. Uncle Astor, the previous majordomo, could have lived a hundred more years, and Auden would have had no need to expand his repertoire.

Deep in his thoughts, Auden found himself wandering into a small modiste's shop, more to get out of the wind than to buy anything. Spirits knew he did not have much in the way of frivolous spending money, but the stripes and ribbons drew his attention anyway. He did always enjoy a bit of frippery.

There were three young women in the store, two browsing the ribbons and one behind the counter. They all looked to the windblown pair as they entered, and Auden forced a bright smile.

"Good day, good day. A bit blustery, I'm afraid," he said, patting the front of his vest as if it might agree with him on the subject. One never could go wrong discussing the weather in mixed company.

"Good day, sir," said the striking young woman behind the counter. Her thick, glossy black hair was pinned somewhat haphazardly with an enormous gold and blue enamelled hairpin, framing her heart-shaped face. Her eyes—brimstone! Full of cleverness and dark as a lake at midnight, and framed by arched, dense brows. She wore a velvet collar on her saffron-hued topcoat—a terribly modern outfit for such an out-of-the way locale—which brought out the gorgeous bronze of her skin. Auden had to tear his eyes from her in order to avoid looking rude. Very beautiful. Distractingly so.

"I'm Mr Garcliffe," Auden said. This was not, exactly, the best way of going about such an introduction to townsfolk, but he did not have a valet to aid him. "And this is Henry. We've come from Netherford Hall."

Both of the other women turned in concert, then, their bonnets framing their faces, like sunflowers flipping in a vase. Sisters, he was sure of it: their brows and lips bore the same sweet lines, their dense curls the same black-brown hue. One was starkly prim, with perfectly curled forelocks, a flawlessly starched collar, and not one thread out of place on the elaborate hem of her frock. The other, her hair haphazardly thrown up under her bonnet, was earthier, taller, and strong; yet her intense gaze struck Auden immediately with its piercing intelligence.

"This is Miss Viola and Miss Poppy Brightwell," said the shop owner, as each of the women curtseyed. Viola was the immaculate one; Poppy the one with the disconcertingly enchanting eyes and, Auden noticed, a soiled hemline.

"And this is Miss Rawlings-Vijay," said Viola, gesturing to the modiste with a pristine gloved hand. "She's the owner and proprietor of this much cherished business."

"How grand," said Auden. "I am quite relieved to see such a lovely shop in town. Liege Rookwood is in need of a new suit—I presume you are able to accommodate such a request?"

Viola's eyes went wide at the mention of the gentlewitch herself, but Poppy looked almost bored. Curious woman, Auden decided, but rather than linger on her, he turned to Miss Rawlings-Vijay.

"Indeed, I am capable of attiring both men and women, and anyone in between," Miss Rawlings-Vijay said smoothly.

"Wonderful. I shall return with more specific instructions. Today, however—Henry, please leave those baubles alone—I am not here shopping but rather seeking advice. You see, we've been in and out of the house for a few weeks now, but we are in need of..." Auden hadn't yet figured out how to say this exactly, for it sounded so strange. "Assistance."

Miss Rawlings-Vijay's cheery face went a bit blank for a moment, and then she nodded. "Yes, of course. My condolences, as well. We all grieved to hear the news."

Auden could not say why, but the sincerity of Miss Rawlings-Vijay's kind words made him blink back tears. The Brightwell women nodded and repeated their sympathies.

"For assistance with gentlewitch matters, you'd start at the pub, of course," said Poppy Brightwell, pulling ahead of her sister. There was some resistance there, Viola vainly trying to grab her sister's hand and keep her out of the conversation.

"The pub?" asked Auden. "They are—ah, well, *prepared* for this sort of thing, I assume?"

Viola answered instead of Poppy. "Indeed, the staff at the Holly and Sickle have always been the most welcoming in town for such things. But what my sister means is that the Hodes are Warders."

"It's a point of pride, I should say, in towns like Netherford, to always be ready and prepared for such a circumstance," said Poppy. "You'll want to talk to Molly Hode first."

There was a lingering note of judgment in Poppy's voice, though, and Auden tucked that away in his mind for later. She was not *disapproving*, exactly, but she did imply what Auden knew to be a potential wedge between Edith and the townsfolk: it had been generations since a Rookwood gentlewitch had deigned to come to the country. And Netherford Hall, itself, was in disrepair. It reflected badly on the townsfolk, even if they had no say in the matter.

Still, the young Brightwell women were curiously keen on this subject, Auden thought, for country gentlefolk. But perhaps he had just spent too long in the city, taking advantage of the coven's considerable resources. If you needed appropriate staff, you simply went to the Coven Housing Bureau. He'd never imagined visiting a pub to find a Warder.

Moving to the country had its drawbacks, but he was trying to enumerate the positives and finding himself overwhelmed. He missed the press and bustle of London like an absent lover; what he wouldn't give to smell the belching coal fires, hear the carriages constantly shuffling by, and eat Gadsby's fish pie again!

"Our first line of business will be finding a cook, I imagine," said Auden, steering the conversation back to seeking a recommendation from Miss Rawlings-Vijay and the Brightwells. "There are just three of us right now, but we are sadly out of sorts when it comes to the kitchen."

"Uncle Auden is a terrible cook," said Henry, making a face. "He gave me cheese yesterday that tasted like old socks."

"Say nothing more," said Miss Rawlings-Vijay, with a kindness that Auden appreciated after Henry's damning, if fair, assessment. "In the interim, do not hesitate to take whatever you need from the shrine, of course. It's an old practice, and no doubt a little confusing if you're unfamiliar with country ways."

"There's more than we can carry, Uncle," Henry said, pulling on Auden's cuff, "but the berries looked delicious."

"We can arrange for our gardener to deliver them to you at the gate," said Viola, as her sister scowled at her.

"I would appreciate that immensely," said Auden, smiling through embarrassment. Not for the last time, he quite wished he'd spent more time in London learning about keeping house for a gentlewitch than carousing with the lads.

Viola smiled. "Say nothing of it. It's the least we can do."

"Of course," said Poppy, though the reluctance in her voice did not escape Auden. "We are here to help."

THE RAIN BEGAN in earnest just as Auden and Henry left the clothier's, but thankfully the pub—the Holly and Sickle—was easy to find and both open and dry. It smelled as so many pubs did, of sawdust and salt and ale, but it was neat and bright. In fact, the Holly and Sickle was *pristine*. The floors were smooth, pale wood, the walls matched the wattle and daub of the exterior, and the bar top gleamed in copper and tile, shades of green and gold accenting the hammered spiral motifs.

The ceiling was strewn with ribbons tied with witch's wishes, not terribly uncommon in pubs, but unusual in such numbers. Amidst the long, colourful ribbons were bunches of herbs, mostly culinary, in neat rows and patterns. There was a kind of symmetry to the whole business.

Still, the pub's protective spells washed over Auden as he passed over the threshold, a welcome familiarity. He knew the feel of magic, and this reminded him of fresh baked bread, malt syrup, tart apples, and oats. Rather appropriate, he thought, as his stomach grumbled.

There were two figures behind the bar top, one man and one woman, and they were so alike in bearing and colouring that they had to be siblings, if not twins. Each of them was broad about the shoulders, square of jaw, and red of hair. Twin pale eyes set in freckled faces. But the woman's face was interrupted by a web of scars that obliterated one eyebrow and curled down the edges of her eye. The man wore a dusty apron, and the woman wore her hair in a long, thick braid. The man was slim, however, where the woman was all muscle.

At the chiming of the bell—or perhaps alerted by the wards—they both turned to Auden and Henry and nodded.

"Well, it's about time," said the woman, in a deep, honeyed voice.

Auden, not accustomed to being spoken to with such familiarity from pub staff, looked behind him a moment to make sure someone else wasn't standing there.

"Oh, yes," he said, awkwardly. "I am here."

"*She* is here," corrected the man. "I suppose you're ready to begin staffing now."

Feeling his face flush at this stunning lack of decorum,

but being too well-mannered to question it, Auden nodded. "Indeed. I'm looking for Molly Hode."

"You've found her," said the woman, rolling up her sleeves and coming around the bar to get a better look at Auden. "I'm Molly."

"Good," said Auden, as it was the only thing he could think to say with any conviction. Truly, he was wondering if Molly was planning on using her impressive biceps to deliver a blow to the side of his head.

"I'm Henry! I like birds. And I'm very hungry. It smells like apples in here. Do you have apples?" Henry said.

They all turned to look at the boy, who seemed entirely unaware of the woman's looming menace.

"Well, Henry, I've got quite an affinity for birds myself," said Molly, her tone softening. "And this, over here, is my brother, Basil. While I don't think birds are quite his fancy, food is. If you hop up on the barstool there, he'll see you fed."

Henry's eyes went wide as saucers, a brilliant smile spreading on his lips. Before Auden could stop him, the boy was clambering up the barstool and making conversation with Basil who, at least from this distance, appeared to be considerably gentler and more softly spoken than his sister.

Molly wasted no time.

"My office," she said to Auden. When he hesitated slightly, glancing back at the boy, she snorted and said, "He'll be safe. Even if I wanted to hurt him, I couldn't."

Which wasn't a wholly comforting thought.

Molly's office was a picture of practicality: a writing desk, a high-backed wicker chair, neatly folded journals, and a small window, high up. It smelled of beeswax and cigar smoke and dog, the latter on account of the wolfhound asleep by the sparse little fire.

Auden took the seat Molly indicated, prepared to listen.

Molly slowly sank into her own seat. For a woman without means beyond an inn, she was nonetheless commander of the space. Her slightly lopsided stare made Auden—already physically her inferior—feel even smaller and he wondered if he should have tried harder to convince Edith to join him.

Not that anything he did could have convinced her. When Edith set her mind to something, no matter how unreasonable or incongruous, there really was no room for debate. And as she was the witch of the family now, Auden had to concede eventually. They were both new at their jobs, both still reeling from grief mingled with guilt at having escaped their family's fate; it was acceptable that they endure missteps. And yet, Auden could not help but feel entirely out of his element. He'd spent most of his time flirting, drinking, and impressing the non-preternatural sector with his poor enchanting skills while the rest of his family did the hard work.

"It's been more than one hundred years since we had a gentlewitch here in Netherford" Molly said. "It used to be that Netherford Hall saw at least some occupants in the warmer months, considering the location, but I have to admit I never thought I'd see the day a majordomo walked into my inn asking for help."

Auden, already confused, offered a simple reply: "In my defence, I am a very new majordomo. In fact, to date, you are the only person to actually use that title, since, well, everything that's happened."

"Lucky me," said Molly, apparently unconcerned with extending sympathies. "I take it you are unfamiliar with the situation, then. The requirements. The rules and regulations."

"Well, I've lived my entire life in London," Auden said, as if that was enough to explain away his near-childlike understanding of his duties.

Molly's lips thinned. "Ah. I suppose you just went straight to the Bureau whenever you needed help up at the house. Hatchney, wasn't it?"

"Yes, that was what we called the house," Auden replied. It felt like speaking of the dead. In a way it was.

"My father worked there for a few years when things were meagre around here," Molly mused. "Told me it was 'a Baroque nightmare.' Had a love of architecture, Dad did. But no matter where in the world he'd been, Netherford Hall was always his favourite house. In fact, it's my family—and a few others in the town—who've kept up the house over the years."

It was hard to imagine anyone had *ever* 'kept Netherford Hall up,' but Auden conceded that it could have—and likely should have—been worse. Bats and guano aside, the hearths were clean for the most part, the furniture was covered and tied, the musical instruments stored in dry areas, and someone had even gone to the trouble of repairing some of the roof tiles. It was an ancient house, and it had ancient house problems, but nothing truly derelict.

"Thank you for that," Auden said.

"In London," continued Molly, holding up a thick finger, "the Pact is done perfunctorily. Much the way someone goes into any apprenticeship. But there are dozens, if not hundreds, of witches in London to choose from, and that magic is... *broad*, for lack of a better term."

Molly knew so much more about any of this, and Auden wished for a brief moment that he could simply back out of the tavern altogether and go back to the modiste's. At least there was pleasant conversation there, and ribbons without bones tied to them.

"Yes, I'm familiar with general contracts," he agreed, having not even the faintest idea that there were other ways of hiring help through the Pact.

"London is a place of wonders, and I do not want you to think I disrespect its old, meandering magic. But it is not the way we do business here. Netherford village has four hundred residents. The nearby hamlets of Gorge and Mornock have another two hundred combined. We have eleven great houses within that boundary, and they employ the vast majority of folk here. Yet many people in Pact families have spent generations in waiting."

"Waiting?"

Molly gave him a pitying look. "They really didn't tell you a thing, did they?"

"They might have," said Auden, feeling sheepish. "But I'm afraid I might not have always been the best listener."

"You're the son of witches," said Molly with a shrug. "I know the sort."

He would have argued, but she had a point.

"So, what is required? Is there a handbook? A pamphlet?" Auden had scarcely said the words out loud before he regretted them. Molly gave him such a look of disgust that he flushed.

"No. We do not have... *pamphlets*," Molly said, voice dripping disdain. "You have *me*. I run the Holly and Sickle. My family has had an establishment here since before the Domesday Book. We don't have fancy titles, but we do hold the key to two very important aspects of work here: like all witch pubs in England, we have a portal; and like all Warders, we make wards."

Now Auden was utterly shocked. Portal pubs were quite common in London—they were the best way to travel around the city, established by none other than Virginia Cawley, the High Witch herself—but he never imagined somewhere as far out as Netherford would be so connected.

Molly continued, and if she noted Auden's look of surprise, she gave no indication. "It's an old portal, and not as fast or reliable as the sort you're likely familiar with in London. It hasn't been used for some time and is in need of repair. But we should be able to do just that."

"So I can get to London if I needed?"

"Not at present, but once it's fixed, yes. It's not limited to England, either. It's trans-continental and bi-directional."

By all the rivers above and below. Auden had used many of the London pub portals in his day, usually half-drunk and half-mad, but they didn't possess any of the complexities of design like Molly described.

"I'm quite certain Edith will do everything she can to help with this matter," Auden said, even though he had no idea if she had a proclivity for such magic. Likely not.

But a quick escape to London? It was too good to be true.

However, though he might not have been the brightest man in the country, he knew an adversary when he saw one. She was clever. Molly had something he needed, and he would have to play by her rules.

"I would hope so," Molly said. She reached into one of the top drawers of her desk and pulled out a long scroll. It looked older than Netherford Hall, and at least half covered in a scribble of old calligraphy and marginalia. "Now, to the matter at hand."

"Yes, of course."

"There were thirteen Pact families. The Dute family line tragically ended about sixty years ago when Mam Dute vanished. The Harpoles are the most numerous, but they also have a reputation for eccentricity. Which may or may not be something the gentlewitch is looking for."

"Truly, we just need reliable staff. I can do most of the interviews," Auden offered.

"It's very kind of you to offer, Mr. Garcliffe, but there is no way to go about this work without direct collaboration between the gentlewitch herself, the majordomo, and the

Warder." She paused for effect. "That's me. And, technically, my brother. We're twins, and so we share the title."

Warders had a single kind of magic: protective charms. And every gentlewitch needed that. Good, deep magic was only possible with the safety provided by a Warder, and when they collaborated well, the town would prosper. London had its own Warder Guard, so it was not necessary to employ individuals—one of the many benefits of living there.

Of course, the converse was also true. Should the Warder and the gentlewitch fail to work together, it could usher in a season of ruin.

"I see," said Auden, although he truly did not.

"I suggest we begin tomorrow morning. I simply need a formal invitation to begin the process."

Auden tapped his pocket for paper he knew wasn't there, as if he could will a glorious invitation into being, in gold writing, with just enough of a spell to move the ink. It was the sort of thing his sister Cassandra would have loved. She had always been fond of the fanciful.

"I am afraid you have once again found me lacking," said Auden.

Molly grinned, showing her white, uneven teeth. "Oh, no formalities required. I simply need a verbal invitation for our first visit. As majordomo, you hold that power."

"Oh." He paused. "Does the wording matter?" He was sweating now, his armpits damp and his neck prickling with it.

"Not really," Molly said, standing.

He stood, and held out his hand. "Then I formally invite you, Molly Hode, and your brother Basil, to Netherford Hall, at the request of the gentlewitch herself. Tomorrow morning. After breakfast. But not too soon after breakfast."

"That will do, I suppose," Molly said, holding out her hand to clasp his own.

At first, Auden felt nothing. Just the calloused skin of the Warder's palms against his own. He was about to let go, worrying about the growing sweatiness he presented, when he jolted like a hooked fish. Indeed, that's what it felt like: as if someone had twisted a fishline around his spine and pulled.

Molly nodded. "There we go. Set in bone."

Auden did not stay long enough to inquire as to what that meant. He had quite enough of today's adventures, thank you very much.

CHAPTER TWO
HARROW HOUSE

"I CANNOT IMAGINE such a man surviving Molly Hode!" Mama was saying as Poppy described the scene at Miss Rawlings-Vijay's. "Oh, Poppy, you should have given him some warning."

Poppy nudged the last bit of jam from her toast to the edge of her spoon and gave her mother a wicked smile. "Well, who else would I have sent him to? We're not a Pact family. I was just being as helpful as possible."

Papa, who was sketching in his notebook in preparation for another of his watercolors, looked up. "You could have considered sending them to Burrier's, you know. At least they'd have had a good meal before being thrown directly into the flames. You must remember that the gentlewitch and her family are Londoners."

"Well, neither Miss Rawlings-Vijay nor Viola were any help," Poppy said. "Everyone was just gawking at Mr. Garcliffe and his damask waistcoat—and I admit he is a handsome fellow, if you measure him by the standards of London, but that's no excuse to be useless."

"I was not 'useless,'" Viola protested from the doorway. She had just come in from outside, her cheeks flushed from the cool air, looking lovely in that way she always managed without any effort. "I have just directed Hounslow to take the cart and ensure that Netherford Hall has enough food for a week. And we've got some townsfolk now to help with any other deliveries."

"That was very thoughtful of you, darling," said Mama, walking to her eldest daughter and putting her arm around her shoulders. Side by side, Viola and Margella Brightwell could have been sisters, though Margella's hair had long ago turned altogether white—prematurely, but strikingly. They were both willowy and petite, pretty in the way that made portrait painters swoon, though Viola had the coppery skin of the Brightwell family, rather than her mother's pale fawn tones.

Poppy and Viola shared a certain strength of brow, and strength of will, but they were otherwise quite different. Viola was a socialite, a matchmaker. She revelled in connecting people and was almost offensively outgoing. Poppy, with her earthy roundness, was affable when the opportunity allowed, but took to wandering around the countryside when she wasn't about her studies, preferring to spend time alone whenever possible. This gave her a wild quality that no application of pin or petticoat could alter.

There were, as well, two brothers generally found at Harrow House: Heath and Oliver. Heath was the eldest child, two years Viola's senior, and was currently away at King's College, Cambridge studying law. Oliver was the youngest at just sixteen last winter, two years younger than Poppy. He had a predilection for studying insects, particularly moths and beetles, and was a keen musician. Like Poppy, he preferred to be out of doors, and was, at the moment, speaking animatedly to Hounslow, their footman, while he put the finishing touches on the wagon set for Netherford Hall.

"I still don't understand the fuss," said Poppy, reaching for another slice of toast. Mrs. Pratt, their cook, gave her an approving look. "We don't even know if the gentlewitch will stay."

Papa glanced up from his sketching and peered over at his daughter; he was still in his favourite banyan of chartreuse paisley. On this quiet Saturday afternoon, he was in no rush to make himself presentable.

"The Old Ways are a bit complicated," he said, gesturing with his pencil. "Witches are tied to their land. What happened to our gentlewitch is a tragedy of immense proportions—and, perhaps, without precedent. All that's left to the Rookwoods is Netherford Hall. Their home in London was burned beyond the boundaries of magical recovery, from what the papers said, and their family with it."

Mama clicked her tongue. "The poor dears. And them all alone, and the gentlewitch herself so young and with so much responsibility."

"Well, if she's smart, she'll start looking for a wife," said Viola, taking a seat next to her sister at the table. "There are quite a number of families in the area, I imagine, who will be queuing up for an audience as soon as she decides she's ready. I heard that the Durlings and the Greenstreets are already planning dances and dinners."

"I hope that doesn't mean *we* have to go," moaned Poppy, who actually enjoyed the dancing and revelry of such events, but not the social preening and primping. "It's so insufferable to have to watch Antonella Greenstreet go on about which shade of muslin is in this season from atop her golden dais."

"Well, should you find yourself invited," said Mama, "you should be grateful."

Poppy frowned around her mouth full of toast. "I hate when people feel bad for us."

"We are a *good* family," said Papa, who had heard this argument from Poppy before and was no longer shocked. "We've simply fallen on difficult times. And we have enough."

Mama tutted at her youngest daughter. "I would not trade it. Not for one second."

And that was the crux of the problem: they had traded their lives, *her* life, for this meagre existence. When Poppy was six, she fell gravely ill. Doctors were confounded, and it was at last determined she had been cursed. The removal of a curse so nefarious and deep required the intervention of an unregistered hedge witch, and at a price to match the curse: what was left of Margella's dowry, their home in Canterbury, and Redmond Brightwell's ability to walk.

Not a day went by without Poppy feeling that guilt. They lived off Papa's illustration work for the papers, Mama's tutoring, research, and lacework, and the frequent assistance of the Dowager Viscountess St. Albans, their father's godmother, who had married into a good family and who lived nearby awaiting the return of her heir, Viscount St. Albans, from Paris. Lady St. Albans was their primary reason for moving to Netherford in the first place. The children all tended to her on a rotating schedule, escorting her to the opera or the shrine when required, playing card games, and helping to keep the old woman occupied. She lived in a sprawling house called Burkley and did not have a kind opinion of witches.

"Which reminds me," said Papa, wheeling away from his desk and coming to put his long, fingers gently on Viola's shoulder. "I believe it's your turn to visit the dowager viscountess tomorrow afternoon. I know she'll want to know all the gossip, and you are so much better at relaying a story than the rest of us."

"I do enjoy my time with her, even if she is a little old-fashioned," Viola said, beaming at her father.

"You could spend a little more time considering your own future than tending to old women," ventured Mama. "You cannot hide at Burkley House forever. Your next Season is upon you, my dear."

Viola pouted and Poppy tried to hide her smirk.

"And don't think *you're* free of your responsibilities, Poppy," said Papa, helping himself to another cup of tea. Mama frowned at him—he knew too much tea gave him dyspepsia, but there was absolutely no stopping him. "You can't traipse around the countryside for the rest of your life."

"Why not?" Poppy asked. "I think it's a perfectly acceptable way of living. I can practically forage for whatever I need on my own."

"No child of mine will *forage*," said Mama.

"Well, I could always apply to be part of the Pact, given that we have a gentlewitch in residence now. That would mean regular employment."

"Oh, darling," said Mama, tutting. "I take it back. Foraging is a better alternative."

The Brightwells were not ash-touched, and they had remained outside the realm of influence of the coven families for time out of mind. But Poppy was nothing if not unconventional; and she did love scandalising her mother whenever possible. Mama was notoriously sceptical of witches and the like. With good reason, of course.

Poppy frowned at her mother. "Working for the gentlewitch wouldn't be so bad. Even considering the neighbouring towns, I doubt there will be staff, let alone anyone with local knowledge."

"I will not hear of it," said Papa, and he gave an uncharacteristic grunt.

Poppy felt frustration rising in her, first as a heat in her ears and then as a simmering in her heart. She wanted a way back inside Netherford Hall—or at least, one that was sanctioned by her parents. Her only hope was to become Pact-bound. The idea of separating herself from the house forever felt a bit like dying.

"Oh, Papa," said Poppy. "There are far worse fates than the protection of a High Witch. I only ask that you consider."

"And I only ask that you not bring it up again," Mama said, standing up abruptly from her chair. She pointedly picked up her skirts and made a dramatic exit.

As THEY STILL had no direct staff to speak of, it was Auden who greeted the small caravan of townsfolk and food as they made their deliveries. It took an hour, half of it in the driving rain, to unload the food and wares—and many decorations and trinkets, bundles of logs tied with ribbons, books, and other miscellanea—and another two hours to find appropriate storage for it all in the house.

Auden had not been sleeping well. His dreams were riddled with blinking eyes and strange omens he could never quite remember; all he wanted was a nap, but life, it seemed, conspired against him.

He was preparing to sit down, rub his aching feet, and settle into a glass of brandy, when he heard Edith calling him from the foyer.

With an heroic effort, he mustered his strength and meandered across the squeaky-floored corridor to find his niece standing at the same window he'd left her earlier in the day.

"There is a hatless, barefoot woman chasing a flock of sheep across our front lawn," said Edith, calmly. "She is dressed well enough, so I don't expect that she's a farmer's wife."

Auden peered out the window. "You are quite right, my liege," he said.

"She's even got through the hawthorn hedge."

"That—that isn't supposed to happen," he observed. "We have wards for that." When the ensuing silence continued a moment longer than absolutely necessary, he added, "Should I go to her?"

Edith's look was enough to send Auden for his coat, which he had only just shucked, and down the long drive, past the babbling brook and the rising fog, to where the madwoman was now sitting, legs askew, leaning on a very large, pregnant sheep.

"You again," she said, when Auden drew close enough. She was even muddier now, but unmistakably one of the Brightwell women he'd met at the modiste's shop. "No damask waistcoat today, I see."

The observation made him pause. "I only wear damask when—no, never mind. You've upset the gentlewitch," Auden said. "Please dispense yourself."

"Well, my apologies to her," said Poppy Brightwell, brushing away the long curls that had plastered against her face. "But I was trying to protect the grounds from these errant sheep. I'm something of a hero in that respect."

"Are you, now?" Auden asked. He was shivering in his wool coat, wishing for a muffler and gloves, but somehow this wild woman looked as comfortable as a cat by a fireplace.

"I'm sure it doesn't look like it from there," Poppy replied.

"Well, regardless, can you please...?" Auden made an awkward gesture in the direction from which he thought she might have come, but then caught himself halfway through and changed course. "Leave."

The look the woman gave him, of such fury and keen-eyed brilliance, made Auden take a step back. He'd spent much of his life with witches, and he knew when he was outmatched. Not that she was a witch—the Brightwells were not that kind of family—but she possessed a similar forcefulness. It was harrowing, indeed.

Poppy stood up, then, and didn't even bother to brush the dirt from her frock or tidy her hair. "You tell the gentlewitch herself, then," she said with a calm that belied the fire in her eyes, "that if she prefers errant sheep running through her pastures to someone *actually* taking care of them, then by all means, shoo me away. We do share property lines, after all. I was only helping."

"My apologies, Miss Brightwell," said Auden. "I should invite you in for tea and better conversation on the matter—I am but the majordomo and can only speak to my best judgement—"

"Tea? You're speaking of tea, now?"

"Well, yes. In fact, all my breeding compels me to do such a thing; tea between strangers is the best way to foster friendships. But as it is now, given the present circumstances..."

"Yes, as it is now, with me helping you and ruining my dress, the appearance might be lacking?"

"No, I didn't mean that!" Confound the woman.

"Ah, I see. Just a first impression. Setting the boundaries?"

It occurred to Auden that his attempt at diplomacy, if it could be called such a thing, was having the very opposite reaction he had intended. Had he slept better, and had he not had to concern himself with the likes of Molly Hode and Poppy Brightwell, he would not now be standing on the driveway in a damp coat, feet aching and half-dazed, remonstrating with a rather muddy young woman with a gravid ewe.

But Poppy was right, at least on one count: the Rookwood family had practically ignored Netherford Hall for a hundred years, deeming it too far out and too feudal to concern themselves with. And they were going to have to work together.

So, he put on his most brilliant smile, even though his lips were chapped and his teeth were dry. He likely looked like a flushed corpse. But if Auden Garcliffe had any strength, it was in his charm.

"Here, take my coat," said Auden, "and my sincerest apologies. I'd like to make it up to you."

Poppy snorted. "I seriously doubt that."

"Well," Auden continued, ignoring her insolence, "since you are our tenants, and familiar with this township, please consider this a formal invitation to Netherford Hall for tea next Saturday afternoon."

Briefly, Auden was convinced that he had further infuriated the Brightwell woman, but she snatched the topcoat and put it on with more ease and comfort than he'd ever managed.

"I'll come next Thursday," she said, pulling down the sleeves. "Saturday afternoon we have a prior engagement."

"Very well," said Auden.

As Auden watched Poppy Brightwell stalk off through the gathering mist, sheep manure and grass clinging to her soiled petticoats, he knew she heralded trouble.

"YOU GOT AN invitation for tea after chasing down the flock?"

When Poppy limped back to Harrow House, she was exhausted and filthy, but thankfully the only other member of the family at home to see her arrive had been Oliver.

"After chasing a flock of sheep *into forbidden lands*," Poppy said, shaking out the last of her wet curls. The bath had helped ease some of her muscles, and Isabella, their housemaid, had been refreshingly free of judgment. Now, though, she was taking the moment of quiet to eat a little and reorder her thoughts.

Auden Garcliffe was a strange man. Charming and nervous. Quite a combination.

"You really are a brave person, Poppy," said Oliver sitting down beside her on their faded sofa. It was closest to the fire, and their favourite place to read and discuss; as the two youngest, they had a long history of whispered moments, shared stories, and mischief.

Before Poppy could continue the conversation, their immense grey tomcat Thorne jumped up on her lap and began purring and pressing his head into her shoulder. His amber eyes glittered in the firelight like jewels.

"Not now, Thorne," Poppy said, with no intention of moving the cat. His fur was soft as down, long and luxurious. "You are such a pest."

"Yes, but he's a beautiful pest, and somehow we forgive him," said Oliver, which was true. "Do you think they'll want me for tea, too? The gentlewitch and her brother, I mean."

"Oh, darling, tea will bore you to tears."

"But I like tea."

"It isn't polite to put seven cubes of sugar in your tea before a gentlewitch," she admonished. "But regardless of your attendance, I am rather perplexed by this whole business. Our conversation began with Mr. Garcliffe chastising me for trespass and ended with an invitation to call."

"Did he have any insight into your wandering?"

Oliver was the only one who knew the actual extent of Poppy's Netherford Hall adventures. Viola knew she'd gone to the grounds on occasion, but that was all she could confess to her practical older sister. In reality, there was hardly a corner of the old house *or* grounds she didn't know. She dreamed of it at night, and sometimes woke up wondering if she had somehow sleep-walked into the long, gloomy corridors.

The first time she trespassed at Netherford Hall, she'd been only seven years old. It was a complete accident, losing her way in the fog off the downs. She'd been turned around and had found herself in the graveyard, mottled stones rising out of the mist with strange old Rookwood and Darnley names.

She should have been afraid, but she wasn't. This was not necessarily unusual for Poppy; as her mother noted many times in her life, she had a perpetual fearlessness which defied reason.

As Netherford Hall loomed ahead of her, day by day, week by week, year by year, she began to creep ever closer to it. Now and again the Hodes would come by, as was their right as Warders, but Poppy learned their schedules and how to avoid them.

Derelict as it was, Poppy never wanted to change a single thing about the house. And even now, many years later, she still sometimes found new corners of Netherford Hall: passageways, new carvings, strange books, pieces of jewellery. She never altered a mote of dust, but was obsessed with knowing and understanding Netherford Hall. So she catalogued the flowers in the spring and summer, mapped the hallways in her sketchbooks, and traced the provenance of the fabrics when she made her way to the library in Tonbridge.

"Well, I didn't intend to get caught," said Poppy.

"You never do."

"The flock only ruined *some* of the lawn, but without me they very likely could have turned over half the crocuses, which would have been unforgivable. Mr. Garcliffe was not impressed with my wrangling, though. Merely flustered over my trespassing."

"Flustered?"

"Flummoxed. Angry? He had a great many emotions regarding me."

Oliver leaned forward over his bony knees, the hems of his trousers rising over his ankles. He was growing out of everything, and would soon be taller than Heath. "You do have that effect on people, Poppy. Who knows, perhaps you're a witch yourself?"

"Doubtful. We all know witches require discipline and birthright, of which I have neither. No, my eccentric brand of magic has developed over time, and I take some pride in it."

Oliver snorted, and Thorne jumped into his lap, and they both laughed as the cat howled as if in approval.

CHAPTER THREE
THE HODES

THE WARDERS, MOLLY and Basil Hode, were precisely on time, and were much changed from Auden's last interaction with them at the Holly and Sickle. In an unexpected turn, they had unearthed some sort of rural costumes that must have once implied their status, though they were surely a hundred years out of date and moth-eaten. Comprised of voluminous blue and gold rose brocade and matching vests—Molly's was a bit snug—their silver buttons were nonetheless shining with care. They both wore hammered torcs, as well, just above their tufted collars, each set with an uncut stone in the middle.

If Auden had not seen them before, he'd have guessed they were traveling minstrels who'd been left outside too long without shelter.

Acting as butler yet again, Auden ushered them through the main entrance and into the great hall, which should have been a point of pride but at the moment was a bit of a dusty holding bin for various odds and ends, unwieldy furniture, and the remnants of their things from London. They'd lost most of their belongings in the fire, but there'd been enough furniture in storage that they at least had a start.

Thankfully, the withdrawing room—truly one of the gems of the old house—looked presentable no matter the situation, what with the wall of windows and the peaked ceilings falling like meringues above their heads. To say nothing of the gigantic fireplace. The furniture within was sparse but sturdy, and though far from modern, the room was rather more comfortable than the overwhelming great hall, which would have been more at home in King Arthur's court.

Within, Edith awaited. She had few suits, having had little chance to fill out her wardrobe since her arrival, but Auden approved of the mulberry-coloured ensemble she'd chosen. Though no giantess like Molly, Edith still possessed a great presence and bearing. Auden had expected her to diminish slightly under the weight of their family's tragedy—certainly he had, judging by the new lines in his face and the grey hairs at his temples—but she had not. Edith had always been made of stern stuff.

As she turned around to face her guests, Auden felt a sudden well of pride: She looked every inch the gentlewitch, her dark blue eyes catching the light from the windows and flashing like topaz, her mouth in a serious, straight line, her hands out, gloved, and splayed, in a gesture of peace and welcome.

"Welcome to Netherford Hall, Warders," she said, her voice low and resonant. "I am Edith Rookwood, Gentlewitch of the High House of Greystrand. I am indebted to you."

"This is Miss Molly and Mr. Basil Hode, of Netherford. Warders," said Auden, since no one was there to announce them directly.

They took their seats, and there was nothing to offer but stale biscuits, so once again Auden felt a now-familiar mortification twisting about his belly.

"The correct phrasing," said Basil, without any of the temerity that his looks would insinuate, "is 'the Hallowed Warders Netherford, Mary and Basil Hode.'"

"Though you can call us Molly and Basil," said Molly. "The other is a bit of a mouthful."

Edith nodded, her expression unreadable. "Yes, I can understand that. And Liege Rookwood is ample for me."

Molly nodded slowly, and for the first time Auden saw just a hint of nervousness in the Hode woman. Her pinky finger twitched slightly. He was no expert in matters of expression, but he had played a great deal of cards during his days in London and had learned to notice nervous tells, if only because they had so often caused his own downfall.

"Very well," said Basil, then. He took out an old journal from his pocket, the leather worn shiny and smooth, the edges stained like an old tea towel. "I suppose we best dispense with pleasantries. It's clear we have a great deal of work to do."

"Indeed," said Edith, and only because Auden knew her well enough did he see that she was already growing impatient.

"Thank you again," Auden added, taking his own seat, a rickety wicker nightmare that would have served far better as kindling. "We do appreciate you coming to see us."

Basil, unperturbed, thumbed through the pages of the little booklet, and said, "Well, we may not have had a gentlewitch in Netherford in some time, but it is our family's duty to serve. I can tell you we have a very good selection of Pact families, and a surprisingly impressive number of ash-touched in the area."

Edith leaned over, just ever so slightly, tilting her head to try and get a look at the writing within the journal, but it was impossible. Molly's glare was acid enough to curdle milk still in the udder.

Molly frowned, putting her hand protectively on her brother's shoulder. "It has been our life's work, and the work of ancestors, as far back as we can trace."

"I assure you, the effort is greatly appreciated," said Edith. But, as was the way so often with the gentlewitch, she did not sound particularly sincere. Auden rarely saw his niece express much in any way of enthusiasm about anything, save her history books and old scrolls. "But, pray—would you take a moment to enlighten me, before we commence with business? You see, as a London-raised gentlewitch, I'm afraid I'm quite ignorant in the ways of identifying ash-touched people or, indeed, how Pact families come to be in the country. My area of expertise is Parliamentary history in regards to the Coven body politic, and not more quotidian matters."

A pause. The fire crackled, and somewhere off in the manor house, something fell.

"Mice," said Edith, and, "Owls," said Auden, at the same time.

Basil licked his lips. "Well, 'quotidian matters,' as it were, are *my* area of expertise. The Pact families, as they remain, have been in our ledgers—kept within the *Booke of the Coveyne*—since the founding of the town and certified in the Rote of Coveyne passed by Parliament in 1441. Much of the notes here go into detail about other preternatural groups— vampires, werewolves, the like—and how Netherford was welcoming to most. Though, given the diminished populations of such groups, excepting witches, less of an issue now." He thumbed down the scroll. "The town was established as Nitharford in 669, by Navia the First's great-granddaughter Astrid, and there were three main families besides the Rookwoods: the Poles, the Rivers, and Blythes. Only the Poles were Pact, but through marriage lines and inheritances, the families prospered and grew."

The Warder unfolded one of the pages from his ledger and unfurled it down his leg. Even from where Auden sat, he could see the progression of lettering: from scratchy runes at his thigh to a clean hand in deep ochre red by his ankle.

"This is just the family heads," added Basil, looking a little embarrassed. "I can't carry around the full ledger, for I'd need sturdier arms and legs for such a thing. If you would like to join us back at the Holly and Sickle later in your stay, we could arrange—"

"Basil, this is not a lecture," said Molly, not unkindly, but firmly.

"Yes, of course," Basil said, his moustache working a moment. His smile was childlike and kind. "The ash-touched are the easiest to explain. Our midwives, like all midwives in the region, are all ash-touched themselves, so every child born is screened for potential. It takes an apple, a gold pin, and a great deal of patience, but it can be done, and with great certainty. Though in recent years, the ash-touched population too has dwindled."

There were ash-touched servants all over London. Hundreds, if not thousands. Their power lay in their abilities to handle magical objects without harm. A witch's library, for example, could not be overseen by a mortal; touching the books was poisonous, in some cases, or would drive them mad. As such, the ash-touched could command great salaries. The rare ash-touched children even of Pact families could rise to the most impressive circles, though not Coven born themselves.

"Which brings us to our local ash-touched families. The Pole family became the Harpoles, and they are sturdy folk. There are still twenty-six Harpoles in the surrounding areas, and five of whom we feel would be best suited for the position of head of house."

Molly was the one to continue. "My personal recommendation would be Miss Angelica Harpole. She is twenty-seven, Cambridge-educated, and currently working in apprenticeship with the Greenstreets."

"Cambridge-educated?" Edith's brows went up high

enough to vanish a moment beneath her russet curls. "And working as an apprentice?"

"Well, we couldn't have her beholden to anyone else," said Basil, simply. "Not when there was a chance the gentlewitch would return."

Glancing uncomfortably at Auden, it appeared Edith was beginning to understand the depth of the Warder's discomfort and, presumably, rather dogged loyalty. "You said there were six candidates. Are they all so well-educated and similarly situated?"

"Of course," said Molly. "They range in age, of course, and the only reason we would not suggest Miss Agnes Doutwater, for example, is that she is just shy of her eighty-sixth birthday and has begun to show signs of extensive myopia."

"*Eighty-six?*" Auden hadn't meant to say it out loud, but the gravity of the situation truly dawned on him. "She's been an apprentice all this time?"

"Head of house is an exceptionally important position," said Molly. "It is considered an honour to have spent one's life in preparation for the gentlewitch."

Edith stood up, paling, her hands balled into fists, her tea long forgotten. "Well, that is—I mean to say—I am quite—"

"Quite, indeed," said Auden, mopping his suddenly sodden brow.

"Did you know this, Uncle?" Edith asked, accusingly.

Auden, who found direct questions painfully uncomfortable, swallowed hard. "Well, not to this extent. As you know, I was not expected to rise to my position any more than you, given my age and status and…" *Recklessness.* Rakishness. General ineptitude? The words felt like ash in his mouth, and he was terrified to make eye contact with either of the Warders.

He was absolutely *ashamed*. If the family had been a bit less concerned about London style and status, he should have been given the same education as his sisters. He would have studied the family lore and been prepared.

As it stood, the depth of his moral and intellectual shortcomings felt like a shroud of lead around his shoulders. Hot lead. Then cold. Like clinging rain.

"Uncle?"

"Yes?"

"I asked you a question." Edith was not amused, and she still hadn't taken her seat again.

The Warders, for all their pomp and circumstance, were remarkably placid. Auden assumed the conversation was proceeding precisely as they had expected.

"I'm sorry. I was…" Mortified? "Distracted."

"Was my mother aware of such proceedings?" Edith's voice was deadly calm now, and that was more frightening than volume by a grand measure.

"Most likely," Auden said, looking desperately at the Hodes, but finding nothing but matching, pale gazes of indifference. "There were the Netherford reports. I never read them myself, but I know they were delivered because, as long as I lived, they'd be delivered on the thirteenth of the month wrapped in red leather and sealed with at least a dozen different seals."

"Twenty-six," Basil offered.

His tone was mild, Auden realised, but terribly calculating.

And no surprise, really. Given what their troth meant, their unwavering dedication to a gentlewitch who had cast less than a shadow upon their doorsteps for two lifetimes. Auden had only heard the name 'Netherford' in passing, and in the way one speaks of a moon-touched aunt sent out to the countryside, not of a town full of people who had dedicated years of their lives *across generations*.

Edith gathered herself. "I cannot undo the generations of grief. Nor can I undo the feelings of abandonment or of alienation. I wish I was half the gentlewitch that you all deserved, but I fear that I am all that remains. And, as you can see by the state of our affairs, there is very little in that calculus. I must beg your patience with us."

She did not beg forgiveness, thank the saints, for that would have been most inappropriate. Auden had to give credit to Edith for that: unlike her hot-headed mother and aunt, she maintained a remarkable sense of calm even in the direst of situations.

They could not afford to have angry warders. Or an angry head of house. And certainly not angry cooks! Dying of poison was the most unromantic thing he could consider.

But, it seemed, Auden's fears were unfounded. With Edith's words, plain but true, the Hodes visibly relaxed. They did not thaw entirely, and Auden expected they never quite would. That was not the goal.

"We are here to serve," said Basil.

"We are here to build," said Molly. "And we will bring as much patience as we can."

THEY WORKED TOGETHER and decided upon interviews for the main positions, those which they had to fill without delay. It would be a long next couple of days, and Auden could not see how he would manage enough sleep to endure it.

When Henry came to him later in the day, covered in dirt and ant bites, it was all he could do to not howl in fury and pain along with him. But he did as he had done so often since the fire that took their family: he washed little Henry, he spoke to him quietly, he tended to his cuts and scrapes and wounds, then told him stories of the Green Man and his magical flute.

As he tucked him in bed, Henry took Auden's head in his own little hands and said: "Is there a charm cousin Edie can do to help me sleep?"

"You usually sleep so soundly, my dear. What do you mean?"

Henry sighed, turning his head away. "I have bad dreams."

"Oh, you know the Green Man can chase those terrible dreams away," said Auden. But he could understand: Netherford Hall was eerie even in the broadest of daylight. Sleeping alone in a room like this, with the constant creaking and shifting and persistent chill, would have frightened Auden as a boy, too. If he was honest, it frightened him as a man.

"I dream of a beast with six eyes," said Henry, almost too quiet to hear. "She breathes in my ears and tells me to let the spiders in."

Nightmares were a common thread among the Garcliffe men, but this was a strange coincidence: Auden had dreamed of a six-eyed beast himself, just days before. It emerged from a mist, rising from the river. At the time, he hadn't thought much of it save that he ought not eat sweets before bed. But now he shivered.

"Well, that's quite silly," said Auden, tweaking Henry's nose. "What would a beast do with six eyes?"

"It could look inside me," said Henry. "Through the spiders."

"Well. I'll tell you what. I'll go down and see if I can find some lavender and hawthorn berries in the pantry. It's a good ward against bad dreams. But first, I'll tell you another story of the Green Man and his magical flute— and of the time he visited Stirling Castle to put a family of vampires to sleep."

He forced himself through the story, trying to cast aside the gnawing fear from Henry's shared dream. Eventually it worked.

Henry was sound asleep just a few minutes when he saw Edith's shadow in the doorway. If she'd sought him out, she must indeed be in need of counsel.

It ached to battle the selfishness within him, and for a very sharp moment he nearly feigned sleep to avoid another conversation. But she, and Henry, were all that he had left in the world of his family. Of the whole Rookwood line. Of their hopes, and their future, even if it was a future in this drafty old house half-crumbling into the landscape. Nightmares and dreams, hopes and fears, all of it.

It occurred to him that someday, no matter how well everything worked, Netherford Hall would be a ruin. It was not a consideration he had in London, for old and new lived side-by-side, the conglomerations growing into each other without beginning or end. Nothing died in London, but was merely consumed by the landscape around it, incorporated into an ever-shifting mass that grew across time and space.

But here in Netherford, change came slowly. The manor itself was so old that its plumbing was barely rudimentary, the architecture more medieval than Tudor, and the feeling of decay pervaded all around them. They lived away from the constantly shifting world of London, and it was not difficult to think of it falling into disrepair—really, it would only take a few years to start the real deterioration.

And the thought of it made Auden lose his breath a moment. He steadied himself, trying to understand the growing dread in the pit of his stomach. It couldn't have just been the dream, could it? He could not think of a single thing he liked about this house. Not a single stick of furniture felt his own, or reflected his style. Yet the idea of the grand dining table reduced to splinters, or the hearth crumbled to rubble, sent a horrid chill through him.

When he finally managed to get himself into the hallway, Edith's pensive expression shifted to worry.

"Uncle, you look as if you've seen a ghost," she said, holding up the lantern to examine his face.

"This house," he said, putting a hand up to the rough plaster wall to steady himself. "It makes one think strange thoughts sometimes. And I've been having strange dreams."

Edith, always the sober sceptic, surprised him by saying, "I wander it in my dreams, you know. Though the layout is never quite the same. Every night since we've been here, I have roamed the halls alone. And there are always voices in the rooms, but no one that I can see. Yet I feel eyes on me."

Auden's hair rose on the back of his chest. He was used to the uncanny nature of witches, but Edith was not the sort to whom he normally ascribed such strangeness. She had always seemed so pleasantly boring.

But now he saw, in her eyes, the same fever-bright look he'd known in his sisters.

"I just felt the most peculiar grief, I suppose," he said. "A kind of mad concern, a feeling of possessiveness for this place. And yet, if you were to tell me that I would have felt such emotion a few weeks ago, I would have laughed."

"I wonder if it has to do with your being majordomo. I've heard tales, old tales, of such a thing. A kind of connection to the home. Did you do anything unusual before it happened?"

"I just feel like such a failure to you," he said, unable to hold the tears at bay. The depth of his exhaustion was impossible to ignore.

"Fate has drawn us together," said Edith mildly, taking his hands. "And it appears, for all your lack of preparation, you are still, somehow, intuitively connected. You love this house, just as Uncle Astor loved Hatchney."

"I miss them," said Auden, and heavens, it was true. "I should have been there."

Edith shook her head slowly. "If you weren't drunk on the stoop of the Blake, and I hadn't gone looking for you, we would both be dead. Your intemperance is what saved the family."

Cassandra. Georgina. Horace. Uncle Astor. Old Rust. Jolly and Toff. The six tabby cats he never could differentiate. Cook Brown and Cook Dunn. There weren't even bones left to count, save a few teeth.

"It feels so heavy sometimes," Auden said, finally finding his handkerchief and mopping at his face.

"I know," said Edith. Hey eyes, as ever, were dry—yet not empty. Whatever the young witch *felt*, it was ever at a distance. She'd been the same as a child: she would fall and break her skin, or crack her head, breathe deeply, bite her lip, and limp on. "And though so much is lost, we have Netherford Hall. I feel myself growing attuned to it; my powers, though they are not ever going to be remarkable, feel more comfortable. And we made true progress with the Hodes today, and I do believe they will be our allies. Hearing that Netherford was established by one of Navia's descendants made me feel strangely proud. Like perhaps we do belong here, among these good folk."

It was that reminder that sent Auden's stomach twisting in recollection.

"I forgot to mention. I invited the Brightwells for tea."

"Tea?"

"Yes. Thursday; apparently Saturday wasn't a good option."

"I thought I sent you out with explicit orders to dispense with the interloper." Edith was irritated, but not furious.

Auden folded his handkerchief, trying to measure his words. "There is something strange about her. She is able to come to the grounds with absolutely no trouble. And she is knowledgeable. And headstrong. And clearly not concerned with social lines, even when a gentlewitch such as yourself is involved."

"'She'? Did you not get her name?"

"Poppy, I believe."

"Are all the Brightwell children named after greenery?"

He hadn't asked, but he suspected that was the case. "It appears to be in fashion. But to my point—they are our tenants. And we must at least extend the barest of civility."

"Do you suspect she's ash-touched?"

"I don't know. Uncle Astor would have known—he was a *proper* majordomo," Auden said. "But at least this means that Poppy won't bother us until then. She seems to be persistent."

"She sounds like a nightmare," Edith said, dubiously. "But if you have made them a promise, as my majordomo, your invitation must be honoured. Hopefully we will have a half-competent cook by then and we won't have to serve them stale biscuits. And once it's over, we'll only have to consider the Brightwells when we collect their rent."

Auden laughed, and it felt like a spring uncoiling inside him. "Speaking of biscuits. I think I cracked my tooth on one of those," he said, as they began walking back down the long hall to their rooms. "No wonder the mice didn't bother with them."

CHAPTER FOUR
TEA AT THE ESTATE

EVEN WITH THE beginnings of a household, Edith still had to take responsibilities beyond her experience. Regardless of the ridiculous tea engagement this afternoon, she had work to do—for Auden was a terror with numbers. They had agreed, after those first dark days, that Edith would take responsibility for their financial records. Auden would have to manage payments and post.

So, as she sat down to her desk and opened the first of her letters, dreading meeting the Brightwells later in the day, she was not quite prepared for the letter from Pendle's Bank.

There was money, well over a hundred thousand pounds in all—enough to build anew in London and live comfortably for a long time. Calpurnia Southern, their coven representative, wrote in a sprawling, red ink, providing all details.

But Edith's hopes were immediately dashed: The trouble was not in the sum, but in where it was due.

The benefactor of the estate should be, Calpurnia explained, the nearest living relative—which they had all assumed would be Edith.

Except that it seemed there were three others contesting Edith's inheritance.

She rubbed at her eyes and read it again: her grandmother Bette and grand-uncle Astor had a sibling, a bit older than they, who'd left for America, and now had resurfaced in London with a son and daughter. They had heard of the fire and came to the bank with convincing papers, convincing stories, and, most importantly, family artifacts and sigils. All authentic.

Edith's stomach churned as she read the letter once again, her mind struggling to accept this new information.

> *There is little precedent for this situation, and though the timing is suspicious we must abide by the laws of the High Houses and of the Coven Itself. I anticipate resolution at some point, but there will likely be a significant wait before the funds are allotted.*
>
> *Due to the unusual situation, however, and thanks to the generosity of neighbouring covens, we can extend a significant loan to cover the majority of the expenses, as well as a small policy taken out in your name specifically in the sum of...*

Tracing her fingers over the names of her heretofore unknown great aunt and cousins, Edith frowned. Beatrix Rookwood-Nourse, Petronilla Rookwood-Nourse, Giles Rookwood-Nourse. Were she trained, or even mildly talented, in the ways of divination, she might have gathered some psychic sense about the three—faces, favourite perfumes, locations, *something* to go from—merely by touching their names with her fingers. She begged for a clue, something to settle the pit in her stomach.

But she gained nothing. No insight. Just a shiver from the infernally cold study walls which creaked with the wind. Tea with a tenant now seemed an intolerable and vexatious imposition.

*   *   *

FOR POPPY BRIGHTWELL, tea at Netherford Hall was cause for great anxiety. She would have to maintain the pretence that she didn't know the lay of the house the whole time she was there with her mother and sister.

The task became less daunting when she was greeted by Hattie Knightley, the gentlewitch's new head of house, at the immense front doors.

Hattie was an energetic, intelligent woman of extensive education. Like all the women of her family, Pact-born as they were, she'd returned to Netherford after her schooling and had opened up a small law firm in town.

When Hattie opened the front door, Poppy couldn't help but marvel a little: the lawyer was wearing her robes of status, the violet uniform of the gentlewitch's head of house. Judging by the crispness and rich hue of the material, it was brand new. Poppy had only ever seen such uniforms at a distance before, having never seen an official head of house at close quarters: the buttons were arranged in three lines down Hattie's breast, all of tortoiseshell and carved with little spirals so they looked like shining snails. In place of a skirt, she wore loose pantaloons in deep aubergine, two shades darker than the high-necked bodice, which was strung with three bands of pearls over each epaulet.

The sunny yellow curls at her brow, however, were all Hattie, as was the gentle slope of her nose between her bold-lashed brown eyes.

"You are our first guests," said Hattie, directing the Brightwells over the threshold and into the great hall.

Poppy had to remind herself to look up in wonder at the arching medieval ceiling, for it truly was a marvel, especially now it was so much cleaner.

But it wasn't just the great hall that had been transformed. Netherford Hall itself was changing, down to its scent. The pervasive smell of the place lingered—chestnuts, tree resin, beeswax, ash—but joined now by something else. And it made her terribly sad.

"Are you crying, Poppy?" Viola whispered in Poppy's ear.

"No, of course not," she said back, trying to avoid Hattie's stern gaze. "It's rather dusty in here."

"Girls, please," said Mama batting her fan at her daughter. Poppy had tried to dissuade her mother from bringing that old fan—an ivory contraption barely held together with green silk and faded laces—but there was no dissuading her. It clashed terribly with her raspberry-red bonnet and yellow scarf.

Oliver was back at home with Papa, who could not make the trip in the current weather, but Poppy wished he could see it. He loved the bones of things, the structures, and was always trying to figure out how things were made. The thousands of windows, the arcing timbers from ancient trees, and the carvings, paintings, sculptures...

"This way, please," Hattie said, as two footmen—boys from the Grant family, Poppy thought—took their capes and hats. Although, she reflected, she could have done with the warmth.

Poppy caught sight of a young boy peering out of a hallway corridor, tousled hair over his dark eyes. He had smudges on his face, and a curious if slightly haunted expression on his face.

When she went to give him a little wave and a smile, he vanished.

Well, she would have to ask later. For now, they were to meet the gentlewitch in the withdrawing room.

And what a transformation it had seen! Much of the house was still draped in cloth and untidy, but the withdrawing room was resplendent. The ceiling—always her favourite feature, falling in peaks like well-whipped cream—was scrubbed clean, and lit by the rose windows on one side and the flickering fireplace on the other. And oh! Now, there was new furniture in deep forest greens and mulberry hues, woven in playful brocade. There was a harpsichord, too, gilded and set with a large bouquet of heather and holly. It smelled of fresh coffee and old books.

"There they are," said Auden Garcliffe as he stepped into the room. He was dressed for tea in a jaunty ensemble of yellow and blue stripes. "Welcome."

They made their introductions, and Mama blushed so deeply she almost matched her dress. Hattie helped everyone find seats, and then left them all.

The sofa was imminently comfortable, Poppy found, expecting springs and the creak of wood but meeting only softness and support. It was difficult not to run her hands over the material, it was so soft.

"The house is coming along quite well, Mr. Garcliffe," said Mama, as if it were hers to comment upon. "I had no idea such splendour lurked beneath."

Mr. Garcliffe leaned forward, his hands on his knees, and beamed. "Why thank you, Mrs. Brightwell. I am growing quite fond of it. We're working diligently to get things back to their proper working condition."

"Well, if this is but the beginning, I am truly anticipating the final result," said Mrs. Brightwell.

"As am I," came a woman's voice behind them, low and with a slight rasp. "However, a home of this provenance and complication leads me to believe that there is not any final state. As we tidy up one wing, another will begin to fall into disrepair."

Then the gentlewitch herself, Liege Rookwood, came into view. She wore a tailored suit of slate grey shot with metallic blue floss, closely fitted over her broad chest and narrow waist, the chains and chatelaine of her station in plain view. She was tall, so much taller than Poppy had imagined—for she had only ever glimpsed Liege Rookwood at a distance—and had almost Roman features: a pair of deep blue, soulful eyes, an aquiline nose, and a round chin.

And she was russet haired. Not like an orange cat, but like copper, like nutmeg and clove and the first morning light in the autumn. Her hair curled, not by the application of iron or press, but in a natural wave that cut across her fair, smooth brow.

"It is good to meet you," said the gentlewitch when no one replied to her—albeit out of surprise rather than shame. "I am Edith, Gentlewitch of Netherford Hall."

"Liege Rookwood," said Mama, standing, and then making a strange half-curtsey as she pulled her daughters up with her. "May I—may I present my daughters Viola and Poppy Brightwell, of, at the moment, Harrow House? They are suitable. Suited. Sweet? No, I mean, they are quite pleased. To be here, with you, at Netherford Hall."

Mama had apparently lost all sense. But then, perhaps she didn't have much to begin with where her daughters were concerned.

Viola was already batting her eyelashes—a nervous habit she'd had since childhood—in mortification at Mama's curious display, but Poppy felt an odd calm.

For Poppy could not draw her attention away from the gentlewitch. She was compelled to stare at her, as if by some magnetic force. Poppy had never been around a witch before, let alone a gentlewitch. And she was surprisingly alluring. Not in the way of forbidden things, but in the way of a flower blooming out of season or a moon rising in startling hues of blue or red. The world was winter, and Liege Rookwood was an unexpected briar rose. Or at least a very colourful, defiant mushroom, what with that hair.

"We are most pleased to meet you, my liege," Poppy said, when Viola continued in mute embarrassment.

"The pleasure is ours," said the gentlewitch, sitting by them, but not looking at them directly. In fact, Poppy noticed that the gentlewitch appeared to go to great lengths to avoid catching her eye.

Then the witch's attention shifted, and Poppy's temper flared. Alluring though she might be, Liege Rookwood was very clearly *suffering* through this without any attempt to disguise her discomfort. A shame, truly, that one given so much would be so cold.

Viola regained her composure, perhaps also picking up on the gentlewitch's mood. She took her seat and said, "I hope you are enjoying your time so far in Netherford."

"I would not use the word *enjoy*," said Liege Rookwood, paying more attention to her hands than current company. Her uncle coughed, and the gentlewitch amended, "But I appreciate your concern on the matter."

"It was very kind to have us up, my liege. We would be most pleased to help you get accustomed to the town as much as possible," Viola said, her voice losing some of its initial enthusiasm.

"Thank you, but I have my majordomo for such things," said the gentlewitch.

"My sister does not offer her guidance to just anyone, my liege," Poppy said, unable to keep silent. "You would be lucky to have her as a guide."

This did draw the gaze of the gentlewitch. She betrayed no hint of merriment, nor of anger; just a glassy reserve. Like the eyes of a stuffed trophy werewolf. "As I said, the sentiment is appreciated, but I have no need of additional services at this time.."

"But Viola knows the town. Mr. Garcliffe is practically a stranger," said Poppy, knowing immediately that she'd chosen her words ill.

Liege Rookwood raised an eyebrow and leaned back,

finally levelling a stare at Poppy, and suddenly she found herself having second thoughts. "Miss Brightwell, unless I am mistaken, your family is neither Pact nor ash-born. Nor are they landed gentry."

"That is correct," said Poppy. "My liege."

The gentlewitch continued. "As such, and given your status, there is little reason for us to engage beyond our necessary relationship as landowner and tenant. Which should be courteous, of course. I expect, should you like, you could even join us at the house for occasional events. It is good to mingle, I'm told, and fashionable, even, for folk such as yourself."

It was good that someone had set tea before Mrs. Brightwell and not Poppy, at that moment, or else the gentlewitch could have found herself fending off a teacup aimed directly at her head.

No one spoke. Mr. Garcliffe stared intently at his teacup and cleared his throat.

"Do I make myself clear, Miss Brightwell?" It might have been her imagination, but Poppy thought she saw the gentlewitch's eyes flash amber. Furniture rumbled above them—someone moving a bed or a trunk on one of the upper levels.

"Indeed," intruded Viola, clasping her sister's hand hard enough to hurt. But it did the trick. Poppy's temper was a live thing now, an adder poised to strike, and it should not be permitted to cost them their reputation. Not this soon into their acquaintance with their new landlord.

"Indeed, indeed," echoed Mama, tossing her ribbon strings at her collar and letting out a nervous laugh. "I daresay it is quite refreshing to know *precisely* where one stands. It does save a great deal of energy trying to decipher otherwise."

It might have been the nastiest thing Poppy ever heard Mama say. Not just in her words, but in her clipped tone.

She was positively incandescent with rage, and it was a beautiful thing.

"Yes," echoed Poppy, blinking as if awaking from a dream. "It most certainly is."

"The Great Peace relies on such an understanding—we are the arbiters and protectors of magic, now that Faerie is closed forever," said the gentlewitch, and now she did look directly at Poppy. "We live in a modern society, and a harmonious existence depends upon knowing one's place."

And heavens above and below, Poppy read those eyes like a sonnet. She felt the air rush out of her and knew, without a doubt, just how much her trespass into the field had enraged Liege Edith. And that the gentlewitch would have been well within her rights to punish her for it, to shame her. And though shame was an emotion Poppy rarely felt, the gravity of her error filled the room like an invisible fog.

This was not about tea. This was not about society. It was about *laws*, ancient and immovable, and Poppy understanding just who it was she was dealing with.

And she was in trouble.

THE WALK HOME to Harrow House was silent, rainy, and cold. Mrs. Brightwell had to shoo one of the cats from the threshold when they entered, and the beast howled its offence, while the three women stood together, shivering, in the dim light of the entryway. Thorne was the only cat allowed indoors, but a veritable pride of the animals lived between Netherford Hall and Harrow House.

Viola was the first to speak. "Well, that did not go as I imagined."

"No," said Mama, her voice cracking with that one syllable. "No, it most certainly did not."

Oliver, sleepy and tousled, emerged in the doorway, his

feet bare. He looked like a deer in a night shirt, with pale, narrow ankles. "Oh, you look like ghosts."

"We do feel a bit ghastly," said Poppy, as Isabella went to work with their cloaks and bonnets, indicating that there would be warm cider and biscuits awaiting them in the foyer.

The simple comforts of Harrow House, plain as it was, helped to cast the dark shroud of Netherford Hall and its pompous gentlewitch from her mind. But not the threat, not the bone-deep knowledge that she would be held accountable for her actions should she ever trespass again.

The three Brightwell women then all sat in silence together before the roaring fire, the damp slowly evaporating from their hair, their hearts dazed.

"What a wretched creature!" Viola covered her mouth as soon as she had said it, and even Poppy felt a stab of fear.

"Viola!" scolded Poppy. "I have never heard you speak so."

"With good reason," said Viola. "I have never been so affronted in my life. I cannot imagine the cause of her disdain."

Mama frowned. "Well, whatever the cause: I make no excuses. I only know that the gentlewitch has lived a very different life from our own and may see and understand things in ways we cannot. As tenants, we must maintain the property and our payment, but, thank the stars, we are not beholden to her in any other way."

"I have no intention of ever seeing that horrid woman ever again," said Poppy, and she had to choke back tears. Tears! Poppy was far from the weeping sort, but Edith Rookwood had made her afraid, and Poppy was not used to being afraid of anyone.

The tears were for more than that, though. In that moment, Poppy knew she had truly lost Netherford Hall. From now on, she could never set foot there again. She would work Oliver through his lessons, wheel Papa around, go to town to shop for ribbons—and the whole time, seeing the lights of Netherford Hall from her window as it was restored to a new age of beauty and status and power.

Thankfully, Poppy was spared further embarrassment by Oliver, who slipped into the parlour holding a large letter, a grin on his face.

"In all this fuss, I forgot to mention," he said, handing it to Mama. "This is from the Greenstreets—they're having a ball next weekend, in honour of the gentlewitch herself."

A ball. With the Greenstreets! Even Poppy had to feel a bit elated at that news. The Greenstreets were an old family, but they were celebrated for their balls, not to mention their taste in food and fashion and games.

And she couldn't help but wonder what the gentlewitch would look like in an embroidered waistcoat.

"You keep staring at their house," Auden said, joining Edith in their second parlour, now almost clean enough to entertain. It had been the day's work for the staff, and he was pleased with the results.

The Brightwells had left almost an hour ago. Auden could not say that the meeting was a success by any measure, and he'd had the distinct understanding that Edith wanted to be rid of them. Yet, here she still was.

"I think I might have a been a bit too harsh with them," she said.

That was surprising. Auden had known Edith a very long time, and he could count the number of instances she had admitted to any error of temper or etiquette on one hand. Maybe on one finger.

"Well," he said in return. "I don't think they will be regaling your hospitality all throughout the realm. You said you didn't want them having airs, given their proximity to us."

"I didn't mean it that way. And I wanted to simply reiterate the fact that they were our tenants, that our relationship was primarily transactional. It is only—"

"Only?"

Edith turned slowly to look at Auden. "The younger one. You're right. There is something truly strange about her. I *sensed* her in a way that I have only been able to do with a very select few, and always those in the coven. I could feel her mind, somehow. Her emotions. Distantly, but unmistakably."

"Do you think you are attuning to the house, then? Is this something new?"

"I have sensed something, yes. My meagre abilities are deepening. But this feels separate. As if it encompasses another space within my being. Like a room in a house, where the fire has been kindled for the first time."

"But she isn't a witch," said Auden.

"Assuredly not," Edith said. "But that remains my problem. She isn't ash-touched, she isn't Pact, she isn't a witch. I don't think she's a vampire, or a werewolf. But she is *something*, and I do not know what."

"My dear, you may learn in this life that not everything is attained through knowledge."

"That is precisely my point."

Auden could not contain the long sigh. "I'm afraid you have lost me."

Edith gave her uncle a soft smile. "She meets no criteria for any arcane-gifted mortal I can think of—and it's a subject I've researched extensively. If I don't know *what* she is, how can I protect her?"

"Protect her?"

"Protecting the people here is my only duty. I am at Netherford Hall, on the wings of tragedy, with little more than my name and the pitiable reputation we've built for ourselves. When Mother and Aunt Cassandra were alive, her power was great enough to keep Netherford safe from afar. But I must build the lines of protection again, fortify the Warders' work. I must establish the house and the town, and protect it from any nefarious workings."

Auden felt a shiver run through him. "Have you felt something?"

"Henry has whispered of bad dreams," she said softly. "And we both know, he dreamed of flames before the fire."

"I try not to remember that," sighed Auden. Dreaming of fire was considered a generational curse, of sorts, among certain men of the line.

"I feel a darkness here, somewhere, lingering at the edges, but I cannot see it." She let out a long breath, shaking her head. "I feel the debt of what happened at Hatchney House on me every day—feel my lacking and insufficiency."

"Oh, Edith. I thought you gave up on finding out what happened," Auden said, because he had truly hoped so.

"I never will," said Edith. "I cannot rid myself of the image of Henry, surrounded by rubble, naked as a babe, unscathed."

"He still doesn't remember," Auden said, hating to talk about the boy when he was not near. "But he may, yet."

"The Cleromancers did not see him in their investigation. A true warlock has not been born in many ages," Edith said. "But I will continue to research, and you will continue to monitor the boy."

"Of course," said Auden, though he felt himself the least qualified person in the entirety of Great Britain.

It was then Edith noticed the ornate invitation in Auden's hands. "What on earth is that?"

Auden had forgotten about the invitation entirely. Helplessly, he handed it to her. "The Greenstreets," he said, by way of explanation.

Edith flicked her gaze over the ornate invitation, gilded and sealed with long, scarlet ribbons. "A ball," she said, in the way one would describe a newly-discovered slug beneath a rock.

"I'm afraid you are the guest of honour," said Auden, which was a bold, if predictable move from the Greenstreets. No doubt the other landed families would follow suit, and their winter would be one long procession of balls and dances and soirees. "There were also delivered, by separate post, at least six requests to dance. Apparently, the rumour that you may be looking to marry to secure your title has multiplied."

"Well," said Edith, throwing the invitation into the fire and watching it burn with particular satisfaction, "At very least, it is an excuse for a few new waistcoats."

CHAPTER FIVE
THE GREENSTREETS' BALL

HARROW HOUSE WAS a thrill of excitement, albeit shot through with a vein of anxiety. Dresses were costly, and neither Viola nor Poppy had means for a new gown, especially considering the rumours that this would not be the last ball of the winter.

Every day new carts arrived from Tonbridge, London, and beyond, with decorations, furniture, fabric, and every kind of frippery imaginable toward the Greenstreets' house. It was said the family had hired three illusory witches—an unbelievable sum—for water charming and centrepieces. And a cornucopia of new dresses had been delivered to Hoyt's Clothiers, Miss Rawlings-Vijay's prime competitor.

Poppy was just about to check on Miss Rawlings-Vijay's work—she was collaborating with the modiste on a dress alteration for Viola—when she heard someone speak her name.

Slowly, Poppy turned to see Antonella Greenstreet approaching her, flanked by Jessimina Finch and Elizabeth Wayfair. Antonella was a veritable layer cake of fox fur and velvet, her smooth, pink skin bright against the high ruffles and perfectly angled hood of her cape.

Poppy knew, intellectually, that Antonella Greenstreet was very beautiful, the most beautiful among her sisters—

perhaps among the whole town, if not all of Kent. She had a wide, sharp-featured face, lovely lips, and eyes of a grey-green hue that seemed to change colour with the seasons, the sky, and her mood. Poetic, really. Not to mention that she was enviably lush and round, with dimpled elbows and soft chin and curving, round shoulders. To say nothing of her hair, which was black as jet and curled in tight, glossy ringlets. Her sumptuous body moved with a kind of languid grace, and her dancing was the talk of the town: she was passionate about learning new dances and had musicians playing new music at whatever party she threw.

But there was nonetheless something about her that Poppy found repugnant. To look at her, she could find no flaw. Even Antonella's fingernails were pristine, white crescents against her porcelain skin. Beneath the beauty, however, Poppy knew lurked a viper, made so by generations of wealth, power, and influence.

"If it isn't Poppy Brightwell," said Antonella, as though pointing out a mildly interesting roadside wildflower.

"Good afternoon, Miss Greenstreet," said Poppy, giving a perfunctory curtsey. She had not expected that Antonella would deign to shop in town, and she was suddenly aware of every pulled thread and stain in Mama's old cloak, not to mention the state of her shoes.

"We've just been to Hoyt's," said Elizabeth, peering askance at Poppy. "You should see the ribbons. I haven't seen anything so fine since I was last in Paris."

"Have you been to Paris, Poppy?" Jessimina asked.

"I have not," said Poppy, who had not even been to London. "But Mama has, a few times. She said there were too many werewolves there for her tastes."

Antonella ran one of her white gloves over her fox fur muff. "Well, werewolves aside, that's where I got this from.

Paris. From a *real* modiste there. I wonder if the gentlewitch has been to Paris."

All three women looked pointedly at Poppy, who simply said: "I haven't the faintest idea."

"Well," said Antonella. "We've heard you had tea at Netherford Hall."

Poppy had been trying to forget that horrid afternoon ever since, but knowing that Antonella—and thereby the whole town—was aware, she felt her stomach sink. "We did. It was jolly."

"Jolly? My goodness. You have such a curious way of speaking, Poppy," Antonella said. "But tell me. What should I do to impress the gentlewitch?"

"I'm afraid I can't say," said Poppy, because she couldn't. And she also knew that if anyone in the whole town was an ideal match for the gentlewitch, it was Antonella. "We did not discuss much."

"Oh, she's just keeping the details to herself so she can charm the gentlewitch on her own," said Jessimina.

"Hardly," said Antonella. "Imagine a gentlewitch wooing their *tenant*."

All three girls laughed as if were the most hilarious jape in the history of comedy, but Poppy stood frozen, the insult stinging anew.

"Oh, there you are, Poppy!" Miss Rawlings-Vijay was suddenly beside Poppy, taking her by the shoulder. "I have something to show you in the store. I hope you are not otherwise engaged?"

Poppy gritted her teeth. "Not at all. There is absolutely nothing keeping me here, save spite."

Antonella and her flock of taffeta-shrouded admirers began laughing again, but Poppy allowed Miss Rawlings-Vijay to pull her into the shop, and it was very satisfying to slam the door once they were inside.

The application of a cup of strong tea, three shortbread biscuits, and some restrained ranting later, and Poppy felt more herself.

Miss Rawlings-Vijay was always good for cheer. They had gone to school together, though Miss Rawlings-Vijay was a few years older than she. Both shared a love of fashion, flowers, and frippery, and were fierce friends to this day.

"You do always know how to cheer me up, Jamini," she said kindly.

"Well, Miss Greenstreet was in earlier, insulting my ribbons," Jamini said. "She had this coming to her. My grosgrain is not 'unremarkable.' She needs spectacles."

"Your ribbons are divine," Poppy said. "And I was on my way to admire them—and to check on Viola's dress. But if you hadn't interrupted, I just might have shoved Antonella into the muddy street."

"She would have deserved it, but I'm glad that you did not cause such a fuss. Come, let me show you the dress."

Viola believed the dress in question was in a pattern of her own choosing, fashioned from one of Mama's old silk dresses and another she'd worn two years ago to the summer celebration for Hypatia Greenstreet's birthday, along with a bit of taffeta Poppy had salvaged from a mending project.

But Poppy's vision was for so much more.

Miss Rawlings-Vijay ducked into the room behind the counter and came out with the dress, Poppy gave an involuntary sigh. It was high-waisted, pale green, with sheer lace across the shoulders that Poppy had from Dolly Munns in exchange for rebinding a volume of encyclopaedias. Now, bleached and laid across the top bodice, the end result was nothing short of stunning. The taffeta had been repurposed into piping along the seams, then folded into perfect pale green flowers and leaves.

"We'll need matching ribbon for her hair, of course,"

Miss Rawlings-Vijay said, when Poppy did not react.

"It's a masterpiece," said Poppy, and she meant it. True, it was not the kind of finery in satin that the Greenstreets would be wearing, nor was it even the kind of whitework that would turn heads with its gossamer layers. But Miss Rawlings-Vijay had worked tirelessly to create a gown that would be complete only when Viola wore it.

Viola would be the belle of the ball, and it was high time others noticed. Poppy's sister was a talented gardener, with a near perfect memory for plants, and an eye for painting them almost as real as life. But she also had the kindest heart Poppy knew, and read on a variety of topics that would impress even the most judgmental scholars. The Greenstreets were always in the company of professors and barristers and politicians, besides eligible folk from all walks of life. If Viola shone well enough, even in the shadows of the gentlewitch's presence, she could make the impression she deserved to.

"I also found these," Miss Rawlings-Vijay said, pulling out some silk slippers that looked reconditioned, but which matched the green hue perfectly. "Consider them a gift."

"Oh, my dear, this is just too much," said Poppy. "You elevated this to art. And I don't think half this fabric is what I gave you."

"I won't tell."

"*Jamini*," said Poppy.

"I won't hear your protests," said Miss Rawlings-Vijay. "I have you to thank for the bulk of my work. I might not look busy, but we've been working directly with the gentlewitch's modiste, George Morley, who came all the way from London, to put together their ensembles. It was Mr. Garcliffe himself who came to us."

"Yes, *charming* Mr. Garcliffe," Poppy said. "He's a very handsome face, but I fear a bit scattered. Then again, I would be the same way if I had to work in such company."

Miss Rawlings-Vijay stilled in the way deer do when they've been spotted across the field. "I take it you have reservations about your new landlord."

Poppy was no gossip. In truth, she gained far more enjoyment in life by speaking her mind than she would by bloviating. Bluntness was an art, and she its most devoted mistress. By the same token, it was unwise to share her personal distaste for the gentlewitch.

"Oh, nothing," said Poppy, folding the dress back up and giving it a good pat. "Merely the frustrations of a tenant in a house with a newly proximate owner. I did feel as if we had privacy up there on the slope, and now we must see all the lights on and the comings and goings."

"Harder to run about undetected," Miss Rawlings-Vijay pointed out.

"I would never 'run about,' Jamini. I am an exceptionally boring young woman."

"Why, that is the greatest fabrication I've ever heard!"

"So speaks the modiste."

Miss Rawlings-Vijay laughed. "But tell me: have you finished *your* dress?"

"I don't think I shall be attending," said Poppy, opting for nonchalance and examining the intricate piping around Viola's new cuffs.

"Oh, Poppy, no!"

"Don't be so scandalised, my friend. You know well enough I'm more suited to barns and fiddles than great halls and pianofortes."

Miss Rawlings-Vijay was not convinced, and tutted. "That may be. But I suspect a deeper deception: you didn't finish the dress. Even after I gave you the ribbon. And the edging. And that bit of lace."

Poppy tried to mask her embarrassment, but it was futile. "I didn't even begin upon it."

"You wouldn't have made the dress if Virginia Cawley, the High Witch herself showed up to ask for it," sighed the modiste. "And your mother will be so cross!"

"Let her. This should be Viola's moment, not mine."

Just then, before the modiste could express any more shock, Mr. Garcliffe himself entered the salon from the showroom, trailed again by little Henry, both red-cheeked from the cold and dressed far more appropriately than they had been on their first visit.

Mr. Garcliffe's expression remained cordial, though his discomfort was evident in his continual blinking. "Well, we hadn't anticipated seeing you so soon again, Miss Brightwell."

"Good afternoon, Mr. Garcliffe," said Poppy, affecting her most generous smile. "I was just departing."

"Oh, please, do stay a moment. I hoped you might be able to give me a little advice," Mr. Garcliffe said, to Poppy's surprise. "Since you are a person of feminine leanings, and I am in need of assistance."

"I am not the expert in such matters," she said, gesturing to Miss Rawlings-Vijay. "You seek this woman's most tenacious and artful eye."

"Perhaps," Mr. Garcliffe said carefully. "But—well, all respect to Miss Rawlings-Vijay, but she and I have been working together on the gentlewitch's ensemble and cannot agree on the cuffs."

"Oh, Miss Brightwell always has opinions to spare," said Miss Rawlings-Vijay, and were it not *wholly* outside the bounds of propriety, Poppy would have pulled her bonnet down over her chin. "Here, let me fetch the items in question."

Rather than speak to Mr. Garcliffe, Poppy leaned down to greet little Henry. "I hope you're up to as much trouble as possible," she said to him. "Tell me, have you been on adventures?"

Henry beamed, his darling gap-tooth on display. "Oh, I have. There are so many places in Netherford Hall," he said.

"I suppose it might take a lifetime to know all those rooms," said Mr. Garcliffe. "But darned if the boy isn't trying to pack it into a week."

"I found a grand dragon!" said Henry. "On a piece of stained glass. It was so dirty when I found it that I thought it was just an ugly red blotch. But when I cleaned it, it was a dragon. With feathers!"

Poppy could not help her stab of jealousy at his words. She, too, would have loved to find hidden dragons at Netherford Hall. But if she could not, at least someone was enjoying the gifts the manse had to offer. "Perhaps you will find a whole family of dragons," she suggested. "You must name them, and tell me all about their personalities."

"Oh, I would like that very much," said Henry. "Thank you, Miss Brightwell."

Miss Rawlings-Vijay reappeared with the shirt in question, along with the matching cuffs. The cuffs were a detachable affair of Miss Rawlings-Vijay's own invention, affixed by metal clasps that wound about the buttons.

In this case, Miss Rawlings-Vijay had created the finest set that Poppy had ever seen. These cuffs were embroidered in gold, green, blue, and pink floss, in a pattern of bee flower orchids studded with honeycomb bosses. They ended in gold buttons, set with what had to be alexandrite.

"Here we are," said Mr. Garcliffe. "It's adapted from a few pieces of family jewellery. The gentlewitch isn't much for rings or baubles, but I think this should suit her well."

"It needs a green line," said Poppy, surprised to have spoken, and indeed, to have formed an opinion at all. There was nothing wrong with the piece, really. Except the contrast. "On either side of the embroidery. Oh, Miss Rawlings-Vijay, they're absolutely beautiful in every way!

But if you were to expand upon the outer edges, perhaps with some satin or velvet ribbon in a bright green, the result would be even more striking."

"Well, the waistcoat is also green, so now I'm feeling a bit ashamed that I hadn't thought of that," said Miss Rawlings-Vijay. "What do you think, Mr. Garcliffe?"

Mr. Garcliffe drew his eyes away from the cuffs and looked between Poppy and Miss Rawlings-Vijay before saying, "I think that's a brilliant suggestion. I agree. Green will work well against her colouring."

Poppy thought for a moment, again, of that brilliant sunrise russet hair, and those dark, knowing eyes. But then she remembered the cold, deathlike grasp the gentlewitch had put on her heart and she could no longer summon up the romance.

"Very well, it's settled," said Miss Rawlings-Vijay. "I can have the alterations finished in time for the last fitting. I assume that Mr. Morley will be by?"

"Possibly," said Mr. Garcliffe, clearing his throat. "But if you would like to visit the house, Miss Rawlings-Vijay, you have—well—an official invitation. I was actually bringing it here, for you."

Mr. Garcliffe presented Miss Rawlings-Vijay with a little cylinder, containing, Poppy presumed, a scroll. She had heard of these before. On the great spectrum of magical implements, they were very basic, but would admit someone onto the grounds of the estate, as per invitation, as long and as often as they liked. It was, in essence, an open door.

The look on Miss Rawlings-Vijay's face was nothing short of awed. "I would be honoured," said the modiste at last. "I can deliver these myself, then. Perhaps two o'clock tomorrow?"

"Yes, that should suit," said Mr. Garcliffe with a smile. It was a nice smile, and that was the truly deplorable thing about him: every time you tried to dislike Mr. Garcliffe, he would smile and absolutely ruin the attempt.

And Miss Rawlings-Vijay was certainly enchanted by Mr. Garcliffe. Poppy sincerely hoped it would not end in heartbreak, as it so often did for Miss Rawlings-Vijay. She loved too easily and too quickly, already fashioning wedding attire before the first glow of love had dimmed.

Still, as Poppy Brightwell made her way back to Harrow House, she was not as doleful as she had been on the way down. Though she would not attend the Greenstreets' ball, she was full of the anticipation of generosity. How lovely Viola would be, and how happy! That was all that really mattered. And perhaps Miss Rawlings-Vijay nursing a loving spark, even if unrequited, would put a spring in her step.

And, she supposed, she had saved the gentlewitch from a potential sartorial mistake. That had to count for something.

EDITH ROOKWOOD HAD been in town, some distance behind her uncle and cousin. She saw them enter Miss Rawlings-Vijay's shop, and had even gone so far as to step upon the threshold, when she caught a familiar voice: Poppy Brightwell. The woman, it seemed, had a knack for being wherever the Rookwoods needed to be. But rather than showing herself, and truly being entirely mortified by their last conversation, Edith instead slipped into the shadows to listen.

She was not the most accomplished witch, but melting into the environment was a gift at which she excelled, and a rather rare one at that. It had served her well throughout her life, and she did not wish to see the Brightwell woman so soon after their last parting.

Yet Poppy had known what to do with the cuffs without any consideration, and without a sharp word for Edith. It felt strangely intimate.

When Poppy had gone—*whistling*, of all things, as she headed back to Harrow House—Edith joined her uncle and Miss Rawlings-Vijay at the large counter where the cuffs were still laid out.

"Apologies, Miss Rawlings-Vijay," Edith said, when the modiste began fretting and fussing over her arrival. "I do not wish to cause any distress. And I must agree with Miss Brightwell's observations—a green background will make an excellent addition."

"Of course," said Miss Rawlings-Vijay, fingers trembling as she began packing away the new chemise. "I am humbled by your invitation to Netherford Hall, my liege."

"Temper your excitement, miss," said Mr. Garcliffe. "The house is still in a state of utter madness. But it will be far easier for us to receive the suit there, than come to collect it here."

"Well, the exterior work looks quite lovely," said Miss Rawlings-Vijay, off-hand, pulling out a large drawer of ribbon and selecting a few green samples to measure against the colous on the cuffs.

"Exterior work?" Edith hadn't done a thing to the exterior; at least, not on purpose. She didn't believe Uncle Auden had begun looking for contractors, either, considering the weather.

Miss Rawlings-Vijay did not register her surprise. "Oh, yes. Don't think we didn't notice! I've been staring up at Netherford Hall every day for my entire life, and I'd been wondering about those patches in the roof by the east wing — I was concerned they might fall through."

Edith looked over at Auden, hoping he might have some kind of enlightenment on the subject, but he was just as confused as she was. That, and he was still mooning over Miss Rawlings-Vijay's eyelashes, which were, to her credit, most beautiful.

AFTER SPEAKING WITH Miss Rawlings-Vijay regarding one more tailoring project, Edith decided to walk with Uncle Auden and Henry the long way home, rather than take the carriage. She had to admit, she hadn't spent much time looking at the outside of Netherford Hall, because living on the inside took such willpower day-to-day not to reduce it to rubble.

Thankfully, the fog had lifted, and as they took the bend around from Baker's Lane, they could see Netherford Hall in its full glory, laid out across the little slope above Harrow House. And it was true: the roof was somehow much restored.

"I just want to be clear," said Uncle Auden. "I did not authorise any roof repairs. This is very strange, indeed."

Edith did not answer him right away. She knew her silence bothered him, but the problem with Uncle Auden—at least the most obvious to her—was that he filled up silence with too many words. The man could scarcely keep a thought to himself. It was as if his speech needed more grammatical structure. Or perhaps his brain did.

"I think it's magic," she said, at last, tightening her scarf around her neck and glaring in the direction of Netherford Hall.

"Magic? I didn't know you knew those kinds of spells," said Auden.

"I don't. But that does not mean it isn't magic."

Henry blew his nose on his handkerchief. "Magic is everywhere," he said simply. "Everyone knows that, Uncle Auden."

"Well, yes," said Uncle Auden. "But managing entire

renovations unbeknownst to me? How do you know such a thing, Edith?"

She shrugged. "As Uncle Astor might have said: it's a bit of a hunch, a buzzing in the back of the head, a right gut-feeling."

Great Uncle Astor. How she missed his staunch presence! He had been trying to help Edith with her own magics, which were modest at best and steadfastly underwhelming at worst. It was why they had pinned their hopes on another, more powerful witch, hoping that Aunt Cassandra's next child might prove more acceptable.

That sick, hollow feeling she had felt the moment she'd seen the belching pillars of smoke rising from Hatchney returned again: worthless, untalented, useless. She smothered it down.

Reclaiming Netherford Hall had been her sole focus since the tragedy. Every day they had remained in London, her powers had weakened; for Hatchney House hadn't just been destroyed, it had been *expunged*. All trace of magical connection to their High House, decimated. Netherford Hall was her last hope for any kind of power.

House magic was old magic, and not an exact practice in the way of illusion or necromancy, or any of the coven disciplines. It was the magic of *place*. It was a connection between the land and its gentlewitch, and ancient as the earth itself.

Netherford Hall had stood upon this slope for time out of mind—the original structure was even mentioned in the Domesday Book. But the Rookwoods had become detached from it.

Until now.

"I can't say," Edith said, picking up her pace again as Henry and Uncle Auden caught up to her. "But it gives me a glimmer of hope."

The relief in Uncle Auden's eyes was nearly enough to break through Edith's stalwart defences, but not quite.

"THIS MUST BE a dream. Oh, Poppy, I don't know how you did it!" Viola exclaimed, turning this way in that in Mama's long mirror.

"Oh, stop crying, you'll ruin the lace," said Poppy, holding back her own tears.

Mama and Papa watched in awe as their eldest daughter made a show of the truly breathtaking gown Poppy had bestowed upon her. There had been much embracing, sighing, and fawning, and after a few family heirlooms found their way to Viola's wrists, ears, and fingers, she was declared perfection.

"Now, show us *your* dress, Poppy dear," Viola said, when all the adulation came to an end. "You absolutely must."

Poppy was prepared to admit she had absolutely no intent of going to the ball, and not only because she would have rather painted tar over her toes than spend another moment in the presence of the gentlewitch, but also because she had failed to start on her own gown, when the front bell began clanging, followed by Oliver's shouts.

In a moment, amidst a flurry of clothing and bodies, Heath Brightwell emerged into the parlour, hat askew, Oliver hanging off one elbow, and two of the cats curling around his legs.

Heath had only been gone about three months, but he was changed. That head of coarse black curls, so like Poppy's own, was tamed and oiled—though a little ruffled on account of his enthusiastic brother—and his face was leaner, tougher, looking so much like their late Uncle Regus, Papa's brother.

"What a day of surprises!" Viola said, encircling

Heath yet again in an embrace, and kissing him on the cheek. "Heath!"

"I believe I have stumbled into a fairy tale," Heath said, looking at Viola. "You're a vision, sister."

"It's all on account of Poppy," said Viola, drawing her sister in with one hand and squeezing her. "It was just the most remarkable of surprises. I swear, Poppy is an enchantress in her own right."

Thorne had jumped up on Papa's lap and was now prodding at a loose bit of newspaper. Papa, looked around at his family with tears in his eyes and smiled. "Heath, you didn't even write, my boy."

"I know, and I am a churl for it," Heath said, drawing his father's hand to his lips and kissing it. "But you see, news has made it all the way to Cambridge: the Gentlewitch of Netherford has returned. And the Greenstreets are having a ball. Since I hadn't been home in some time, and my advisor had fallen curiously ill, I decided to study for exams here. And it affords me the joy of accompanying my sisters to the ball, as well. Unless they've escorts I'm not aware of?"

Both sisters said nothing, but that was well enough, because Mama had not had enough embracing her eldest child and did so now without restraint.

"Now what is this fanfare all about?" Heath asked.

"We were just waiting to see Poppy's gown," said Viola. "But she was being evasive."

"I was not," Poppy explained. "It's only that, you know how I am about such festivities, and there just really wasn't the time—"

"Oh, Poppy, you didn't!" Viola said, knowing full well exactly that Poppy had, indeed.

"Didn't what?" Papa asked. "The child has barely said a word."

"Of course," said Oliver. "It's obvious."

"What's obvious?" Mama asked, wiping at her eyes. "Someone explain what is going on."

And just as Poppy again steeled herself for a long-winded explanation about witches and well-to-do families and the resources it took to put together an outfit, the front bell rang. Mrs. Pratt gave a startled cry from the foyer.

Oliver reached Mrs. Pratt first and returned the bearer—quite literally—of the news. An enormous package tied in green ribbon and dried flowers and wrapped in lovely cotton cloth.

"It's for you, Poppy." Oliver looked as confused as anyone. He alone knew just how little Poppy had prepared for the ball.

And this box had no markings, no return address, and no courier.

"More surprises," mused Viola, though clearly unconvinced.

Poppy approached the box as one might a hostile badger. Tied to the top was a card with broad, blackletter writing: *For P.B.* Keeping herself steady, Poppy unfolded the letter and read the simple note inside: *Let me be that I am and seek not to alter me.* Shakespeare. How curious!

The top slid off easily, and the colour immediately captured Poppy's attention, accompanied by the hushed whispers of her family—it was pale red, almost pink, but diaphanous. The overdress was light as air, muslin shot with brighter pink rosettes. The gown beneath was actual silk, a deeper purple that contrasted with the petals embellishing the shoulders and sleeves. And the bodice was very nearly *scandalous*.

Or would be, if she wore it.

Poppy had finished examining the dress, and felt the gazes of her entire family resting upon her.

She had no explanation.

Except—no. The gentlewitch would never dare. And this

was not the work of Miss Rawlings-Vijay, either; she knew her stitchwork too well.

"It appears I have an admirer," said Poppy, closing the box, or trying to, as Viola descended and began her own inspection.

"The letter isn't even signed," said Heath, turning it over in his hands. "Not terribly gentlemanly."

"Well, Poppy has always been a child of remarkable circumstances," her father said, and she could not mistake the warmth in his voice. "Perhaps the Dowager Viscountess has extended her generosity."

"I doubt *that*," said Poppy, trying not to snort. "The last time I was there, she said I breathed like a frog. It's Viola she adores."

"What about your dress you've been working on?" Mama pressed; as usual, she was far less convinced.

"There was no dress," said Poppy. "I was too caught up in work on Viola's, you see."

"Well. It seems that doesn't matter now," Mama said, clicking her tongue. "But do not trust this to happen again. Next time—providing there *is* a next time, I will have to spend more time looking over your shoulder. Which is surely beneath the both of us, considering your age and my schedule."

"There is no need to scold, Mama," Viola said, her voice sweet as treacle. "This is a miracle dress, and it will somehow be even more lovely in contrast to mine. Oh, what a day we shall have at the Greenstreets!"

What a day, indeed. Poppy forced a smile, but she had truly been hoping to avoid the comb and primping and attention the next days would bring—in spite of the lovely gown, she was somewhat disappointed.

* * *

THE GREENSTREETS' MANSION, Jasper House, was everything a great country home should be, and for some reason that cast Auden into a foul mood. He was envious of this resplendent mansion, every inch gleaming wood and marble, every corner orchestrated with the perfect balance of paintings, glass sculptures, statues, lush fabrics, and gilding. He didn't even like what he was looking at, but he still felt Netherford Hall was entirely lacking.

He felt like a pauper.

And his ensemble felt tight. Itchy. He had declined a fitting by Miss Rawlings-Vijay, mostly because he lived in abject fear of what would happen to him if he allowed the modiste any nearer to him. It was well enough to admit to himself that he enjoyed their flirtation, and yes, he had come up with every reason possible to frequent the modiste's shop from that first moment he saw her. But their last exchange...

The ballroom at Jasper House was, he supposed, the reason for its name: the entirety of the room was jasper and red marble. Normally, he might have considered the contrast rather appealing, but he was feeling both melancholic—a rarity for him—and discomfited, and it reminded him, instead, of streaked blood.

As if the architecture weren't enough, the great hall was alive with magic, courtesy of the illusion witches, who'd spun elaborate spells to look like curtains of falling snow, holly bushes blooming and twisting into great columns in the shapes of dragons, horses, and elephants. The artistry was there, for certain, but the constant wavering and changing had his stomach a bit at unease. And the fact that half the guests had illusions flickering in their hairpieces didn't help.

"You look like you've swallowed a maggot," said his niece, walking up to him with a silver and jade flagon of fragrant wine.

Auden swallowed. "If there are maggots in the canapés, please alert me."

This elicited the barest of smiles from Edith. True to her station, she was the centre of attention wherever she went. Throngs of young, eligible suitors kept to the edges, whispering over fans and averting eyes the moment she glanced their way. It was a pastel-and-creme nightmare, topped with curls and twirling fascinators.

"You don't have to suffer," Edith said softly, watching Auden quaff his drink with hardly a breath. "I can manage."

"This place makes me ill," he said, reaching behind his head and finding his neck absolutely thick with sweat. "Witchcraft paraded around for parlour tricks."

"You lived in London for your whole life, Uncle, surely that can't be what's bothering you!"

"You're right. It's the news you gave me earlier."

Edith had shared with him, that morning over breakfast, word of their newfound relatives, the Rookwood-Nourses. Not only did they have a claim to the house, their fortune, and the coven's seat, but they were coming to visit, as well.

"It is a strange circumstance," said Edith. "But I am willing to entertain them, to assume the best before I discover the worst."

"Wise, as always." Auden frowned, looking into the murky bottom of his flagon. The music picked up, and some of the guests began moving in a new dance he had never seen before. Or perhaps it was an old country dance that just hadn't made its way to London. Either way, he dreaded any more movement. "This whole business just makes me feel inadequate."

"Well, you *are* inadequate," said Edith in her typically blunt way. "And so am I. We will need to learn together."

Auden was about to say something sentimental, when the music swelled and a small cluster of new guests arrived.

Two were easy to recognise: Viola and Poppy Brightwell looked every inch women of style, far beyond what Auden would have thought them capable given their status. The man on whose arms they entered was surely their brother.

Edith's attention was caught, as well. Viola, to no surprise, was a wonder in a delightful gown that accentuated her long neck, dark hair, and delicate bone structure.

But *Poppy*. And her gown. Even amidst all the illusion, she was the most magical thing in the vast hall. Her gown was constructed of layers, the exterior a diaphanous pink hue, and fell long on her arms down to her wrists. She was not a petite woman, and the ample swell of her breasts and the arch of her shoulders was on display in a way Auden could never have expected. She wore three plain silk roses, white with green petals, against her black curls, looking for a moment like a princess out of a tale of yore. Her dark hair had been swirled into three high buns, like a coronet.

Edith saw. Oh, heavens, did she see.

Yet there was no time for discussion or explanation: for the Greenstreet girls arrived then, all five of them, pushing through the Brightwells as if they were nothing more than servants, in matching moiré taffeta. Carine and Carlotta were identical twins, so the effect was even more startling. The youngest, Antonella, the main attraction of the festivities, had the gall to wear a crown made of coral, ensorcelled to sway as if it was underwater.

And if that wasn't offensive enough, behind the Greenstreets came two very familiar figures, smiling and smirking as if they owned the place: Laertes and Ophelia Byrne.

Vampires.

And, in the case of Laertes, Auden's former suitor.

Auden might have vomited, if he hadn't been jostled by the parting crowd. Antonella climbed up a little dais apparently raised for the purpose.

* * *

As Poppy entered the Greenstreets' ballroom, trailing behind Viola and Heath, she nearly lost her footing when Antonella and her courtiers came by, disregarding the Brightwells entirely. The crowd seemed to sigh as one as Antonella rose before them, resplendent in a dress of seafoam green, absolutely littered with diamonds and dripping with enchantments.

"It's like biting into a perfect apple to find a worm inside," Heath said under his breath. "Every time I see her, it takes a moment to remember just how poisonous she is."

"I do wish I could fill out a dress that way," Viola said, shaking her head. "And that colour—heavens! She looks like a sea goddess."

Poppy was about to add to the conversation, if not a very nice addition, when she felt an unexpected warmth at her chest and felt her gaze pulled up, as if compelled.

Edith Rookwood stood, arms folded before her, staring back at Poppy. Not at Antonella, which was the proper and the obvious thing to do.

Flushing, Poppy tried not to think just how perfectly handsome the gentlewitch looked. The cuffs were lovely, and the green she'd chosen a truly smart decision—but that was just the half of it. Liege Rookwood was every inch a gentlewitch from the long tailcoat—a purple so dark it was almost black—to the gold and green of her waist coat and her glittering chatelaine of office. And those eyes. Even at this distance, Poppy could still see those blue-grey depths, and for one strange, disorienting minute, she felt as if she were right beside the gentlewitch. She felt her hand rise to separate those lustrous red curls.

Poppy was either going to burst into giggling or else vomit profusely.

Thankfully, Heath had her by the shoulder, Viola pressed a cup into her hand, and Antonella began speaking to the guests.

The Greenstreet girl's voice was resonant: she was, after all, a trained opera singer. Were she from a lesser family, it might have been acceptable for her to travel and perform. But, as Mr. Brightwell was fond of saying, there are chains for every class; some are just forged from finer metals.

"Welcome, all, to Jasper House," Antonella said. With every swoop of her hands, the diamond-and-sapphire bangles around her wrists and fingers glittered, leaving little trails of light behind, like spectral comets.

"Not only am I celebrating my twenty-second birthday, a most auspicious year, but I am officially presented, on behalf of my father and mother, to society," she said with mock-humility. "I will be attending the next London season, should I not find a match before then. Though, I will say, my heart will always be in Kent, and so I have every hope to stay as the shepherd of Jasper House." Antonella twirled, the lights twirling with her, looking now like flower petals in the dimmed lights.

The musicians began playing a soft, old rendition of a local song that Poppy knew by melody, though not the words.

"And of course, this is a new age for Netherford. I am so very pleased to welcome to Jasper House, on her first engagement since returning, the gentlewitch herself, Liege Edith Rookwood, High Witch of Greystrand. Please, darling, come to the dais with me so everyone can see you."

Darling?

That was uncalled for.

It was impossible to see where the gentlewitch now resided in the crowd, but judging by the uncomfortable delay it took for her to reach the dais, she was reluctant.

Yet there she was, slowly ascending the stairs toward luminous Antonella Greenstreet. Liege Edith looked like she'd just swallowed a slug, and Poppy could not explain why this made her so gleeful.

When it became clear Antonella expected Liege Edith to speak, the gentlewitch brushed aside one of the twinkling illusions—which melted away from her touch in a most impressive way—lifted her head and looked across the room. "Thank you for having me."

Then she turned on her heel and left the dais, without so much as a glance to Antonella, and was absorbed again by the crowd.

HUNGRY THOUGH SHE was, Poppy couldn't manage much in the way of food, and that was highly unusual. Everything looked terribly greasy, or else was shrouded in illusions so as to surprise the guest upon eating. After biting into a piece of cheese and jam to find a mouthful of crab, she'd sworn off anything more.

The pull of boredom threatened Poppy, and with it came the familiar agitation she'd known since childhood. She had to move her feet. And more than anything, she needed some fresh air. What was it about so many people moving together in a single space? It made her long for the sound of the river and the swaying grasses outside.

She was just within reach of the large double doors leading out to the balcony when Poppy heard her name. Her heart lurched as it had so many times last spring.

Captain Horatio Evans. Her first love. Her first heartbreak. Her first passion.

"You're supposed to be in India," she said as she turned.

Tall, kind, generous, and possessed of eyes so blue they rivalled the robin's egg. Captain Evans was taller than

Poppy, and broad from his work in the military. His family, like hers, had fallen from grace through ill-luck, and he was all but orphaned. Two summers ago, he had worked on Harrow House repairing all manner of broken windows, leaky roof tiles, and uneven floors. He asked only to eat with the family and for good conversation.

Then last spring, he had asked for her hand.

But Poppy did not desire marriage, nor did she desire children. And Captain Evans did.

"I took a bad step," he said, leaning down just slightly to knock on his shin with his knuckles. Even with the noise coming from the party, Poppy could hear the hollow sound. "Though, all things considered, it could have been much worse."

"Oh, by the speckled firmament!" Poppy breathed. He hadn't written her. But then, she hadn't written him, either.

"Do not fret, my dear. It was no foul play. I quite literally fell in a hole on a dock, getting ready to embark on my next assignment. I didn't see it, and I should have been paying attention. Then the wound festered and, though I do not want to bother you with the details, no amount of magic or medicine could help, and we made the decision to relieve me of my ailment altogether."

"Does it hurt?"

"Not today. Sometimes I forget it isn't there, when I wake in the night." He rubbed at his head and laughed. Poppy had forgotten just how musical his laugh was. It made her stomach flutter.

Poppy gazed up at him, speechless for a moment. She always found it difficult to capture words around Captain Evans. Theirs was a language older and quieter.

"But you're on the mend now, I hope," she said.

"Yes. It was months of work to walk again, and I was in bad shape there for a bit, but they let me come home through the New Year. I arrived just yesterday, and the Greenstreets made sure I knew I was welcome. I was hoping to see you."

"Well, here I am," she said, giving an awkward curtsey. "More or less."

"Always more," Captain Evans said. "You are resplendent."

"You know I find balls tedious."

"You do not," said Captain Evans, taking a step forward. Poppy could not help but remember when they had been unable to keep away from one another. When her days, and nights, had been filled with nothing but the nearness of him: his lips, his hands, his breath.

Heavens, he just smelled delightful. Warm, spicy, welcoming. Like a sweater dried by the fire over lavender.

"Well, *today* I find it tedious," she corrected. "Having to fawn over Antonella and her clucking entourage is exhausting."

"Now *that* sounds like the Poppy I know. Mercurial and clever. Antonella Greenstreet still sets your teeth on edge, I see."

"Is it so obvious?"

He chuckled. "Tell me, how is your family?"

"Much the same, I suppose. Mama will be going back to Cambridge with Heath, as he's found her a short-term tutoring position, and it's been far too long since she's been able to research her beloved history tomes. Papa gave us a bit of a scare last winter, falling out of his chair and hitting his head. He recovered well, but he still has frightful days."

"He's such a good man," said Captain Evans, and indeed, they had been fast friends. "I miss his diatribes on portrait etiquette. And his jokes."

"I'm sure he'd love the audience. Poor Oliver is tiring of his repertoire. Oh, and Oliver! You should see him. He's all angles and elbows. I think he may even outpace Heath at this point. He's nearly taller than me."

"But still very much your darling?"

"Always. We are of a kind, and would be blissfully happy living among the trees and woodland creatures, and never speaking a word to another human being."

"Given your passion for speaking, I find *that* hard to believe."

Poppy actually laughed. It felt good to laugh like this, to fall again into Captain Evans's easy teasing conversation. His gaze was so warm, so honest. And she felt great affection for him, even if it was tinged with grief.

"I said speaking to other *humans*. I've compiled lengthy dramas and sermons for the fireflies and fairies, I'll have you know," she clarified.

And then *he* laughed, and Poppy nearly melted to hear it. Some men could laugh, and it sounded so cold, so detached, like a rehearsal of joy rather than an expression of it. But when Captain Evans laughed it filled her heart, it coursed through her like a low, resonant bell. And she wanted nothing more in the world than to make him laugh more.

Ah, her fickle heart. It was reason that had kept her from a life with Captain Evans, but sometimes it was feeling that spoke loudest, and she gave way to impulse.

So when Captain Evans asked, "May I call on you later in the week?"

She of course said yes.

EDITH HAD INTENDED to avoid dancing at all costs, but as the speeches ended and a pair of pale faces started working their way through the crowd towards her, she found herself presented with a very clear choice: dance, or speak to the vampires. As much as she abhorred dancing, conversing with the Byrne siblings was an even darker fate.

So, before she could think too much about the situation, and shoving her cloyingly sweet drink at Uncle Auden, she thrust herself into the middle of the dance floor, just as one of the reels began. This, of course, caused immediate mayhem, as half the attendees fumbled for her hand to begin. So many gloved hands, rings and bangles—so much artful giggling. It really was untoward.

Then, she saw, to the side of the dance, a familiar face. Poppy Brightwell. She was not directly dancing, but just out of the way, distancing herself from a very tall man in a captain's uniform who looked at her with—well, Edith was not so cloistered to be unaware of *that* look.

It was not jealousy that made her do it. It could not be jealousy. It was *panic*. Or that's what Edith Rookwood told herself as she twisted through a group of tittering dancers to take Poppy's hands.

God, but those eyes.

Poppy was shocked, and almost angry, but Edith knew, without a doubt, that she had the upper hand. Perhaps Poppy would rebuke her and insult her in private, but never here, before the rest of Netherford.

"Forgive me," said Edith, drawing Poppy in closer, whispering into her ear. She didn't know why she did it. It was intimate. And Poppy smelled *lovely*, with a delicate, floral hint. Like lilac and fresh pepper.

The reel was quick, but danced at close quarters, and Poppy was not a good dancer.

"Ow, sorry, ow!" Poppy said as they tried to get into rhythm and failed, yet again. It was supposed to be a promenade, but it was more like a limping skip.

"It's my fault," Edith said softly, again into the soft curls by Poppy's ear.

"What's your fault, my liege?"

"Well, a great many things, but mostly that I dragged you here to this dance," Edith replied, trying to avoid looking into Poppy's eyes again. They were dark, fathomless. She had the sudden desire to see those eyes in all sorts of lighting, to find the amber hints and the maroon and the deep, rain-washed bark.

Edith was beginning to wonder if she was demented. Her head felt too full, her thoughts languid, and *most* scandalous. Poppy's full lips were so ripe for kissing. And her floral perfume—jasmine, honeysuckle, and a bright, citrus note—simply goaded Edith on, swirling around her own erotic contemplations.

"Well, in your defence," said Poppy Brightwell, turning her chin up defiantly, revealing the curve of her neck. "You were being swallowed up by a gaggle of Greenstreets and pursued by a fierce woman who looked like she wanted to eat you alive. I took pity upon you, my liege."

"I think Antonella Greenstreet would marry me at this precise moment if I consented," said Edith, who found their hostess beautiful but vapid. "Given the elaborate décor, it would not have even felt out of place."

"Oh, do not jest. She is very used to getting what she wants. And she is obscenely rich. Although, perhaps, that is precisely what a gentlewitch like yourself is looking for."

Edith felt affronted, a flare of anger mingling with the increasing sense of arousal being this close to Poppy Brightwell. Had her eyes always been this beguiling?

Edith did not have time for a response before the dance separated into two lines. This part of the dance entailed some quite ridiculous hand flapping. Edith watched as Poppy made a piteous attempt to follow along, but it was no use.

A few more minutes and they were reunited again. Poppy's hair had started to come out of the delicate flowers at her temple, and the result was no less lovely. She most certainly did not need witchcraft to accentuate her virtues.

Edith, again, resisted the urge to touch Poppy's cheek, to run her fingers along the length of her neck and across her collarbones—along her lower lip.

"I believe I have you to thank, though," said Poppy, breaking Edith out of her reverie.

"You do? For what?" Edith asked haltingly.

"Well, I have been thinking." Heavens, but how Poppy's bosom rose and fell with her breath, the skin so smooth and delicate! How soft it must feel. How yielding. "This dress. The note. It was you, wasn't it, who sent it?"

"The dress is very lovely," said Edith, who was not contemplating Poppy in the dress, but rather her vision of the young woman out of it. "But I'm afraid I did not—"

"But the colours, and surely someone overheard me at Miss Rawlings-Vijay's?"

Edith just stared, infatuated with the way Poppy's lips moved over her teeth with every word, and said nothing.

"Oh, I'm sorry. I must have made a mistake. It was only for a moment, of course you'd never do such a thing."

Poppy was still talking, her voice quavering and thick with embarrassment or perhaps holding back tears, but Edith could barely make out the words as the realisation hit her: chest tingling, lips hot, a coiling pressure between her legs...

Edith was not just *demented*.

She was *enchanted*. And she had missed it. A novice's mistake; she had performed a charm to detect potions like this one—brewed to entice mortals to lusty thoughts, but terribly toxic to gentlewitches—but her working must have been flawed. She should have been alerted to it. Now, she was sick in heart and in stomach.

Edith's shame was a hot tide, threatening to choke her. Could she do *nothing* correctly? A memory of her mother came to her then, that feeling of despair and abject disappointment: *A middling witch. Of no consequence. So unlike the Rookwood line.*

Edith only managed: "Oh, this is terrible."

The crowd was so wrapped up in clapping that they did not notice, at least right away, as Edith led Poppy out to the balcony. She cast up a small net of obscuring, one of her few reliable spells, and bent over, trying to stop the bout of dizziness and stop the ringing in her ears.

"You could have just said 'no,'" said Poppy, crossing her arms and looking down indignantly at Edith. This helped nothing in terms of Edith's stoked ardour, as it pushed her bosom up even higher. "Really, there's no need for such theatrics."

Edith was trembling now, and she began to worry that the situation was going to degrade even further. A love potion! It was insulting. And dangerous.

"I must leave now," Edith said, through gritted teeth. "I need you to—to fetch one of the footmen and call my carriage. Then tell Mr. Garcliffe to meet me outside. Do it quietly."

Poppy gaped, tears brimming in her marvellous, enchanting eyes. Edith hated herself for causing that hurt.

"Please, I need you to get away from me," Edith moaned, and it sounded awful, like she was rejecting Poppy in the most indelicate way possible. But whatever they had given her was working its way through her, and making her angry and sick. And incapable of controlling her own desire for Miss Brightwell. Which she would far prefer to nurse in quiet and solitude, not in public.

"Poppy, please, I beg you—call the coach and leave me!"

Poppy ran, still cloaked in Edith's spell. Well, at least *that* worked on the Brightwell girl—she could be obscured. Edith's head was beginning to throb at the temples, and the nausea grew inside her. She leaned over the balustrade, trying to take in the cold air, trying to clear her eyes.

Edith's tenuous magic was slipping through her fingers, becoming unreliable. So she strained to listen below, where the front entrance cast golden light on the gravel and lit the carriage windows. Poppy's voice was easy to pick out, but so was the trembling in it. The fear. The hurt.

But there were vampires within, and decidedly incautious witches, and mortals. And Edith could not risk the danger to salve Poppy's feelings.

Edith waited until she could hear her carriage's wheels approaching, and she swept up her tailcoat and twisted down from the balcony, landing softly on the gravel below, still cloaked in her magic, but breathing heavily. That would be enough for her, tonight, of any kind of spell.

As Uncle Auden approached her, eyes wide with concern, she did the only reasonable thing she could. She vomited all over his shoes.

Vomit-stained shoes were the least of Auden Garcliffe's concerns. Someone had made Edith very ill, and he was not capable of helping her. He hoped it was an innocent mistake. Likely, someone had the idea that a love-stricken gentlewitch would be either entertaining or fortuitous, but they did not realise the hazards.

Neither did Auden, for that matter.

Which was why he called for Molly and Basil Hode as soon as he'd arranged Edith in one of the settees in the withdrawing room. It might not have been the best choice for her convalescence, but it was Edith's favourite room, and he thought that might help.

It was Basil Hode who arrived shortly, a narrow apparition in the doorway, windblown and red-nosed. It looked as if he'd been in the middle of working, as his sleeves were still up around his elbows and he smelled faintly of malt and sawdust.

"We may need to get some reinforcements," said Auden as Basil approached, taking in the scene.

Edith was tossing, face pale, vomit all down the front of her marvellous waistcoat, one of her splendid new cuffs missing. What an utter shame that was.

"We think it was a love potion," said Auden. "Perhaps the doing of a hedge witch or local mage."

Basil leaned offer, sniffing. "I smell it on her breath. Mandragora, oleander, a bit of bay leaf."

"Someone gave her a goblet, just before the dancing began," said Auden, choosing his words carefully to spare Edith later shame. "It must have been well concealed. The gentlewitch drank it down, then went dancing. Then Miss Brightwell found me and reported the symptoms."

"We'll need some goat's milk," said Basil. "Still warm, if you can. And some honey." He paused, taking a little book out of his pocket—the man was a portable library!—and consulted within. "And then I will need some lavender, a twist of oak bark, holly berries, and some black salt. Do you have all those in the kitchen?"

Auden had absolutely no idea. He called in the cook, and she was doubtful, saying that they hadn't had enough time for such detail while stocking the ancient pantry.

"If the gentlewitch believed it was a love draught, then I concur," said Basil softly, almost as if he were attempting to calm Auden down. "I am not a complicated man, but I am a Warder. And one of our first rules, though unwritten and not practised in Netherford in quite some time, is to allow the gentlewitch to lead by Her intuition." He grinned, and Auden had not noticed the man's single dimple before. Then again, he had not seen Basil Hode smile before, either.

"But I am most experienced with drunkenness and the best ways around such a circumstance, and it is concerning the spell was strong enough to conceal such a simple draught."

The cook arrived in short order with all the requisite items, stirred together and presented in a rather ostentatious pewter goblet.

"Well, that will do," said Auden, taking the cup.

Leaning forward, and timing it just right, he managed to get Edith to sit up straight and take a few sips of the brew. She did not make a face as he had expected; nor did she let loose its contents.

But she did not wake, but she seemed to relax, with a soft sigh.

"Every hour, if you can, have them make another batch," said Basil, apparently quite pleased with the outcome. He looked relieved, thought Auden. "The first *warm* sips are the most powerful and soothing."

"Thank you," said Auden. "In London, this sort of thing would have never happened. Witches never partake of mortal draughts."

And Edith should have known how to detect them.

The Warder gazed at the gentlewitch for a moment before answering. "At this dose, it could have been fatal for her."

"Do you think they knew?" Auden half-whispered the words.

He felt his skin crawl. He pushed himself up from his chair and began pacing the room, worrying his fingers through his beard in a way his mother would have been scandalised to see. She always said it made him look like a maniac.

Well, he might become one, if what precious little was left of his family was still in dire peril.

"I hope not. For all our sakes," said Basil. "Did you notice anything odd leading up to the event?"

Aside from his and Henry's continual nightmares, no.

But Auden did not want to share his childish dreams of ghouls. "I don't understand why anyone would attempt such a thing," said Auden. Edith settled more in the settee. Her cheeks were pink, now, and it was a great relief.

"Well, Molly is making sure the house wards are safe," said the Warder. "And it is possible that the ingredients in the draught were accidentally poisonous. Vomiting was probably helpful, given the situation."

"That's the first I've heard of it," said Auden. "And my shoes will never be the same."

"It may be best—if I am allowed to be so forward, sir—if we take up residence closer to the gentlewitch. Just for a time. Though we do not possess any great powers of our own, we do have considerable ancestral knowledge. And though Molly is a middling apothecary, she's a dab hand with a club."

Auden did not want to trust anyone with protecting the gentlewitch, but he was in dire straits.

"I understand your hesitation," said Basil, and his gentle manner almost brought tears to Auden's eyes. His genuine bearing was a relief. "And it is not something I offer lightly. Think on it, tonight, as she improves—if she continues to do so. And in the morning, when the sun rises and she gains her strength again, we can discuss."

"What should I do in the meantime?"

Basil gave Auden a sad smile. "Rest, Mr. Garcliffe. There may be a more dangerous road ahead."

CHAPTER SIX
DEATH'S DOOR

THE WINTERY WEEKS passed with little change, though gossip ran rampant concerning the gentlewitch's abrupt departure from the Greenstreet's ball—as along with Poppy Brightwell's curious behaviour, and the Byrnes returning from the London Season and taking up residence at old Howarth castle. The vampires had indicated that they would remain through the following summer as well, prompting much gossip.

For her part, Poppy tried to keep to quiet. Her ego had been terribly bruised, and the idea of seeing anyone from the ball, especially Antonella Greenstreet and her friends, made her physically ill. She'd spent two straight days in bed doing nothing but reading, sketching, and drinking tea. Her tolerant parents, familiar with her approach to matters of the heart, did not bother her until the third day.

"Captain Evans is on his way," said Mr. Brightwell, meeting his youngest daughter in the hallway as she went to raid the pantry for more food. "We just heard. And you might want to consider tidying yourself up?"

Captain Evans.

Heavens above! Poppy had entirely forgotten.

Mrs. Brightwell and Heath were in town, preparing for their return to Cambridge, and Viola was at her singing lessons down the lane. Oliver, as usual, was half-asleep in the living room, a book on his lap.

So, when Captain Evans arrived, it was just Poppy and Mr. Brightwell who greeted him, the former a little the worse for wear. She'd put her hair up in a loose, lace bonnet and washed her face, then haphazardly wrapped herself in a cotton dress at least two inches too short.

Captain Evans, no longer in his dress uniform, still looked as crisp as a freshly painted portrait. The bright lighting at the ball had revealed the changes in his face, but now, as she gazed up at him, he seemed almost his old self.

Poppy kept herself busy serving fruit and cakes, which also meant she got the first and best choice; perhaps it was selfish of her, but she was feeling indulgent, and nothing soothed her soul quite so much as a tidy cheese plate.

When he and Mr. Brightwell finally caught up, Captain Evans very politely asked if it would be acceptable to take Poppy for a walk, to which Mr. Brightwell laughed, and said, "As she has demonstrated time and again in her life, captain, it is entirely up to her."

But Poppy relented; a walk seemed an appealing prospect. It did take some time to find the right coat, as the wind was still chilly, but the sun was shining brightly and she never did argue when it came to time outside.

Captain Evans was a good walking companion. Like Poppy, he had long, strong legs, and kept a good pace. Oliver and Viola were always dawdling on their walks, never serious about the actual exercise and only interested in chatter. A good walk could include chatter, Poppy believed, but it shouldn't be the sole purpose.

Which was another reason she had always liked Captain Evans. He didn't have to fill up space with unnecessary conversation. And the moments of quiet between them were comfortable.

"I'm off to London this evening for a few weeks," said Captain Evans. They were now on the hill above the house, not far from the confounded property line of Netherford Hall. From where they stood, they could see the long sprawl of the old Tudor mansion, dark grey plumes of smoke rising from its chimneys like a sleeping dragon.

"London?" So far. So soon.

"Yes," he said, pausing a moment to reach down and adjust his leg. "There's some family business I need to attend to there. Nothing exciting, I'm afraid. And paperwork. They'll be transferring me to Tunbridge Wells for a clerk position in the service. Unfortunately, my days on the field are behind me."

"I've never been to London," said Poppy. Although it was not something she dreamed of, or even really considered. "But that's where *they're* from." She gestured to Netherford Hall. "And I don't think it brings out the best in people."

"Oh, London is a place of wonders. And it's filled with parks and beautiful gardens. I do think you would enjoy it."

"I'm afraid I must dislike it on principal."

Captain Evans examined her a moment, and she felt he was trying to peer into her soul. Well, no one peered into Poppy Brightwell's soul unless invited.

"May I be frank with you, Poppy?" he asked.

"I would have you be no other way."

He laughed. "When I saw you dancing with the gentlewitch, I wondered if perhaps she had taken your heart. The way you looked at her, well..."

"That's nonsense," Poppy said, turning her head away to hide the blush rising on her cheeks. "How would you know a thing about the way I look?"

Gently, he took her hand in his. "Because you looked at me that way once, my dear."

His gloves were thick, but somehow still conveyed his warmth to her hands.

"I know," he continued, shaking his head so the shadow

cast by his hat came and went from his marvellous eyes. "I know, we've been through this before. And I admit, part of me was hoping that when I returned to Netherford, you would have reconsidered. That you would have changed."

"Oh, Horatio," Poppy said, her voice thick in her throat. She wanted to cry. She wanted to *explain* to him. "I am not bewitched, I can tell you that. You do not need to worry about me."

"It isn't that I worry about you," Captain Evans said. "It's that I am, apparently, capable of jealousy. And I want every happiness for you. I had hoped, perhaps foolishly, that I could be the one to bring you that happiness."

Poppy felt the hot tears course down her cheeks before she could stop them. Captain Evans gently brushed them away.

"I do not want children," she said, and not for the first time. "I do not want marriage. Not now, and not ever."

"What do you want, Poppy? And why does it make you weep, so?"

"I do not *know*," she admitted to him, because she knew he was a friend, in spite of their unmatched hearts. "And that frightens me sometimes. I feel as if I owe it to Mama and Papa, to be something more—"

Because I am broken—and they are broken, because of me.

She couldn't tell him that. She couldn't reveal that secret shame. That her parents had sacrificed everything for her life, and she had done nothing of consequence with it.

"My darling, my bright Poppy," said Captain Evans, and he embraced her. And she allowed it. "Don't ever think you aren't enough, precisely as you are. Every part of you is exactly as it ought to be. Perhaps not forever, but for now."

No one had ever said that to her. "I can't do anything useful."

"Oh, Poppy. You can do so, so much."

"But I am only middling at any one thing."

"The dress you created for Viola was far from middling."

"I had help."

"You had vision! That is a rare thing, indeed."

She buried her head in his jacket again. "You are too good to me. I'm sorry I cannot be your wife," she said into the prickly wool. Her voice was muffled, but clear.

"You do not need to apologise. I was a fool for bringing it up again. Jealousy is not a welcome emotion, but I am just a man."

"You are a good man. And I wish—I very much wish—I could be the sort of woman who could make you happy," she said.

"I think you would make me happy, but I do not think I could make you happy."

He squeezed her one more time, and Poppy knew he would not ask her again. It was both a relief and a deep, bone-aching sorrow. Such was her mind; at times, she knew the truth of a thing, and no matter how many times she examined it, in her heart it would not change.

"We should get back," she said, looking down toward Harrow House. Its white and grey roof tiles looked almost like a chessboard from her vantage point, blurred as it was with tears. "But I would very much enjoy it if you wrote to me from London. I might even return the favour."

"I should be immensely flattered if you did," said Captain Evans.

Poppy turned away from Netherford Hall, her arm looped through Captain Evans's, and took one last look at the old Tudor before she went toward Harrow House again. She couldn't say for certain, but it seemed to her that the roof was a bit shabbier than it had been the week before. And some of the windows looked frostier than they ought.

But perhaps it was just the blurring from the tears in her eyes.

* * *

THE NEXT DAY, Poppy drove the cart to Tonbridge and back, to arrange passage for her brother and mother by coach to Cambridge. Mama was cheerful and excited. Like Viola, she enjoyed the constant movement of larger cities, and the opportunity to do research had her chattering incessantly on the way there. Heath was quiet, but patient. It was good of him to have helped Mama; they could certainly use the money.

On the return trip, Poppy kept going over the conversation with Captain Evans the day before. In no way did she question her answer to him, but she did wonder about what exactly had happened with the gentlewitch. She'd been avoiding thinking about it—what it had felt like to be in her arms, to be felt and not just seen.

Edith Rookwood could sense Poppy in a way that no one else ever had before, she was sure of it. And the liege was strange, yes: cold, and perplexing. And it was apparent that the gentlewitch did not even like being *around* Poppy— except that she had asked her to dance with her. Of all the great beauties at the ball, it was Poppy she had asked.

What a bother, having a heart!

When the rain picked up, and the sun sank out of sight, Poppy's thoughts turned to the warmth of home. As dearly as she loved her adventures outside, coming home to Harrow House was always the greatest joy. The house didn't have to be hers to matter. It was home.

The Kent lanes were treacherous when muddy, and the wheels of the carriage caught more than once. By the time the carriage drew up outside the house, Poppy was dreaming of a cup of tea and more cheese with a particular fervour.

But when she came in through the front door, Isabella was white-faced and shaking.

"Why, Isabella," Poppy asked, "whatever is the matter?"

* * *

EDITH RECOVERED SWIFTLY from her brush with poisoning, and after a few days began working more closely with the Hodes to protect Netherford Hall, and its inhabitants, as best as they were capable. That meant more wards, which had to be maintained daily, and required concentration on Edith's part that she frankly didn't have.

Such is life when you have been targeted for assassination; although that was only one of many concerns. Something still felt out of place in the house—and there was the impending issue of her estate and the Rookwood-Nourses.

Auden was frustrated that Edith did not want to hire someone to look into the issue of her poisoning, and mistook her hesitation for disinterest. But really, she did not want to rile the locals. They were already talking about her in every corner of the county, and it was going to be a long time before they forgot what happened. Someone was responsible, yes, and Edith had her ideas, but at the moment she just needed to get stronger and stay home. There was also the matter of the Rookwood-Nourses. And the Byrnes. *And* the Brightwells.

Edith longed for normalcy, for any shred of routine she could manage. But the house seemed more opposed to her than ever. One corner of the withdrawing room had collapsed in the rains a week before, and now she had to retreat to the room they called the 'small library,' because it was where the books that weren't ruined by time, rot, and insects resided. It had an old, potbellied stove, rather than a fireplace, and enough room for a desk, a chaise, and a little antique table that looked more like it belonged in a church than in a house. It smelled by turns of lemon and dirt and was cold no matter what Edith did.

Then came the deluge. The windows shook and rattled in

the wind; the walls creaked ceaselessly. Edith felt the strain on the house in her bones and worried that it wouldn't hold up against the weather.

She was about to go and see if she could find Auden, who had taken to spending time in one of the parlours— the one with the large windows and enough room for a billiard table—when she heard a ruckus at the front of the house. Her first, and likely wisest, inclination was to avoid it altogether. Edith had far better things to do than worry about strangers at the front door, and was too tired from her recent sickness to consider the ramifications of yet another cave-in.

But then she heard Hattie's voice: "I'm sorry, Miss Brightwell, but the gentlewitch has retired for the evening."

It could only be Poppy. Again.

"Please, I just need the gentlewitch. Just for a moment," Poppy was saying. "I don't know what else to do."

Hattie Knightly was doing her best, aided by Horace Poole, one of their footmen, to calm Poppy and also help her exit. But there was a note of desperation in Poppy's voice.

With no potion to blame this time, Edith could only ascribe her next actions to pure impulse.

"What is this nonsense?" Edith asked. It was not the kind thing to say, and she immediately regretted it when Poppy turned tearful eyes on her.

Hattie looked spooked, but indignant. "Mr. Brightwell is ill, my liege."

"Well, send Basil," Edith said simply, preparing to leave. Shows of strong emotion made her uncomfortable, even when the source was lovely to look at. "He's still here, I believe."

"But—it's a *curse*," Poppy blurted, through hiccupping sobs.

Edith shivered. She had the distinct sense there was more to the story than Poppy could share in present company.

"There is a price for such a thing," said Edith to Poppy. "I do not know how familiar you are with the ways of witches, let alone of a gentlewitch."

Poppy did not look afraid, but she *felt* afraid. A flash memory of their dance flitted through her mind before Edith was able to bat it away.

"I know," said Poppy. "He will die if I cannot help him."

"I will exact a price from you as I see fit," Edith continued. "You are also trespassing here, against my explicit orders."

"I would be anywhere else if I could," said Poppy—and oh, the anger roiling off of her! "The bridge to town washed away; I have no other choice. Even if I could get to old Salvinia, the hedge witch, she wouldn't know what to do."

"Very well," said Edith. "Horace, get me a coat. And find some umbrellas, would you? And a warmer coat for Miss Brightwell. She's soaked through, and this damned old drafty house certainly isn't helping matters."

BY THE TIME they arrived at Harrow House, Basil Hode in tow, all three were soaked to the bone. The Brightwell's house did little to remedy this—though Edith had never stepped foot inside the place, she could not help but be embarrassed how drafty her property was. Her eyes were used to the dazzle of London and the crowded, if crumbling, opulence of Netherford Hall. Harrow House was old, uneven, and simple in construction, but clearly loved. Every corner of the house, even in the gloom, showed signs of life: newspapers, sketches, embroidery, open books, pressed flowers, and the smell of good local food and mild spices.

How strange that love could so fill up a space in the absence of the family. Even in the best days at Hatchney, the Rookwoods were too busy to congregate for dinners, outside of engagements; expansive and modern as it was, it had never felt as much of a home as Harrow House did.

A scarecrow-thin boy met them on the way through the house, and Edith presumed it was the youngest Brightwell boy.

"How is he, Oliver?" Poppy asked. She was shivering, and the housemaid—it appeared they only had one—was trying to help her out of her old jacket and wrap her in blankets.

Edith allowed herself an old, tattered quilt, shucking off her long tailcoat and hat.

The boy—Oliver—shook his head. "The same." He looked Edith over, appraising her as a man might size up a wolf at the edge of his lawn. Clearly, he was made of sterner stuff than he seemed. "This is the gentlewitch?"

"This is," said Edith.

"My liege," said the boy with an awkward bow. He nodded to Basil. "Hello, Mr. Hode."

Edith cleared her throat. "Poppy tells me your father is ill."

"Papa is *always* ill," said Oliver, sighing, standing aside and gesturing into the next room, lit only with a few flickering tapers. The wind howled again outside, and Edith felt drafts at her feet. "But he's gone some place we can't find him tonight."

Poppy leaned over and kissed her brother on his forehead. Tall though she was, it wouldn't be long before he outgrew her. "Stay here and keep an eye out while we tend to Papa."

Oliver looked relieved at this and waved the three of them through.

Mr. Brightwell was laid out on a small, threadbare sofa, covered in a heap of blankets. He was a tall man, but not hardy. Beside the sofa was a wooden wheeled chair, the sort Edith had seen soldiers in after the war in London. It was a rather old thing, rickety, but well-used, its ratty cushion once detailed embroidery with daisies and ivy, perhaps.

The room reeked of sick and urine. A fire burned low, and Mr. Brightwell breathed very shallowly, his eyes open but seeing nothing.

Edith knelt beside Mr. Brightwell to get a better look.

"I don't know where to begin," Poppy said. She was looking at Mr. Hode. "It's been a secret in our family so long."

Basil put a comforting hand on Poppy's shoulder. "I am in the service of the gentlewitch, Poppy. You may speak freely."

"You said he was cursed," Edith pressed. She did not expect this was the case. People, non-witches, saw curses everywhere. It was usually just bad luck or ill-fortune, seen through the eyes of a fear of magic, which still flourished in spite of hundreds of years of witches living peacefully among mortals. Such prejudices die hard.

But when Poppy began speaking, Edith learned very quickly that what she was dealing with was indeed arcane, and deadly dangerous.

"When I was a child," Poppy began, taking the small chair by the fire while Edith and Mr. Hode arranged themselves more comfortably around Mr. Brightwell. "I almost died. This was back when we lived in Northamptonshire, where Papa was a teacher, and he sometimes sold antiquities to make extra money. We had a lovely house, so they say, with wide, sweeping fields, horses, and strawberry fields.

"One day," she continued, looking down at her hands now, "I fell into a fever, and would not rouse. They brought in doctor after doctor, at great expense, but nothing helped. That was when Mama and Papa sought the help of a hedge witch. They struck a bargain, but the price was heavy: our life savings, and the house, and Papa was cursed, never to walk again."

Poppy looked over at her father and swallowed back more tears. "I do not remember a time where Papa walked. I only know him as the man in the chair. Saving my life ruined them, ruined him."

Edith did not mock Poppy, nor did she question her explanation. Instead, she nodded, and then asked gently, "May I look at his legs?"

Poppy nodded slowly.

"Did he fall?" asked Basil, who was rummaging through his large bag, looking for something.

"Oliver says he just found him, lolled over in his chair," said Poppy, taking a handkerchief that Edith proffered. "This evening, just after the storm began."

Edith went back to her examination and pulled up the blankets by Mr. Brightwell's legs. His long bones shone clear, muscle barely visible on his too-thin legs, knobbed and darkened at the knees and ankles. The skin was smooth and hairless, and motley with the marks of what might have been a burn.

Living in London, Edith had seen the infirm plenty of times, but never at such close quarters. Her training and inclination toward healing was minimal, and it only required a short study to grasp the basics. Yet she did not need to have significant expertise to know that this man must bear a great deal of pain almost constantly, and the ruin of his legs was a twisted tale, indeed.

Basil pulled a cushion over and knelt beside Edith, his clear grey eyes dull in the firelight as he examined the man along with her. She did not want to look at his face long, though, or the pity lining his face so deeply. Though much more used to caring for the ill, he was clearly shocked at what he saw, just as much as Edith was.

"Tell me a bit more," she said, clearing her throat. She had to keep Poppy talking, to dispel the oppressive silence in the room. "Since the—incident—how often has he been ill?"

Poppy took a deep breath before answering, fiddling with

the edge of the blanket now resting at her lap. "The cold and the damp are the worst. A few summers ago, he had some hives that we thought might have been related, but it may have just been stinging nettles or a bee."

"But nothing to this extent?" Edith asked, replacing the coverlet now, and gently placing her hand on Mr. Brightwell's legs.

"Nothing I wasn't able to tackle myself," Poppy said. "He has moments of melancholy, or needs help around the house, but I've always been able to attend to him. We've all learned how to, if only to give Mama a break."

"I make poultices for him," Basil said. "Various ointments for his pain. Mrs. Brightwell comes in and helps, some nights, with organising the herbs, and Poppy here has always been good about finding what she can in the wild. I appreciate her keen eye."

"And what say you, Mr. Hode, about the nature of this illness?" Edith asked him.

Basil looked momentarily taken aback, and Edith knew she'd been too harsh with him too often. It was a habit she ought to break.

"Although Miss Brightwell's testimony is compelling, I have never sensed anything supernatural about the circumstances," Basil said, measuring his words carefully. "Which could mean very, very little. I am an apothecary and a Warder. Magic and the supernatural are part of my life, but not my personal expertise."

"Have you some belladonna?" Edith asked him.

"A little here, but not much," he answered, immediately rummaging again in his satchel. In a moment, he retrieved a little black vial with a scarlet label, the ink worn off.

"I don't need much," Edith said.

"No!" Poppy stood up, understanding at least in part. "You would put yourself in danger, my liege."

Edith gazed up at Poppy standing before her, lit from behind like a goddess, black hair drying just barely at the edges and curling into almost red accents about her. She felt humbled, somehow, that she had been recognised as Poppy's liege, but the emotion was deeper than that. Poppy was genuinely worried for her, which was surprising; especially considering Edith had given Poppy little reason for any kind of affection.

"I have been using belladonna for a long time, Poppy," Edith said gently, trying to put her at ease. "It is used often to help with the Sight, especially for those of us in the coven who are not gifted with it. My expertise lies elsewhere." Which was not entirely true, but Edith was not about to disclose her own weaknesses at the moment, especially with Mr. Brightwell's life in the balance. "It is not so dangerous for witches."

Poppy sat down, wilting like a flower in the frost. "Very well," she said, her voice so quiet the popping fire almost drowned it out. "Just, please be careful."

The vial of belladonna was heavy for its size, the glass cool against her palm. When Edith turned it around in her hand, she saw the remnants of an old stamp on it. She would have to examine it later, because it was vaguely familiar.

But not now. A quick sniff confirmed the quality—the sharp, bright scent reminded her of her time working with Aunt Cassandra on spells, cloistered together in the high tower at Hatchney House. For a brief moment she could see her aunt's face, a rounder, softer version of her own mother's, with dark brows and kind eyes. In her heart of hearts, it was Cassandra whom she most missed, for Georgina was more of a witch about town than a mother and a teacher, who had never really seen Edith for who she was beyond a disappointment and a too-serious child.

This was no time to linger in the past, though.

"Basil, I'll take his hand," said Edith calmly, though her insides began roiling the moment she said it. "You know what to do if I become unmanageable."

"Unmanageable?" That was Poppy.

"Sometimes, Miss Brightwell," explained Edith, "if there is any residual magic, or if the spell itself is warded, it can backfire. I could become infected with the spirit, or I could go a bit mad for a time."

"You said belladonna was safe!"

"I did. And it is not the belladonna that could hurt me, but the transmission. I will be slipping into your father's…" She searched for a word that Poppy would understand. "His *spiritual memory*. Magic always leaves a signature. He will not feel a thing, but it will help me to better trace what happened to him and what is currently amiss. If it is just an illness, it will be like dipping into a hot bath for a little too long. If it is a complex curse, I will need Mr. Hode to help me back."

"We will do everything we can to ensure everyone is safe," said Basil, checking Mr. Brightwell's pulse and frowning. "But time is running out."

Tearfully, and without words, Poppy nodded.

Edith put three drops of the belladonna tincture on her tongue and then took Mr. Brightwell's hand in her own.

THE SKY IS *the colour of slate, the ruins of the old church dark in the setting sun. From where he stands, Redmond can see the outline of St. John's Well, a gaping maw in the foundation of the ancient structure. It is frigid, biting cold, and he cradles his young daughter in his arm, her form lifeless and limp.*

He is racked with worry, with fear. They've been warned about Old Gam, but they cannot sit by and watch their daughter die. He would rather perish than endure such a thing.

And what else can *he do? His pleas to the High Coven went unanswered. Even with his ties to the Cawley family.*

When Old Gam crawls out of the well, something about her presence sets his hair on end. Though there is nothing old *about her at all, at least from what he can see. She is all eyes, and long hair, and smooth, pale skin.*

"I see you, Redmond Brightwell, and I hear your heart beating," Old Gam says, her voice hushed.

"I've come to ask you a favour, witch of the well," he says, because it is what he has been told to say. A hedge witch showed him the way, and taught him the ritual to summon the creature.

Old Gam laughs, and without warning she is before him. Her skin shines like pearls in moonlight, her lips stretched over sharp teeth. For all the power in her, and all the wilfulness in him, he still sees her for what she is: a beautiful, broken monster.

"Witch of the well, is it?" Old Gam cackles and draws one of her long, wet locks across Redmond's forearm. It is warm, sticky, and makes him feel ill. "I suppose that will do well enough. What have you brought me, mortal man?"

"My daughter is ill, and we have tried everything to save her. But she will not wake." His voice breaks. He has told this story a thousand times, yet now the wounds feel fresh.

"And you have come to ask me to wake her." Old Gam observes, her body moving at odd angles to her head. Redmond tries not to stare.

"Yes. I am here to ask you for a boon."

Old Gam leans forward and sniffs, deep and strange, drawing in the child's scent. She shivers, then stumbles back, licking her forearm with a long, black tongue.

"She is half-dead. I will need half a life."

"I will give it," says Redmond without hesitation.

"So hasty. Listen to me. A life is not merely the force that drives your flesh. It is all you have won. It is good fortune. It is progress. You will not know what you have lost until it is gone."

"Will she live?"

"She will wake, she will speak, she will dance and eat and love again," says Old Gam.

Redmond is pleased with the answer. "If you promise all those things, then I will give half of what I have. You may take my home, my wealth—so long as my family remains safe."

"Redmond! Redmond Brightwell!"

The sound of his name cuts through the fog in his brain, and Redmond turns to see a woman standing behind him. At first, he thinks it must be Margella, for who else would have followed him?

Then he sees her more clearly—it is Virginia Cawley, the High Witch.

She holds a high, white staff, and the end of it pulses against the dark, like a distant sun. In the other hand, she cradles a globe. It has been long since he saw her, and his heart still stops at the sight of her.

"It's too late, foolish child," Old Gam says to him. "You are too late."

"Return to the darkness from whence you slithered," the High Witch says.

Old Gam laughs. "Ah, but it is your fault I am even here, High Witch."

There is a great clash, the sound of magic searing across the stones and through their bodies. Redmond falls to his knees as Old Gam descends upon him, teeth bared, and little Poppy rolls away from his grasp, the edges of her white blanket taken up in a strange, warm wind.

Virginia's staff connects with Old Gam, and they spit and fight. Something pulses painfully in Redmond's lower back, but he cannot feel his legs at all. He cannot stand. He reaches back to feel a sharp protrusion, hot with blood: a thorn. He has fallen on a thorn.

Together, Old Gam and Virginia fight until, at last, the High Witch swings her staff and the wretch screams. A bolt of light streaks from the sky, violet lightning, and Old Gam is forced into the ground. Another flash follows, and when Redmond's eyes adjust again there is a great tree where the monstrosity was, a tree with glass leaves tinkling in the breeze.

Poppy stirs, calls her father's name.

"Oh, Redmond," says Virginia. "I told you this day would come. And you did not listen."

"Ginny..."

Virginia stands tall, her long, white hair across her shoulders and down to her waist, parts of it dangling from being pulled. "You have brought a great darkness to your family."

Poppy begins to cry, but Redmond cannot reach her. Virginia leans down and picks her up, brushing the thick black hair from her forehead. Tears trickle down Virginia's face and land on Poppy's blanket, pattering softly.

"She lives," Redmond says. "Oh, praise the heavens. She lives. There would be no greater darkness than a life without Poppy."

"She is changed," Virginia says, pain in her expression. "The monster still took her price. The child's soul is sundered, and the wretch yet lives."

"What can I do?" Redmond is in such pain, and not just from the injury.

Virginia leans down and wipes his brow with a strange familiarity. "Dear child, why did you not wait for me?" And now the tears streak her face with blood.

*   *   *

EDITH OPENED HER eyes to darkness; the dim lamp in the corner of a room might as well have been a league away. She felt a heaviness in her limbs, exhaustion pulling at her eyelids. She focused on breathing, and struggled to remember what she was here for—*who* she was here for.

Her tongue was tart and thick from the belladonna. She had never found herself in such an encompassing memory of magic. And what she had learned...

Mr. Brightwell had not traded his health for Poppy's life. The injury to his legs was a foul accident. Which meant, unfortunately, that his current woes were not rooted in magic.

And Poppy did not know the truth. Perhaps none of the Brightwells did.

Old Gam was worse than an errant hedge witch. She was a dark soul, corroded with time and burdened with great magic, escaped from somewhere. The fae, perhaps? No, the Coven Council had sealed that way for over a thousand years. The Brightwells would have had to be truly desperate to have allowed her near Poppy. In some ways, Old Gam was more powerful than a witch; that it had taken Virginia Cawley, High Witch of the Empire, to imprison her was shocking indeed.

"Try not to judge them, dear," said a voice.

Edith turned, or she tried to. In this strange, dark place, between memory and reality, there was no up and no down.

The distant light was not a lamp, it turned out, but a woman, glowing in the gloom. And one whom she recognised immediately from the memory as Virginia Cawley.

They knew one another, vaguely, back in London. Virginia was head of the Coven Council, and a living legend. All about her was pale—eyes, skin, hair—but all with a tinge of rose gold, down to the long, gauze dress she wore.

"My Lady Cawley," said Edith, for that was her official title. "How are you here?"

"I am not *here*," Virginia replied easily. "You are caught in a pocket of time, space, and magic. I call them *liminales*. I design them, constrain them—they are the heart of witch portals, you see. It's one element of my studies. I am impressed. I had honestly thought I was alone in accessing them."

"I came here to try and help a man who you appear to know, somehow," said Edith. "Redmond Brightwell."

Virginia drifted closer, angling towards her like an eel. She floated, almost angelic, above Edith's head, her face but inches away.

"Yes, the poor man. He is my sister's godson. The Brightwells are of little consequence, but dear to the St. Albans family—and yes, they would do well to live under the protection of a gentlewitch. But you have probably already concluded that. They are unusual."

"Poppy, his daughter—she blamed their misfortune on the curse of a witch. But that was no witch I saw."

Virginia sighed. "No. That creature was no witch."

"Poppy thinks her father gave up his health for her," Edith explained. "And he is still simply ill."

"His body and his mind, his choices and his debts, they all live together within him. You may help untangle some of it for him, and I can show you how. But he will need to be strong to come through unharmed."

"What *was* Old Gam?"

Settling as though on an invisible chair, Virginia leaned forward on the edge of her palm. "Redmond was impatient, and full of fear. That creature in St. John's Well was beyond any magic he could fathom, and she would have taken every last drop of Poppy's life had I not intervened."

"Stars and the rivers of the dead!"

Virginia sighed. "Poppy has half her soul intact. The other half, I'm afraid, we had to keep safe. It was the best I could do, given the circumstances."

"Why do you not help them *now?* I did not realise how close they were to destitution," said Edith.

"The Brightwells are kept comfortable enough through my sister's favour; she cares for Redmond, still, as he was raised beside her own nephew."

It was strange to imagine the Dowager St. Albans finding the Brightwells anything but pitiable. But non-preternaturals were perplexing.

"It's an odd circumstance," said Edith. She liked the feeling here, she decided, now that she was getting used to the weightlessness of this in-between world.

"Perhaps. But my sister is also an irascible old woman with her own prejudices," said Virginia lightly. "We came from poverty ourselves, you know, and she developed rather a distaste for it. Mr. Brightwell has never invested very sensibly, and it has mostly been due to the women in the family that they've gotten on as well as they have."

"Poppy needs protection," said Edith. "I've never even heard of someone with a sundered soul. She could be at risk of a thousand different arcane assaults. If part of Old Gam still exists—"

"Do not try," Virginia said again. "There are some paths even the most accomplished witches ought to balk at. I have made the attempt, my dear. The risk is too high."

"But surely the soul exists, bound in captivity with Old Gam."

Virginia did not need to say it so baldly, but her words brought the reality home: "Old Gam is a corrupt, ancient power, greater than you can fathom; it is best that someone of your limitations remains out of its reach."

Limitations. It was Edith's 'limitations' that had allowed her to be poisoned on her first night among the townsfolk, and her 'limitations' that had left her useless as a gentlewitch—unworthy of passing knowledge from her mother and aunt. Edith felt like she was going to be sick. "The Brightwell girl seems impenetrable to magic; that is my responsibility."

"She is not. But she is *resistant*. She is something new. I have been monitoring her situation for years now and done everything in my power to assure that she lives a full life—and there is no sign she is anything other than whole and happy."

Edith clenched her fists. "But what can I do to protect her?"

"Oh, my darling, Poppy Brightwell does not need much in the way of protecting. Witch she may not be, but her heart and will are as strong as any. To say nothing of her body."

There were many things Edith could say about Poppy's body, but none of them were appropriate in present company. "And what of Mr. Brightwell? You said you could help me."

Virginia nodded, and then pulled a small orb from within the folds of her dress. It spun on its own little axis, like a golden moon, and gleamed in the darkness. "This is a celestial orb I designed. Take it and use it when you return. Just pass it over Redmond's body. I have done as much for him in the past, in the early days before they left the Midlands."

The orb floated over to Edith and shrank as it reached her outstretched hands. It was warm, and pulsed, like a little heart.

Virginia continued: "It will scour his body for impurities and give him some strength. But he will wane again, my dear. His injuries are mortal, and always have been. For some, it only takes time. But his ailment was an accident— no more."

"Thank you, My Lady Witch. I am in your debt," said Edith.

"Then, please write me. I would appreciate knowing what is happening at Harrow House, even if dear Redmond will not have me."

"Of course," said Edith.

"And one more thing. I am very glad that you have discovered this *liminalis*," said Virginia. "However, I ask that you avoid making or visiting such spaces for now. Perhaps, in time, you and I can engage in formal training, but until then it is best you remain within your realm of experience."

"Yes, My Lady Witch," said Edith, that feeling of inadequacy building inside of her.

"Edith." Virginia stared at her a moment. "Please heed my warning."

The light of the celestial orb began pulsing more brightly, dismissing the gloom around them.

Virginia's voice echoed as Edith felt her body grow lighter, and the space in which they spoke faded. "I am so dreadfully sorry to hear what happened to your family, Edith. But Netherford has needed a gentlewitch for a long time. I hope you find strength in that. And be careful. Be watchful. There are corrupt forces still at play, and closer than you think..."

AT FIRST, IT appeared Edith had just fallen asleep sitting up. She twitched a bit, and Basil put his arms around her to ensure she wouldn't fall over. He assured Poppy that— though he had very little experience with witches directly—

this sort of thing was absolutely expected, and that it wouldn't take very long.

He was mistaken.

Two hours passed. Oliver came in half a dozen times, and was scolded each time for leaving his post.

Then, just as Poppy was about to go ask for another kettle of tea from Mrs. Pratt, who was nervously pacing the kitchen and baking bread for the following morning, Liege Edith began convulsing.

It was slow, at first. But within minutes, she was shuddering, her head snapping back. Her eyes were open, but they were white—not rolled back in her head, but glowing an uncanny pearlescent shade. The room smelled of flowers, sunshine, and loam.

Basil shouted, "I can't hold her much longer—Poppy, get my satchel—there's some smelling salts."

With trembling fingers, Poppy found the bottle and held it carefully under Edith's nose.

The reaction was instantaneous and terrifying. The gentlewitch ceased her convulsions, her nose erupted in blood and she half-fainted in Basil's arms.

Poppy shrieked, then flew into action, grabbing the cloths she'd seen in Basil's satchel and sending Oliver back to the kitchen to get hot water. Thankfully, by the time he returned, Liege Edith was conscious again, her eyes blazing with something between annoyance, indignance, and bruised pride.

Back to her old self.

"I'm sorry," the gentlewitch said, which was a surprise in and of itself. Poppy had not spent a great deal of time with the gentlewitch, but the phrase seemed positively divested from her vocabulary. "That was a bit more challenging than I had expected."

"You had only *just* recovered," Basil pointed out.

Poppy, who was likely nosier than she should have been and quite truly emotionally exhausted, said, "Recover from what?"

Basil gave an apologetic look to the gentlewitch, who nodded to him in assent while she mopped her nose and blouse.

"The gentlewitch was indisposed by something at the ball," said the Warder. "It weakened her somewhat."

"I'm fine," insisted the gentlewitch. "None of it had anything to do with Miss Brightwell. Give me a moment to compose myself."

Poppy's guilt descended like a hot kettle of water over her skin. But with it came a strange glimmer of hope. If *hope* was the right word. Was hope what remained when someone, in their heart of hearts, wanted to be admired by another, whom they found insufferable and yet alluring? During their dance, Poppy had felt something kindling between them: the way Liege Rookwood looked deeply into her eyes, the way she spoke with such sweetness.

Then it had ended so abruptly.

She would have to speak of it later. If there *was* a later.

"I didn't know," Poppy said, crossing back over to her father. He seemed entirely unaffected by the distressing situation.

"I am not done yet," said the gentlewitch, stumbling to a stand. Her face still stained a ruddy red from her nosebleed, Liege Rookwood knelt again by Mr. Brightwell's side, tilting her head to scrutinise him.

Poppy's mouth had gone very dry. "What—what did you see?"

Liege Edith went still. For a moment, Poppy was certain she had given offence. Her breath was the only sign she moved, her shoulders rising and falling gently as she gazed at Mr. Brightwell's lined, dear face.

What did she see, Poppy wondered, in that visage? Poppy knew every ridge and valley of her father's features: the wide nose, the creased brow, the long, white, curling whiskers, the surprisingly smooth cheeks above. But to Edith, perhaps he was just another mortal man, of no particular importance. How much of him did she know now, having read the lines of his soul?

"His current ailment is not arcane in origin," Liege Edith finally said. "But I know enough to help."

"Not arcane? But how can that be?" Poppy was confused. The family knew what Mr. Brightwell had given, what sacrifice he had made, in order to keep Poppy alive. It was a most terrible price. How could his troubles be simply due to age and hardship?

Edith reached into her waistcoat pocket and pulled out a small, silver bauble that could only be magic. It looked as if painted on her hand by an artist not of this world. She had never seen silver so bright, nor so smooth.

"Consider this, Poppy," said the gentlewitch, holding out the bauble. "Your father's illness was not caused by magic, but his body has for many years lived under the effects of a powerful curse, which has made him more susceptible to worldly afflictions. It may be that he can sense something we cannot. Or, that his body simply has tired and needs rest. Either way, this will help."

"Well, whatever the case, that wretched witch is to blame," Poppy said, before she considered her present company.

At this, Edith finally wrenched her attention from Mr. Brightwell. She looked Poppy in the eye, which was not a great distance as she and Basil were huddled, one on each side of the gentlewitch, before their patient. Edith seemed to wrestle with an inner question as she looked into Poppy's face, struggling to keep eye contact. At last, some inner turmoil resolved, she said simply:

"This was not the magic of a witch."

"But that's impossible," said Poppy.

"The creature who did this to your father, and who took the sickness from your body," corrected the gentlewitch, "was not a witch; it was older than some of the oldest witches that walk the earth. And the price they exacted—" The gentlewitch paused, her gaze returning to the bauble in her hand. "A witch would never do such a thing."

"But witches take payment all the time," Poppy interrupted. "They bribe and they barter and they—"

"Hedge witches and charlatans," said the gentlewitch. "Not *gentlewitches*."

"You do not need to lie to preserve your reputation," snapped Poppy.

"Poppy, enough," said Basil, and she knew she had crossed a line.

Very well. But she could not believe the gentlewitch would say such a thing—to contradict what Poppy knew very well to be a fact—in a moment as this.

The bauble in the gentlewitch's hand began glowing softly, producing tiny golden sparks, each of which vanished before landing on her hand. The effect was haunting and beautiful, and before Poppy could wonder at it, Liege Edith whispered a string of words which resonated with each pulse of the bauble.

Then, to Poppy's great surprise, the bauble slowly rose to float above Papa's navel. The sparks began extending into streaks of light, which remained, creating an intricate net of light, like a strange golden spiderweb.

The net of light spread over Papa's body, casting light on their faces, and then settled on him and vanished.

It might have been her imagination, but some colour returned to his face. The room felt warmer, smelled a little fairer.

But the gentlewitch looked exhausted. Pale enough that Poppy noticed a dusting of freckles on her cheeks, even in the dim light. She slumped forward a little and both Poppy and Basil leaned to try and compensate. Thankfully, Liege Rookwood was able to right herself.

"He will improve over the next few days," said the gentlewitch, her voice raspy with the effort. "If he wakes, feed him nettle tea. Do you have any?"

Poppy nodded, sitting down on the floor as the gentlewitch rose and slowly drew on her overcoat, wincing in the process. She looked untidy, her shock of red curls up in six different angles, her face and scarf still dark with blood.

"Good. Basil will send you more if you need. Get some lavender water as well, and wash his face and his hands each morning," continued the gentlewitch. "Once he is able to move around a little more, I recommend oat cakes twice a day, followed by lemon water and tea."

"What did—? How did…?" Poppy couldn't find the right words. "That bauble—the net and the…"

Basil cast a confused look at Liege Rookwood, but she did not reply to his silent query.

"I have helped untie some of the complex snags inside of him," said the gentlewitch. "Old age and exposure to magic often combine to make the bodies of mortals resistant to healing. I can help it along. I cannot heal him of his ailment, but I was able, at least, to urge his body toward healing."

Poppy barely whispered, "Thank you."

Then, as the storm had let up, and there being nothing more to do, the gentlewitch departed Harrow House, Basil Hode in her wake.

Poppy sat by her father through the rest of the night, waiting for any sign of life. At dawn she realised, with a strange jolt of guilt and shock, that the gentlewitch had not asked anything of her in return.

CHAPTER SEVEN
OLD PARAMOURS

VAMPIRES WERE NEVER frightening in the way mortals imagined. They did not drink the blood of the unwilling except in times of war, and only then with special dispensation. They were not necessarily susceptible to the sun, though they did burn readily. They had no issue with religion, with crosses, or with silver—or any other metal, for that matter.

And they were not *entirely* undead.

Just mostly.

Auden Garcliffe knew this most intimately because, for a few months, he and his family had entertained the idea of marriage to Laertes Byrne. Rarely did witches and vampires marry, but Auden was no witch or warlock, or even a minor mage. He could marry as he pleased, and an alliance with the Byrnes would have been a significant boon to their house.

And Laertes was a rather dashing fellow, easily as rakish as Auden himself. Truth be told, Auden had been smitten with the vampire. And who could blame him?

Like most vampires in England, he had black 'spider-silk' hair, named for its lack of gleam; it did not catch the light as a living human's or witch's hair might. He did not grow it long, as was the fashion among vampires, preferring a shoulder-length cut which accentuated his sharp features. Laertes may have originally been from Scotland, if Auden remembered correctly, but his accent had softened over the years. He had bright blue eyes, thick brows, soft pink lips, and smooth, fair skin. He dressed fashionably, yet always managed to look a little medieval.

And Auden had never been able to keep his wits around Laertes, even after their affair had ended.

Even now, as they sat across from one another in the green parlour, the newly renovated room Auden had claimed while the withdrawing room underwent repairs, it was difficult to pay attention to exactly what Laertes Byrne was saying rather than focus on the movement of his lips over his teeth.

"My apologies," Auden said, and not for the first time. "Could you explain that last part again?"

Laertes smirked and leaned back in the plush velvet chair they'd just reupholstered. Its blood-red damask made the vampire's gold and chartreuse suit look even more stunning in contrast, as if he'd orchestrated the redesign in anticipation of this very moment.

"It isn't an *official* betrothal," Laertes explained. "But there was absolutely intent on either side."

If it wasn't bad enough that the Rookwood-Nourses were arriving in three days and the house was in such a state of disrepair that Auden had awoken to a puddle at the bottom of his wardrobe, the Byrnes were now asserting that, prior to their deaths, Georgina and Cassandra Rookwood had discussed with the Byrnes about a betrothal between Ophelia and Edith. That it had been nearly completed, in the eyes of the heads of both families.

Of course, no one had taken the time to explain any of this to Auden before. There was no record of an agreement. Just the vampires' 'good word.' Which was never much to begin with.

"Did anyone plan on informing the intended parties?" Auden asked.

"I believe the intention was to do so at the Solstice Gala in London," said Laertes. "And to my credit, I *did* try and get your attention at the Greenstreets' quaint little ball. But you were quite intent on avoiding me at all costs."

"We had very little time for carousing," said Auden. "But to be quite honest, I don't know that we could entertain such a union now."

"Strange, considering the current rumours," said Laertes, in that damnable, arrogant air that managed to be insufferable and delicious at the same time.

"Do enlighten me, Mr. Byrne."

Laertes barked a laugh. "Oh, come now. The Rookwood-Nourses have been writing every great family from here to Ceylon."

"Mr. Byrne," managed Auden, swallowing down unwanted rage. "You presume too much."

"Do I?" The vampire picked an imaginary speck off his cuff before adding, idly, "I've met them, you know."

"You—what?"

"The Rookwood-Nourses. They made quite an impression on Mother during dinner last week in London. You know they have ten thousand a year? They invested in stagecoach routes between New York and Boston, trying to inspire their fledgling nation to higher purposes. It's all very admirable."

"Delightful," said Auden, standing now, because sitting was making his legs hurt with the stress flooding through his body.

The Rookwood-Nourses were rich? And if Laertes was this excited about them, they were surely beautiful as well. "Then why don't you marry Ophelia off to one of them? Frankly, sir, I haven't the time for such nonsense."

"Oh, my darling, you used to *love* my nonsense," said Laertes.

He had, it was true. Regularly, in fact.

"Do not try to flirt with me," said Auden. Dealing with vampires always meant propriety went out the door. Along with impulse control.

"You truly have become a nincompoop. Tell me, are you the governess now, too?"

"Henry is my ward," said Auden. "My nephew. I take my duty to him very seriously."

"You once told me you'd rather wade through boiling acid than have a child."

"*Some* of us mature with age," Auden replied with a sniff.

Laertes pouted. "I suppose it's to be expected, given the tragedy you've endured, but I was hoping there would be some glimmer of the rakish boy I fell so madly in love with."

"That time has passed. That *boy* is no longer," said Auden, hoping that the vampire would get the point.

He did not. In fact, Laertes looked like he was making himself more comfortable, running his hands down the silky arms of the chair, nestling in just a little deeper.

"You can't tell me you're not curious as to what they're like," the vampire said.

"Of course I'm curious. I'm out of my mind with it. But I also know that you always exact a price from me, and I do not want my niece used as a pawn in your machinations."

"You are so striking when you're alight with furious indignation," Laertes said, flashing a sharp-toothed grin. "And I'm flattered you think I have *machinations*. Usually it's Ophelia who has the reputation for intrigue."

Was the room warm? It shouldn't be. The creature had a habit of getting, quite literally, under Auden's collar. And pantaloons.

"Enough," Auden said, and this time he sounded desperate.

Laertes relented, if just a little. He looked at Auden with what he could only interpret as disappointed pity.

"Allow us to at least entertain you for dinner," Laertes said, finally, his cold gaze full of mischief. "You and the gentlewitch. We can share what we know and discuss any potential complications for your niece and my sister."

"I will not entertain notions of—" Auden tried to interrupt.

"I have said nothing of betrothal, only of dinner. In exchange for one evening of your attention, we can discuss the matter of your cousins."

Auden tried to recall his diary. "I am quite overscheduled at the moment, and with our guests arriving in two days—"

"Then, of course, tomorrow night suffices," said Laertes.

Edith would not be happy. But then, Auden supposed, she so rarely was, that another upset hardly seemed an inconvenience. Perhaps once he explained things to her, she would warm to the idea of keeping the Byrnes at a comfortable arm's length. They knew more than they were letting on; likely, Laertes wanted to share some information directly with Edith. Which was insulting, but also a relief. Auden did not like the idea of being trusted with important information. It gave him a headache.

"Fine," said Auden, at last. "We shall join you tomorrow night. Weather allowing."

"Excellent," said Laertes, finally standing and preparing for his departure. He brushed his dark sleeves. "I hope you learn to see that, though you may be without a family, you are not without allies—if you play the game well."

AUDEN RETURNED TO his office, and enjoyed a little cider, which always helped his spirits. He had begun a correspondence with Severina Jones, the majordomo of House Whitebriar, in hopes that he could make surreptitious pleas for assistance with their situation. But like the Rookwoods, most of the coven houses had abandoned the country in favour of larger cities. Those few who had kept their homes in the country had sprawling families and many heirs. He honestly didn't know how long it had been since a witch had established a house, let alone resurrected one from neglect.

This business with the vampires wasn't helping anything. It made him itchy just thinking that Laertes and Ophelia were so nearby. He may have said otherwise, but Auden was certain their claim to Edith's hand was significant. Why else had they come to the county?

But that got Auden thinking, as well. There must have been something more to the story, to inspire such sudden action.

He just had no idea what it was.

His candle had burned low when Edith knocked and entered. On seeing her state, Auden rose to his feet, ready to rush to her side. She was white as a sheet. Her hands trembled as she clutched a glass of apple brandy.

"Edith! You shouldn't be up. You look ghastly!" His heart thumped about in his chest fearfully, but she waved him back down.

"Your candour is appreciated," she said softly, taking a slow sip of her drink before sitting down across from Auden in the red tufted chair.

"Is it?" Auden's nerves were already frayed. Edith looked sick, but calm. "You haven't given me any indication of what exactly occurred last night."

She looked at him, a wicked gleam in her eye. "I believe I may have discovered my proclivity, Uncle."

"Are you certain?" This would be good news. Edith's lacklustre magical abilities had been a cause of concern her whole life.

"Not entirely. I will need to do some research, of course. And I plan to. It did not come without pain," she said, reaching up to touch her nose. "I know you've seen and experienced far worse with Mother and Aunt Cassandra."

Yes, growing up with Georgina and Cassandra was an adventure in maintaining one's constitution. Neither had excelled in the gentler arts of herbs and tinctures or enchantments, or even illusion. Necromancers, both of them, they had worked with—to put it delicately—raw materials. It was a most respected profession, and a remarkable calling, but terribly messy.

"Are you attempting to be vague, or is this a side-effect of exhaustion?" Auden asked his niece.

"I must do some research," she replied. "I need to go attain some volumes from Oxford, I think, and write to a few of my old instructors. That should do."

"You're being quite cryptic," said Auden.

"I'm not asking for permission, I'm just informing you," said Edith, that haughty tone back in her voice. She looked like she was going to stand up and leave, but then leaned forward in her chair instead and sniffed the air.

"What?"

Edith narrowed her eyes at him. "Have you been entertaining a vampire?"

Auden couldn't deny it. Lying straight to the gentlewitch's face was not a good idea, regardless of the situation.

"You were asleep," Auden insisted.

"Uncle. I am your gentlewitch, not the child I once was."

Oh, he knew that. Children grew too fast and broke your heart; even Henry was well past needing him. Perhaps Laertes was right—he should have been a governess.

"I didn't want to wake you. You came in this morning, drenched with blood, and now you're surprised I didn't interrupt you when a vampire showed up at the door?"

"I'm assuming this is *the* vampire we all know and adore."

Auden frowned into his cold tea. "Laertes Byrne is not a man I hold in much affection."

"Not these days."

"Edith."

"It's only that, in the years that I've known you, at times your rationality has been somewhat compromised when he saunters into a room," observed Edith, plainly. Auden clenched his teeth. "It's important that we, as gentlewitch and majordomo, discuss any causes for concern, and communicate honestly with one another."

"I did not let down my guard," said Auden, becoming more frustrated by the minute. "I was steadfast."

Clearly, the gentlewitch was not convinced. "Well, what did Mr. Byrne desire of you?" Edith asked.

Auden was conflicted. He wanted to look into their claims more thoroughly, but he really hadn't the slightest idea how to explain any of what had transpired between them. At least not in a way that left him looking anything but bumbling and idiotic.

"They want us for dinner. Tomorrow night. At Howarth Castle," said Auden, deciding at that moment to look very intently at the paper in front of him. It had nothing but an ink splotch on it, and the more he looked at it the more it looked like a very tired rabbit. Which quite reflected his current mood.

Edith moaned with frustration. "And you allowed it?"

He struggled to find the right way to say this. "They... have information about our new cousins."

Yes, that was better. Bringing up marriage, especially a marriage that may or may not have been arranged by her mother and aunt, was not wise. Edith had a very strong outward appearance, but Auden remembered her well, both as a child, and as an adult ruined by the fire. He was not a man of deep emotion either, at least not the more distressing emotions, but he knew that Edith's composure was sure to shatter soon.

"Today just continues with its surprises. I suppose there is no way for us to respectfully decline?" Edith asked.

"Not unless you wish to meet our cousins head on with absolutely no idea of who they are or what they want," he continued. "And, quite frankly, given our isolation, I think it's the best we've got right now. Unless you've any new information?"

"I've barely left the house," Edith said.

"So, I made the right call. You can be angry with me all you want, but I'm afraid everyone around us appears to have the upper hand."

Saying it out loud to Edith made it suddenly real. He didn't like being the majordomo, and dealing with majordomo business. But he was going to have to if they were to survive.

To his surprise, Edith relented. "Very well," she said. "I will go to dinner with you. Miss Rawlings-Vijay has the two new embroidered pieces I ordered, anyway, so at least I'll look the part. I must send someone to her in the morning."

"That reminds me: Molly Hode was by earlier looking for you. She said..." Auden tried to recall what exactly the Warder was concerned about. "Oh, yes. I know. The ladies' maid you liked. Miss Appleworth. She can't start until June. Something about an ill parent and her current employment."

A strange look crossed Edith's face as she rose. Auden had expected more of a reaction to the news: it had been very, very difficult to get Miss Appleworth, and Edith had dismissed dozens of candidates out of hand. She had exceptionally high standards.

"What is it?"

"I think I have a temporary solution," said Edith.

"You do?"

She nodded, her long fingers tapping on the back of the chair she'd been in just moments before. "She isn't ash-touched, or coven-born, but she's like nothing I've ever seen before."

"You're not talking about the Brightwell girl, are you?" When Edith hesitated, Auden pleaded, "Edith, my dear, that young woman brings trouble."

"I just saved her father's life," Edith said. "She is bound to serve, if I ask."

Auden stood out of sheer surprise. "You did what?"

"I healed her father. She came to me for help, knowing there would be a price."

"Foolish business, I say. I've seen how you look at that girl," said Auden.

"Nonsense. This was their *father*, Uncle. I could scarcely deny her."

Indeed, Auden didn't think Edith was capable of denying Poppy Brightwell anything, whether or not she was ready to admit it.

CHAPTER EIGHT
INCENDIARY AND ILLUSORY

IT WAS AN uncommonly sunny winter day, the sky a cloudless periwinkle expanse, and the kitchen and dining room were bathed in golden hues. Poppy appreciated whoever had designed the house for this reason, it maximised the best of the sunrises and sunsets, and meant that the lighting was ideal for Papa and his painting.

But no amount of sunshine could lighten Mama's mood.

The gentlewitch had written and claimed her price for healing Papa—and, Poppy suspected, for risking her life. Poppy would serve as her lady's maid until June. She would have one week off out of three, in order to help with the family. It was, the witch insisted, payment and not a bargain.

"No daughter of mine will be a *maid*," said Mama. Thankfully, Papa was still resting. He had improved every day since the gentlewitch's visit, though he still needed significant rest, as Edith had said he might. Basil Hode dropped by daily to check on him.

Mama was called back from Cambridge, and was none too happy about it, though of course she was concerned for her husband.

"Mama, I made an oath," said Poppy, and the sudden flush on her mother's face told her it was the wrong thing to say.

"And haven't witches already taken enough from us?" Mama asked, voice shrill enough to crack glassware.

"It wasn't like that," Poppy said. True, it was not ideal, but of all the things Edith could have asked, this was far from the worst. Besides, it would mean Poppy could be back at Netherford Hall again.

Mama was positively venomous. "Witches take far more than they give, be they hedge or high."

Viola, who had been standing by the window as they spoke, turned to her mother and said, "Mama, we have Edith to thank that Papa is alive."

It was an unexpected moment of bravery from Viola, who rarely spoke up in front of Mama, especially when she was so upset.

"We spoke at length after the incident," said Poppy, keeping her voice calm even though she wanted to shout. "The gentlewitch said that the creature that cursed Papa is often mistaken for a witch, but is something far more dangerous."

"Nonsense—it was a *witch*," said Mama obstinately. "Whatever happened, your father and I have paid the price, over and over. And now we shall be the laughingstock of the whole town."

Poppy was losing her patience, now. "Mama—we cannot afford to be on the gentlewitch's bad side. And no one needs to know, particularly."

"People will talk," said Mama.

"They do anyway," Viola added. "The wealthy, landed families will always look down on us because we are not fine enough, and the farmers and workers will always feel we are too elevated for our own good."

Mama frowned, looking at her tea as if it had offended her personally. "I have just hoped for more. I am ashamed that we must live so simply, and now—this."

"It isn't forever, Mama," said Poppy. "It's just until June, when the lady's maid they've hired can begin."

"It's dangerous. You never know what can happen in a witch's den," said Mama. "Before long, they'll let all of Faerie in, to our doom."

Both girls were stunned to silence. It was not a kind thing to say. Were they in a city like London or Oxford or Coventry, such words would have been trouble— particularly mentioning the pact with the fae. One simply did not say such things of witches, regardless of their class, but *especially* not of a gentlewitch.

And even if Poppy secretly wished that the fae had never banished. What the world must have been like!

But she was beginning to see that Mama had a very different idea of what transpired the day Poppy's life was saved. Perhaps her father would be more forthcoming about the events at a later date.

The silence got to Mama eventually, who got up from the table. "I don't know what to say, Poppy. I only hope that June, somehow, comes more quickly this year. Between the witches and the vampires, I'm afraid our little town is changing, and not for the better."

MOLLY HODE MET Poppy at Netherford Hall later that day. The Warder loomed large in the doorframe, and seemed glad to see her.

Poppy had only packed her necessities. Home was close enough that she needn't have packed anything, but she imagined that the gentlewitch would keep her busy enough that her life would be significantly easier without a trek back and forth. She expected some sort of uniform, but a cursory glance as they walked through the great hall suggested that was unlikely. They passed many servants, some faces familiar to her, but they were all in, more or less, their outdoor clothes.

"The house really is expansive," Poppy said.

Molly grinned. "It is, isn't it? I spent most of my life wondering what it would take to restore it after so long. It felt like a fool's dream. It's been the honour of my life to oversee the renovations."

"And you should be proud, Molly," Poppy said. "There is so much glass! From the outside it always looked so foggy, but now I'm on the inside, it's as clear as the first winter's ice."

Following her gaze up to the immense east-facing windows, Molly's brows rose up in surprise. "I don't know who finally got to those, though," she said. "I don't remember assigning that job." She trailed off, and looked around, as if hoping to find someone else. "Never you mind. There's a dinner tonight, and the gentlewitch is going to need you to help with preparations."

"I should point out that I have little to no experience as a lady's maid," Poppy said, not without a little hesitation.

Molly sighed like the bellows and shook her head. "If I could help you there, I would. It's a strange circumstance but, as you've demonstrated numerous times, the house seems to accept you as you are."

The house seems to accept you as you are.

As they meandered their way through the narrow hallways, and up to the second floor where Poppy's room would be, those words echoed in her mind. It was hard not to feel as if she was returning home, as if the house itself was glad that she was back. And why not? Netherford Hall had been her place of seclusion. Seeing the floors gleaming now, where they had been so dusty and covered in mildew; noting rooms full of unveiled furniture, now-straightened paintings, new carpets bringing unexpected light and contrast to the familiar twists and turns, was a brilliant, private joy.

They came at last to the servants' wing. When she'd had the run of the house, back before the Rookwoods had returned, the room Molly showed her was full of old furniture. But now she was pleased to see it tidily situated, the walls painted a muted greyish purple.

Her room contained a small, wrought iron bed, an ancient looking chest that must have been original to the house, a washbasin, and a wardrobe. It was by no means elaborate, as rooms went, but it was not anything to be ashamed of.

Molly left Poppy to putting away her things and informed her that the gentlewitch would call for her when it was time to prepare for their dinner at the Byrnes'.

Strangely, however, Poppy found she could not open the wardrobe. She stepped back, looking again at its construction, trying to see if perhaps she'd had the wrong idea. Built in the familiar, almost rustic style of the reigns of Henry VIII and Elizabeth I—the witch-burner and the witch-champion—it had been given a good dusting. The carvings were clearer now: a pastoral, perhaps, with acanthus flowers in the border, almost like an old illuminated manuscript. There were iron findings on it, but nothing even remotely resembling a key.

How strange. She felt a bit insulted, really.

Thankfully, the equally ancient chest—which still smelled of sweet cedar—opened without incident, and Poppy sat for a little, a book in hand, waiting for her summons.

A quarter of an hour passed, and Poppy started at the sound of knocking—not from the door to her room, but from the wardrobe.

Hesitantly, Poppy stood and approached the ancient doors, which swung open on well-oiled hinges before she could touch them.

Into Liege Rookwood's room.

The gentlewitch herself stood there, plain as day, half-dressed, peering expectantly at her. The expansive 'king's quarters,' as Poppy knew them, rose behind her, rather than the master's suite.

"There you are," said the gentlewitch, as if they'd just met on the road.

Poppy looked behind her. Her book lay half-open on the bed. She could feel the warmth coming from the gentlewitch's room, and smell a citrusy incense.

"Did I fall asleep? Is this a dream?" Poppy asked. It was not an intelligent question, but they were the only coherent words she could think to utter.

"Oh," said Liege Rookwood, gesturing to the little passageway that now existed between rooms. "I hope this isn't *too* strange for you. It's old magic, but useful, called a Janus Garderobe. Old portal magic."

"And it really leads straight into your room?" Poppy asked.

"It does," said the gentlewitch. She stepped aside, as though to let Poppy pass.

Gingerly, Poppy stepped up into the wardrobe and felt the wood bend slightly under her weight. She was a little tall for it, and had to crouch, but in just a few steps, she found herself standing before the ceiling-high fireplace in Liege Rookwood's room. This late in winter, the evening came quickly, so it was already awash in lanterns and candles.

"By the speckled firmament!" murmured Poppy, now peering back into her room.

The gentlewitch gave what might have been a suppressed smile. "It takes a bit of getting used to, but it's better than taking the stairs."

Poppy immediately thought how such an enchanted item could help her father. If only magic items, were available to average mortals. One had to be very wealthy, or else very destitute, to be given dispensation.

"I don't mind the walk," said Poppy. "Though I'm certain Papa would marvel at it even more than me."

"Yes, how is your father?" asked the gentlewitch, closing the door to the wardrobe.

Looking up to meet the gentlewitch's eyes—which in the firelight were that same near-black they'd been the night she'd helped Papa—Poppy straightened a little. "He is well, my liege," she said, "Though he sleeps more than before. The tinctures Basil brings give him comfort, and we hope he'll have his strength back come the summer. The warmer weather always gives him a bit of encouragement."

"I'm glad to hear of it," said the gentlewitch. "He's made of sturdy stuff." She sniffed. "Can you get my overcoat? The green one over there. I'd like to see it with this vest."

Just like that.

Poppy froze for a moment, dazed. No one had ever asked her help with dressing in that *tone*. It felt like a blow, somehow, diminishing her.

The overcoat was very fine, with a slight iridescence to the thread. Poppy recalled Miss Rawlings-Vijay saying once that some witch clothiers were able to incorporate beetle wings into the thread, through a kind of alchemical process. Perhaps that was how this was made.

The gentlewitch held out her arms, and Poppy helped her put on the overcoat, one arm at a time. Apparently, this was acceptable, for after scrutinising herself in the mirror a moment, the gentlewitch asked, "Now, the blue one, please."

So they went, trying on overcoats. Then onto waistcoats, and different combinations, with cuffs, scarves, and pantaloons.

Liege Rookwood certainly valued her appearance. Never had Poppy doubted that the gentlewitch was a woman of pristine circumstance, but she had simply thought it good breeding, and perhaps magic, rather than her choice of clothes.

Yet, as she watched as Liege Rookwood went about matching every cuff, every pin, and the very feather on her hat, Poppy recognised a strange, and familiar, pattern: for Edith Rookwood, sartorial elegance was an art. In absolutely every sense. And Poppy saw textures and patterns in a similar way.

Most of Poppy's job was simply to say *yes* or *no*, to reach for different items, or to observe as the gentlewitch adjusted herself. So she could not truly take any credit for the final result—which was, in a word, breathtaking. The gentlewitch's body, what little Poppy had seen and a few times felt of it, was muscular and strong, but poised, like a dancer's. Nearly even with Poppy's own considerable height, the gentlewitch could be easily mistaken for a man at a distance.

"Miss Brightwell?"

Snapping to attention, Poppy hastily dismissed any thoughts of Edith Rookwood's body from her mind. Even though she was standing right there...

"I'm sorry, my liege," Poppy said quickly. "I must have missed what you said. This is all very new to me."

"I asked: the peacock or the quail feather?" The gentlewitch was holding up one in each hand. "For the hat?"

The peacock father was from an onyx peacock, the sort only witches were allowed to breed, and shone in an iridescent rainbow over a deep purple, which would go well with the aubergine suit. But the quail feather was simple, with a touch of the country in it, bringing to mind wild hunts and the deep forest, rather than the fussiness of onyx witches.

"The quail, my liege," Poppy replied.

The gentlewitch spun the feather in her hand. "And why, might I ask?"

"It's suits you better, somehow. It feels more like, well, like Netherford Hall itself, I suppose. Onyx peacocks are very expensive and mostly kept in captivity, aren't they?"

"Yes, it's a terrible practice. But I suppose you are right. The quail will pick up the hue of my hair rather than fight it. And heavens know, there is no hiding this colour. Thank you for your good consultation, Miss Brightwell."

"Of course, my liege," said Poppy, dipping into what she hoped was an acceptable curtsey.

In a few more minutes, Liege Rookwood was prepared to meet Auden downstairs. Their carriage had already pulled up to the front of the house, and the horses' snickering drifted through the windows, slightly cracked as they were in the very warm quarters.

"I hope not to return too late," said Liege Rookwood, checking her cuffs one last time. "I will expect you to help me prepare for bed when I return."

"Of course, my liege," said Poppy, swallowing against the fluttering sensation in her stomach. Dressing the gentlewitch was one thing: undressing her was quite another.

THE PROBLEM WITH Ophelia Byrne was never lack of grace. She was, Edith reflected, a paragon of beauty and poise.

Ophelia stood with the command of a goddess, though she was considerably shorter than average. Her black hair was a riot of curls, each defined with absolute precision. Her skin was milky pale, her eyes pools of black, her lips always a shade of deep berry. Her form was round and pleasing, with full breasts and wide hips, and she dressed to emphasise each and every curve.

Vampires avoided natural light, which gave them nausea

and headaches. So, the interior of Howarth Castle was done up in deep plum and azure, thick velvet damask fabrics pulled tight over the windows. What light there was inside came from witch-lights, quite popular among vampires—and provided, of course, by common witches. In a human home, the appearance of such golden-hued globes, dancing around the ceiling and following guests around, would be shocking. But vampires welcomed the spectacle. And that golden witch light absolutely played to every gift Ophelia had.

Edith could be helplessly distracted around Ophelia Byrne, in much the same way that Auden was with Laertes. But while their passions ran deeper, for they connected on a level beside the physical, Edith found Ophelia terribly tiresome; they had absolutely nothing in common. The vampire mistress was an expert libertine, a woman who sucked the marrow out of life—literally. She wanted adventure, she wanted passion, and she wanted sex.

Not that Edith was opposed to any of those things—she just was very English about it. She had, from a very young age, been a sober individual. Edith was not comfortable flaunting her desires, and finding closeness took time. She needed to *understand* a woman to be attracted to her, or to seek intimacy. Her few affairs had been brief and rather awkward.

Ophelia, in turn, lived up to every expectation—and then cleared them, by a considerable margin—just in the way she greeted the gentlewitch and her majordomo.

The house was taken care of by thralls, humans pledged to the vampires—brought in from the city, no doubt—who ushered Edith and Auden in through narrow corridors that seemed to twist and turn without any real architectural reasoning.

And when finally they arrived in the dining room, there sat Ophelia and Laertes, at opposite ends of an enormous table. Truly, the tree from which such lumber had been hewn was unfathomable, even to Edith.

Ophelia was wearing a French-inspired gown, indulging the daring new trend of bared breasts. Hers, as Edith knew from brief experience, were most lovely, and now only covered in the scantest tulle beaded with pearls and silver charms, which glittered and drew more attention to their placement as Ophelia rose and stretched out her arms in greeting.

Edith was not going to embrace a vampire, no matter how inviting her bosom.

So, she bowed. And Auden bowed, as well.

"Welcome, welcome, at last," said Ophelia, her voice as clear and as sweet as fresh-poured honey. Her singing voice was legendary, and she spoke every word with the practised diction of an opera singer.

"Let's hope this is better than the last vampire dinner we had," muttered Auden, as he was led down one long side to the single plate next to Laertes.

Ah, so that was the game: divide and conquer.

Their last vampire dinner had consisted of more bread than any human being would ever eat, served with undercooked fowl and unshelled nuts. It's said that Ophelia and Laertes were human for a while in their lives, but apparently it had been long enough that they had completely forgotten how to cook for themselves, and their thralls were too busy focusing on their *duties* to provide much insight into what a family of means would eat.

A cursory look at the table showed a good assortment of cheeses, a small duck or two, and fruit and bread. This ancient way of feasting, all the food out on the table at once, was common for folk of magical derivation, though what Poppy and her family would think of it, Edith could hardly say.

But she ought not think about Poppy right now. Or how she had looked just an hour before, her eyes sparkling in the firelight as she watched Edith in the mirror.

Well, that shouldn't be too difficult when Ophelia was before her.

"Hello, darling," Ophelia said to Edith as she sat down. "You look absolutely dashing this evening."

"Thank you, Miss Byrne," said Edith, pulling at the napkin before her and bringing it to her lap.

Edith fixed her eyes on the gold plate before her. It was a pretty setting but must weigh as much as a small terrier. Vampires have a taste for gold, and hoard it like dragons were once rumoured to. Such place settings are considered a sign of respect.

"How was the carriage ride?" Ophelia picked up her goblet and took a tiny sip, her eyes never leaving Edith. "Not too treacherous, I hope?"

"Not in the least. It isn't too great a distance," Edith replied. She reached for her own goblet, then changed course and went for some fruit instead.

Her last drink in the presence of these vampires had not gone well.

"Well, you can't chide a woman for trying to make conversation with such a fetching guest," said Ophelia. "I honestly can't imagine what you spend your days doing up in that crumbling old house. Howarth Castle is old, certainly, but we have staff tending to its every need. Tell me, do you plan on ever having your own ball? It would be so good for you to have a coming out, officially, without the interference of the likes of the Greenstreets."

The idea had not even once occurred to Edith. Half of Netherford Hall was still in various states of decay and degradation. Though there were parts of it, throughout, she'd grown to take pride in—or nearly so—it was such a grand departure from the opulence and modernity of the Greenstreets and their ilk, that the mere thought of it made her sweat.

"We have a grand hall, but even so, it is better suited to feasts than dancing," Edith said, trying to exude coolness in her reply.

"Yes, Laertes said it was quite impressive. So many panes of glass! Did you know that the glass was fixed, rather miraculously, about fifteen years ago? It was the talk of the town."

"I didn't know you had such deep ties to Netherford. You and your brother had always struck me as London vampires, born and bred."

"Oh, *au contraire,* Liege Rookwood. We are citizens of the world," Ophelia laughed in her tinkling, half-mad way, and finally leaned back enough so that the immediate intrusion of her bosom upon Edith's plate was no longer a concern. "We've had a home in Netherford for time out of mind, though Howarth Castle here is a new purchase. But that's how I know the history of your house. I'm an avid reader, you know, I find history absolutely enthralling."

No matter how much Edith chewed at the fig she'd selected, it would not reduce itself to within consumable margins. She was trying to figure out if there was any possible way that she could spit it out without making a fool of herself.

"I'm afraid I am only beginning to learn my family's history," said Edith, finding at last a better turn of conversation for her purpose. "Uncle informs me that you also knew a bit about our unexpected relatives."

Ophelia arced one of her brows, a dark smudge above her captivating eyes. "Oh, indeed. I wanted to speak to you about it at the Greenstreets' ball, but you seemed quite otherwise captivated with that young tenant of yours. And then you vanished."

"I assure you, that was all a misunderstanding. I detected a love potion in my drink, and felt I was no longer welcome." Edith did not think that the vampires were behind the potion, but she wanted to ensure she made herself clear. If Ophelia wanted to share more information, she was more than welcome. "Or perhaps that doesn't surprise you at all?"

"Oh, my liege, you know if I wanted you in my bed I would never resort to a *potion*. I would want you fully available for my every whim," said Ophelia, dropping her voice low.

Edith felt her face warm, and she did her best to shove down her shame. "We have yet to determine who it was," she said.

"A childish, mortal prank," said Ophelia.

"Indeed, some of the greatest enchanters of our ages have been 'mere mortals'—and many have gone on to threaten your kind's very existence," Edith reminded her.

"Well, I could find out, if you were in need of such services, who among them dared to make such an attempt," said Ophelia, drawing a finger down the smooth curve of her shoulder. "I am quite compelling, you know."

"No doubt. Which is why we are here in the first place," said Edith. "I am told you might have knowledge of our newfound relatives, the Rookwood-Nourses. At least, it was that expectation which convinced Auden to accept your invitation to dinner."

"Oh, I'm quite certain there was very little convincing required when it comes to those two," Ophelia said, pointing to the two men, who were both laughing. For all his protestations, he would forever be easily ensnared by that vampire.

Edith gave a small sigh and reached for bread. She'd finally managed to swallow the fig, and sincerely hoped something more substantial would help. Saints and mavens, she was hungry.

Ophelia, apparently not so obtuse as to be unaware of Edith's tension, sobered slightly and continued. "It is a shame what happened to your family, Liege Rookwood. But it is also a shame that they did not share with you the secrets of your inheritance, or of the complicated relationship between your mother and her sisters."

"Well, I was never intended to inherit the title. And even had I, I would not have been privy to their secrets until I had come of age. Which, in our family, is around fifty. I am barely halfway there."

"Oh, you witches and your traditions. It's all so confusing. I don't understand why you can't just all speak to one another plainly."

"Because magic is dangerous. And witchcraft even more so, especially in a family of necromancers."

Ophelia grinned. "Of course. Well, I knew Beatrix Rookwood quite well before she left for the colonies. From what I know, she had an argument with the family and was cast out."

"Strange you never mentioned it before," said Edith.

"Oh, we must have been oath-given. When your family passed, I found I could speak of her again."

"Oath-given. That's an expensive enchantment," said Edith.

Oath-giving was an old, and somewhat dated, method of preserving secrets between witches and vampires—or, on occasion, particularly clever werewolves. It could not be used on someone like Auden, who would have no mental barriers to withstand the psychic force of the spell.

"Indeed," said Ophelia. "But not entirely unexpected. Beatrix was unconventional. She had dreams of expanding witchcraft to the uninitiated, bridging the gap between hedge and gentlewitch."

"I do not think my foremothers would have approved," said Edith, understanding now a little more why they'd take such extreme steps to silence Beatrix. "But I do not see why I wouldn't have been given a warning."

"Are you questioning the source of the fire?" Ophelia asked very carefully.

"I have written to Bow Street to see if they have any new evidence," said Edith, not wanting to divulge too much. "There were multiple inquests. We literally raked the coals, and all signs point to just an *accident*." She hated saying that word.

"The boy you live with. He survived," Ophelia pressed. "Did he see anything?"

"He was asleep," said Edith, shaking her head. "And it is not a topic I wish to discuss. Now, I was asking about the Rookwood-Nourses."

Somewhat cowed, Ophelia leaned back on her chair. "Well, besides their rather obscene addiction to 'justice' and 'progress,' they are relatively innocuous people. They are not unusual witches, not that I'm aware. Whatever passed between Beatrix and her sisters, she'll have to tell you."

"And my cousins?" The word felt stale in her mouth.

"They were but children when they left for the colonies," said the vampire. "Couldn't have risen past my knee. I barely remember them."

Edith was going to ask another question when Laertes stood at the end of the table.

"We have gathered here this evening for a number of reasons. As you may have gleaned, and suspected, we are not here purely on matters of friendship and general gossip, though those things are not without value, and certainly are always appreciated," said Laertes. He tossed back some of his dull locks of hair, that same light-choking black as his sister's.

Here it came.

"Liege Rookwood, we are humbled by your presence

here," Laertes continued. "But you must know we have some points of business to discuss."

"Very well," said Edith, flatly. "But I assure you, at the moment, the banks and executors are still untangling my finances. Any investments or..."

She knew very well that they weren't talking about investments. A woman didn't dress like Ophelia without reason. She was on show.

Laertes grinned again, laughing brightly. "Oh, I am not speaking of *bank* investments."

He loved a show, but he was also too much of a gossip to keep from spilling his story too early.

"You're speaking of marriage," said Edith, sparing a glance at Auden. For his part, her uncle looked embarrassed, which meant he'd known about this. But of course he had. She would have kept it from him, were their roles reversed. She'd never have stepped foot into this house, they'd never have learned a thing about the Rookwood-Nourses, and she'd never have had to swallow down that fig. "To Auden."

Naturally her uncle hadn't known how to broach the subject, especially considering the last few days. And the Greenstreets' ball had been rocky at best. So, she would let him dangle just a moment more.

"No, of course not," Laertes said. It was still insulting, though he made an attempt at bashfulness. "I'm speaking of marriage between you—and Ophelia."

"This is not the first time you've tried to marry into our family; I had hoped you were done with such machinations," Edith said smoothly.

Laertes put a hand to his chest as if he had been struck with an arrow. "My love for Auden was singular. What would I have gained from such an alliance? He is the son of a witch. He is entirely mortal, and without inheritance or title."

"Thank you for that reminder," said Auden. He looked as

if he might crawl under the ridiculous table at any moment.

"No offense meant, my dove," said Ophelia. "Let us calm ourselves. Given the current circumstances, an alliance between the Rookwoods and the Byrnes would put us in a remarkable position in society, *and* within the arcane community. To say nothing of your situation in regard to those unwanted family members. We could pay them out or pay them off. Then we could all return to London like this never happened."

"And it isn't without precedent," pointed out Laertes. "As strange as it may sound to you, vampires and witches aren't so different. We are all descended of the first witch—just by different sires."

Edith took a deep breath. She did not want to lose her temper, especially not here, knowing that they would take pleasure from it—even nourishment. So, flattening her hands on the tabletop, she rose and met Laertes' gaze. "We eat food, and you do not. And that is just the beginning of our differences. If the 'precedent' you speak of is that of Mira Rookwood and De Laure, theirs was a storied romance of the ages. Hardly what we're speaking of here."

"But surely romance could blossom in time," Ophelia said. "I know you desire me, darling. Your eyes betray you."

"I cannot argue that, physically if nothing else, you do not offer an enticing prospect. But I am a new gentlewitch, and I am not a woman of society, nor will I ever be."

"She hasn't *actually* said no," observed Laertes.

"I have said it is not something I wish to discuss," clarified Edith. Anger simmered beneath the surface, hot and defiant. "I am still grieving my family. At present, I have no desire to return to London. The very air is darkened with the ash of my lost family." An unexpected well of emotion rose to meet her, and Edith had to take a moment. "That ground is no longer home, no longer sacred to me."

Ophelia huffed and sighed. "Witches die in London all the time. It shouldn't change the way your magic works."

"And tell me, lovely Ophelia, what you know about witchcraft?" Edith asked.

"Well, very little, of course."

"Of course," said Edith. "I could no more explain to you the nuances of witchcraft than a snake could tell a bird how to slither. Such an offer from you is no temptation."

"But money might be," said Laertes. He looked positively wicked now, and Edith was certain he knew more than he let on.

Ophelia cleared her throat. "The rumour is that the Rookwood-Nourses have the deed to Netherford Hall *in hand*."

It was true that they had not been able to find the original deed to the house in the family's lockbox, but there was plenty of anecdotal evidence on their side. Edith had thought perhaps it had been burned in the fire along with everything else.

"I don't understand how you'd know that," said Auden, standing now. His napkin was still plastered to his jacket and Edith would have laughed if she wasn't trying too hard to keep her emotions in check.

"You always seem to forget that vampires are better suited in a number of matters," said Laertes, turning one of the forks in his hands as if it might be a much more dangerous weapon, more suited to human hearts than pickled beets. "Especially in travel. And in surreption."

"That," said Ophelia, "and the fact that we have been in contact with your aunt and cousins for quite some time. Beatrix did not wish to be found. And as I said to Liege Rookwood just now, we were oath-given, until recently."

It didn't prevent them from lying once the oath was dissolved, though. And vampires loved lying almost as much as they loved blood. Well, perhaps *lying* was a little harsh—but they blurred the lines of reality and elaboration whenever possible.

"We will be speaking with the Rookwood-Nourses shortly, and I'm sure we'll have everything sorted out," said Edith, though she was certain of no such thing. The only thing she could say for sure was that she did not want to be in the vampires' home a moment longer. And she needed a word with her uncle.

"Please do consider the offer," said Laertes, sitting down now. He was, at least, a good sport; and he knew the conversation was over. "I can even send you along official papers if you'd like. That way you can see how the numbers look. I know you have a great many distractions at the moment."

Edith did not consider herself a romantic woman. She had never really entertained notions of marriage, because she so enjoyed being alone. However, the idea that the decision could be reduced to entries in a ledger made her half-sick. Should she marry, and that was a reality she would have to consider given the Rookwood-Nourses and her very tenuous grasp on Netherford Hall, it would at least be with someone she found companionable.

"We thank you for dinner," said Edith, as some of the thralls scuttled out of her way and off to get her overcoat. "Perhaps, once all the sums are counted and peoples accounted for, we can return the favour."

It was as polite as she could manage, and frankly more than they deserved.

ON THE CARRIAGE ride home, Edith was perfectly silent, staring out the window into the veil of darkness, the lamp swinging at the head of the carriage occasionally bringing out a red flush across her forehead.

Auden found her silence absolutely terrifying.

"This was not a good visit," he said, at last. "I'm sorry."

Edith turned slowly to him, and though he expected wrath, she seemed genuinely sad. Why was that worse? Why did her sorrow cut him to the bone? Well, of course it did. Because though her face had thinned and hardened, though her brow was marked with wear and worry, she was still the little dimpled child he'd loved and coddled, and perhaps understood, more than anyone else.

"Calm yourself, Uncle," said Edith, and there was real warmth in her voice. "We knew the vultures would come. I may not have much of a fortune, especially if they're right about the Rookwood-Nourses, but I do have status within the Circle and among the High Houses. I would help elevate their position significantly. I cannot fault them for their interest."

"You're not considering it, are you?" Auden was shocked to hear her speak so soberly about the Byrnes.

Edith shook her head, but it wasn't exactly a denial. "There is very little of the Rookwood family left in the world, Uncle. I do not know *what* I should consider."

"You should consider your happiness."

"Happiness is a matter for simple folk. I have never sought happiness, nor even dreamed of it. Not from the youngest of ages."

"What do you want, then?"

Edith said nothing for a moment. It might have been the trick of the light, but Auden could swear he saw tears in her eyes.

"I want to be useful," she said eventually, her voice low and a little husky. "I want to mean something. I do not wish to be the dregs of a long-lost house, left to ash and rubble in the middle of London, to the trickery of love potions and false proposals. I must make my way, somehow."

"You were always too good for my sisters," said Auden, dabbing at his own eyes with his handkerchief. "They just couldn't see past your eccentricities."

"They wanted a daughter that looked more like Ophelia Byrne, I suppose," Edith said, shaking her head. "I could never fill out a dress like that, even with the best stays and enchantments a woman could buy."

"Well, she was not filling it out tonight—she was spilling over. I was quite certain she was going to fall into your soup," said Auden, now finding he had room to laugh a little.

"I wouldn't have argued," said Edith. "I think we all deserve a little show every now and again."

"Agreed," said Auden, and they fell into an easier silence on the way home.

POPPY HAD FALLEN asleep in the kitchen while folding napkins for Reena, one of the scullery maids, when someone roused her to inform her that the carriage had been spotted. She excused herself and ran up the long stairway, taking the stairs two at a time, before she realised she couldn't remember how to get to Liege Rookwood's rooms from where she was.

That was truly strange. She knew the house as well as she knew the lines of her own palm, but somehow in all the changes the house had seen, she kept getting turned around.

So, she did as she had the night before. She went to the wardrobe in her room and knocked softly on the other side.

There was the gentlewitch, her overcoat slung over one shoulder, eyes slightly red. She did not smell of alcohol, but had a tinge of copper about her. Poppy supposed that dinner with vampires would leave a lingering metallic taste.

"I'm sorry, my liege," said Poppy, falling into another very stilted curtsey. "I'm very new at this, and I..."

"My nightclothes are in the second wardrobe," said the gentlewitch, her voice rough with fatigue. She gestured to one of the very large cabinets built right into the wall, the door rendered in a thousand little diamonds of glass.

Inside the wardrobe were many different night robes, but Poppy chose the one that she felt most suited Liege Rookwood, in a dark purple so deep it was almost black. She loved the way the colour looked against the gentlewitch's hair.

When she turned around, Poppy started. The gentlewitch scarcely a breath away from her. Her eyes were so arresting, so sorrowful.

"What do you see when you look at me, Poppy?" Liege Rookwood asked almost without inflection, her gaze penetrating.

"I see the gentlewitch," Poppy said, which was only part of what she wanted to say.

"I see," said Liege Rookwood, and began to turn away.

"But I also see a woman who has endured a great hardship," rushed Poppy, clutching the nightclothes as a kind of barrier between the two of them. Her heart was pounding in her chest, her stomach felt like she'd just had bright, warm tea. "Who wears the pain of it on her shoulders, who went to great lengths to help a man who meant nothing to her."

The gentlewitch looked away, down at the pile of deep purple fabric. "I am your gentlewitch. It is my duty, as antiquated as it is, to come to your aid. I exact a price for the work. It isn't merely kindness."

"You were kind to him, though," Poppy said. "And to me."

"I did as I ought," said the gentlewitch. "I am sorry you have had to deal with such things, and sorrier still that I had to exact a price from you. I know this sort of work cannot be easy for you."

"There is nothing I wouldn't do to help Papa," said Poppy, setting her jaw determinately. "He broke his body for me. I owe him my life."

"You owe no one your life, Poppy," said the gentlewitch. "But that is not a discussion for tonight. Please, would you assist me?"

Liege Rookwood held out her arms, and Poppy tucked the nightclothes under her elbow and helped her take off her waistcoat. Then, she helped her undo the laces to her pantaloons so she could shuck them off, along with her stockings.

"I need help with the stays," said the gentlewitch, turning so that Poppy could help remove her shirt.

Poppy could not say why her fingers trembled so; she had helped friends out of clothing the same way. This did not feel at all the same. Once the smooth material slid off the gentlewitch's shoulders, Poppy could not wrest her attention away. Liege Rookwood's skin was freckled as a sparrow's egg, and covered with the finest down of hair. The stays she wore were not the sort that Poppy herself wore: the gentlewitch's were short in the old fashioned style, called 'jumps.' They bound her small breasts beneath what looked like a vest.

Poppy worked as swiftly as she could to undo the lacing—which was all of a finer quality material than she had ever seen used before—and then rolled up the stays and placed them on a chair.

Poppy glanced over her shoulder in time to see Liege Rookwood leaning over to pull her night clothes over her head. The firelight illuminated her skin and hair, along the very slight curve of her hips and breast, and Poppy suddenly could not breathe. She had never wanted to touch someone so much; a frightening need coiled inside of her in that moment. And not only could she see the beauty of

Edith Rookwood, the woman, but she could sense a sorrow and power in her, mingled like twin flames. And her body thrummed with the desire to feel the warmth of that skin against her own.

Slowly, the gentlewitch approached Poppy, one step at a time. Their eyes met, and Poppy was caught between wanting to run back into the wardrobe, and straight into the gentlewitch's arms.

Just as Liege Rookwood was about to close the distance, however, Poppy felt the weight of a ball of clothing in her arms.

"These will need to be cleaned," said the gentlewitch. "I trust you know what to do."

"Of course, my liege," Poppy managed. "Of course."

CHAPTER NINE
HOT SOUP AND HOT TEMPERS

"You look like you could use some hot soup."

Molly Hode found Poppy alone in the kitchen, sitting and staring into space, later that night.

"Oh!" Poppy was surprised at the booming voice. "Soup?"

"It's just the thing for tired feet," said the Warder, taking a seat with a sigh, and placing a bowl before Poppy. Potato and leek, one of her favourites.

Poppy took a big spoonful of the soup and savoured the warm, briny taste. "I truly underestimated how much I'd be on my feet. And I've *sorely* underestimated the work of Mrs. Pratt and the house staff."

"Indeed," said Molly. She had also procured some crusty loaves of bread; she handed one over to Poppy. "A little sense of humility never hurt anyone."

"Least of all me. I do tend to get into my own head."

"Basil tells me your father is improving," said Molly.

"Indeed," said Poppy. "On the way to mending, I think. Though it's bound to be a hard road. We're accustomed to it, but it's never easy with Papa."

Molly shook her shaggy head. "No one should have to endure what he's had, Poppy. He's a good man, and you're a worthy daughter."

Poppy concentrated most diligently upon her soup to conceal her embarrassment.

"What keeps you up so late and with such..." Poppy indicated Molly's muddy boots. "Intensity?"

The Warder took a thoughtful bite of her bread and leaned back, stool creaking. "Warder business with a gentlewitch in the house is more work than I bargained for, too. Much of the work my ancestors did was more theoretical than anything. I've had to do a significant amount of travelling across the shire for assistance—our wards keep breaking. I'm baffled. I'm just returned from repairing another."

"You have had quite the adventure," said Poppy, who was truly a bit jealous. The idea of gallivanting around the county at the behest of the gentlewitch felt terribly romantic.

Molly's laugh was a comfort. Big, boisterous, and bright. "It isn't exactly as heroic as all that. It's a complex business, but best spoken of directly to Liege Rookwood."

"I'm afraid I know very little about the Warder's life," said Poppy, knowing she had trod into a conversation well above her own understanding, and that was never a place she liked to tread.

"Well, for one, it's unusual that there's both Basil and me. Warders are the *de facto* stewards of the home, but typically it's a sole inheritor. Our gifts are small but mighty. Protection is key, here. Yes, Basil does tend to lean toward the gentler gifts, but healing is a kind of protection, isn't it? Protection from the unseen. The illnesses of body and soul and mind that so often plague mortals and witches alike."

"We are grateful for that kind of protection, too," said Poppy.

"He's damned good at it. So, I specialise in defense," said Molly, and her eyes were bright. Clearly, the woman loved her job. "You can't see them or feel them, but we've protected this house and the surrounds most impressively, with the wards. It's a webwork of interlacing spells. We use special sigils to build up the defences, and we carve them into trees, stones, stiles—anything really. Especially places that mark boundaries."

"And being a witch is so dangerous as to require such a proliferation of wards and protections?"

Molly looked surprised. "You really don't know much about witches, do you?"

"Given my family's history with them, you can imagine my lack of education on the subject was entirely intentional."

"To the contrary, I would have thought your parents would go to great lengths to ensure you aren't unprepared for a hedge witch or minor mage."

"Well, judging by your reaction, and the gentlewitch's, my unusual condition is a bit unsettling."

Molly nodded, hesitating a little. "Wards... don't work on you. And neither do witch's spells. Any other person would have needed to go through extensive work, and preferably come from a Pact house with generations of allegiance to magical families, to do such a thing. Pact families simply acclimatise to magic better than others. Your sister and brothers, for instance, would likely feel continually ill in the house without proper wards on my behalf, and considerable work on the gentlewitch's. You, meanwhile, saunter into the house as if you'd owned it. I didn't need to do a single thing to accommodate you."

"I feel quite well here," said Poppy. She scooped up the last of the soup. Were she in a bolder mood, she might have requested more. "It's always felt that way."

"Always?"

"Well," said Poppy, trying to change the subject. She was too tired to keep sharp. "Since first stumbling in this direction."

Molly fell silent and then nodded. "Whatever the cause, we should do some work to discover it. The little research I've encountered comes up surprisingly short. I've found no indication of families of your ilk with magical resistance *and* ward neutrality. The only creatures known to combine such traits are ghosts, and well, you are clearly alive and in this realm."

"Clearly," laughed Poppy, standing from her seat. She was warm now, but wary, as well. The conversation had meandered too close to her secrets. "I am not a ghost. Or, if I am, I've never been informed of it."

"Whatever you are, we should do what we can to discover it, Poppy," said Molly, her tone unusually tight and even a little concerned. "A gentlewitch is nothing if she is not a defender of her household, her town, and her shire."

AUDEN WISHED HE'D never heard the name Rookwood-Nourse. As he scuttled around the house, ordering the staff and servants to their work, his stomach churned like a stormy sea. He had to continually quaff the little cordials Basil prepared for him and his peptic tendencies. It helped, briefly, but then the discomfort roiled up again in him and he was off to another branch of the house, horrified that there was, yet again, the unfortunate leavings of owls setting on some of the furniture in the day room, a nest of wrens in the chapel, and new cracked glass in the withdrawing room—which had just undergone repairs the week before.

At very least, Auden was committed to providing good food and making a good show of both gentlewitch and majordomo. Which required a great deal of oversight of menu planning and tailoring, neither of which Auden considered his strength.

It was in this dizzying mania, the evening before the Rookwood-Nourses were due, that he ended up nose-to-hose with Jamini Rawlings-Vijay in the hallway and caused a small hurricane of fabric.

"Oh, Miss Rawlings-Vijay, my great apologies," said Auden, scrambling up from the sideboard which he'd barely managed not to dent, or knock over the vases atop it. "Are you injured?"

Miss Rawlings-Vijay was half-buried beneath a mountain of cloth, one bright brown eye visible between damask and moiré silk. "Hardly," said the modiste, somewhat muffled. "The only bruise is my pride, I'm afraid."

Auden reached down to grab the modiste's arm and hoist her up as a flurry of staff appeared, relieving Miss Rawlings-Vijay of her burden and folding and neatly tucking away the rest into parcels.

"Please take these to the darning room," said Auden to the staff, and Miss Rawlings-Vijay nodded enthusiastically, still straightening her own clothing.

"Your—scarf," said Auden, leaning forward before he could think anything of it, and adjusting the fabric just so. He was keenly aware of the heat from Miss Rawlings-Vijay, the subtle fragrance of jasmine and oud, and the very closeness of his fingers to the Modiste's slim jaw. There was a freckle there, just so.

Jamini Rawlings-Vijay was a distractingly attractive woman, possessed of fine skin and bright eyes and a wicked half-tilted smile—a countenance more frequently found in galleries than behind mounds of fabric.

"Thank you, sir," said Miss Rawlings-Vijay as Auden pulled away. She touched her throat ever so lightly, gently, almost in reverence.

Auden's blood thudded in his ears. "I—well, I hope you have been well. I'm glad you were able to help us out on such short notice. It has been nonstop since the Greenstreets' ball."

The modiste gave a helpless smile. "Yes, I will not soon forget that week. I still have people clamouring for Poppy Brightwell's dress."

"As well you should. It was a vision."

Miss Rawlings-Vijay chuckled. "I had nothing to do with that dress, though I wish I had. There is nothing so frustrating as being asked to produce a gown which you know is well outside your own capacity."

"Truly?" Auden was shocked. Poppy's dress was such a masterwork, he could imagine no-one other than Miss Rawlings-Vijay at the helm.

"On my absolute honour, sir. Would that I had, for I'd be a richer woman for it."

There was no trace of deceit in the woman, Auden was sure, and therefore he found it all the more perplexing that the issue of the dress still gnawed at him. Could it have been Edith after all?

"Well, if you do hear who the perpetrator was," said Auden with an air of mock-consternation, "do let me know. It's quite the mystery."

"And you are well, sir?" Miss Rawlings-Vijay levelled her intense gaze at Auden, and, despite his better judgement, he could not look away. He could lose himself in her eyes, in the way her black lashes framed the deep, dark pools of her irises.

"I persist. As you can tell by the current state of the house, there is no end to my work here." He gestured to his messy tie. "I don't think I've slept well in months."

"I'm sorry to hear that," said Miss Rawlings-Vijay. "I hope you know that the town thinks well of you. If there's anything that can be done, please let me know. You may not be the gentlewitch herself, but you're cared for."

Auden found his ability to speak was suspiciously out of reach. It was already difficult to think of proper prose when the modiste's lips were so fine, let alone when shaping such kind words.

"You could always come into town to just relax one of

these days, engage yourself with the common folk," the modiste continued, slowly disengaging herself from the conversation. She glanced over her shoulder. "I'd always be happy to share a drink with you. Or two."

IT TOOK NEARLY an hour, but after his rather ruffling experience with Miss Rawlings-Vijay, Auden at last located his niece. The day was a bit warmer than expected, and she was out in one of the solariums, a large volume of poetry in her hand. At least, Auden assumed it was poetry. The gentlewitch never did cater much to fiction outside of verse.

In the bright winter light she looked younger than her years, and Auden waited a moment before announcing himself. He was impossibly proud of Edith. He had loved her, as a child, near enough in age to be a playmate. They had shared a similar sense of otherness from the rest of the family; he was too wild and she was too tame. They were Rookwood extremes, and the family never seemed to want to go out of their way to understand either of them.

Sitting, her long legs stretched out on an ottoman, her brow creased in concentration, she looked like she belonged in Netherford, belonged in a way that she had never done in London. Auden didn't have the heart to tell her what he'd heard about her on the streets, how her so-called friends and acquaintances laughed about her strange ways.

And Edith Rookwood *was* strange, even for a witch. She had a unique way of seeing the world, of seeing people, and a quiet manner that was so at odds with what people expected of an enchanter. She was not showy, she was not proud or boastful, she did not revel in the spectacle of illusion.

He loved her as he loved nothing else in his life, and in the moment, it was almost too much for him to bear.

"I can see you, you know," she said, not turning to look at him, but instead speaking down at her book.

"Have you learned how to see through your eyelids, now?" He cleared his throat, trying to affect an assured tone.

"Hardly. I can see your reflection in the glass," she said, gesturing with one boot. And indeed, he was confronted with a near perfect reflection of his form, limned in half-dead plants. They would have to do something about the greenery, and soon.

"Oh," said Auden. He took a few meandering steps and then sat on one of the yellow leather tuffets in the room. There was a curious proliferation of tuffets, he thought. They looked a bit like mushrooms, and he couldn't help but almost like them.

Finally, Edith looked up. "I hope you're not getting sentimental on me, Uncle."

"Of course not. I'm only a man, however, and there is no denying our family, what little of it there is left, has been through quite an ordeal. And seeing you, here, sitting and reading as you once did in Hatchney House—well, it kindled memories long muted by drink and carousing and the other rather neglectful behaviours of my youth. You seem almost suited to this place."

"It is shaping up rather well," Edith agreed, looking up at the glass ceiling. Moisture gathered up there, refracting the light and clouding some of the panes, but it was still a marvellous structure. "I have to admit, you and the staff have done a truly remarkable job. I am feeling almost grounded."

"That's beyond my wildest hope," said Auden.

"I said *almost*."

"But you never did so in Hatchney," he said, lowering his voice.

"No, I never did."

It was their own secret, really, that Edith had never

attuned to Hatchney. Witches, and especially those in the High Houses, drew much of their magic from ancestral items, places, and structures. Hatchney House had been built in the 17th century to precise measurements and filled with more relics and tomes than could even be catalogued, all to empower the Rookwoods and propel them forward into the society.

Little good it did for Edith in the end.

"Perhaps I was too hasty in celebrating my mediocrity," she mused when Auden didn't respond, deep as he was in thought. "Or perhaps the cloud of so much magic in London was detrimental to my own abilities. It does feel easier here."

"That might come in handy, considering…" He gestured vaguely to the chaos about them.

"Are you implying that I should hex our guests?"

"I would never."

"Of course not. Because even you know that you can't hex witches within your own house without provoking all-out war," Edith said, as if he were the dullest candle in the chandelier.

"War may be worth it."

"I will defer my judgment until they arrive."

"You are kinder than I am."

"I have to be," Edith said, and Auden saw how weary the whole business had her.

"I wish it didn't fall to you, for all of our sakes. Henry does not know yet how lucky he is to have you, but I do."

Edith gave him a weary smile. "Well, our newfound relatives are due by noon tomorrow."

Auden frowned. "And we have no strategy."

"We could ask Miss Brightwell, the wild shepherdess of Harrow House. She has words and ideas for everything, it seems."

"I cannot tell if that is a positive appraisal or a cry for help."

"Neither," she replied. "Simply a thought. For now, we can only meet the Rookwood-Nourses as they are and see what comes of it."

The clock in the hallway began a doleful chime, marking the hour. It warbled, rather, for a clock, but the sound did not bother Auden as much as it had when they first moved in. If he didn't know any better, he would have thought it had somewhat righted itself.

"Oh," said Edith, tossing a letter from her lap over to Auden. It was written in Ophelia Byrne's wandering script. "I almost forgot. We found our culprit."

"Culprit?"

"The poisoning. At the dance."

Auden opened the letter and scanned it quickly. They had been able to trace the love potion to the town hedge witch, Salvinia. But she had been under the impression it was for a desperate wife married hastily to an unloving husband. Instead it had ended up in the hands of Elizabeth Wayfair, Antonella Greenstreet's closest friend and confidante, and thence in Edith's cup.

"I don't think they had any concept of what they were doing, but we may need to put closer eyes on Salvinia, though I am loath to do so considering our already tenuous relationships with the hedge witches," sighed Edith.

"You have no plan for punishment?"

"I do not believe it was done in malice, and I do not wish to begin my tenure as gentlewitch with a heavy hand. Or with admission of my considerable limitations."

"You are too good for them."

"That is arguable. But I am all they have ever known, so I must try and be at least good enough."

*　　*　　*

THE ROOKWOOD-NOURSES ARRIVED in a flutter of chaos, done up in all the most recent London winter fashions, tip to toe in Spitalfields silk and trimmed with vibrant ribbon and furs. Poppy spied them from the alcove by the great hall: all three of them were petite and fine-boned, with clever bright eyes and mounds of deep brown hair.

There was no denying a family resemblance, though, for what the Rookwood-Nourses lacked in stature they made up for in features. Especially Beatrix, who had the same dark blue eyes as Edith, though her hair was a darker auburn. Their noses were practically the same, too, turned up just at the end and complimenting the bow of their lips just so.

Poppy scolded herself again for contemplating the bow of Edith Rookwood's lips. And then again for peering at the guests with such intensity.

Jamini Rawlings-Vijay, who was crouching beside Poppy, was equally transfixed. "I've never even *seen* such silk—those patterns must be straight from the loom."

Poppy swallowed back a less-than-enthusiastic remark about Petronilla's shoes, just as someone cleared their throat behind her. She turned to see Mr. Garcliffe looking at her sternly.

"Oh, Mr. Garcliffe," she said, falling into one of her spectacularly lopsided curtseys.

"Please attend to Lady Rookwood-Nourse," said Mr. Garcliffe. "She has had a long journey."

"But what about Liege Rookwood?" Poppy knew immediately from Mr Garcliffe's quirked eyebrow that she had been too enthusiastic.

"You can attend to her once our guests are settled," he clarified.

"Very well, sir," said Poppy, straightening her dress. "Of course."

Following the procession behind the Rookwood-Nourses—toward the powder room, which was recently restored and finally useable, and the ball and spire rooms, named for the decorations on their elaborate windows—Poppy had to swallow down her own pride.

The Rookwood-Nourses smelled of roses and sea salt, a cloying, sharp note that made Poppy's nose tingle.

Lingering in the hallway as Mr. Garcliffe helped his relatives into their respective rooms, Poppy took a few breaths to still herself. This would pass. Today, she was an invisible servant, that was all.

As Mr. Garcliffe passed her in the hall, he took her elbow and said, "Miss Brightwell. Be wary. They do not know what you are."

The hair on Poppy's neck rose. Yes, she supposed the Rookwood-Nourses would be witches of some repute, given they were related directly to the Rookwood line. She had not considered her own safety, however.

"They are old, far older than they look," said Mr. Garcliffe, dropping his voice lower. "If you feel out of your depth, the gentlewitch wanted me to give you this."

Poppy felt the cold press of metal into her hand and glanced down to see a part of the gentlewitch's chatelaine: a key in the shape of an octopus. Years of tarnish had left the long arms blackened, but the underside was smooth-worn silver.

"It will bring you back to the wardrobe," said the majordomo, with a knowing wink.

In spite of her better efforts, Poppy's heart leapt to her throat, and she squeaked out her reply: "Thank you, sir. Tell the gentlewitch I appreciate the gesture."

"I'll leave you to make yourselves comfortable," said Mr. Garcliffe loudly, as they all arrived on the landing. Then, he was down the stairs and out of view.

Thankfully, Essie also was attending the Rookwood-Nourses, so Poppy had a better idea of what to do. Liege Rookwood might tolerate her bumbling, but she doubted that the new guests would. Poppy trailed the maid, her head down, behind the guests.

"Well, it certainly is a relic," said Giles Rookwood-Nourse, poking his head into the powder room, where Poppy and Essie were hefting trunks and arranging the room.

Lady Rookwood-Nourse did not look disgusted, at least outwardly. She had a strong, kind voice. "We can unpack the large trunk on our own, but please do attend to our clothes," she said to Essie, waving her finger in a circular motion. The room snapped cold, just for a heartbeat, and then that smell of roses filled Poppy's nose again.

"Thank you, my dears," said Petronilla, her voice sweet as caramel.

"Of course," said Essie, her own tone gone dreamlike. "Whatever you need, Lady Rookwood-Nourse."

It was a spell. And, clever as she was, Poppy knew to repeat the same words in the same tone, her hand reflexively going to the octopus key in her pocket. The edges of Lady Rookwood-Nourse's eyes crinkled slightly as she nodded, pleased.

Poppy had felt witchcraft before, but this magic was different. It had a sound, and a resonant dissonance that made her eardrums ache. Her instinct was to clench her teeth together, but she knew that would draw attention. So she kept her breath easy and waited until Essie began going over to one of the large striped trunks and began putting things away as if pulled along on invisible strings.

"It is so dreadfully easy to charm staff these days," said Lady Rookwood-Nourse, removing her ornate bonnet—a velvet and silk affair with enamelled flowers all about it—

and thrusting it toward Poppy as she passed. "You'd think they'd have a *modicum* of training for such things."

"You judge too harshly," said Petronilla, glancing toward Poppy. "You can't blame poor Edith. She's been out to sea for so long, alone—and in London, where one can forget that the countryside is *full* of such flocks."

Poppy pushed against every instinct to keep her shoulders and expression slack. Though she had great fondness for the sheep of Netherford Hall, she did not appreciate being compared to them.

"Not to mention the *actual* sheep," said Giles. "I've never seen such a herd." He gave a wide, gap-toothed smile that made his boyish appearance even more pronounced. But he was foxlike in his smallness and sharpness, like a wild child forced into the trappings of gentility.

"I'm so tired my nails ache," said Petronilla, falling back into one of the overstuffed chairs. "What a dreadful ride. And it's so cold in here! Heavens, it's practically medieval."

"Not practically. It is in fact medieval," said Giles, running his finger over the windowsill, checking for dust.

"Imagine the trees they'd need for such timbers," said Petronilla, glancing up at the wide-beamed ceilings. "You'd think the beams would have rotted away ages ago."

Lady Rookwood-Nourse walked the periphery of the room, ignoring her children. Slight and delicate she may be, but Poppy recognised a steeliness in her gait neither of her children managed.

"Children, gather yourselves," said Lady Rookwood-Nourse. She slowly removed one of her pristine white gloves and put her bare hand on the beam above the fireplace, closed her eyes, and fell silent. "I need silence. I must listen."

The quiet was punctuated only with the occasional rustle of fabric, the squeaking of trunks, and the popping of the fire, while the old gentlewitch meditated and concentrated. Poppy did not wish to draw too much attention to herself, so she only caught the barest of glances, but she could have sworn that the witch was in pain.

"Mother?" asked Giles.

"Strange," she said, pulling her hand away and examining her fingers, as one might after being burned by a hot iron. "I thought I sensed a presence when we first entered, but I mistook it for wards."

"What is it?" Petronilla pressed. "Now you're just being mysterious."

Lady Rookwood-Nourse glanced toward the maids a moment, then spoke, quieter this time: "There is power here. Deep, ancient power I do not recognise."

"Do you think it's Edith?" Petronilla asked.

"Or perhaps it's that ghost of a boy who has been lurking about," said Giles.

"He has a name," said Lady Rookwood-Nourse. "Henry Garcliffe. And no. I do not believe it is the boy, though he *is* touched in some way. But it is not Edith, either. At least not directly. But I did not think her capable of plotting against us."

Plotting, indeed! Liege Rookwood was genteel, courteous, and kind. She might be aloof, moody, and altogether odd at times, but she was fully incapable of malice. Not to mention she had invited the Rookwood-Nourses here in a spirit of good will.

"Are you certain it isn't just despair at the atrocious state of the manor?" Giles asked, picking up his hand as if it had been sullied.

Poppy's breath hitched. *Atrocious?*

"You have both been coddled beyond belief," said Lady Rookwood-Nourse. "The colonies are far too pristine. The house is, indeed, in a state, but not beyond repair."

"A state indeed," said Giles, "if we do end up with the place, we'll probably have to raze it to the ground rather than do any renovations."

Lady Rookwood-Nourse looked shocked at her son's words, but before she could reply, the window facing North—featuring the Rookwood family crests all lined up like magnificent jewels—shattered inward in a cascade of rainbow shards of glass.

There was a great deal of screaming.

"EXPLAIN IT TO me once again, Miss Brightwell, this time pausing between words," said Edith Rookwood, once the house had settled and Poppy was with her in her study, alone, and without hysterical relatives demanding explanation.

It had not been an auspicious beginning.

Poppy's face was still scratched but, thanks to Basil's quick work, no longer bleeding. Her dark eyes were swollen, her nose ran, and the top of her white frock blossomed with crimson splotches of her own blood.

"I think they tried to charm me, my liege," Poppy managed. "Lady Rookwood-Nourse said she sensed a presence, a power in the house."

Edith shivered. Was it the same she felt? The same that came to Henry in his dreams? "Your observations are much appreciated, Miss Brightwell."

"Essie was not herself," said Poppy. "So, I mimicked her behaviour. The Rookwood-Nourses spoke as if I could not hear them. But, of course, I could."

"That spell you sensed is a dampening charm," said Edith, trying to find the best words to describe it to the young woman. "Basic charms and incantations are exempt from the treaty in terms of privacy. You understand, ages ago, the High Houses fought against one another, before we joined Parliament. Frankly, I would be concerned if they weren't using precautions. Even though I'm hardly a threat to them."

"But they…" Poppy went to paw at her red face, but Edith caught her before she did too much damage, holding her hand for a moment and letting go. Poppy blinked, breathing rapidly a moment, before saying, "They said terrible things about the house."

Edith was rather delighted that Poppy took such offence on her behalf. This fondness was growing. And had she imagined Poppy's reaction to her touch? "When I first arrived at Netherford Hall, I was not impressed either."

"Even so, such behaviour from them—! The glass went everywhere. Did they try and attack us?"

"I do not think so. The glass broke inwardly. And it caused them harm, as well," said Edith gently. "Here, let me look at that cut on your temple, Miss Brightwell, it's still bleeding."

Clearly, Poppy wanted to say more—so she was most assuredly back to her usual self—but she snapped her mouth shut and turned to the side so Edith could take a look.

"Do you mind?" Edith asked. She had a small jar of comfrey salve in her office, and it did wonders on her own scratches.

"Please," said Poppy. "I made sure Basil went to tend to the Rookwood-Nourses, and he may have missed this one, my liege."

"It hurts?" Edith found her chest ached knowing Poppy was still in pain.

Poppy nodded, tears brimming again. "Yes, my liege."

"Considering you spend most of your time among nettles and brambles, I'm inclined to believe this as rather severe pain."

Edith dabbed her finger into the metal box, taking a small amount of the waxy substance, and then gently applied it to Poppy's temple. Basil would have to come and have a look at it again, though; Edith truly hoped it wasn't going to require any intervention as barbaric as stitches. Although, come to think of it, a few scars would be rather roguish on that already darling face.

Poppy let out a small moan, her shoulders relaxing. "Oh, goodness—that helps a great deal, my liege."

They locked eyes. Edith felt Poppy's gaze go through her, sizzling nerves from her stomach to her toes. Brimstone, the Brightwell girl had no business having such intelligent eyes! The way her lashes clustered, wet from tears, felt like the artful hand of a painter placed them there. So often, Edith avoided eye contact as it made her uncomfortable. But Poppy's eyes made her feel emboldened, comfortable— vulnerable. She wanted nothing more than to see those eyes heavy-lidded with desire, beholding Edith with the same want that thrummed inside of her.

Clearly, the love potion had only amplified what Edith was too afraid to identify: a deep and complete desire to know Poppy Brightwell most intimately.

A loud knock on the door startled Edith back to her senses; she rose abruptly. It was Hattie, holding out a message on a silver tray she must have found in storage. It warmed Edith's heart to see it. A brief reminder of how things were before the fire.

The missive was from Auden, the ink was still wet at the bottom.

Edith had to read it twice before she folded it and put it away.

"What is it?"

Edith had lost her train of thought, once again, thinking about Poppy's lips, and what tasting them might be like.

Would she kiss back with force, or perhaps she would soften, or open her mouth just so and allow for a delightful play of tongues? "Pardon?"

"The note," Poppy said, a bit of shyness creeping into her voice.

"The note." Edith cleared her throat and paced, trying to decide if she should share this news with Poppy or not.

"Well, now you're frowning and I'm desperately curious."

"I am not *frowning*," Edith said, now massaging the channel that had most certainly been crushed into existence between her eyebrows. "I'm considering."

Poppy was picking at the hem of her dress. Somehow, even when embarrassed, she was still devastatingly beautiful. "You can't spell me to keep from lying to you. You can't even take my oath in blood, or pact, or whatever flavour of enchantment such a thing might require. You must trust me."

Edith had never thought of it that way. But it was an astute observation. Even though she was a witch of but middling capacity, she had relied on the old tricks of her trade to keep secrets among mortals. She could not do so with Poppy Brightwell.

"You put it so succinctly," Edith finally replied. "But I suppose you're right. I've never had to deal with a mortal woman who I could not manipulate in some way. I am not used to trusting people."

"I did not mean to become entangled up in this business, but, well," said Poppy, a hint of her liveliness returning as she gave a little smirk, gesturing to her face. "I now bear scars of battle for House Rookwood."

It did not take as long as it should have for Edith to consider sharing this kindling between the two of them. Trust. Confidence. Connection. Those were rare elements in Edith Rookwood's life, and perhaps it is why she reached out for them in that moment. Not for the first time, she discovered that time alone with the Brightwell girl rather addled her otherwise judicious thoughts.

"The room has healed itself," said Edith without inflection, gesturing to the note.

"Healed itself, my liege?" Poppy whispered the words in awe.

Edith both detested and revelled in that title coming from Poppy's mouth. By the speckled firmament, she couldn't spend more time alone with this woman.

"Auden writes, hastily and with many smudges, that he went to examine the room, assess the damage, and found that although the ground was certainly littered with an impressive amount of glass, the windows themselves were unharmed and good as new. Better, in fact. Apparently, there is now a portrait of—well, me. In glass."

"And this is shocking?" asked Poppy, as if Edith were the pre-eminent scholar on self-healing houses.

Once again, Edith felt the great gulf between them open wide, all that she knew and understood about the world of witches, and Faerie itself—or as it had once been. To share such information with a mortal woman, especially one of such minor circumstance, would be both improper and scandalous.

Edith did not want to sound pedantic, and she knew well that it was often her standard approach. She was a terribly clever witch, partially due to her lack of power, and was not used to having to explain herself in the least. In London, her near encyclopedic knowledge of witch history had made her indispensable, if something of a boring companion to many of the more modern witches who considered fashion above history.

Not that Edith was opposed to fashion. Quite the opposite. It was only that she did not appreciate, or truly even care, about the trends and customs of modern witches.

And the longer she spent away from London, the more she became aware of just how much energy it had taken to pretend to enjoy that life. Truly, it had only been to mollify her mother and aunt. And now, without them, there was a lightness to her bearing she had only begun to understand.

And to Poppy, she could be anyone. She could slowly weave a net of lies, or she could begin with truths.

"The kind of witch needed to perform that kind of spell no longer exists."

"Whatever do you mean? I've heard of witches mending things. It's quite common," said Poppy.

"Mending, of course. But it is not about the act, my dear. It is about the composition, and the effort required. Different witches have different affinities."

"Oh," Poppy said, though she most certainly had no idea. "Of course."

Edith sat down again next to Poppy. It was a long, complex history to explain in short order. "Blood magic is the magic of healing, of life. I have a basic working knowledge of it, and if you were not as you are, I could close small wounds on your face and use your own life forces within to protect you." For some reason, the idea of not being able to do so made Edith's stomach twist again. She had to look away from Poppy while speaking to her. The whole business was just so unnerving. "But glass is, at its most base level, stone. And the petromancer line died out in the late thirteenth century with the Whettings of Norwich. Since that time, before the Peace, it has only been through ingenuity and the sweat of human hands that we have built such houses and gardens and temples and churches, never through the power of witchcraft. All that remain are the cleromancers, those who divine the future; necromancers, those who commune with the dead; blood witches, healers and sometimes warriors; pyromancers, who command fire; illusionists;

and the Triune Druid sisterhood who command water, plants, and animals."

Poppy was rapt as Edith spoke, her dark eyes wide and bright. "That seems like a great many kinds of witches. And you have to pick one?"

"Not necessarily. Many have aptitude in more than a single discipline, but it's typical to be strongest in one," said Edith. "My family were primarily necromancers."

"Then you must be a powerful witch indeed. Which kind are you? No, let me guess—"

"Poppy, it's rather rude to ask such a thing of a witch," said Edith.

"Am I Poppy now?"

"I misspoke. Miss Brightwell," said Edith, though the damage was done.

"Well, Liege Rookwood, I suppose you will have to forgive me. I am but a poor, strange young woman, who breaks almost all the rules of magic and perplexes you at every turn. But I do not wish to embarrass you or befuddle you further."

"You do not embarrass me."

"There, I think I've finally stopped bleeding," said Poppy, raising her chin to display her rather sad-looking face. She looked as if she'd been in a bad fight with an irascible cat.

"I have never found a significant proclivity," Edith muttered, frowning into her neck scarf a little.

Poppy turned. "What was that?" The woman had a penchant for missing out on quieter speech; likely her thoughts were too loud.

"You asked me about my abilities as a witch. I am, admittedly, more of a scholar on the subject than a practitioner. I am certainly no cleromancer, nor am I affiliated with the Druid Triune. I can light candles and fireplaces, heal minor wounds, and I have been known on occasion to cast an illusion or two when needed. But, in spite of my family line and their most sincere hopes in me, I was not deemed strong enough by their standards."

Poppy did not laugh, nor did she give Edith the pitying glance that she had expected. Instead, she considered the gentlewitch a moment before standing and brushing the front of her dress. "Well, I used to say the same sort of thing to my mother all the time. Heath was always meant to be a barrister; he could argue the chasuble off a priest when he was six years old. And Viola, well, Viola has always wanted to be a mother and wife. And I followed along with her, picking up the loose ends of her embroidery, making my own dresses, reading Heath's discarded books, but I have never felt that I belonged to any one thing. I never saw myself as a woman of letters, nor as a mother. I do not want children. It is not in my nature, I do not think."

In another life, Edith might have laughed at Poppy's openness, her comparing her own, simple life with that of a gentlewitch. But her candour could not be mocked. She had a keen feeling Poppy had not spoken this openly on the subject to anyone.

"Go on," Edith said, when Poppy stopped to gather herself.

"You know, my name isn't even really Poppy. It's my nickname. My parents named me Persephone. But my siblings were all named after flora. So I became Poppy. I used to think I had to choose something to be myself, to fully be Poppy. But one day, my mother went on a long walk with me, and we climbed up to Bambree Hill, overlooking half of Netherford, and I cried and told my mother that I must be broken because I had no calling in life. She held me and told me that perhaps what I was simply hadn't been conceived of yet."

"Your mother is a wise woman," Edith said, finding the words cutting through her own heart. Her mother would never have uttered such comfort. Georgina Rookwood had been, first and foremost, a gentlewitch of good breeding and nobility—one's duty outstripped any personal desires. That Edith could never adhere to one discipline or another had long been her sorrow.

Poppy laughed. "Most days, she makes me a little mad, but I suppose I do the same for her. I was given a second chance at life, and my parents have done everything to ensure that I treasure it. I am not always happy, but nor am I always sad. It brings to mind something that Lady St. Albans says often, in between her falling asleep to my most abhorrent pianoforte. Would you like to hear it?"

"I have the sense you would tell me even if I did not," said Edith.

Poppy rose her chin and said in an impeccable, imperious tone: "'What remains is not all that there was.'"

"That is a curious saying, indeed."

"It reminds me of your petromancers. Perhaps there is more to the story than you know."

"I have no doubt. But I do not think my relatives are such witches. Nor is there one living secretly in the house. As to my new family, well, we shall hear what transpires at dinner. Or, rather, I will. I *almost*—"

"Almost?"

Poppy was close now, leaning over, tilting her head like a curious cat. Regardless of her dishevelled state—and likely because of it—Edith understood the Brightwell girl to be the most beautiful creature she had ever seen. Her heart thrummed in her chest, and she wanted nothing more than to bring her closer, to feel the heat of her body again as they had when they'd danced at the Greenstreets'.

The door rattled. Edith nearly jumped out of her skin.

"My liege," came Auden's familiar voice. "Dinner is upon us. Do I need to send for Basil again? I believe he's finished up with Miss Rookwood-Nourse."

"Of course," Edith said, a bit too loudly. No, she could not blame this on a potion. But nor could she allow the Brightwell girl to cloud her judgement. To Poppy she said, "I wondered if you should take the rest of the day off."

"But don't you need my help?"

"I think today's adventure displayed that your help may be putting you in danger. They will ask questions about your unhealed face. And although you are a remarkable woman, you are a barely passable lady's maid. I will see if Molly Hode can find me a replacement for their stay—though I wish you to return to work once they are gone. It should not be more than a few days."

Poppy stood, smoothing the front of her stained frock. She did not look at Edith as she said, "And this is truly what you want? For me to leave?"

Oh, it was the wrong thing to say, but Edith said it anyway. "Yes, that is what I wish."

"Very well," Poppy said, rising and walking over to the door. She hesitated a moment. "I hope it goes well this evening, my liege. Thank you. For the salve."

Then Poppy Brightwell was gone, the oak door shuddering in her wake, the iron latches making a clatter. Auden's surprised voice came, muffled from the other end.

In all truth, Edith could not say if she was glad, or absolutely heartbroken at her departure.

CHAPTER TEN
WHAT REMAINS

THOUGH THE PLATES and chafing dishes were piping hot, the temperature in the great hall was frigid. Auden had done all he could to ensure the aesthetics of the room reflected Edith's station, status, and rank, but given the gloomy skies and the strange incident in the Powder Room earlier in the day, the company and conversation were stiff.

Auden had not had a great deal of time with the Rookwood-Nourses, but he did not think they were terrible people. A bit straightforward for gentlewitches, he supposed, but living in the Americas would account for that. They were not rude, exactly; but their directness was unsettling, like tea with an unusual spice. Auden had once been given tea with a pinch of cardamom in it, and he had not yet recovered from that shock. Good, plain, English tea was good enough on its own. Anything more was simply gauche.

"I must thank you again, Liege Edith, for having us at such short notice," said Lady Rookwood-Nourse while they waited for the second course. "It was quite a shock to us to arrive in London and find, well, such tragedy. We did not know the extent or terms of the oath, but I never would have wanted it to end in such a way."

"It was indeed a great tragedy," said Edith, not glancing up from her plate. "For all of us. But time has passed, and the wounds begin to heal. Being here in the house has helped me greatly."

"Has no one looked into the cause of the fire?" Giles asked. Apparently his impertinence did not surprise his mother or his sister, for they merely turned to Auden and his niece with expectant expressions upon their faces.

Now, Edith did look up. Then, she reached for her goblet of mead and swallowed a rather impressive gulp. "I would have it no other way. Uncle Auden and I stayed in London for almost a year," said the liege. "We had the parish constables and the night watch tracking down known troublemakers, and the Bow Street Runners investigated at length. The Witchery Protocol themselves sifted through the remains. We did not find any instance of foul play, magical interference, or anything else. It was a fire. A fast-moving fire. An act, as the local vicar might say, of God."

"And yet there was a survivor," said Petronilla. "Our cousin, little Henry. I have not seen him about."

"He is young, and best served by keeping to his studies. He's with his tutors at present," said Edith. "Though I do hope you aren't insinuating that he had anything to do with the fires."

"There have been stranger stories," said Petronilla. "He may not have caused it, but the circumstances around his survival are certainly curious."

"I don't suppose someone has questioned the lad?" added Lady Rookwood-Nourse.

Edith pulled at her cuffs, and Auden inwardly cringed. She was already losing her patience. "He endured more hardship in a single day than most do in a lifetime. I cannot allow more trauma to be thrust upon him. It is our duty to protect him, body and soul."

"Of course," said Petronilla, with a nervous laugh. "He

just seems like a rather skittish child. Staying here, all alone, with no other children."

"I assure you, Henry has received the best possible education," said Auden, now feeling the need to speak up. "I raised Edith, and she was much the same."

The Rookwood-Nourses fell silent, exchanging uncomfortable glances.

At last, Lady Rookwood-Nourse spoke. "I know our appearance is something of a surprise to you, Liege Rookwood, and we shall not meander around our purpose: we have a vested interest in this house and its surrounds. Our years in exile were spent well, but we have been cut off from our ancestral seat for too long."

"I hadn't heard a whisper about you until the bank wrote me," said Edith. "Oath or not, you can't have made that much of an impression."

"Oh, my dear, there are a great many things about our extended family of which I do not believe you have been made aware, intentionally or otherwise," said Lady Rookwood-Nourse, her voice dropping low. "Just ask the High Witch."

"I have a mind to," Edith replied.

Lady Rookwood-Nourse leaned forward. "I am over two centuries old, my dear. And my children, though they scarcely look much older than you, are in their seventies. It is the benefit of the line, or at least for some of us."

My dear, indeed!

"That is not a surprise to me," said the gentlewitch. "And I assure you, though I am young, I have had extensive education, both in the arts and the traditions of Coven Law."

"I have no doubt you are most erudite, Liege," said Lady Rookwood-Nourse. "Would that knowledge were the only way to tell such things! I am willing to brush aside the violent acts committed against myself and my children earlier today."

"I assure you, Lady Rookwood-Nourse, the situation in the Powder Room was in no way orchestrated or—"

Lady Rookwood-Nourse frowned even deeper now, her eyes flashing a most strange violet hue for just a moment. Power sizzled through the room.

"I may not be recognised as your liege at present, but I would beg you: do not interrupt me as your elder," she chastised.

"Very well," Edith said, biting out the words as if they pained her.

"We share a common ancestor. Harriet Rookwood was my mother, your great-grandmother. She did not live long, but she sired three children: Elizabeth, your grandmother; Astor, our brother; and me. When I married outside of the coven, to a Mr. Felix Nourse of Boston, I was formally excommunicated from the family, and banished from the shores of England until such time as the famed Hatchney House fell upon its own foundations, Oath-given. I assumed the oath would endure the rest of my life. But, four months ago, as my children and I were sitting in our New York apartments, we were all unchained from the restrictions of the curse. I wrote to your mother and aunt, my nieces, in hopes of welcome or explanation, but when none came, I feared the worse."

"Mortal love is far from scandalous in the covens. It's how we bolstered our ranks in the fifteenth century after the last of the fires. I don't see what the issue would have been," said Edith. "I knew Uncle Astor until his death, and he was a most treasured majordomo to my mother and my aunt. And Grandmother, what I knew of her, was all meekness and gentleness."

"Then perhaps you will hear me: my sister Elizabeth," said Lady Rookwood-Nourse, "was used as a siphon for her brother Astor. This is what I discovered. *That* is why I suffered such castigation."

Auden managed to stammer, "Th-that is absolute madness."

"It is truth," said Giles. "Though it is strange. I, too, have a vein of magic within me, but I would never resort to such parasitic practices. And when we heard of the situation, we worried that perhaps you, Mr. Garcliffe, or young Henry might have inherited the same troubles."

Edith sat stock-still, her face pale and her hands splayed on the deep chestnut table, reflected like a mirror at her fingertips.

She breathed so deeply, so measuredly, that it frightened Auden.

"Explain your accusation," said Edith.

"Your grandmother was a talented, but unfocused witch. There was a concern that, as the eldest, she would not be able to reach the standards expected for a Rookwood," said Lady Rookwood-Nourse smoothly. "Astor had potential, but no power. So, they used her as a siphon. They drugged her and tethered her to Astor's soul."

"Astor was a majordomo," said Auden, helpless. "He was a kindly old man."

"I do not know what transpired after the birth of my nieces—your mother and aunt—but what reports I gained indicated they knew nothing of the exchange. Tell me: did you ever see your grandmother perform magic?"

Edith whispered the words: "Never once. She died when I was a child."

"I understand this is a great deal to take in." Lady Rookwood-Nourse looked uncomfortable. "And I assure you, I have certified testimonies and have worked with cleromancers both here and in the Americas to corroborate the authenticity of the Oath-given charms, as well as our testimonies."

Giles acknowledged Edith with a curt nod. "You have no reason to take our word for anything, but you must understand our circumstances. We do not wish to depose you, Liege Rookwood, but there are precedents and protocols. We only wish to make clear where we stand."

"So, you wish to formally challenge the house and my position?" said Edith. "Just so we are clear. I am not one for oblique discussions. I prefer frankness."

Lady Rookwood-Nourse gave the gentlewitch a sad smile. "You cannot imagine that under the law we would do anything else. Having been ostracised and—"

"Very well," said Edith, standing. She pulled down on the edge of her waistcoat and swept the table with an imperious, cold-eyed gaze. "You are welcome to stay for dinner, but you must make arrangements to be housed elsewhere. You understand, I'm sure, given the circumstances. I will be calling upon my barrister, as well as the Coven Council, to discuss our options moving forward. We will conduct a full Measuring, and barring that, a Rite of Place. Good day."

And Edith marched across the room and out of the dining hall, leaving her guests staring in shock. A Measuring was a legal proceeding to weigh claims to a single property; a Rite of Place was a far less civilised tradition setting witches against one another in combat. The outcomes would leave no doubt to the house's ownership.

It was the right decision, Auden knew that, but he could not suppress the dread creeping down his spine. There were so few options left. Edith was not liege by her skill, but by the mere fact of surviving all her forebears. It was devastating. They could not win this.

Petronilla pouted into her glass of wine. "Well, that went about as well as I expected it."

Auden searched for words but found nothing more than a buzzing between his ears.

"Our apologies for the inconvenience, Mr. Garcliffe," said Giles, and he did look sincere. "We understand this is not an easy situation."

Above them, the hall's timbers creaked like old oaks tossed in the wind. At the hearth, Auden could have sworn that the stag horns looked sharper than they had before dinner.

"Poppy! Faith and heavens!" Mama was shouting the phrases over and over in between bouts of sobbing and hollering for Isabella and Mrs. Pratt to fetch Basil, or anyone in the entire town capable of sound medical treatment.

It was all quite overwrought, and even Viola was losing patience with their mother.

"Truly, Mama," said Viola, once the servants had been dispersed and the parlour fell into a fitful silence. "You can see Poppy is perfectly well."

"I will leave that determination to a proper physician," said Mama. She had been in the middle of writing to Heath when she'd been disturbed and was now covered in ink all down the front of her frock. She'd then gone and touched Poppy's face, and it was likely that the cuts and scrapes looked worse for the dark blotches Mama had left.

"Mama, listen to Viola," said Poppy, though it was not a phrase she enjoyed uttering one whit. "My pride is bruised deeper than my face."

"Well, why on earth didn't the witch fix it?" Mama was teetering again on the shocking by avoiding Liege Rookwood's proper address. "What do we have a witch for if she cannot heal scrapes and gashes?"

"I assure you, there was simply no time," said Poppy. "What with the guests arriving. I was just clumsy." That was a good cover. Mama could not know the extent to which Poppy was resistant to magic, and it must remain that way. Else Poppy would never be allowed to set foot in Netherford Hall again.

The look in Viola's eyes, however, was all suspicion.

"The cuts are not deep," said Viola, examining again, and helping dot the still-seeping blood from Poppy's face. It had been raining again, and in her progress from the hall, her face had undergone a gruesome transformation. Once the blood was smoothed away, what was left was very minor indeed. "And Poppy already has some good salve."

Indeed, Poppy had accidentally taken the comfrey salve from the gentlewitch in her hurried exit.

Mama was pacing again, knotting one of her handkerchiefs. "This increasingly seems like such a terrible idea. And what with the news from Lady St. Albans…"

"Oh, no—is she unwell?" asked Poppy.

"What is the trouble, Mama? I do hope she is not ill." Viola—for once, all did not seem to know the business of Lady St. Albans, in spite of her many visits to Burkley House.

"Far from it," said Mama, shaking her head, bonnet trembling. "But the same cannot be said of her brother—old Lord Titus St. Albans has died, it seems. And now their son, the new St. Albans—reared in *France,* of all places—is moving in. They say he's bound for Parliament, too, in a summer or so."

"Oh, goodness—Netherford is becoming quite the cosmopolitan retreat," said Poppy. That would mean a great deal more strain on the good town, and its eligible population. "Not to mention that half the house is still under renovation."

"Indeed, and now progress will move even faster," said Mrs. Brightwell, "and the Dowager Viscountess has requested you girls help her with the management of the house, seeing as young Lord St. Albans is unattached, and she is no longer capable."

Poppy bridled at Mama's glancing blow. Her mother knew well that she had no desire for marriage, and she had no desire for a family. She had known this since the youngest of ages.

And it was her right, thanks to witching law, whether or not Mama appreciated it—which she was sure she did not. Though succession still heavily favoured men, *inheritance* did not, or not always. Women, many of whom would have been considered spinsters before the Great Peace founded in the reign of Queen Elizabeth, could marry other women in the same way witches did, to secure their own financial situations. They did not receive dowries, unfortunately, and there were a great many other legal considerations: but it meant for women like Lady St. Albans, who had achieved her status through clever marriage, her title and money could go wherever she chose. And she had chosen her nephew, the new Viscount, Lord St. Albans. Poppy supposed her mother had held out hope that her godson might inherit something.

"Well, I can scarcely spend the time," said Poppy, already overwhelmed. "I do have to return shortly."

"You won't be at Netherford Hall forever," said Mama, almost hopefully. "And if there is even a slight chance that the dowager takes a shine to one of you…"

"I do think it's a little late for that, Mama," said Viola, finally turning from fussing over Poppy to address their mother more directly. "I am her helper, and nothing more."

Poppy gave her sister a kind squeeze. "I do think you underestimate just how kind and lovely you are. The dowager adores you."

"Very well," said Viola, and everyone was surprised at how quickly she relented. "I will go forth to Burkley in a week. Perhaps I can coax a smile from her at least once."

Poppy snorted. "Best of luck, darling sister. My mere existence irritated her. Last month when I visited, she said that my hair was an offensive shade of black. As if that was something I could control."

"Oh, she is an old woman, with old views on the world, my dears," said Mama. "We must be patient with her. Viola—darling." She came over to her eldest daughter and put her hands on her soft, flushed cheeks: "You are braver than I could ever hope. If your father weren't in such a terrible situation, I wouldn't press the matter so. The dowager viscountess favoured him very much in his youth, and I can hope that in time, perhaps, she will extend her charity even a little further."

Poppy wished she did not still feel the sting of blame for their difficulties, no matter what the gentlewitch said, but she could not help herself.

Her discomfort was not on that matter alone, however. Netherford was changing. It had begun changing the moment that Edith Rookwood crossed the threshold of Netherford Hall.

Yet, in that moment, looking upon her mother's hopeful expression and her sister's bright eyes, and Oliver curled up with Erasmus's head on his lap, she was beset with an unexpected longing for the old house: to smell the evening smells, when the candlewicks were snuffed and that sweet smoke rose to the timbers; to breathe in the cozy, lingering spices of dinner; to hear the distant shuffle of feet and the murmur of conversation as the whole house creaked and moved in the wind.

And perhaps, she even had to admit to herself, what she missed most of all was the sight of Edith Rookwood, her hair and face lit by the fire: quiet, resolute, and desperately handsome.

*　*　*

POPPY EVENTUALLY RELAXED enough to order her thoughts, bathed and mended as far as possible, and was taking a cup of tea, when Oliver tapped at the door to her room. He looked impish, grinning like a cat and clutching a small calling card.

"Who's here?" asked Poppy when Oliver did nothing but giggle.

"It's the gentlewitch herself. Asking for you." He whispered it, conspiracy glittering in his eyes.

Poppy's stomach dropped, nerves ricocheting to life. She froze, trying to take account of her own feelings—but she could not. They were all layers and contradictions.

"Why are you whispering?" Poppy asked, hoping to give herself time.

Oliver grinned. "She's by the servants' kitchen. Basil let Mrs. Pratt know, and Mrs. Pratt let me know."

"Well, there is no getting past Mrs. Pratt."

"Not at all. Mrs. Pratt is already baking three platters of Mama's favourite scones to help soothe her after this day's excitements."

"Quite the politician," said Poppy.

"Well, yes, but only so far. Your guest is waiting at the servants' table," said Oliver, raising an eyebrow. "I do have to admit, she cuts a most fetching figure."

Poppy had to agree. Gathering her courage, and her skirts, she brushed past her brother and made her way to the servants' kitchen, wishing her heart would stop pounding against her ribs like a frightened bird. Poppy Brightwell was not afraid of anything.

THE GENTLEWITCH SHONE like a burnished garnet at the old, worn table. Her hair, her clothes, her manners—she was refined and polished and perfect. But, Poppy thought, she looked tired. Worried, even.

"Miss Brightwell," the gentlewitch said, standing and giving a neat bow.

"My liege," said Poppy, her voice rough with exhaustion. She returned a half-hearted curtsey.

No one else was in the kitchen, now, but there were scones on the counter, and the table was festooned with currants, herbs, spices, and half-polished silver. It was warm and cozy and quiet.

"I couldn't sleep. The whole house felt wrong. And I..." The liege trailed off, running a hand through her hair. "I wanted to see if you were on the mend." She took a deep breath, and added: "Are you?"

"Am I what?" Poppy asked.

"On the mend."

"Oh. Yes." Poppy put a hand to her face. It felt warm and tight, but she would heal in time. "Would you like some tea?"

It was a simple offer, but it felt oddly intimate to make it. Symbolic, almost, of the subtle changes in their relationship.

The gentlewitch replied quickly, her dark gaze meeting Poppy's. "Tea would be lovely."

The trouble, Poppy now realised, was that she had no idea how to start tea in her own kitchen. Mrs. Pratt was asleep, as she should be, three floors away. For though Poppy's reputation was undoubtedly wild, prone as she was to long walks, extensive reading, and a near-encyclopaedic knowledge of herbs and plants, she was still born to the gentry, and she had never had cause to boil water herself for tea.

And as for the gentlewitch. Well, perhaps there were spells and incantations for warming steeping tea, but it would be unforgivably rude to ask, even for Poppy.

Three big water crocks stood side-by-side by the back door, the worn old wooden ladle resting across the top. A safe place for Poppy to begin, as she'd snuck many a sip in her childhood from this very contrivance, and the first step to brewing tea was water. She popped open the stopper, but realised that she did not have a suitable container into which she could pour the water, and spilling half of it on her way to the stove was unlikely to make the best impression.

"What kind of tea do you prefer?" Poppy asked, taking a detour to the shelf where the teapots sat in neat order. "We have a little bohea left, which is Papa's favourite, but at a time like this I'd think something like simple chamomile might suffice. I collect it in the summer, and Mrs. Pratt dries it for me."

"Delightful," said the gentlewitch, her eyes never leaving Poppy's form as she moved—which Poppy found she did not mind. "You are quite the botanist."

"Hardly," said Poppy. "Viola is the expert. I am just cursed with a perpetually curious mind. That, and I can't see the point of such delicious tea being left to trample by the local flocks. Seems such a waste, really."

The old copper kettle in the middle row up on the shelf was rather battered, but lighter than the cast iron—which would, at any rate, have required stoking the fire rather than using the remaining heat of the stove. Poppy could almost see the old design etched on the kettle's burnished sides; the interlacing sweet-pea vines had been worn nearly indistinguishable by use.

"We got the cooktop stove only last year," Poppy continued, now that she'd chosen her implement. "So I'm afraid I'm a little unused—"

"Here, let me help," said Liege Rookwood, standing immediately, as if glad to be of service. "Perhaps you're not used to such advances at Harrow House, but in London we had one like this, and as I endured many a night awake, I learned its mysteries—not wishing to bother the staff, of course."

For a highborn gentlewitch, Liege Edith Rookwood moved about the stove with remarkable familiarity. Poppy had noted how athletic the gentlewitch was, of course. But it was the ease with which she carried herself that was truly remarkable. She removed her jacket, rolled up her sleeves and buttoned them, then located the kindling and matches, and had started a low, crackling fire in minutes.

"There, I think it's warm enough to begin the kettle," said the gentlewitch, standing and clapping her hands together. "It's been a while since I've done such a thing, but it's good to know that my abilities haven't vanished altogether."

"Marvellous," said Poppy, putting the kettle on. "You will have to show me. I cannot always rely upon the staff."

"I hardly think they'd allow such a thing," said Liege Rookwood with a grin. "But you do not strike me as a woman who will be swayed once her mind is made. If I do not teach you, you will find some other helpless wretch to pass on the knowledge."

"You would be correct, my liege," replied Poppy, finding the teapot she wanted. It came from the Empire of Japan, her mother had told her, and depicted a heron, blossoming cherry trees, and a river.

She didn't have to ask if the gentlewitch liked honey in her tea, for by now she was quite aware Edith Rookwood had a fondness for sweets that rivalled young Oliver's.

At last, the kettle began its sweet song, and before it got loud enough to bother the rest of the house, Poppy went to work filling the pot to steep. And because she took any excuse she could to nibble, she found a box of Lady York biscuits, her brother Heath's favourite.

She poured their cups and added a drop of milk, and the

two women fell into a comfortable silence as they sipped and nibbled in the gloom.

"I wouldn't blame you if you didn't want to come back," said Liege Rookwood as she went to select another cookie. "To the house."

"Nonsense," said Poppy. She had already consumed her first cup of tea and was going for the teapot again. Did she want to come up with a reason to keep the gentlewitch here longer? Yes, she found she most certainly did. She looked so captivating when she was flustered. "I owe you a debt. We all do."

"Surely, I can figure something else out," said the gentlewitch. "Something that would not put you in harm's way."

"I agree that your relatives pose a unique challenge, but I somehow doubt they will be staying long at Netherford Hall."

Liege Rookwood laughed. "Yes, well. I may have already asked them to depart."

"Dinner was that bad?"

"Abysmal."

"Well, let me know when it is safe to do so, and I shall return to you post haste." Poppy nibbled thoughtfully at the edge of her biscuit, enjoying the crumbles that melted to sweet paste in her mouth. "Oh, but perhaps we could be even *more* adventurous."

"Who said we were being adventurous?" The gentlewitch crooked an eyebrow, her eyes dipping to Poppy's mouth before returning again to her eyes.

Poppy's heart fluttered as she swallowed. "You can place a lantern in the withdrawing room window, the second to the end where the edge has been worn away ever so slightly, you know the one?"

Liege Rookwood looked a bit confused, but nodded. "And that should function as some sort of signal?"

"I will look up and see that you've put on the lantern, and I will come at once," said Poppy, clapping her hands. Oh, it was all so very romantic.

"It might be faster to send Hattie or Mr. Yates."

Poppy tried not to sigh. Edith was being very practical. So she leaned forward a little, noticing how the gentlewitch marked her every movement. "But it isn't anywhere near as exciting."

Edith smiled. "You are right, of course."

"We shall compromise, then. If I don't answer right away—or within the half hour, at nighttime—you can send someone. Or a letter. Perhaps via pigeon. Do we have trained pigeons?"

"Not yet, I'm afraid. You—you really *are* well, Miss Brightwell?"

Poppy chuckled. "I am afraid I might be close to giddy from lack of sleep at this point, but I am entirely well. I feel almost elated."

"As long as you are comfortable. Poppy—" The gentlewitch corrected herself: "Miss Brightwell—"

Poppy?

Liege Rookwood was suddenly very close. The scent of her, that dark cherry and leather perfume, rose about them, and Poppy had to stop herself from closing her eyes and breathing it in at once. The gentlewitch did look so very dashing.

"My liege?" Poppy asked. Her heart continued its enthusiastic thumping, a knot of nerves twisting in her stomach. The anticipation made her shiver.

The back door banged open, and a caped figure came half-tumbling in. "Oh! Liege Rookwood, my apologies! Poppy! What happened to your face?"

Heath was soaking wet, and covered with mud to his knees, looking like he could well have been out tending the wards with Molly Hode.

Liege Rookwood stood, bowing neatly at the waist, her face once again assuming the mask of dignity and propriety. "Mr. Brightwell."

"Pleasure," Heath said, glancing just briefly at his sister before shutting the door behind him. He clapped his arms at his sides, shaking the chill and damp from his jacket. "I do think we're in for snow, but I got in just in time. Didn't expect to find anyone up, this late at night. I trust you're taking good care of Poppy."

"I assure you, she's the one who takes care of me," said Liege Rookwood. She added, haltingly, "There was a slight mishap at the house, but she'll be well enough soon."

"A mishap indeed. Did you run into a pack of stray dogs, P?" Heath was the only human being on the face of the earth that Poppy permitted to call her 'P.' To her credit, Liege Rookwood did not so much as flicker an eyelid in reaction.

Poppy cleared her throat. "Of course not. We think it was—"

"The wind," finished Liege Rookwood. "Something about the structure of the old manor. Poppy just happened to be in the wrong place at the wrong time."

"Indeed," said Heath, drawing up to his sister now. He put a cold, gloved hand on her cheek. "Well, it isn't as if you're not used to scratches."

Poppy batted her brother's hand away. "I am not some wild animal."

"Your words, not mine," said Heath, and Poppy shoved him.

The room fell silent, then, and Poppy wished her meddlesome brother would go back into the night where he belonged. They were about to have a moment before he ruined everything!

The gentlewitch bowed deeply. "Well, I have intruded too long. I must bid you both good night. Miss Brightwell, I will send for you, by whatever method I can devise, once we are rid of our houseguests."

Poppy truly wished she could come up with a reason to keep Liege Rookwood there. She felt more comfortable, somehow, in the gentlewitch's company, which was not something she would have admitted to even a few days before.

"Goodnight, my liege," said Poppy.

To her surprise, Liege Rookwood came up to Poppy and planted a soft kiss on her cheek. The closeness sent Poppy's breath into a gasp, and wordless she stared up at the gentlewitch.

"Thank you for the tea," Liege Rookwood said, before replacing her hat.

There was no time to think it through. Not now.

"I'll see you out, my liege," said Poppy, in a rush, before Heath could tell her otherwise. And given the face he made, he would have had much to say.

It was windy outside, and the shingles of Harrow House rattled as Poppy closed the kitchen door behind her. After the bright warmth of the hearth, Poppy could barely make out the gentlewitch's profile, but she could *feel* her. A pressure, a warmth, a confidence, a longing. It was truly strange.

Liege Rookwood spoke first. "Perhaps, when your debt is discharged, you can join me for tea more often. Up at the house."

The tea and confections had made Poppy a little bold. "Oh, but the village will talk, my liege," she said, swaying her hips. Her eyes adjusted, and she realised just how close the gentlewitch was. The nearness of her alone felt inevitable. Delicious.

"What makes you think they keep silent now?" The gentlewitch's voice was low; she knew the game Poppy was playing, even if Poppy herself did not.

Despite the chill, Poppy felt a flush spread across her cheeks. Her belly began a dance of butterflies again, spiralling lower. "Well, they will always gossip. But their whisperings are unfounded."

"Indeed," said the gentlewitch, her voice low, half distracted. "Entirely unfounded."

"Positively," whispered Poppy, leaning toward the gentlewitch as naturally as a bluebell in the breeze.

"Baseless," said Liege Rookwood, her hand rising up to gently push back the curl at Poppy's ear. That moment of contact sent a frisson down Poppy's spine and she sighed. She could not help herself.

The gentlewitch's breathing became heavier, too. The scent of dark cherries and leather filled the space between them. A welcoming, lulling sensation pulled at Poppy's body, magnetic yet gentle. The drowsy pull of a dream.

"Entirely circumspect," said Poppy, and she could hold back no longer. She needed to be closer to the gentlewitch, to touch again; even this small distance felt painful.

But she was too slow. The gentlewitch said: "I'm going to kiss you now."

"As you like," Poppy replied.

And in one smooth motion, Liege Rookwood wrapped a strong arm around Poppy's middle and drew her in, pressing their lips together. The gentlewitch's lips were full, warm, and insistent. The cuts on Poppy's face stung with the exertion, but sweetness overcame the pain as the kiss deepened, and lips and tongues explored with intermingled breath. The magic of that kiss danced down her throat, skittered through her breath, and down to her very core. A kiss still barely restrained, yet full of sumptuous promise and decadence. Poppy's hands slipped to the side of Edith's face, and she felt the temptation in the dance of their bodies: this pleasure would take its time, but it would be sweet torture every step.

By the stars, Poppy's legs felt weak. She could live inside a kiss like this forever.

Then it was over, and the gentlewitch was breathing against Poppy's ear. "Goodnight, Miss Brightwell," she said, one finger gently tracing Poppy's lower lip in reverence. "You taste of wildflower honey."

Pulling away, Poppy shivered, lost in the look of desire still blanketing the gentlewitch's features. She wanted to reply, but words felt long gone. Her body thrummed with passion, but she could only look on while the gentlewitch turned, cloak flapping, and began the ascent up the hill to Netherford Hall.

"WELL, THAT WAS unexpected," Heath said as Poppy returned to the kitchen. He'd found a bottle of wine and was already pouring some for her. "You and the gentlewitch appear to be on exceptionally good terms. I would have thought such an indenture would have you frothing at the mouth."

She was glad of the rising fury, it helped mitigate the lingering spell of the gentlewitch's kiss. Poppy snorted. "I do not *froth;* it's unladylike. I *percolate.* With grace and aplomb."

"And since when has being ladylike ever been a consideration for you?"

"I am not the one traipsing through the mud in the middle of the night. And clearly, Mama has been writing to you on every detail of my life," Poppy said. The wine was good, at least. More than good.

Heath grinned, undoing his neck scarf with a sigh. "Yes, Mama and Viola do keep me apprised of the goings on, especially when one of my only sisters is working as a lady's maid."

"It's just temporary."

"It's *beneath* you." The humour had gone from his expression, and she did not like the tone in his voice.

"You wouldn't say such a thing to the Hodes, or half the other people working at Netherford Hall."

"I wouldn't say it to them, but I would think it. Listen, dear sister. I know we are far from the most affluent of families, but we are still a family of standing. This is temporary. I hope you remember that."

"Liege Rookwood saved father's life."

Heath looked down into the deep crimson wine in his glass, swirling it slightly. "I know. I understand. I think."

"You think?"

"Witches have a reputation for such things. For illusion and trickery. For seduction."

"I assure you, this is nothing of the sort."

"I am simply asking you to be careful."

"I *am* careful."

He glanced at her forehead, still swollen and red. "Not just with your footing, my dear. With your heart."

There were a great many things she wanted to say to her brother, but between the exhaustion and the emotion of the day, she knew anything she said would end in tears. So she stood from the table, drained her wine in one gulp, and excused herself, returning to the shelter of her own bed.

You taste of wildflower honey.

CHAPTER ELEVEN
BLOOD TIES

"I'M JUST SAYING, you need to take these things into consideration," Auden said as Edith loomed large over his desk the next morning. "You cannot do this alone."

Edith was very angry. Over what, he could not precisely say. His niece was rarely upset over her present situation; that much he knew, having practically raised her as a child. But she was in a state nonetheless: hair tousled, shirt untucked, dark smudges from lack of sleep under her eyes. And the moment he had brought up considering an advantageous marriage, the situation had deteriorated.

"I do not wish to take a wife," said Edith. "I know it will make our case more appealing against the Rookwood-Nourses, but the very thought makes me sick. I will not put someone in such a position. And do not bring up Ophelia Byrne again."

"There are other women, Edith," he countered, leaning back in his chair as Edith continued to press toward him. "Or you could choose a marriage of bond only."

He had a feeling he knew precisely what—or who—this was about.

Edith's expression could have withered the fresh buds off the cherry trees outside the window. Not for the first time, Auden was glad that his niece did not possess the storied arcane powers of her family, or he would have been reduced to bones on the spot.

"There are other methods," Edith said. She slapped Auden's desk with both hands before wheeling across the carpet, freeing her uncle from her gaze. "Older avenues."

Auden might not have been a witch, but he knew what she meant. She had said as much to the Rookwood-Nourses, but he had hoped to avoid discussing it again. The Rite of Place. You could scarcely go to an inn in all of the country without hearing some version of 'The Ballad of Celeste,' a long and sordid chronicle of a witch who had been challenged for her ancestral home and made the entire garden grow to encapsulate the house, thereby preventing her rival from claiming it.

"You are no Celeste," said Auden. Which was, yet again, the wrong thing to say.

Edith looked positively stricken.

"I'm sorry. I didn't mean it that way, Edith," he tried. Was it too early for brandy?

"But what if I *could* be?" The gentlewitch had turned to stare out the windows once again. The woman never could turn away from the light, even though she dressed as if she were attending the funeral of a necromancer.

"Well, then, we wouldn't have to spend so much money on landscape maintenance."

"Uncle."

"I'm sorry," he said, though it had been a good joke.

"I am aware Beatrix Rookwood-Nourse is a powerful witch, and her daughter likewise. But there must be an answer, and I think it has to do with Poppy Brightwell."

"Once again, and most certainly not for the last time, I am utterly in the dark."

Edith gave him a sardonic grin, eyes flickering a bit. "I think I know someone who can help us."

"Oh?"

"Yes. Virginia Cawley."

"The High Witch of Great Britain."

"Yes, that is her title."

"You are a very remarkable witch, Edith, but I do not think she will be interested in mitigating a land dispute between two witches of a minor family."

Edith continued, disregarding his ill-chosen words. "She's already helped us, to some extent. You recall when I went to help Mr. Brightwell? I came home, and you asked me if all was well, and I said it was—except there was a strange occurrence I couldn't explain at the time. I still can't, exactly."

"I do recall that."

"I had to use belladonna to do it, but I was able to drop into Mr. Brightwell's mind, and I saw in his memories that he knew Virginia Cawley, that she was a witness to what happened to him, and how Poppy Brightwell's life was saved."

Well, this was new information. And even if Auden did find the Brightwells a bit overly bucolic for his tastes, there was something very curious about them. Especially the girl.

"You just *dropped into* Mr. Brightwell's mind?"

"I did."

"This is exceptional news. But also terrifying. Is there a word for both sensations at once? You could have killed him. *Ruined* him. Turned his brains to soup—"

"I know the risks, Uncle, I am aware. But he was in a very bad way. And Poppy was there; I don't think that I could have forgiven myself for a moment if I didn't try something."

Poppy. So, she was *Poppy* now. Auden filed away that knowledge for later. Edith was too excited to be derailed. "And it worked?" Auden felt a faint, tentative flame of hope. Could Edith actually have capabilities they hadn't noticed before?

"I was able to help along Mr. Brightwell's healing. But I also saw some strange memories, regarding Poppy's purported 'witch' healing. It was not a witch who helped her, but some dark creature by the name of Old Gam. I think Miss Brightwell is right about one thing: that creature is not done with the Brightwells. And I am stronger, magically, when Poppy is near. I know it."

"But you said Virginia Cawley." He shuddered at the idea of a monster lurking in the house nearest their own.

"I saw Virginia Cawley in the memory. And then I was with her, somehow, in the now." Edith looked a bit confused a moment before she continued. "She told me to keep away from this newfound gift until she could oversee my training, that it was dangerous. And that Poppy..." Edith stalled.

"Poppy what?"

"She has only half a soul. Old Gam took the other half. It was the price for saving her life."

A woman, living and breathing and seemingly whole, with half a soul? Heavens above, and the roiling rivers below—what she would be like with a *whole* soul? She'd burn the whole town down.

"Does she know?" Auden asked this very quietly, for it felt like a delicate question.

Edith frowned. "No. But I believe her parents do. It made me think about what Lady Rookwood-Nourse said about Uncle Astor. And then I remembered the soulless."

"I don't like talking about them."

"No one does. It was a very wicked mark, indeed, on witch history. But I'm not sure that even you know the whole story—"

"Siphons." Auden shuddered. "You don't believe Uncle Astor could have done such a thing, do you?"

Something in Edith's expression frightened him. "I do not know."

It was relatively early and he'd already had two cups of tea, but Auden was suddenly quite exhausted. There were many things to expect in a place like Netherford, but talk of the soulless was not one of them. It made his skin crawl. "I do not like where this conversation is headed, my dear."

"Siphoning began on mortals, draining their souls for power," said Edith. "It was a kind of ritual between the town and the resident witch in times of extreme difficulty: invasion, famine, war. Together, a witch and her soulless could amplify her magic, but the consequences were dire. When the soul was drained, they became a conduit—but a beacon, too, for other, more nefarious interruptions—drawing more insidious powers from Faerie."

"What of it?"

"What if there is a gentler way?"

"You think Poppy amplifies your magic—by accident of her healing?"

"I think, somehow, that Poppy was channelling *my* magic when the windows shattered. I have read that the ties between soulless and witch could be fraught if they did not work together. She was shaken, exceptionally emotional. She may not have been aware of what she was doing."

"Did you feel anything?"

Edith shook her head. No, the pieces of the puzzle weren't so easily connected, he didn't think. They were missing something.

"We must think on it," said Auden, when Edith offered no more explanation. "If anyone found out, it would be..."

"Death for her. Excommunication for me. Ruination."

"But you didn't know. You didn't do it on purpose. If you did anything."

"No, but there is a way to find out."

"Edith, what are you planning?"

"I need to get closer to Miss Brightwell."

Auden did not think the suggestion was in any sense motivated by investigation. "Edith... It's very clear that you have a fondness for her..."

"It has nothing to do with that. It's a matter of utmost importance."

"If you say so." Auden tried to give his niece a smile, but he had a sinking feeling she had lost her wits to her desire. He should know, he had done the same countless times in his life. But he also knew well enough that trying to dissuade her was pointless. "Just guard yourself. And keep her safe. Meddling with witches rarely ends well for mortals."

EDITH WANTED NEW suits, and regardless of propriety or necessity, that required another trip to Miss Rawlings-Vijay's shop; and rather than stay one more moment in the wastes of Netherford Hall, Auden jumped on the opportunity.

It would be no exaggeration to say that every second thought of his had been about the keen-eyed modiste since he last ran into her while they were preparing for the Rookwood-Nourses' visit. It was so rare he was able to venture out alone these days; merely leaving the house felt a little rebellious.

Regardless, Auden had been asked, directly, for new clothes for the gentlewitch. He was, after all, only following orders.

Passing a row of young women in neat lines, all wearing fashionable red cloaks and straw bonnets, Auden took a moment to assess his own garb. He worried for a moment if he was fashionable or not. Was he? He certainly did not have the sartorial flare of the gentlewitch, but he did like a good pattern or two. But there was something of an age gap between himself and Miss Rawlings-Vijay—would Miss Rawlings-Vijay think him old-fashioned?

Never mind old-fashioned, was he getting *old*?

That thought was enough to wrest him from his reverie. He pushed through the front door of the modiste's shop, plastered a smile onto his face and saw Laertes Byrne leaning over the counter within, fingering the long chain of Miss Rawlings-Vijay's pocket watch.

They both sprang apart when Auden came in through the door. Miss Rawlings-Vijay looked briefly embarrassed, while Laertes was positively vulpine.

"Good afternoon, Mr. Garcliffe," said Miss Rawlings-Vijay. "I—was hoping you might come visit. So we could go for that drink?"

A cold calm came over Auden, something he was familiar with from his younger days in more rakish circumstances. It'd been a while since he endured such a sensation: a distinct shuttering of his heart, a closing of his emotions. Seeing Miss Rawlings-Vijay in such close proximity to Laertes hammered home a very clear understanding. Auden had mistaken friendliness for fondness, and not for the first time.

"Ah, no drinks for me tonight," said Auden, adopting the same brusque approach he'd seen his great uncle use in the presence of his servants. That was before servants in a witch house were called the *staff*. "The gentlewitch has requested a new ensemble."

"I can get to work on it right away," said Miss Rawlings-Vijay, smooth and easy, all business. "We've got a new apprentice coming from Canterbury this afternoon, so we should be even faster than before. And I've got a lovely deep green I was thinking the gentlewitch herself might enjoy."

Auden frowned, shaking his head. "No, no. This is to be something else. We are looking for a different kind of design. Black. All black. The deepest, most intense black you can manage. And we want her chains of rank to be the centre of the design. Add some more links if you must. We also need a new chatelaine."

"How morose," the vampire said. "What are you up to, Audie?"

"I am up to nothing of your concern, Mr. Byrne," said Auden. He smiled, though it burned his face to do it.

To his credit, Laertes took the hint and straightened, not saying anything more.

"Of course, Mr. Garcliffe," said Miss Rawlings-Vijay. She turned to Laertes. "I'm afraid we'll have to take a bit longer on your piece, Mr. Byrne. You understand, the gentlewitch takes precedence over everything."

"Indeed," said Laertes. "So long as she reigns."

CHAPTER TWELVE
So It Begins

Viola was long past worried about her younger sister. Coming home covered in cuts and bruises, her eyes hollow and strange, it was quite clear that Poppy was in over her head at Netherford Hall. It wasn't that she was against a good connection with the gentlewitch and their family, but she was beginning to think that something nefarious was afoot.

For every ounce of whimsy Poppy had, Viola had an equal measure of sense and a rather impressive ability to tease out the truth.

Now, as Poppy sat in the parlour at Harrow House, staring down at a book and *not reading it,* Viola had simply had enough.

Viola stopped playing the pianoforte and said, "Oh, truly, Poppy. If you don't tell me what dark cloud has got you so melancholy, I am going to commence tearing out my own hair."

With a little start, Poppy turned her attention to her sister. "Am I bothering you?"

"Bothering me? No, of course not. You never bother me."

"That is patently untrue. I have spent the better part of my life doing my very best to bother you."

Viola huffed. "Well, perhaps that's the problem, then. You're just *sitting* there. Doing nothing. Are you unwell?"

"I am as well as I can be," muttered Poppy. Muttered! Poppy Brightwell did not *mutter*. She had a wide variety of less than amiable qualities, many of which bordered on offence daily, but *muttering* was not one of them.

"Poppy, my darling. Need I remind you of the bond between us? I know perfectly well that you're upset. And if you don't want to share with me, well, that is your prerogative. But know that I *will* find out."

"I don't even know how to begin," said Poppy. She really did look distressed, her brows drawn and her lips trembling.

Viola felt a shiver as she tried to imagine what in the entirety of England could have her sister in such a state. She immediately rose and went to Poppy's side, taking her hands in her own. They were so cold!

"Was it the gentlewitch?" Viola just managed to whisper it. "Did she... hurt you?"

It was a very ridiculous thought, but for a moment she worried that Liege Rookwood might be listening in on their conversation.

"No, the gentlewitch has been beyond kind," said Poppy.

"But you are not yourself."

"No, I am not."

Viola felt tears spring to her own eyes, and she clasped Poppy's hands harder. "Please, let me help you—let me listen at least, so you may not feel so burdened."

Poppy drew a deep breath and said: "I think there's something unnatural about me. I think I am *broken*."

"Broken? Poppy, you are the most whole and unique person I know. Has someone spoken harshly about the time you are spending at Netherford Hall? Are they spreading rumours?"

"Oh, you know that wouldn't bother me."

Viola relaxed at that. Some in England still found the idea of women and men choosing their partners from among the ranks of their own sex abhorrent, but they were generally viewed as backward and hateful. The heavens wouldn't quell her fury if Poppy had endured such spite.

So it must be what she feared most.

"Are you in love with the gentlewitch? Is she in love with you?" Viola asked in a rush.

This line of questioning gave Poppy pause. She tilted her head and gazed at her sister as if she were some divining orb of wonder.

"I cannot say. She is mercurial, to say the least. I do very much enjoy being around her, and there are moments that pass between us where we connect, where there is a kind of warmth between us..." Poppy's cheeks deepened as she spoke, and she averted her eyes.

"Persephone Brightwell," said Viola. "You *are* in love."

"All I know is that when I'm not at Netherford Hall, I'm miserable. In my marrow I am distraught. And the more time I spend there, the more painful it is to leave. Painful to be here, in my own home!"

"Oh, Poppy."

"But I am a lady's maid for now, and it's very likely that the gentlewitch has no intentions toward me. That I'm just confusing my love of a place with the love of a person."

"You think she intends to marry you?"

"I hope not."

"Oh, Poppy, you never will be swayed."

"If Captain Evans could not sway me, the gentlewitch will surely not," Poppy pointed out. "But herein is the problem: I've heard rumours that she's entertaining engagements to save the mansion, and it makes me so gravely uncomfortable I feel as if I should scream. Oh, I shouldn't be telling you this!" Poppy hid her face in her hands.

Viola moved a little closer on the sofa, her skirts crinkling against the straw-stuffed cushions. "I won't tell a soul. On my honour as your sister."

Poppy appeared to consider for a moment, but her resolve waned quickly, like a lump of sugar melting into hot tea. "The Rookwood-Nourses are here."

"Yes, I've heard," said Viola. "The news is all over town, and they were seen turned out of Netherford Hall, too."

"Oh, dear," said Poppy. "That cannot be good. I just have this *terrible* feeling. Not at all like what I felt when Liege Rookwood helped Papa. Like the very opposite."

"What did you feel then?"

"A lightness. A freeing sensation. As if I had been breathing water all my life and for the first time, I was breathing air," said Poppy. It was the most romantic thing Viola had ever heard her say. "But there's more. About what the gentlewitch saw."

As loath as she was to admit it, Viola was getting lost. "Saw? Don't tell me you're still on about this monster business."

"I never said it was a monster," replied her sister. "I said it wasn't a witch. But that is the crux of the matter: Liege Rookwood said that she was able to go back into Papa's memories and see what happened the night I was brought back from the edge of death. I cannot imagine she would have lied about Old Gam not being a witch."

"Well, that's ridiculous," said Viola. Except it wasn't, but she did not know what else to say to her little sister. Their parents had always painted a neat picture of the events leading up to Poppy's miraculous healing, and Viola had been old enough to remember some of what transpired, including that her sister had seemed different when she'd returned. She would never say such a thing to her, of course. She loved her as much. But Poppy never *smelled* the same. She smelled... like an apple pie without the grains of paradise.

Poppy took a deep, measured breath, smoothing her skirts. "I've had time to think it over, and to see the gentlewitch in person going about her daily life. She is not a duplicitous person. Aloof, yes. Frustrating? Almost every day. I do think she lives most of her life in her own head! But have you ever noticed that we moved to one of the few towns in all of England that didn't have a witch in residence? And we rarely travel. I'm certain Mama and Papa gave up a great deal for me, but I do wonder."

"There is that," said Viola. "At times I think Mama and Papa have conversations in a kind of language only they understand."

"And Mama, in particular, is rather defensive about witches. Especially lately."

"You could ask Liege Rookwood more," said Viola. "Tally your suspicions and then we could confront them together."

Viola felt a prickling sensation dance down her back. She did not like the idea of sneaking around on her parents, but she also believed her father too weak to endure more stress. "Perhaps that would be to our benefit. Oh, Poppy, don't give me that look. I want to help you."

"You are too good to me, Viola."

"I will do what I can. If it means looking through papers—if it means going where I ought not—I will. If you are, by some strange stroke of ill-luck, in more danger from the powers of witches and mages, we need to know. I wish I could just speak to Mama about it, but I know she will build up a great wall and never let me in."

"And I will speak to the gentlewitch herself," said Poppy, "or at least do surreptitious research in her library."

"Oh! And I will be your spy in town," said Viola, feeling a very real thrill of excitement. "We know the Rookwood-Nourses are about, and they gave you terrible dread—so I will discover their secrets where I can. Well, we all know how small a town Netherford is. They're certain to have left an impression, and they're going to have to try and make alliances."

"And everyone loves you, so we will know immediately," Poppy exclaimed, bringing her sister into a tight embrace. "But none of them love you as much as I do."

EDITH WAS SITTING, ensconced in yet more legal proceedings, when Poppy announced they were having a picnic on the lawn together, declaring: "To do otherwise would feel an absolute insult to a glorious day."

And the girl would not be deterred. She stood at the entrance to the withdrawing room, clad in her walking dress—slightly rumpled, but clean, at least—basket held aloft, and face beaming with anticipation. Edith looked on from her paperwork, trying to untangle the mess of their finances and the volumes of legal documents from the Rookwood-Nourses.

"You look vexed," said Poppy when Edith did not immediately respond to her enthusiasm.

"I am not vexed," said Edith. "Merely surprised. I don't know if I have suitable dress for such an endeavour, let alone the constitution." She was also remembering their kiss. And the taste of Poppy's lips. And how she had not been able to sleep without falling into dreams of tasting more, at least not without satisfying her more pressing need herself.

"You can come as you are," said Poppy. "It isn't as if you have to worry about petticoats."

"This was an expensive pair of pantaloons, I'll have you know," said Edith, trying very hard not to smile. It would not do to be seen in the yard partaking in such a country diversion, but that gave Edith an idea. "Though there is a way I think I can give us a little privacy. If you would be amenable to such a scandalous concept."

Poppy gave her a dark, curious, and entirely heartbreaking look, full of wisdom and wickedness. "You can't enchant me, my liege. I am a creature of unknown resistance."

Edith stood and closed the distance between the two of them. "You are that. But we have both observed that the wardrobe works when you walk through it. This is similar; in fact, I have a theory that those old garderobes are the surviving remnants of a magical talent I may have rediscovered."

"But we don't have wardrobes outside." Poppy tilted her head, curls shuffling against her printed cotton dress. It was deep red chintz and brought out the warm tones of her skin. She smelled like the out of doors, and Edith wanted to reach out and trace the same dizzying patterns on her skin as on the fabric of her dress.

"No," Edith said softly, "but imagine rather than building a wardrobe, I'm building a pocket of space in the yard that I can conceal. We would stay within the property, but apart from prying eyes."

It was new magic, and the kind Virginia Cawley had warned her against. But it was small enough, and necessary enough, that Edith banished the High Witch's warning from her mind. She couldn't very well open up their little tryst to the entirety of the staff.

Poppy swayed, her skirts swishing at her ankles. "Our own private bower, perhaps?"

"If you like." Edith liked the clandestine implications. "And so long as you're certain the location is suitable."

"I promise you, I've searched the area extensively for possible dung piles, sinkholes, and errant sticks. But if you're offended by mushrooms, I'm very sorry. I never have the heart to move them."

"I harbour no ill will toward mushrooms. Errant sticks, however, are indeed a situation most perilous."

"Oh, *most* perilous, my liege. My poor mother once tripped on the mere thought of an errant stick."

As they reached the lawn, Edith called upon a very simple enchantment, the sort of spell she thought well within even her own abilities, and concealed them from the view of anyone in the town or at the manor. Emboldened by the ease the magic, she walked side-by-side with Poppy down the gentle slope of the lawn, the spring breeze bringing with it the loamy fragrance of wet grass and newly sprung bulbs.

As they walked, Poppy pointed out every new swath of crocuses. They arced in long rivers of colour across the field, sprinkles of pale lavender, buttery yellow, vivid crimson, and delicate ivory.

A small copse of trees rose to the east of the gardener's cabin, big willows clustered around an oak against the wind and the weather. Poppy had, it seemed, already planned lunch: there lay a blanket, a basket of early spring flowers, and even a little tray.

"You were quite certain of my attendance this afternoon, I see," Edith said.

"I admit to a certain relentless optimism," countered Poppy, twirling a little before settling down in a puff of petticoats and mud-edged skirts. "I sensed you were defenceless against my wiles."

Rather than admit to such a thing—if only she knew!—Edith closed her eyes and tested the edge of her magical barrier. Liminal magic of this sort required more concentration than merely obscuring herself. But the barriers felt surprisingly sturdy—even if, in this case, air and light passed through. It was camouflage of a remarkable sophistication.

"I am confident in our concealment," said Edith, gesturing above her head. "Can you detect it?"

Poppy looked up, tilting her head. "I only see sky, the swaying trees, and you."

"Wait here just a moment," said Edith, pausing to add, "if you are capable of such a thing."

Poppy scoffed and Edith walked about thirty paces north to observe their bower from the outside. She crossed the barrier with no trouble, feeling only a sense of coldness as she passed it.

Edith could not see Poppy at all. An unexpected relief washed over her: she could hide Poppy if she needed. The scarce mentions she'd found to liminality in her library offered no clear instruction. For the first time in her life, Edith Rookwood was working on intuition and feeling— and it was always easiest when Poppy Brightwell was around.

"There you are," said Poppy, when the gentlewitch returned again. "I could only see you in a kind of wavering shadow, and I thought there might be something looming behind you, but—I think it was just a trick of the light."

"I was just making sure the structure was sound; I promise, I was very much alone," said Edith, rubbing her hands together. She was quite pleased with herself. Magic had never come very easily to her, but this was exhilarating.

"Shall we commence, then?" Poppy asked.

"Please, Miss Brightwell, let us dine," said Edith. "I am famished."

There was no pomp, no preening, and no standing on ceremony. Poppy merely approached the basket with her elbows out, tongue peeking between her full lips, and began a haphazard placement of every dish.

"First come the spirits," she said, holding up a single finger. "I stole this. From Papa. He'll never drink it anyway."

She produced a delicate bottle scored around the edges with now-fading designs. It was still waxed and corked, but the state of both hinted further at its age. Thankfully, upon opening this forbidden drink, the contents smelled rich, warm, and bright: raspberry brandy, brewed with something else—perhaps clove?

Edith turned the bottle of brandy over in her hand, and found the handwritten label was in French.

"I'm not much of a brandy drinker, but I came with reinforcements," said Poppy, handing Edith another bottle, this one quite familiar. It was birch beer, likely from their own stores at Netherford Hall. "And here are the mugs." Two small pewter vessels most assuredly from the eclectic and extensive collection at the house.

Edith took a sip of the brandy, surprised by the silky progress the liquor made across her tongue. The sweetness was only there in the beginning; it quickly grew peppery, and then finished with a hint of anise.

"The brandy suffices?" Poppy asked, still practically head-first in the basket.

"Indeed. This is all quite impressive," said Edith as the pile of food before them grew in startling proportion. "Are we expecting someone else?"

Poppy chuckled. "You clearly underestimate my capacity to eat. I took the opportunity to leverage my relationship with our respective cooks. Mrs. Pratt was more than happy to provide our first course."

"*First* course?"

"Yes. There is no code that decrees lunch on one's lawn to be anything other than proper."

"Oh, well, yes. My apologies. Do continue, Miss Brightwell."

"Yes, my liege," said Poppy. She began enumerating the plates before them. "I have Mrs. Pratt's homemade bread and clotted cream, just finished this morning and pilfered immediately; then I present a selection of cheese from Mr. Hamnet in town, which I procured myself at a personal expense of a broken boot heel when I tripped and fell over the threshold."

Edith could not help but laugh. "I do wonder how any of your shoes hold up to their treatment."

"I am a living miracle, my mother always said." Poppy nibbled on the edge of a bit of cheese as she explained: "I also have some early chervil, so I rolled that into the butter myself with Mrs. Pratt's help. And a little rosemary one. I tried to make them look like little cats. Plus, a bit of wildflower honey, since I have yet to meet a cheese that didn't somehow ache for a hint of sweetness."

Aching for sweetness, indeed. This woman. "Wildflower honey is my favourite."

"I know," said Poppy, leaning forward with unfettered flirtation, the front of her gown dipping toward scandal. "You show remarkable restraint, Liege Rookwood, in simply gazing upon the wonder."

But rather than offer up herself, Poppy handed Edith a crusty half-loaf of bread. Ah, so this was the game. She could be patient. So she took the bread and began picking at it, while she watched the light in Poppy's hair, the gleam in her eye. She could be patient. Devouring Poppy Brightwell slowly, from the ankles up, upon a field of blooming crocuses was a delicious prospect, indeed.

Poppy continued, waving a hand over the food. "I decided on a somewhat lighter second course. Meats and some leftover capons. Then some rustic duck rillettes for which I traded two bags of chamomile tea to Mrs. Hamnet. I also went next-door to Mr. Mallson's, who had some summertime sausages."

Poppy might not have been a natural cook, but she did have a way with flavour. Quince paste on the soft-ripened cheese gave it a brightness Edith had never expected. And the rosemary butter brought out floral elements in the bread that otherwise might have remained unknown.

To say nothing of that wildflower honey.

Edith could not remember being so full. Her cheeks ached from smiling, her sides ached from eating, and her lips tingled from the brandy.

"Before the final course, I have a gift," said Poppy.

"Dinner *and* gifts! Miss Brightwell," said Edith, "I must protest."

"I will not hear of it," said Poppy, and she dug down into her embroidered satchel and produced a wrapped parcel the size of a deck of cards and tied with green grosgrain ribbon over a white muslin handkerchief.

Rising to her knees, Poppy leaned forward and handed it to Edith, solemn and expectant.

It was not the most elaborate gift she'd been given, but the gesture itself was so sweet, and so unexpected, that Edith had to swallow back on a suddenly very thick throat.

"Consider it a late birthday present," said Poppy.

"My birthday was in October," laughed Edith, but then she stopped, for the gift's value and artistry became apparent as she freed the contents.

Cuffs for her shirts, embroidered with little orange and red poppies, their delicate petals rendered in such fine floss that they looked as papery and fragile as the real thing. The green background was shot with brighter silk, a coppery hue, and backed with glossy black satin.

"You made these?" said Edith at last.

"Of course. You like them?"

"I don't know what to say."

"Say you will have dessert!" Poppy reached into that endless basket with as much fanfare as a trained illusionist. "This is Mrs. Pratt's shortbread, and I promise, once you eat it you will feel betrayed by every other shortbread you've had in your life. No, here. Let me show you."

Poppy settled close to Edith, who had stored the delicate embroidered cuffs in her breast pocket. Edith had by this time adopted a half-reclining pose, her waistcoat open, her scarf untied, but she sat up a little to meet Poppy's eyes.

Edith was about to say something when Poppy leaned over and put a sizeable morsel of shortbread in her mouth.

She began chewing in earnest, and was overwhelmed by the flavour. There were no such things as kitchen witches—at least not that Edith Rookwood knew of—but by the stars and the great rivers, that shortbread melted as soon as it hit her tongue, leaving behind buttery, fragrant delight.

Edith laughed. "A revelation."

Poppy looked a little smug. There were crumbs on the front ruffle of her bodice, clinging to the smooth skin at her neck. Edith tried not to look, but it seemed the brandy and the cheese had conspired together to release her of any inhibitions.

Under the wavering willow branches, Edith felt the last of her restraint ebbing away.

"Poppy—"

"I'm not finished yet," said Poppy, edging even closer.

Poppy reached into the basket, her dark braid falling down one shoulder and her skirts rustling. It wasn't difficult to maintain the illusion around them—their privacy—but Edith's heart was flipping and twisting in her chest so terribly she was wondering if there was some unknown strain on her magic she could not see.

With a devilish smirk, Poppy produced a little trio of crocuses. She spun them around in her fingers so they dazzled, right below Edith's own nose: saffron and ivory and deepest purple. Then Poppy leaned over and tucked the little bouquet into Edith's waistcoat pocket.

With a palpable effort, Edith tore her gaze from the glory of Poppy's flesh and form and swallowed hard. She had tied another length of green grosgrain ribbon around the bouquet, and now it sat there, just above Edith's own heart.

"No one can see us," Poppy said, decidedly not moving away from Edith. The weight of her body, the long line of her leg and arm, pressed into Edith's side. "No one can hear us."

"Poppy—"

"I'm Persephone, my liege."

"Persephone." The name even tasted sweet. "You bring me flowers, and you—"

"*Edible* flowers," said that wicked, wonderful woman. "The buds and all."

Then Poppy's lips were on Edith's, and they melted together in that springtime sun, crushing and sweet. It was not like their first kiss, tentative and exploratory—no, this was the sum of days of passion withheld, of romantic daydreams and musings, of solitary pleasure taken in secret among dreams of wanting.

Edith felt her own centre grow, blossom, expand, and along with it the familiar tingling of her magical prowess she had come to know from her proximity to Poppy. So much power lurked beneath them, just there, waiting, *begging* to be used. But so, too, was Poppy begging to be touched, to be pleasured, to be plucked in her own way.

And Edith wanted it, too. Yes, it began easily enough, that desire for power. But it had so swiftly changed. She had wanted to get closer to Poppy, to see if she could use her powers to best the Rookwood-Nourses, but this was not right. It felt wrong to indulge her desire when her motives had been confused.

Guilt pulled Edith out of her reverie, and she broke from the kiss, running her hands down Poppy's shoulders and holding her out to get a better look.

"My dear, I cannot," Edith began, shame rising up with anxiety.

"Cannot what?"

When Edith, blinking with the fug of lust, did not reply, Poppy began to pull away, agitation in her expression. "Perhaps I misread you—perhaps I have embarrassed myself."

No, Edith could not allow it. She grasped Poppy's forearms, feeling the heat of her skin through the cotton of her dress. By the speckled firmament, she wanted nothing more than to tear Poppy's dress away, to bury herself in her bosom and be lost in it, to feel this brilliant woman writhe and move beneath her touch. She had never felt so enthralled by another being in all her life, and it both thrilled her and terrified her.

"No," said Edith, loud enough that Poppy's eyes shot wide. Their dark depths pulled the gentlewitch even deeper. "I need you to understand. I did not want this complication, this puzzle of you. But I cannot stop thinking of you, Persephone Brightwell. Is my desire not apparent?"

"You are not a woman of many words," said Poppy.

Edith made a sound, almost like a growl, and it was so unlike her and yet so arousing at the same time that she felt emboldened. "I am a woman of action, it is true. But you have confounded me, bewitched me; my body and my soul ache for you, Persephone. Surely you can see that."

"I thought I did," Poppy replied softly. "I know our pairing is not ideal in your circles, but I had imagined..." She dropped her eyes, as if embarrassed to ask. "Do witches not have mistresses?"

"I will not have you as a mistress," said Edith, too quickly.

"What?" Poppy whispered, hurt on her face.

Edith tried again, smoothing her thumb over the back of Poppy's hand. "I would not relegate you to such a fate. I have already offended you, and your family, by indenturing you for my services. I don't know why I did that—only that I needed more of you."

Poppy pulled away, melting into the folds of her dress.

The words were coming out wrong.

"I *want* you," said Edith. "But you must understand my place in this family, or what is left of it. Netherford Hall is in shambles and I have no way of knowing its future. Your family is—"

"*Poor*. My family is poor. And infirm." Poppy's face was even more terrible now, for she was weeping. And Edith knew it was not simply from sorrow, but from fury. "And of little consequence to the gentlewitches of London."

"You deserve more than life as a consort, as a mistress," Edith pleaded. "I cannot take your future simply because I am able to."

Poppy's expression was of such betrayal Edith felt physically pained. "You dare to think I want you because of your power and position?"

"You cannot deny I have put you in an inferior position. I would be doing you no service."

Poppy stood, a hurricane made woman, and kicked the basket, so what remained of the food went tumbling out in all directions.

Edith knew what she had to do. Leveraging Poppy for her own gain was unthinkable. She would have to figure out how to regain Netherford Hall from the Rookwood-Nourses on her own, or not at all.

Losing Poppy somehow seemed worse. But she could not allow this dance of flirtation to continue under false pretences.

"So you desire me, but you will not have me because you deem me both too inferior for marriage and too worthy for a mistress. But that is not all—you shun me because you believe I was wooed by your power and status," Poppy said, furiously pulling her shawl back around and over her dress.

"I did not mean to give offence," Edith replied. "I did not want you to think..."

"You cannot know what I think. *I* scarcely know what I think when it comes to you!"

"And you are far too naïve to think you are anything less than an open book, Persephone," said the gentlewitch, finding her own temper rising with Poppy's impertinence. "You should not be so willing to give away your body—your *heart*."

"At least I *have* a heart," Poppy spat.

Edith took a deep breath, wishing she could retract her words, wind the clock back by minutes. But she could not. "I do not think I can continue to have you in my service. It would not be fair to you."

"*I* get to decide what is fair to me. And I do not *want* to be in your service, *Edith*," growled Poppy, stomping her foot like a petulant child.

"Please, my dear—I want you—you must know that I--"

"*No.*"

It may have been the shortest sentence Poppy had ever uttered in Edith's presence, and it was like a thunderclap across her senses. The young woman grabbed one of the pewter mugs from the luncheon spread and threw it with all her might.

It shattered through Edith's arcane bower, as surely as if it had been made of sugared glass. Stunned, the lost magic sizzling down her chest and arms, Edith tried to stand and re-summon it, but she could not. She could do nothing but watch Poppy stomp her way back home to Harrow House, her hiccupping sobs dissipating in the distance.

AUDEN WAS ORGANISING his pitiful library again, which kept him calm when his nerves began jangling, which was too often these days. He felt queasy. And useless. If Edith's scheme to get close to Poppy Brightwell didn't work, there was no way they would maintain Netherford Hall on talent alone.

The door to his study creaked, and he looked up to see Henry. He was muddy from the knees down, his feet covered in soot, cheeks bright, but otherwise sound.

"You look terrible," he said to his uncle, with all the gall and aplomb of the young and observant.

"I'm rather fatigued, my boy," said Auden, which was an understatement.

"Edith looked worse."

"Did she, now?" That got his attention. Even on her worse days, Edith was next to immaculate.

"I think she's sad. And angry." Henry reached up to wipe the back of his hand across his nose. "And she was pulling out all the crocuses in the front lawn. I asked her what she was doing, and she shouted some words I didn't understand."

"Oh."

That was really all Auden could say. He went to the window, and indeed beheld the figure of Edith Rookwood, gentlewitch of Netherford, angrily pulling up crocuses in handfuls.

"Should I bring her some tea?" Henry pulled up alongside his uncle and leaned on him.

"I think, in this instance, it is best if we simply wait for her to expend her energy properly, and then have a good conversation. There is no witch on this green earth that I would cross in such a mood."

NOT LONG AFTER, Edith came stomping into the office in a filthier state than Auden had ever observed. She was barely recognisable as she removed her coat, waistcoat, and neck scarf, and was so flushed her nose was the same hue as her hair. And, if he was a betting man, he'd say that she had been crying.

"I want you to find every last detail on Netherford Hall," she said, slapping her hand down on his leather-topped desk. It made his ink bottles tremble, and he had to wonder if there wasn't a bit of magic in that wrath. "Every deed. Every mention. Go to London if you must. I will write to Alistair Dane and ask him to pull any of the archives from the Coven Library. We will provide all we can to the barrister and the Rookwood-Nourses."

"Of course, my liege," said Auden, far more formally than he typically managed. "Should I discuss this with the Hodes as well?"

Edith paused in her fretting and righted a few pieces of paper before continuing. "Not for now. Leave that to me. I see now that I have been otherwise occupied. Unwisely occupied."

"Distracted? Does this have to do with Miss Brightwell?"

"She is no longer in our employ."

"I see," said Auden, finding himself rather disappointed at the news. Miss Brightwell had brought out the best in Edith, he thought.

Turning on her muddy boots, leaving a tract of black soil on the red carpet, she turned at the last moment at the door. "Put out the call out again for a lady's maid. Post haste. Also, and let me reiterate: the Brightwells, *any* of them, are not permitted on the property without my express permission."

"Yes, my liege," he said.

The door shuddered closed, and Auden had to brush tears from his eyes. Had he been hoping Edith had found love? Had he dreamed that kindled connection between her and young Miss Brightwell? Of course, it would have been a terrible match. Disastrous. But they could find some comfort, couldn't they? They both deserved it.

* * *

Viola had never had cause to visit the Holly and Sickle, as it was not the sort of establishment in which she felt at home. It was, as her mother was fond of saying, a place where those who could not find welcome in the other taverns congregated, much like the flotsam and jetsam of a shipwreck. Which was not a very kind picture of Netherford, she now realised, but that was not surprising.

Witches needed places like the Holly and Sickle, however, and she was collecting information about the Rookwood-Nourses, even if it meant sifting through the detritus of town.

Much to her surprise, however, the Holly and Sickle was a pleasant, clean, well-appointed tavern. Though Poppy was something of a regular, finding many of her clients for mending and odd jobs among its patrons, she had always made it sound a bit rough around the edges.

That couldn't be further from the truth. It smelled of baked sourdough, fresh cedar, and crisp cider. The floor was laid with smooth stones which gleamed in the light from the massive hearth. Though it was just before the rush, it was full of quite average folks looking for food and conversation. And overhead, Viola spotted thousands of witch's ribbons, tied with love, trinkets and a good deal of hope.

She was searching for someone in particular, though; an old woman who Poppy knew as Salvinia Pemble. By all accounts, she was a seasoned herbalist and lore-keeper, but she rarely left the Holly and Sickle, and would only speak with you if you had an offering. She was an old hedge witch.

A dangerous business. Hedge witches were not sanctioned by the Grand Coven, and were rumoured to have wild, unpredictable magic. But if anyone knew *anything* about the Rookwood-Nourses, and Netherford Hall itself, it would be her.

Poppy would be absolutely crimson with fury if she knew what Viola was trying to do.

"May I help you, miss?"

Viola turned abruptly, gathering her shawl around her, and came face-to-face with the living portrait of a man she'd seen time and again. His eyes were very dark in the dim light, but she remembered them as deep hazel in the Lady St. Albans's favourite portrait. His hair was shorter, now, in a more contemporary fashion than rendered in paint. She had guessed him, then, to be in his twenties, but now she saw he was a little older than that. Like the rest of the portrait figures in the St. Albans family, he was descended from a herald of Henry VIII, so beloved they'd been titled.

But here, rendered in the flesh, the Viscount St. Albans was so much more than his portrait. His brows were black, a shade darker than his deep brown curls, contrasted against the smooth sable of his skin. And his smile was kind, and knowing. And roguish.

"Your lordship," she said, dipping into a curtsey, her heart pounding in her chest.

When Viola straightened, she could see a quiet kind of merriment in his eyes. "I don't usually get such a formal greeting here. Might I deduce that I am in the presence of Miss Viola Brightwell?"

"The very same, sir," said Viola.

"My great aunt speaks to no end of your talents and patience—which I hope you realise is immensely high praise!" said the viscount. "But she did not tell me of your loveliness."

Well, that was certainly a place to begin. "I'm sure that the Lady St. Albans was being kind."

"On the contrary, she almost never exaggerates. She met Queen Charlotte once and said she was offended by the colour choices at Dutch House."

Viola had already taken off her gloves, so when she gave her hand to the viscount, she felt the touch of his skin on her own.

To his credit, he did not kiss her hand, and only held her gaze for a moment. The spell broken, Viola walked a few paces beside the viscount before he offered her a seat at one of the tables—it was somewhat private, but not so private as to invite unwelcome gossip. She muttered her thanks and only sat because he was clearly waiting for her to do so.

She was trying to remember his name. Lady St. Albans had mentioned it a thousand times in their long afternoons together, especially as his visit came closer. But now she couldn't recall it. Not that it was a particularly difficult name, but it was somewhat unusual. Nothing as boring as James or George or Andrew.

"I am very grateful for Her Ladyship's kindnesses," said Viola. "Not just to me, of course, but for my whole family."

Lord St. Albans gave her another smile, this time a little sad. "Well, kindness is not a characteristic that I would normally ascribe to her, but she seems to have had a rather soft spot for your father since he was a child. I am told he and my uncle Edward played together when they were young; before the fever, of course. A damned shame. I would love to have met him, but the Fates did not have such a tale in mind. Hence my being here at Netherford, and soon taking up residence at Burkley House. At least for the spring and summer."

This was a new development. Viola's father had never mentioned Edward St. Albans as a friend. And neither had the dowager viscountess. But the casual manner in which he'd shared the information was most curious.

"Your family must have had another house in Northamptonshire," said Viola. One of the staff dropped a plate of immaculate little pressed cookies before her, and a flagon of ale.

The viscount looked into his ale a little suspiciously before taking a sip. "Not that I was aware. Why do you say that?"

"I just thought that's where my father grew up," said Viola.

Another strange chink in the armour of Papa's stories.

"Well, he would have had to be in Essex, wouldn't he?" Lord St. Albans lifted a very fine eyebrow in Viola's direction. "At least until my great-aunt moved, which wasn't until I was born, and my mother and father took up residence at Bellechamp—that's where my uncle grew up, you see, as I did, before going to school and relocating to London after my—" He laughed brightly. "I am clearly boring you to pieces with all this genealogy, and shame on me for it. We were talking about you."

"I admit, I didn't expect to see you in town for a few more days," said Viola. "The Dowager Countess let me come home yesterday before going back to help with the rest of the arrangements. And she's planning a banquet on Friday."

"Yes, yes," said Lord St. Albans. "I have heard. And no, she doesn't yet know that I've arrived. I do love her very much, and owe her a great deal, but she is woefully backward in the right way to do things these days, especially when there are witches involved. I wanted to come to town to see if I could have some conversations with the *right people*. And the Holly and Sickle is always the best place to begin. I know you're tenants to the gentlewitch, so you understand, I'm sure."

"I do," said Viola. "But in spite of that, I do not know if the dowager viscountess has ever much approved of the Rookwoods. Or witches in general."

"Which is terribly strange considering she was once very close with them," said the viscount, leaning back in his chair to look over at the fire. "I don't expect you to know all the details, and I don't think she would ever share, but before she married into the St. Albans family, she was a Cawley. She is Virginia Cawley's sister."

"My stars. Is she? I forget witches age differently," Viola said.

"And there are some other interesting ties as well. No one quite knows why the Rookwoods left Netherford Hall in such disastrous shape, but it was through the kindness of the St. Albans family that it was kept up at all. Why, I found invoices from just fifteen years ago for the replacement of every last window in the hall. I've only seen it from a distance, and that is a great, great many panes of glass."

"It is. Thousands, indeed," said Viola. "And most ornate."

The viscount laughed. "It is strange! It is one of the reasons I felt the need to come here. Before my father died, I confronted him on the issue, and he said it was not for debate. I am not one for arguments, I admit, but he was also not the kind of man to leave things unexplained—though he *was* the sort to leave bills unpaid." He paused, sipping his ale again and gazing toward Viola. "And now I hear the ownership of Netherford Hall is in dispute."

Viola tried to act surprised. "I had thought that a simple rumour."

"It was all in the *Times* two days ago."

Viola laughed. "I admit it is difficult to think of Netherford Hall being in the London papers."

"There are many curious happenings in Netherford, Miss Brightwell," said Lord St. Albans. He looked down at his watch and gave a bright laugh. "And alas, I am late for another appointment. Setting up a new home is no mean task—and you have been an immense help, I have heard. Thank you for the conversation, Miss Brightwell. I do hope we meet up again at Burkley, if not before the banquet."

"It was my pleasure, your lordship," said Viola, finding the words so strange. She had met peers before, but they didn't feel so comfortable as the viscount. It wouldn't have been difficult to speak with him all night, she thought, and if she hadn't been guarding her tongue, she might have said even more to him.

"No, I assure you, the pleasure was all mine," said Lord St. Albans, and he took her hand, kissed it, and departed the Holly and Sickle.

It was another hour before Viola was summoned, this time by Tess Hemley, one of the bartenders. She was sixteen if she was a day, and Viola remembered her well as a little plump girl with a mountain of black curls.

"She'll see you now," said Tess.

Viola followed Tess up the creaky stairs, which were thankfully drowned out in the hubbub of the busy tavern and mostly unnoticed. For all those in attendance at the tavern she didn't know, she was surprised to see plenty whom she did and had never expected to be in with the Hodes and the Rookwoods.

The upstairs was narrow and tilted, as were many of the old Tudor buildings in town. And the air felt mustier, as if all the smells from hundreds of years had risen from the common room and collected there. The wallpaper might once have been white, but now was peeling and yellowed, the memory of old portraits or artworks lingering in brighter squares.

They passed three doors on the side before Tess took out a key and put it in the lock. Viola didn't want to ask why Salvinia was behind a locked door. It was better that no questions were asked. It was unusual enough that Tess had ushered her in with no real questions asked. Hedge witches weren't always so amenable to such things. Especially Salvinia.

"There you go. Just knock when you're through and I'll

open the door," said Tess, swinging the door forward. It creaked enough to make Viola startle.

"You're not coming in?" Viola asked.

Tess's scoff was enough to answer that question.

Viola anticipated a witch's den full of strange furniture and hanging herbs, but the room looked like a clerk's office. It was clean, swept, and sparse. Salvinia sat behind a large desk of worn oak, sorting through papers, and drinking something out of a large clay mug.

Viola had never seen Salvinia up close, but she looked remarkably plain now. Just an old woman with undone hair, really. Her face was lined but plump; her dress was homespun but clean. She had long, knotted old fingers, but she was not frightening in any other way.

"Miss Brightwell," said Salvinia, looking up from her desk. The hedge witch even wore spectacles. "You had some questions for me."

The door behind her clicked shut and Viola made herself comfortable on the chair opposite Salvinia. She rather liked the quiet simplicity of the room. The cacophony below was barely audible save for a slight thrumming in the floor below Viola's boots.

"Yes, thank you for taking the time, Mrs. Pemble," said Viola.

"It's *Ms.* Pemble. But please call me Salvinia. And I will call you Viola. And though I quite expected to see your sister when they told me 'Miss Brightwell' was coming to see me, I am still surprised that *either* of you would make your way up here."

Viola tried not to feel as if she were gossiping, but the pressure of her adventure was heavy on her shoulders. "I was wondering, since you've been here longer than just about anyone, if you were familiar at all with the Rookwood-Nourses."

"That's gentlewitch business," said Salvinia, a note of warning in her voice.

"Yes, I'm aware, I only thought—"

"I will, for your sake, assume you are unfamiliar with the workings of hedge witches, and their most frigid relationship with the High Coven," replied the hedge witch. "How, for the majority of the last six centuries, we've been maligned to the edges of society because we are not deemed important enough for the High Coven and their political purposes. We fought the barrier between our world and the fae, and we have paid for it every day since."

Viola swallowed, and she swore it was loud enough to hear across the room. She would not let herself cry, so she gritted her teeth and tried sound apologetic. "I really didn't know, Ms. Pemble."

"How unsurprising," said Salvinia, her shoulders falling somewhat. She held out her sleeve, which fell back to reveal a strange contraption twisted around her wrist and fingers: a shackle bracelet, connected to a set of rings by delicate chains. "These are the prices I pay. The magic binding them to me is far too powerful to ever break. No matter where I go, they know what I am. And most importantly, what I am not."

The metal looked cold: Viola almost expected frost to form on the surface. But then Salvinia put it away. And the room felt warmer again.

"I'm sorry," said Viola, her voice barely a whisper.

"You probably think us backward midwives, wandering the fens for old medicines, and cursing children from the woods," said Salvinia. "If you've come here asking questions about the Rookwoods, I'm afraid I cannot help you much there. Chances are you won't like what I have to say, anyway. They never do."

"I'm simply trying to help my sister," said Viola.

Salvinia folded her hands, and gazed at Viola with disappointment. "Hedge witches are subservient to the Coven-born. We are allowed to practise magic, under the observation of Warders—like our Hodes here in town—and maintain a certain amount of autonomy. But just because I'm a witch doesn't mean I have any greater insight into the world of the High Coven."

Viola wanted nothing more than to leave, but she suspected that would be rude. And she knew Ms. Pemble wasn't quite done with her.

"But I am willing to share a little knowledge, as I am aware of what sisterhood means," said the old woman, to Viola's surprise. "For a price."

"Of course," Viola replied. "I came prepared." She began to take out her purse, but Salvinia's laugh stopped her.

"I do not want your coin. I want your influence. If you could arrange a meeting between me and the majordomo—Mr. Auden Garcliffe, I believe. Do you know him?"

"I do." Viola's stomach clenched. She had the sensation she was walking into a trap.

"If you think you can arrange a meeting between us, then I will tell you what I know."

It didn't seem impossible, she didn't think. Mr. Garcliffe was always about town—he even frequented the Holly and Sickle, she was quite certain.

"Very well," said Viola. "I'll do all that I can to arrange a meeting."

Salvinia nodded, then leaned back in her chair. "The only witches that have been in Netherford longer than the Rookwoods are my people, the Goodys. Oh, that won't be in the gentlewitch's records, nor in the Hode's big books. It wouldn't be. They profit from their version of history, and since the majority of England and the rest of the Empire believe it—well, it's as good as truth.

"But we keep close eyes on the Coven-born. Not for malicious reasons, but to protect ourselves. When they stopped burning the gentlewitches, it took a while to come down to us, and in some counties, we're still often found dead, or maligned, or ruined. We don't hold to the same concepts of purity as the other witches do, and they do so love to call us *indecent*.

"That said, some darkness is coming to Netherford on the heels of the Rookwood-Nourses, and I think the whole town feels it. The fae do not like to be caged. Though I wouldn't say the gentlewitch herself is exactly admired around these parts, there's a general approval for the work she's done to Netherford Hall. No one likes to see a great house fall into disrepair, least of all the hundreds of souls who are supposed to make their livelihoods off it. But I digress."

Salvinia spread out her hands, smoothing the papers in front of her. "I think the answers are right under your nose, my dear. You're practically a ward to the old dowager, from what I know."

"The dowager? How do you know?"

The old hedge witch clicked her tongue. "As I said, we listen. And the Holly and Sickle is a good place to listen."

"Thank you," said Viola. "I will write to Mr. Garcliffe presently."

She went to stand, leaning her hand on Salvinia's desk, but she realised her error immediately.

"One more thing," said Salvinia, a half-whispered command. The hedge witch grabbed Viola by the wrist, and her grip was as sure as iron. She felt her bones groan with the pressure.

When Viola looked down, Salvinia's eyes had gone white, her withered lips trembling over crooked yellow teeth. "*Beware the wandering beast, Viola Brightwell. Beware the places in between. Beware the unbeating heart.*"

The spell snapped and Salvinia staggered back, stammering an apology. But Viola would have nothing of it. Fear had taken control of her, and she had to run. Magic! Oh, she could have gone her whole life without it and been perfectly blissful.

To her credit, Viola did not sob until she was well out of view of the Holly and Sickle, safely ensconced in the space between Miss Rawlings-Vijay's shop and the florist, shaking so violently she thought she might faint.

CHAPTER THIRTEEN
Once Again We Dance

Viola shared her harrowing experience with the hedge witch with Poppy, but did not divulge too many details about the viscount. She could not say why—perhaps because she knew her sister's heart still stubbornly belonged to Edith Rookwood—but it felt a bit tasteless to speak of romantic dealings, even if she never expected anything from it.

They were walking together in town, the weather still holding a bit, side by side and arm in arm, but Poppy was still quite dejected.

"'I see'? I've given you a *wealth* of gossip regarding irate old witches and our very dear dowager viscountess's involvement in Netherford Hall, and all you say can is, 'I see'?"

Poppy scowled into her bonnet. "The gentlewitch was no help. Everything fell apart, Vi. I don't know what it is about her that just makes me a little mad, but I—oh, am I so broken that I can't even keep proper company?"

"You cannot speak so! And you cannot give up. Oh, Poppy, what if you are caught up in this grand adventure, too? With the house, and Papa, and the viscount."

Poppy gave her sister a curious look, one eyebrow raised. "Something has gotten to you, sister. You never used the word 'adventure' unless in distress."

"Oh, can't you feel it? When you're happy, I feel as if the whole town is happy."

When Poppy stopped altogether, Viola's heart jumped a bit, thinking something terrible had happened. And in a way it had:

Standing in a half-circle around the hexafoil were the Rookwood-Nourses, heads bowed in silent prayer. They had quite a gathering around them, too. A few weepy townsfolk, including the butcher—who, to Viola's thinking, was hardly the most prestigious acolyte.

"They're already acting as if they've won," growled Poppy. "Even if I never see the gentlewitch again, I still can't bear the thought of those wretched people living at Netherford Hall. I feel ill whenever I think of it. Ill down to my marrow."

"Come, let us go home," said Viola. "We have both returned from our errands with middling results, and there is but one source of truth untapped."

"Mama and Papa will be out for the evening," said Poppy, turning her face away from the scene at the hexafoil. The threat written on her face made Viola's skin crawl. *Loathing* was not a strong enough word for it.

PAPA'S OFFICE WAS on the east side of the house, always the first to warm up with the morning sun, no matter the time of year. Now, in the evening, it was cold and cheerless, and Poppy noted the mountain of paperwork and sketches left since he'd fallen ill a few months before.

Even in his best years, no one would have ever claimed that Mr. Brightwell was a tidy man. As he'd gotten older, the drifts of paper had grown, and his productivity lessened. Perhaps in his more vibrant days, Mama excused his untidiness for a kind of genius, but the benefits never quite materialized. Poppy had spent many an evening assisting him in organisation and direction, only to find her progress scattered about the next day and a new project begun. And unfortunately, Mr Brightwell applied the same level of disorganization and lack of focus to his investments, to catastrophic result. He was a man one step from greatness at any moment in his life, but without the courage or skill to leap upon that promised shore.

Poppy balked at the enormity of her task. There were, perhaps, clues that she had missed, correspondences that she had overlooked. Did Papa have a journal? She didn't think so. A ledger? He didn't seem the sort.

Whatever their reasons for withholding the truth from Poppy, her parents had done so out of fear of Old Gam. They were afraid of witches, and the powers of the arcane; they were afraid of losing what little they had, most especially their children.

The lock on Papa's desk might have deterred any of the other Brightwell children, but not Poppy. She'd had years of sneaking into places she ought not to be.

With one of her hat pins and some matchsticks, she was able to open the lock on Papa's desk to reveal—well, another pile of old papers. Some kerchiefs in a wad, full of something she had no desire to investigate, scraps of expensive yellow silk, and there, at the bottom, two small ledger books.

One book was clean, if a little untidy. There were enough errors in it to make her head spin, and she was horrified that her mother had let her father work such egregious accounting. Heath would be mortified, as well.

The other book was a smaller one, with a velvet cover, worn with time and use, to a dull sienna hue.

And inside—

Payments.

Not in money, but in vials of blood. To Laertes and Ophelia Byrne, going back at least two years. Every two weeks, right as rain, bled and accounted for, with signatures and everything. According to the transactions, he was only halfway through paying back the loan.

VIOLA AND POPPY didn't often share a bed these days, though they had done so for most of their young lives. But that night, without need for consultation, they gathered under the sheets in Viola's room and spoke in hushed voices.

"What are we to do?" Viola asked, not for the first time.

Poppy was finally warming up, her toes returning to a more sensible temperature now that they had nestled together. "Vampires," she said. "It only raises more questions."

"As if we needed more of those," Viola replied.

"I do have a plan."

"I hoped so. Though I do hope it doesn't involve anything that might get us arrested."

Poppy scoffed. "You think so little of your sister."

"On the contrary, you loom large in my mind—enough to draw attention."

"Well, that's just it. We're not going to draw attention. We're going to be pretty and flirtatious, innocent and whimsical, and when the time is right, we shall strike."

Viola sunk into her pillow, looking up into the tented sheet. "You make it sound so exciting."

"Everything is an adventure."

Poppy couldn't help but worry she had missed out on her greatest adventure yet. It still hurt to think about Edith's rejection, cold and soulless as it was. The ache inside of her only grew as time passed, away from Netherford Hall and that gentle smile. Her mind knew they were doomed, but her heart kept going back to that perfect moment just before it all shattered, and the feeling of the gentlewitch's hands on her shoulders, her lips pressed against her neck.

"Poppy. Are there tears in your eyes?"

Poppy cleared her throat. "No, there aren't." Damn her sister, she could practically *smell* tears.

"You're thinking about her again, aren't you?"

"I wish I could tell my brain to stop torturing me."

"Surely, she must have had her reasons," said Viola.

It was difficult to explain to Viola, who always saw the good in people. She was precious in that way: trusting and open. Poppy approached people in her life with scepticism—trust had to be earned. Perhaps it was for that reason she had so few enduring friends outside her immediate family.

Poppy took a deep breath. "It's the *damned* Rookwood-Nourses."

"Oh, Poppy," scolded her sister, always taken aback by coarse language.

"It's true! I would be a weakness. A lesser creature in their eyes, tied to the gentlewitch."

"Sounds almost gallant to me," said Viola with a romantic sigh. "Did she propose to you?"

"Quite the opposite. She said she could not offer me marriage, but neither could she have me stoop to being her mistress."

Viola pulled at her long braid, the ends curling into a perfect corkscrew. "Well, once your heart is mended, there is always Captain Evans. He is such a darling man."

"You beast," said Poppy, shoving Viola. "You will never know my pain! I feel as if I'm not just losing Liege Rookwood, I'm losing Netherford Hall."

Viola squeezed her sister's hands together and kissed them. "Then we shall go forth, twisted and broken, to discover the truth of all of this, shan't we? My heart tells me that there are answers here. We just have to look harder."

"There's no one else I'd want along as my guide, my dearest Viola. Your hope will steer us both."

* * *

EDITH HAD NEVER been a woman of impulse, but as she pressed through the wardrobe door of Poppy's room in Harrow House, her own judgement was addled. There was, of course, a twin key to the octopus on her chatelaine: a nautilus, in silver and iron, still cold against her hand.

The room was dark, but Edith could see Poppy's imprint on every corner: snippets of news clippings pinned to the walls, sketches half-finished on the desk, fabric swatches strewn in piles by her dresser, and stacks of books bristling with ribbons. There was little rhyme or reason to the room, and yet it was all Poppy.

She slept deeply, hair in a careless plait, mouth open. No bronzed goddess, here, but beautiful still. The curves of her form under the sheet and quilt made Edith sigh a moment, considering the choices before her.

The gentlewitch had come here intent on apologising, proclaiming her love to Poppy again, and promising a life together—in whatever form she wished. She had even considered running away, abandoning Netherford Hall and these constant pressures. Two snifters of brandy in, it had felt like the right decision.

Now, watching Poppy breathe in the dark, unaware of her presence, it felt like a violation.

"Cousin Edith?"

The whisper was so quiet, Edith might have missed it, but it was also accompanied by a tug at the edge of her chemise. Henry had found her.

"Shh, now," Edith said.

"I've had a bad dream," Henry whispered.

"I know."

Quickly, she doused the room in even more darkness—she had cast a simple charm to help her see, but did not want to risk Henry discovering what lay beyond. What a fool she had been! Foolish and careless. Leaving the wardrobe open and forgetting to cast a simple charm of warding.

Her little cousin was bleary-eyed, half asleep still, and she managed to corral him into the wardrobe, shut the door quietly behind them, and usher him back into her own chambers. All without awaking Poppy.

Anyone else might have felt ashamed, but Edith instead felt a kind of clarity, of decision. This business of the heart had made her weak—weak enough that a little boy of no consequence, half in dreams, had managed to take her unawares.

Henry was small for his age, yet he still weighed more than Edith recalled. He hugged her tightly around the neck.

"Let's put you back in bed," she said, starting for the door.

"Can I rest in here with you?" Henry asked, and she had never heard such a pleading in his voice before.

"Is it the same dream as before?" Edith asked.

Henry trembled, voice muffled. "There was a red dragon fighting the monster with the six eyes, but it got swallowed up. And then the monster became a *dragon* with six eyes."

"Very well, you may sleep in here tonight," said Edith, unsettled at the boy's constant dark dreams. She was certain it was trauma from the fire, but there was naught to do but push through. Eventually, he would grow out of it. "But just for tonight."

Once he was situated in a pallet by the fire, Edith took one more longing look at the wardrobe and felt around for the nautilus key in her pocket, but it was gone. She must have left it in Poppy's room.

"Edith?"

"Yes, Henry."

"What were you doing in the wardrobe?"

Edith sighed, gazing into the dwindling flames. "Chasing a dream, my boy. Chasing a dream."

THE NEXT STEP in Viola and Poppy's journey of discovery began at the banquet for the new Viscount St. Albans. Viola, of course, had been part of the planning of the event, and knew ahead of time exactly who would be where. She had been staying with the St. Albanses for almost a week.

Burkley House was just slightly older than the Greenstreets' manse, but it held none of the overwrought angles and obscenely ostentatious balustrades. The Dowager Viscountess St. Albans had spent the last fifteen years renovating the original sixteenth-century home. Now, it was a very modern affair, featuring fifteen bedrooms, and over one hundred acres of pristine gardens and grounds.

As the carriage rattled to a halt, Poppy looked across at her brother and mother, the former adjusting the latter's glove. Mama's hands were too busy shaking to do it herself.

"You look beautiful, Mama," said Poppy, and it was no lie. Even if the dress was a little old-fashioned, the bodice done in a braided crisscross of silver beaded floss, it was still stunning by dint of its craft.

"I may have forgotten how to behave in such company," said Mama with a long breath.

"Nonsense," said Heath. "You are the picture of elegance."

"We all are, thanks to you and Papa," said Poppy, for their parents had scraped together for new gowns for both she and her sister.

"My goodness," said Mama, taking in the house grounds. "I had no idea Burkley House could shine so."

The dowager viscountess had not only chosen the date so the garden would be at its peak, but also so the lighting and decorations would dazzle. She did not employ illusionists of any sort, but relied solely on the beauty of growing things. The garden spilled straight into the house, hydrangeas in purple and pink bursting out of windows, peonies in bowls, rose petals littering the floors, and all manner of greenery standing tall.

"You never described the house like this, Poppy," said Heath, leaning over to his sister, with whom he'd linked arms. "The way you go on about the old wreck at Netherford Hall, you'd never think you'd seen Burkley at all."

"Netherford Hall is an entirely different place," Poppy said, adjusting the front of her dress before taking the first few steps. "And it's just waking up."

"You speak of it like it's a living thing," said Heath, wrinkling his nose in amusement or distaste.

"Miss Brightwell is right, you know. There is more spirit in my house than in some living, breathing people," came a familiar voice.

It was Liege Edith Rookwood.

Of course, it was. And Poppy was stuck, absolutely restrained by the laws of propriety. They had not spoken since their falling out, and though Poppy knew it was a possibility the gentlewitch would attend, she was still unprepared.

Worse even, Liege Rookwood looked so perfectly handsome, so painfully stunning, that Poppy could not find words adequate.

Then she realised the gentlewitch was wearing the very cuffs Poppy had embroidered for her. The ones she'd given to Liege Rookwood that day in their bower, just before their relationship shattered.

Poppy fell into a curtsey behind her mother and brother.

"I'm glad to hear it, my liege," said Mama, giving the gentlewitch a very tight smile. "I'm sure my daughter's service was helpful in that matter."

"Indeed, she is quite the wonder. I have no doubt she will amount to great things," said Liege Rookwood.

"I don't need to *amount* to anything to be of value, my liege. But I am flattered by your assessment," said Poppy curtly, then skittered up the stairs as fast as her silk shoes could take her, leaving the gentlewitch and her family very much in her wake.

For all her huffing and puffing, however, Poppy had to wait for her escort before being announced, which caused her a great deal of consternation. Alone at the top of the stair, she imagined the long stretch of her years before her, the lone child left to take care of her parents, the woman without attachments and without any particular accomplishments. She could see herself wheeling in her infirm mother, her own hair going grey, to a similar soiree with another fresh crop of available nobles vying for attention.

No matter how the society pressed down on her, Poppy Brightwell could not comply. She could not change. If the world was a little kinder to women like her, women who never stopped moving, who treasured muddy boots and windblown hair, who lost time to enumerating leaves and chasing errant gales, then perhaps she could have imagined another life. But as it was, in that moment, she saw naught but disappointment and drear.

"Mrs. Margella Brightwell, Master Heath Brightwell, and Miss Persephone Brightwell of Harrow House," announced one of the many servants, opening the grand doors to admit them.

Though it was no ball, the banquet hall still shone with decorations and the opulence one would expect from someone like the dowager viscountess. Six chandeliers, imported from France if Viola was to be believed, scattered light throughout the space and across the sumptuous dining service. Dozens of servants stood around the mirrored room, prepared to pull out chairs, proffer drinks, and serve the night's delicacies.

Half in a daze, Poppy allowed herself to be steered away from her family and placed at the table. The chair itself likely cost more than her entire wardrobe, and still smelled of beeswax and lacquer; it was carved wood, swans and greyhounds in relief, but gilded in gold and upholstered in deep green velvet. The newness of it was shocking to Poppy, having spent so long at Harrow House and Netherford Hall where every corner was antique, worn, weathered, and loved.

She was seated, unexpectedly, next to Auden Garcliffe. She had requested to Viola that she be positioned beside Carlotta Greenstreet, who chattered so incessantly Poppy's own silence might be overlooked. A cursory glance revealed Liege Rookwood was six seats down and on the same side; at least *that* was as it should be.

The man seated to her right smelled of old roses and dust, and his dull black hair twisted into a low braid, accentuating the sharp angles of his face. He also dressed half a century out of fashion, even if it was well done.

"Good evening, Miss Brightwell," said Mr. Garcliffe, by way of greeting and introduction. "I'm glad to see you again, and in your proper surrounds. I'm not sure you've had a chance to meet Mr. Laertes Byrne. Mr. Byrne, this is Miss Poppy Brightwell of Harrow House."

AUDEN STAMMERED TO a halt. He had dreaded introducing Poppy, though it was the gentlemanly thing to do; but four words in and he had already failed miserably. He had been trying to say that it was good to see her in proper society, and no longer playing lady's maid to the gentlewitch.

Within moments of the clumsy introductions, however, Poppy was entirely focused on Laertes.

Auden could not help but feel he should do something to draw young Miss Brightwell away from the deepening conversation. Antonella Greenstreet was casting curious glances down the table, to say nothing of Edith. He could only catch glimpses of his niece, as she was on the same side and seven seats down, but she was positively glowering.

And who could blame her? Poppy's dress was deep, dusky lilac silk with contrasting stripes, with long sleeves and ruched about the bodice, cuffs, and hem. Auden was minded of bluebells in the shade, the sounds of the River Rothley rushing over rocks, and mossy, hidden places. He was uncertain how a dress on a person could convey so much, yet now that he knew Poppy Brightwell a little more, he supposed it made sense.

Edith saw, and her eyes shone every time Poppy laughed or Laertes leaned over to her. By all accounts, Edith had given up entirely on Persephone Brightwell. Not because the gentlewitch did not love her, but because she believed—stubbornly and perhaps even erroneously—that it was a bad match between them, seeing as the young Brightwell woman did not want marriage of any kind and Edith's own standing in Coven society was bruised enough as it was.

The Rookwood-Nourses had declined this evening's invitation, if the rumours were true. Both Auden and Edith had endured a handful of uncomfortable dinner parties in the intervening weeks, speaking to their relatives only through barristers and Coven missives. At least tonight they were free of that stress.

"Tell me, Mr. Garcliffe, if it is not too indelicate," said Laertes, loud enough that Auden could hear. "How goes the search for the gentlewitch's wife?"

Poppy went still and carefully put down her salad fork to gaze intensely at the tongue in aspic and fennel cream sauce before her.

"Ah, well, no decisions have been made as of yet," said Auden, which was true. But not for want of trying. "We hope to make a decision by the late summer."

"It must be a great strain on you all, seeing that the Rookwood-Nourses have not relinquished their claim on Netherford Hall; let us know if we can do anything, financially or otherwise. Unless you are resorting to the old ways to settle the matter."

Or otherwise, indeed.

"I am confident we will have no need of that," said Auden, trying to discern the look on Poppy's face, but seeing only the back of her elaborate hair. There were little sprigs of Lilly of the Valley tucked between her tight curls. He could smell them.

POPPY DERIVED NO pleasure speaking with Laertes Byrne. He gazed at her as if she were a crooked painting he could not straighten, and it made her squirm.

"Tell me, Mr. Byrne," Poppy said, refusing more wine from one of the servants. She had to be careful tonight. "What do you mean by 'the old ways,' in regards to Netherford Hall and the gentlewitch?"

Mr. Byrne gave a smug grin. "Oh, I forget, little darling, how unfamiliar you are with the ways of the arcane folk."

"Though I've lived here most of my life, we've never had a gentlewitch in that time," she simpered. "And my mother and father never spoke of vampires." Yes, she could play the ingénue if needed.

"Then let me enlighten you. It is said that the fae themselves bestowed powers upon the witch bloodlines, back before the world changed, when we were one people," said Mr. Byrne, breathing in the substance in his glass. He had not been served food in any form other than liquid.

"All three preternatural houses—witches, vampires, and werewolves—are said to be descended from the fae. And it is from the fae that we inherit our traditions."

Poppy suppressed a shudder and forced an interested expression on her face, batting her eyelashes coyly.

"Such sentiment is terribly out of fashion," chimed in Mr. Garcliffe.

Mr. Byrne shrugged. "You short-lived creatures wouldn't know fashion if it was wrapped up in paper and tied with ribbons," he scoffed. "But I digress! Regardless of Mr. Garcliffe's opinions, the 'old ways' are clear on disputes such as these: the contending witches must come to face one another in the Rite of Place. It is a kind of second harrowing."

"Harrowing?" Poppy did not have to feign her ignorance this time.

"That's the test of a witch," said Auden. "It is completed before a witch's twentieth birthday, to discern which branch of witchcraft suits them best."

"It's more complicated than that," said Laertes. He sloshed around whatever substance he was drinking and made a sour expression. "In order to best nurture their strengths, which are typically quite clear during the harrowing, they are attuned to their homes. I doubt even Mr. Garcliffe understands that particular ceremony, as it is shrouded in most sacred secrecy. But a witch, gentle or otherwise, is only as powerful as the land she cares for."

"That's why you came to Netherford," said Poppy, addressing Auden. "And why the Rookwood-Nourses want it so badly."

Mr. Garcliffe gave her a weary nod. "Indeed. But, unlike the larger dynasties, we have limited capacity."

"Such a tragedy," said Mr. Byrne. "The Rookwood-Nourses are looking for a place to put down their own roots. Netherford has old bones, and Netherford Hall most of all.

"At any rate, a Rite of Place is likewise an attunement. It is also a contest, of sorts, for the land itself. An arcane duel."

Poppy felt as if she was missing something. "Why didn't Liege Rookwood bring about the challenge right away?"

"Because," said Auden, "as I said, it is considered somewhat old fashioned. A bit, ah—well, *backwater*. Perhaps not best for someone still trying to improve upon her reputation."

"That, and everyone knows that our liege is not the most, shall we say, dazzling enchanter," said Laertes, voice dropping even lower.

Poppy flushed, shocked at Mr. Byrne's tactlessness. She may no longer be beholden to the gentlewitch, but she had absolute confidence in her abilities. The vampire's words offended her to her marrow.

"Well, I have every bit of faith in her," said Poppy. "And I cannot imagine a situation where she wouldn't find some path to success. Netherford Hall is in her very bones. She belongs there as much as the village belongs between the rivers."

"That is very kind of you to say, Miss Brightwell. Thank you."

Poppy really did have a fondness for Mr. Garcliffe, and it was a shame that things ended so abruptly with the gentlewitch; she had a sense that she and the majordomo could have been friends.

Their conversation meandered to an end as the next course arrived, and Poppy had to pretend she could not feel the weight of Liege Rookwood's gaze upon her, for fear of looking as forlorn and spurned as she still felt.

* * *

EDITH WAS SITUATED across from Miss Antonella Greenstreet, a vision in pale blue muslin, and beside the Viscount St. Albans, who was, in turn, to the right of his aunt. The main course was a remarkable presentation of oysters and pork, fanned out like a great eye and surrounded by roasted apples and sage.

She kept trying to avoid looking at Poppy, but failing miserably. She was in such deep conversation with Laertes Byrne, and it kindled a frustratingly deep jealousy. Edith knew that logically it was best to move on, but her heart could scarcely notice anyone else; Poppy looked beautiful, her lavender silk gown giving her skin a luminescent quality in the candlelight.

No, she would allow her thoughts to meander toward the Brightwells. She would banish them from her mind entirely.

"Tell me, Liege Rookwood," said the viscount, his voice low and polite. "What is your assessment of the Brightwell family?"

Edith straightened, momentarily concerned that she was leaking her own thoughts. But that was not a logical conclusion in the least. She had been infected by Poppy's ebullience and whimsy, perhaps. Or she'd been drinking too much. Or both.

"Why, they are good people and good tenants. Anything beyond that is veering toward the edge of gossip, which is not my forte—nor my interest," said Edith.

The viscount gave her a rather pained look. She knew the man only by reputation, and like most men of his age, he was known as something of a rake.

"I apologise, Liege Rookwood," said the viscount. "My question was indelicate. You must forgive my misstep. My aunt is godmother to Mr. Brightwell—she practically raised him as a child—but I have not had the occasion to learn much of the family. I am only curious."

"Yes, I knew there was some family connection, but I did not know that detail." This was a surprise. Especially since there was that matter of Virginia Cawley, who Edith now knew was the dowager countess's sister. These things must be connected, and yet Edith found herself unable to make sense of it.

Edith had written, twice, to Virginia, but there had been no reply from London. No matter; it would not help her in her current struggles.

"I am yet to have the pleasure of meeting Mr. Brightwell, but I was curious what about the family so endeared my aunt," said the viscount. "She is not a woman easily swayed by charity, I assure you."

"The Brightwells are a surprisingly compelling bunch," said Edith. "They are all cut from a similar cloth and yet fashioned into unique designs."

"There is a rather enchanting quality about them, I cannot deny," said the viscount, eyes drawn down the table to where Viola sat, speaking with all seriousness to the man next to her. She was a vision in buttery taffeta trimmed in lace. Viola was lovely in the way that cut flowers were lovely, all precision and crispness. But it was Poppy that Edith could never quite shake from her mind, all her substance and rough edges and loose ends, her mounds of hair and sweet, smooth skin.

Rivers and the speckled firmament, she could not banish the *taste* of Poppy from her mind now that she was near. The memory alone was intoxicating, making Edith's heart race with the mere thought of another similar conjugation of their bodies. She wanted more of Poppy—of her lips, her laughter, her deviousness. Even in their brief kiss, Poppy had made the most delicious sighing sound and Edith wondered what other sounds she might elicit with even more attention.

She had forgotten to reply.

"You could have any spouse you wanted, St. Albans; far be it from me to judge," said the gentlewitch, clearing her throat against the rising blood in her body. "A young viscount, with a sizable inheritance. London, I recall, is fit to bursting with many women of more significant station and weightier dowries than the Brightwells."

Viscount St. Albans nodded, moving back in his chair as the next course arrived: wild duck poached in pears with a clear sauce studded with anise. Once his dish was properly arrayed, and the sound of voices rose around them again, he continued speaking.

"Well, that is precisely my point, my liege," he said to Edith. "We are in the dawning of a new era, and the way our forebears went about their business feels antiquated to me. Miss Brightwell encapsulates just about everything I could imagine wanting in a woman: wit, winsomeness, and the knowledge of how to run a home. If I am to relocate here in the summer, I must collaborate with someone with local knowledge."

It shouldn't have bothered Edith, yet she found herself bristling. "I assure you, my lord, this is hardly the Hebrides! It is Kent."

He laughed and nodded his acknowledgement. "Of course, it is not so simple as *choosing*. I am beholden to my great aunt's approval." The dowager viscountess frowned into her plate at the other end of the table. "So *any* choice presents some challenge."

"Perhaps you will find the challenge makes the prize all the more valuable," Edith said.

"Why, you are a romantic!" he said. "I had heard that you were quite *against* the idea of involvement with, ah…" He cleared his throat when he registered Edith's scathing look. "My apologies, I dig too deep."

"My duties, I assure you, are quite complicated, St. Albans. And deeply personal. There is little room in my life for the frivolity of love."

The viscount went silent, paying very close attention to the duck. Edith, for her part, tried to remove the currants from view. Something about their little swollen bodies always made her feel a bit ill.

"I am sorry that is the case," said the viscount at last. "My father endured a loveless marriage, and my mother died when I was young; I would not wish such a fate on anyone. Even after she passed, his resentment for her remained. Which must seem odd to you."

"No doubt you have had time to decide what kind of specimen your heart desires since your return from France," said Edith. "London is a city of delights."

The viscount tried to suppress a grin behind his napkin, gently dabbing at the corners of his mouth. "I assure you, I have been a gentleman, though I suppose my reputation suggests otherwise. That is not helped by some of the company I hold: my cousin Roland is another matter altogether. He remains in Paris, though."

"You intend to stay at Burkley House, then?"

"I do, indeed, when I am not in London."

"Well, if you are set on staying here, I suppose you must at least attempt to find into a kind of happiness," said Edith.

"Yes, and it appears I have found myself rather hopelessly attached to the view."

Edith knew what he meant, more than anyone.

WHEN THE DANCING began, Edith was convinced that Poppy would have nothing to do with her. And at first, that seemed true. The girl lingered at the edge of the dance floor through the first few dances, uncomfortably close to

Laertes Byrne, and that did not sit well with the gentlewitch one bit. She tried not to openly seethe.

"Why, Liege Rookwood, I'm sorry I didn't see you there," said a voice behind her.

It was Viola Brightwell, tilting her head at Edith, sizing her up, fluttering a rather ostentatious ivory and gold fan. The musicians were just commencing a new dance, and the awkwardness of the situation pressed around her.

"If you've the inclination, Miss Brightwell, I would love to have you join me in a dance," said Edith, as civility dictated. "Unless you have other arrangements."

"I would be most honoured, my liege," said Viola, bowing low and letting her fan fall to her wrist. The eldest Brightwell girl proffered her hand, and Edith joined the promenade leading up to the dance itself.

Though the song was unfamiliar to Edith, the steps were close enough to many of the more formal affairs she'd endured coming up in London. This was one of the newer waltzes and required very little separation between partners.

"This has been a lovely evening, my liege," said Viola as they passed a glass fountain covered with camellias. "Have you enjoyed yourself?"

"I do believe I may have eaten one too many kinds of meat in one sitting," said Edith. Her stomach was like a brick of hardened dough beneath her waistcoat. "But it was, every bite, delicious. And you?"

"Oh, my, yes. I'm certain you are used to such fare as this, but I admit to being dazzled by every dish," replied Viola. Her voice was higher than Poppy's, and without the rougher edge to it. But it was still pleasing, and similar enough that Edith felt her heart ache. "We typically have to resort to balls for such sumptuous meals, and those are few and far between."

"I admit, I have a rather simpler taste at home," said Edith, holding Viola out at arm's length for a moment, as the dance required, and then bringing her back into a kind of half-embrace.

Poppy's hair was visible from where Edith stood, at the end of the line, now dancing with the viscount. She was smiling.

She must smell divine.

"Do you miss her, my liege?" Viola looked straight up into Edith's face, her dark eyes full of questions. "Poppy, I mean."

Edith blinked. "You are as direct as they come, Miss Brightwell."

Viola smiled demurely. "It's a family trait. But you are not answering my question."

"I am not," Edith said, pulling Viola in a little more closely. She was delicately built, but not fragile.

"And you *will* not, my liege?"

"I don't have to. I'm the gentlewitch—for now, at least."

"Indeed. And interest from a suitor of such stature is a matter of some concern, particularly to overprotective older sisters."

Edith let herself smile a bit. "Yes. I am growing accustomed to such scrutiny. My cosmopolitan upbringing afforded me a measure of anonymity."

Viola leaned in a little closer. "My liege, you know I am not a knowledgeable person in matters of magic, and least of all witches. And I may speak out of turn."

"If you are anything like Persephone, I somehow doubt that will stop you."

"Indeed not. But she has been out of sorts since you dismissed her. I know, she is an unusual sort of person— some might go as far to call her odd."

Edith knew that painfully well. "I do not think her odd. She is singular."

"Poppy loves the house with all her soul, and the more she's away from it, she more lost she seems."

"She looks well enough tonight," said the gentlewitch.

Viola scoffed. "You did not see the effort this required. And it is only because..." She frowned, shaking her head. "I do not mean to meddle, I truly do not. It is only that I have one sister, and I nearly lost her once. I do not wish to lose her again."

Viola's choice of words took Edith aback. She'd never been good at making conversation, but this was far from required niceties. This had layers to it, and she had to pick apart the words to come up with the right response.

"I do not know what the future of Netherford Hall entails," said Edith at last. "But the last thing I would ever want to do is prevent your sister from finding happiness."

"That is up for debate," muttered Viola.

"Miss Brightwell, I do not have to explain myself to anyone."

"No, you do not. Except to yourself, I suppose." The strings swelled again and Viola twirled into Edith's arms. "Be careful with her heart, my liege. Poppy is all brightness and optimism, until she is not. I'm certain that in your life you've seen women like her come and go and you do not need to worry about where their stories end up. But we sisters must."

"Oh, I assure you, Miss Brightwell, I have never encountered another soul like your sister's. And I doubt that I ever will again."

BASIL HODE, DRESSED in his Warder finery, found Auden sitting alone, forlornly watching the dancing. He was thinking about a certain modiste and how he would have enjoyed seeing so many of her gowns on display. Or not on display. Of what she looked like without a gown.

The Warders were in attendance not by invitation, but by necessity: they were the gentlewitch's dedicated security. While Molly preferred to watch from outside, Basil came in and out of the ballroom to update Auden as necessary.

Auden was immediately shaken from his reverie by Basil's drawn appearance. The self-loathing he'd been cultivating in the shadows gave way to fear.

"Is everything alright, old chap?" Auden kept his voice low.

Basil's nose was bright red from the cold, and he removed a handkerchief to dab at it a moment before saying, "A... presence broke through the wards a short time ago. Molly spent some time trying to track it, but then it vanished outright."

"Explain," Auden said, for no other words felt appropriate.

"We've been trying to puzzle out the issue. Initially, we thought it was perhaps the Rookwood-Nourses, thinking they had taken tonight as an opportunity to cross the boundaries into the house, but after consideration, Molly determined..." Basil paused, lowering his voice. "It isn't a human intruder."

Auden felt a prickle of unease crawling down his back, the music distorting in his ears as panic began setting in. Memories of his and Henry's persistent dreams gnawed at him. Should he have told Edith?

"It hasn't left enough of an arcane trace for us to act upon. It's a complex web of wards that we build—including some that we've maintained for centuries. This presence didn't just amble through, it *shattered* our wards, tore them to shreds."

Auden lowered his voice. "Vampires?"

"No, we'd be prepared for that." Basil nodded toward where Ophelia and Antonella Greenstreet were twirling together, dresses in contrasting, draped muslin.

"Werewolves?"

"Most of them are in France, these days. And the few we know would be obvious."

Auden's head pounded, now, as if the next day's hangover had set in early. He was still a little drunk.

"Basil, what do we do?" he asked at last.

Basil took a deep breath. "I don't suppose you can get some reinforcements from London? We've been trying to fix the portal door at the Holly and Sickle, but…"

"Reinforcements? You think it's that bad?"

The Warder gave a curt nod. "I've sent Molly on ahead."

Auden weighed his options; no, Edith was not enjoying herself, but he also did not want to raise alarm in front of the elite here at Burkley House. Decorum at any costs. "I'll tell Edith I've been called away, and send for her when we've made a better determination."

Taking one more glance at the dancing figures, Auden was pleased to see his niece taking up a reel with Antonella Greenstreet. He would slip away and be back before she noticed.

VIOLA COULD NOT find her sister Poppy. Heath was extolling some of his more recent theories on witches in government to a very exhausted looking Mama; Lord St. Albans kept giving Viola sweet, knowing glances, which was not helping at *all*; Captain Evans glared around the room as if hoping his next love might crawl out of the wallpaper.

But the vampires were strangely absent.

"Viola, there you are." The dowager viscountess had snuck up on Viola while she was deep in thought.

"My lady," Viola said, falling into a curtsey. "I hope you have enjoyed this evening as much as I have."

"Oh, indeed, indeed. But you and I need a moment to speak," said Lady St. Albans, looping her arm through

Viola's own. Her skin was papery and soft, almost difficult to distinguish from the mountains of tulle wrapped around her person. "Come. Walk with me."

Leaving the fragrant ballroom, Viola could not deny her father's godmother, though her worry over Poppy's absence grew.

With the dowager beside her, the whole house came alive: servants parted and assembled in their wake, opening the immense doors between rooms, lighting lamps, and making sure all passages were clear of guests and accessible to them.

They walked on in the echoing hall some time until the marble flushed a sweet golden colour in the distance.

"I wanted to thank you for all your work," said the dowager viscountess. "In my younger years I could have managed, but these days I much prefer a book and the quiet of my garden."

"It has been my pleasure," said Viola. Her voice echoed in the hall as she spoke, startling her.

"Well, let me not dither. You know I have enjoyed our time together, but I will not live much longer—and certainly will not be capable of maintaining a home like Burkley House for much longer."

"My lady," Viola found her throat thick with emotion.

"My nephew is enchanted with you," the dowager viscountess said, ever straightforward. "He is not easily impressed; I like to think we have that in common."

"Enchanted? We shared a few dances, and met in town, but..."

Lady St. Albans laughed. "He tells me you were a friend and a stalwart companion during all this planning, that our soiree tonight would have been an embarrassment without your help."

They had enjoyed a few moments together, Viola recalled. She made him laugh, and when he did, the sound thrilled through her whole body. If she was honest with herself, she had worked especially hard to make him smile—he was so *dour*, sometimes. But he never told her much about his life before, he always asked about *her* upbringing. About Harrow House, and Netherford, and her family. He liked to listen to her stories about Poppy and Oliver and Heath making mischief.

She was quite endeared to him.

But this?

Lady St. Albans laughed. "Tell me, my dear: What do *you* think of him?"

Viola tried to calm her nerves; speaking clearly always worked best with the dowager. "He seems a kind man, and a good hope for the future of Burkley House."

The dowager viscountess nodded, her beaded dress making a *shhk-shhk-shhk* sound as they walked. "He does not need money. He does not need land. He needs *grounding*. You did well tonight, my dear. He could not take his eyes off of you."

They had danced, quite a few times. But Viola had never considered—

"I am humbled, my lady," Viola replied.

Lady St. Albans cleared her throat. "Indeed. I would like to give him my blessing—his father never would have approved of a match, but as I am his last living relative and a woman born in similar circumstances to you, I cannot help but feel there is a kind of poetic balance to it. But you are from a lowborn family, whose financial struggles are quite apparent. Were I to approve of this match, there must be no room for even a slight offence."

Viola could not form the words. "Offence?"

Stopping mid-stride, the dowager turned and took Viola's hands in her own, squeezing gently. She had never treated Viola with such intimacy before: so familiar, so kind.

"I helped raise your father," said Lady St. Albans. "And his life has been a sucession of unfortunate circumstances. I have done what I can to keep your family comfortable, but now it is time for you to take that mantle."

"My lady, I'm afraid don't know what to say," said Viola, her breath catching. A match of this standing—to a *viscount*—from the cramped rooms of Harrow House! She had never dared to dream of such a thing.

"These things take time, of course; you do not need to answer now. I certainly wouldn't," said the dowager, patting Viola's hand again. "But I foresee a good future for you, should you be ready to rise to the challenge. But it is a tremendous responsibility, as well. There is no room for a single misstep."

Viola was going to say more, though she could not quite articulate the emotion she felt, when the dowager turned her head toward the end of the hall. They were at the staircase now, above the library.

"That's strange. There's a light on in the library," said Lady St. Albans, and she directed her servants to investigate. "Let us see which guest has trespassed."

Viola felt a well of dread, and a sick certainty: If Poppy liked anything more than food, it was books. But no— surely that was simply Viola's nerves getting away with her. After dancing with the gentlewitch, St. Albans, and speaking with the dowager viscountess, surely she was merely overwhelmed.

Slowly they descended to the library, Viola counting stairs to keep her focus.

As the dowager viscountess and Viola entered the burnished gates of the library, and before she could stand in awe of the veritable forest of books, gold spines glimmering in the lamplight and witch lights, the horror of their trespassers came to glaring life before her:

Laertes Byrne and Poppy. Mingled. Shame-faced. Publicly entwined in such a lewd and unacceptable way that Viola simply burst into tears, shouting, "Poppy! How could you?"

It was over. They were ruined.

CHAPTER FOURTEEN
Dinner with a Vampire

Poppy had no more patience for Laertes Byrne. Initially, she took his loquaciousness as a good omen, but swiftly learned he lacked substance on any other topic than himself. He talked about his wardrobe, his habits, his hobbies, and his travels, with more detail than Poppy could stomach.

Only during their third dance did he ask her a single question, and it immediately set her teeth on edge.

"Ah, now, tell me: Where are your people from, Miss Brightwell?"

"I was born in Northamptonshire and have lived most of my days right here, at Harrow House in Netherford," she replied. Poppy caught the side of the gentlewitch's profile, then quickly turned her attention back to the vampire. She had the feeling Liege Rookwood did not approve of Poppy showing Mr. Byrne favour.

Mr. Byrne gave her a sideways grin. "Yes, but I mean your father's family—you are so exotic. You are like a burnished Amazonian, your hair like soft, dark clouds."

"Certainly, you've spent time in London, Mr. Byrne. I am far from unusual or exotic by the capital's standards. Or even by Netherford's." Poppy could only manage so much more of this.

"I am only curious," he said, squeezing her a little more, that scent of old roses wafting around her head and making her wish she had not indulged so much in the sweet punch.

Poppy kept the same placid, interested expression she had been wearing all evening as she answered. "Regardless of my ancestry, we are all, every one of us, English to our core, I assure you. It's been a long time since the merchant wars with India, and I am proud of my ancestry."

"Of course, of course, no insult meant," said Mr. Byrne. "You must forgive me for the observation. I am a long-lived creature, and human beings so often make such significant distinctions between one another. I am eternally curious."

Mr. Byrne's 'curiosity' was not uncommon, and one that papers to this day often hinted at: Africans, Indians, and beyond were welcome in the peerage of England, and usually recognised great acts of patriotism. At times their blending—like in the St. Albans family—was encouraged and seen as perfectly respectable. But in the lower echelons, there was a growing contingent of politicians and merchant folk who believed they were 'muddying the waters' of English culture, to its detriment. That, perhaps, what constituted as *English* ought to be preserved.

These were often the same sort who felt that witches, and the women representing the covens, held too much power and ought to be curbed.

"I am surprised that Lady St. Albans allowed vampires in at all," said Poppy, hoping that wit could offer a way out of an uncomfortable conversation.

Mr. Byrne laughed. "I deserve that. But we are old family friends. The St. Albans family has been long among our closest allies."

If not now, then never...

"If you have been so long in their favour, you must know my father, Redmond Brightwell." Poppy held her breath, trying to gauge the vampire's perpetually serene expression.

"Yes, I'm familiar with most of the families here in town. We have lived near Netherford for over a hundred years."

"Then you must remember him as a child. I always thought it curious he found such favour with the dowager viscountess. He's always said he was simply in the right place at the right time."

"The joy of serendipity, Miss Brightwell." He gazed into her face—they were of a height—a moment longer than Poppy thought proper. Then he said. "I do remember your father, sometimes, about the house, when he was a child."

"Was he accompanied? Surely he had a family."

"These are questions best posed to your father. I admit, I am not the greatest authority on genealogy. You all do get muddled to me after a while." Mr. Byrne was breathing hard now; strange, for a vampire. Poppy recalled that their bodies did not require much in the way of respiration, and this dance was far from exerting.

"Papa never speaks of it," said Poppy, feigning a truly despondent sigh.

Mr. Byrne's gaze was unfocused for a moment, and then he said, "Well, there's one place we can go—right here, in this very building—that might offer you some answers."

"Truly?" Poppy's heart leapt in spite of herself.

"Yes. But it will require a bit of covertness," he said, whispering in her ear. Was he—was he *sniffing* her?

Much like when she was with the Rookwood-Nourses, Poppy had the distinct sensation that she *ought* to agree, even if her instinct was not to. She knew the path she was *expected* to take, and so she did. Without question, she nodded her head. "That sounds exciting," said Poppy.

The response elicited a smile from Mr. Byrne. He led her around the dance floor, and the waltz turned into a reel—and while the dancers were swirling and finding their new partners, the vampire pressed Poppy up against a panel in a shadowed corner, clicked a button, and they were swung out into the hallway.

This required significantly more clinging to his form than she thought appropriate or amenable, but when they came to a stop, Poppy blinked in the dimness to see they were now in a narrow hallway. In her many years visiting Burkley House, she had never found the door, and part of her was rather frustrated that she had missed it. Hidden doors were her specialty.

Mr. Byrne still kept his voice low. "The library. Come, darling."

Heart thrumming in her chest, Poppy kept pace behind Laertes as he made a serpentine approach to the library. They avoided servants and stragglers from the banquet as they went, taking advantage of the cover of night, and the dark sconces in the hallways.

Then again, Mr. Byrne appeared to attract shadows to himself as he moved.

When at last they reached the library, Mr. Byrne flung wide the doors and let Poppy absorb the truly remarkable space.

The sheer number of books rendered Poppy uncharacteristically silent. Though she was certain great houses all around the country sported such collections, this new construction lovingly cradled what had to be *thousands* of books of every size and colour, nestled in gilded rows of well-cared-for leather. It smelled like fresh wood and old paper, a combination she had hitherto neither imagined nor experienced. There were six rows of volumes, reaching up the arched ceiling, connected by iron-and-wood ladders. On the ground floor, sitting chairs and couches, tables and desks, welcomed them, all upholstered in brocatelle of dark burgundy and silver.

Her first thought was that she wished Edith could see it.

"Take a seat, my darling," said Mr. Byrne, gesturing to the settee near the fire—someone had to have been in the library recently, though the coals were low. "Relax yourself. You must be exhausted."

Yes, she would comply. Poppy wanted to keep him close enough that he would continue to discuss with her, and hopefully she could understand what it was he was doing with her father's blood—and perhaps, from what Mr Byrne hinted at, uncover just why the Lady St. Albans had taken such a shine to Redmond Brightwell in the first place.

But then, before she could even arrange her skirts, Laertes was on her, one leg on either side of her body, pinning her to the chair. He was sweating—no, he was *bleeding*—from his forehead, down his face. His sharp teeth were bared for the first time.

The vampire snarled and pinned Poppy's wrists; the look in his eyes was panicked and feral.

"Tell me what you are," he hissed.

"Unhand me," said Poppy, her voice hushed and ragged. She could not be found like this! If anyone were to see them, they would not understand. Stars, she barely understood!

"Tell me, are you a witch? Some sídhe come to tempt me?" Mr. Byrne was spitting mad, eyes gone white to the pupils.

"Let me go!"

Edith! Her mind rang with the name, but the reality of her predicament settled quickly. How could the gentlewitch forgive her?

"How can you resist me?" Mr. Byrne looked both monstrous and sad, now, like a child with a broken toy.

"Tell me what you did with my father's blood," said Poppy. She hoped to at least claim the element of surprise, as the reality of her situation sunk in. "Tell me, and I will tell you what you want."

That was a lie; there was nothing Poppy could tell him that would make sense.

"That is my sister's business," he said, spittle and blood flecking his lips. "You are an abomination. Now, give in to me!"

"Never!" cried Poppy, spitting in his face. *Abomination,* indeed!

Mr. Byrne collapsed on her with a wretched gurgling noise, and in the same moment, the door to the library clanged open, revealing Viola and the Dowager Viscountess St. Albans. Poppy almost sobbed in relief, except that Laertes collapsed into her, his face going straight into her bosom, and she let out a sound that was evidently misconstrued by the new arrivals.

"My god," said Viola. "Poppy—how could you?"

And then Edith's voice rose above them all: "Come now, everyone, let us be rational."

EDITH FELT HERSELF veiled in a strange calm while the scene unfolded around her. Poppy was still sobbing in one of the library chairs as her mother cooed over her, Ophelia was fretting over her brother's prone body, and the viscount and his great aunt looked both horrified and irritated by the entire situation. Viola stood to the side, wringing her hands, face flushed from tears or fury—or likely both. Her brother Heath was a few paces away. From the angles of their bodies, Edith inferred that they were not speaking to one another at the moment.

Auden and Basil were nowhere to be found—one of the footmen gave her a note as she made her way down to the library: it seemed there was an issue with the wards.

Edith suspected there was more to Poppy's discovery with Laertes Byrne than initially appeared. She had, admittedly, found it easy to believe that Poppy would have recklessly involved herself with the vampire—and not because he was dangerous, but solely because Edith had warned her to stay away. The woman had a remarkable talent for doing precisely the opposite of what she was asked.

But Edith could not ignore that she had heard Poppy shout for her, floors above, just before everything transpired.

At the moment, however, the cacophony was simply too much. Besides, Mrs. Brightwell looked as if she might try and actually murder Laertes Byrne, even if he was already potentially dead. Twice over, if you count him being a vampire.

"Please, silence!" Edith shouted the words, and used a little amplification charm, touching the third link on the chain at her chest.

That worked, a least momentarily, and everyone turned their attention to her. As the most high-ranking member of the group, and the closest gentlewitch by proximity—though certainly not by talent—she had the upper hand.

"But she's nearly murdered my brother!" Ophelia half-moaned, and even in her anguish she was the picture of loveliness.

"I did no such thing," Poppy countered, voice trembling with rage. "I would never. He attacked me!"

"You followed him in here," said Mrs. Brightwell, her delicate hands balled into fists. "You know better than that, Poppy!"

"Now, now, Mrs. Brightwell," said Edith. She mustered all the calm she could, centring herself as she had done in her years of training. "I understand your frustration, but I asked for silence."

Mrs. Brightwell's eyes went wide, but she bowed her head in obeisance.

Now to the matter at hand.

"Miss Brightwell," Edith said, going to Poppy. "Let us speak, as gentlewitch and crofter." Poppy was crouched on the floor in a puddle of skirts, unkempt hair, and tears. But when Edith reached for her, she graciously relented.

To the viscount, Edith said, "St. Albans, please shut and lock the door—and let the servants know to knock the moment they hear from Auden."

St. Albans nodded solemnly. "Of course."

"Let us all take seats and listen to the account of Miss Persephone Brightwell, before we make any judgements," said Edith.

Eventually they were all situated more comfortably, save Ophelia who would not leave her brother upon the floor.

"There, now. Here we are beholden to my demesne, to my power. What is said between us cannot be repeated," said Edith. "As gentlewitch, and as you, all my crofters—yes, even those of you with your own titles and lands—it is my responsibility to ensure we understand what happened, and at my discretion to involve other parties."

Everyone fell silent, and Edith suppressed a rising thrill. She'd never done this sort of thing before. Even Poppy was paying attention to her, luminous eyes deeply sad. "Now, Miss Brightwell. Explain to us how you came to be with Mr. Byrne, alone, in the library this evening."

Poppy's jaw was set, her shoulders back, and she looked absolutely fierce. "Mama, I'm sorry," she said, surprising everyone.

Murmurs began immediately and Edith had to use her charm again to get everyone to settle.

"And not for the reason you think," Poppy continued, brushing tears from her face again. "You see, Viola and I—"

"Poppy, no," interrupted Viola Brightwell, horrified. "Not here."

"I know something is wrong with me, Mama. I feel it

every day. The folk of Netherford feel it; the gentlewitch feels it; even Netherford Hall itself feels it," said Poppy. "And I know you have kept the truth from us."

Mrs. Brightwell put her handkerchief to her lips and hiccupped a sob into it. Her son Heath, his expression perplexed, put a defensive arm around her.

To Edith's utter surprise, however, no one argued with her. Not even Mrs. Brightwell.

"Explain what that means," said Edith, when Poppy lost her nerve a bit.

"I've felt it all my life, but no more so than when you healed Papa a few months ago, my liege," said Poppy, briefly turning her attention to Edith. "You did not detect the signature of a witch's magic, and at first I did not believe you. But then I got to know you, and I decided you were not the sort of person to conceal truths."

"It makes me uncomfortable," said Edith, by way of explanation. "As, I should hope, it does for all."

"If that were only the case," sighed Poppy. "And I learned that witchcraft is not the kind of magic that would have taken Papa's health for my life. That's the work of broken magic, the kind of magic that feeds off fear and pain and desperation."

She *had* been listening.

Poppy continued, looking down at her hands, as if the answers lay there among the bloodstains. "I learned, Mama, that I cannot be harmed by magic, but neither can I be helped. I can be guided by it—I can feel it, sometimes—and I can hide within it. But magic does not impact me. It's how I spent so many years hiding up in Netherford Hall."

"I beg your pardon?" Edith could think of nothing else to say.

"How else did you think I could navigate that labyrinthine house so well?" Poppy asked, boldness returning.

"Poppy!" This was Mrs. Brightwell. "All this time?"

"For years and years, I could wander in without consequence. No ward or lock, no spell could deter me," said Poppy. "And I do not regret it. Even if it led me here."

St. Albans whistled slowly. "A mortal without magical consequence. I could see why you sought answers, Miss Brightwell. And I assume, Liege Rookwood, that you were aware?"

"Until recently, we were still learning," said Edith. Her stomach was in knots where moments ago she had been thrilling with power. Poppy had been visiting Netherford Hall since she was a *child*.

"Well, this is all certainly worth discussion," said Heath. "But I can't imagine what you were thinking, Poppy, putting yourself alone with any man, let alone a *vampire*."

"I can answer that," said Viola hesitantly, worrying her shawl in her hands. "Poppy and I arranged for Mama and Papa to leave the house a few weeks ago, and we found evidence that the Byrnes have been taking vials of Papa's blood, every month, for the last few years. Poppy wanted to get close enough to see if it was true or not, and if it was connected to all this. I helped arrange the seating. We just didn't know where else to look for answers."

Mrs. Brightwell paled to a muslin hue, then flushed red. "Oh, my sweet daughters. It isn't what you think, Poppy— not with the vampires, at least. It has nothing to do with Poppy's *condition*. It was—"

Ophelia squared her shoulders, still stroking her comatose brother's head. "Transactional. All done properly with the correct documentation. Your family had unexpected costs."

The room went eerily silent, and Edith felt ashamed. She knew the Brightwells struggled financially, but that they were *selling* their own blood to vampires…? Poppy and her sister looked positively destroyed.

"Mama," whispered Heath. "The gowns—you said you had more work."

"We had to pay for your schooling somehow, and the girls couldn't come out looking like paupers," snapped Mrs. Brightwell. "Your father gave up his health; I did my part. And now you all come dragging my personal business into the light of day. Well. We tried to shield our children from our private affairs, but, it seems, to little avail."

"It is possible you have shielded them too much, Mrs. Brightwell," said Edith, slowly putting the puzzle together. Laertes had been captivated by Poppy's scent, by her very being, by her blood, so similar to her mother's. He had not understood why—because she was immune to magic and only had half a soul—his power did not work on her. "Though the sale of the blood was not their focus, your daughter tells the truth of what I saw."

Mrs. Brightwell could not have looked more ashamed, and Edith's heart really did hurt for her. "I wish your father was here."

"I don't understand," said Poppy, drawing perilously close to Edith now. "What does this have to do with him? Why did he"—she gestured to Laertes—"attack me?"

"You only have half a soul, Miss Brightwell," said Edith, as kindly as she could, but the shock in the room was still palpable. "The bargain with Old Gam would have taken your whole soul, but—"

"Half a soul?" Poppy whispered, and her mother sobbed.

"It is the reason magic cannot touch you directly, for all magic depends on the absence or presence of a soul, but not one by measures. And Mr. Byrne, well, if he thought you perplexing—he may have inadvertently exerted himself, worried that his own powers of allure were impotent," said Edith. "That would explain the profusion of blood. Vampires do not sweat water, after all. Am I correct, Ophelia?"

Ophelia glanced down at her brother, shaking her head. "You are correct, my liege. And, I admit, it is plausible."

"Mama, tell me you were unaware of this—tell me you did not withhold it from Poppy," said Viola, blinking at her silent mother.

"We were too late," said Mrs. Brightwell, her voice a warbling vibrato. "Virginia Cawley herself tried to intervene, but the thing had already taken half Poppy's soul."

"Virginia Cawley?" The dowager viscountess directed the question at her nephew, even though he hadn't spoken. He shrugged, but judging by the look on his face, something about this situation was not as shocking as it ought to be.

Edith tucked that insight away for later.

"What of Father's afflictions? How did he come by them, if not from a witch's bargain?" Heath asked when Poppy did not appear capable of further discussion.

Mrs. Brightwell shook her head violently when Edith gave her space to speak, so it was up to the gentlewitch to continue: "In the conflict between Old Gam and the High Witch, he was injured.

"And I do not believe 'Old Gam' was its true name," she continued. She was hesitant to share her own research until she was more sure of herself, but they needed to understand the gravity of the situation. "I believe it was a creature known as a Boagane. An ancient, corrupt being known to bargain in souls and provide boons of tremendous power— often with impossible ramifications enduring centuries. They are impenetrable to most magics and used to call Faerie home. It's possible that it was trapped in our world, like some other old magics, when the barrier came down."

Muttering again. A moan from Laertes, who was slowly coming to. Poppy stood still, her hands pressed to her face, staring into the fireplace and saying nothing.

"I have a theory of my own, my liege, if you do not mind

my interference," said St. Albans, stepping forward from his great aunt. "I think I might know why young Poppy Brightwell has had such an affinity for Netherford Hall."

All eyes turned to him, and even Edith found herself, yet again, surprised by the events of the evening. She did not know the young viscount well, but she certainly had not expected that he was schooled in the ways of magic, even if he was connected into—however distantly—the Cawley family.

"That is a piece of the puzzle that I cannot figure out," said Edith. "I welcome your thoughts, St. Albans."

St. Albans nodded deferentially. "You will forgive me, for my assessment of the situation will be somewhat crude. I am no scholar of witchcraft. But I have spent some time with the High Witch and consider myself an avid admirer of your ways."

That was a first. Edith nodded, indicating he ought to continue.

"Before I came here, to Burkley House, I spent months under heaps of paperwork. You must understand, even when renovating a home, there are *hundreds* of years of receipts to go through. Most of is absolutely banal. Except for fifteen years ago, I noticed a very curious transaction regarding both our houses."

The dowager viscountess looked askance at her nephew. "Oh yes. I never like to meddle in the affairs of witches, but I'm afraid I have no choice with her."

Edith thought she heard a rattling outside the door, and hoped for a moment Auden might join them.

"Virginia Cawley is a cleromancer, among other things," said St. Albans. "And she bequeathed a gift to my great uncle and aunt with a very specific request: that they use it to help repair Netherford Hall. At that point, it was near absolute ruin, and at first, I imagined it was because they couldn't stand the sight of such a house falling into disrepair. Until I read the manifest. Mrs. Brightwell—can you tell me how the creature your husband bargained with was captured?"

Mrs. Brightwell glanced fearfully around the room, like a cornered mouse. "Redmond told me that the witch captured that creature in a great oak tree, then exorcised it from there. What was left was a half-petrified tree, with the heartwood and leaves turned to glass."

"And, aunt, tell me—what repairs were done on Netherford Hall fifteen years ago?" St. Albans addressed his great aunt again.

The dowager viscountess pursed her lips. "We replaced the windows—thousands of little, diamond-shaped windows. And the beams."

"You see," said St. Albans. "I think the reason that Poppy is so drawn to Netherford Hall, and likely the reason so many strange things have happened while she is around, is because it contains, well…"

"The other half of my soul," said Poppy. She was looking at Edith now—looking *into* her—as if she were the only other person in the room.

Edith's stomach lurched with a riotous mix of excitement and dread. The glass windows at Netherford Hall were imbued with Poppy's soul and Virginia's magic. The girl had been upset at the Rookwood-Nourses for speaking ill of the house. And of course the wards didn't work! One couldn't protect a person from *themselves*, could they? Auden wouldn't believe it.

But where was he?

"Brimstone," breathed Mrs. Brightwell. "We thought moving to Netherford would distance us from such things."

"On the contrary," said Ophelia, a knowing look in her eyes. "It was calling you to itself."

"Well, it sounds just like Ginny," said the dowager viscountess with a sniff. "Sees things so far-flung that they never make sense until all the pieces fit together. You can imagine what I told her when, as children, she informed me I would inherit a great house—and us with scarcely tuppence to our name!"

"Cleromancy is a powerful but imprecise study," said Edith, walking over to the sideboard and pouring herself a snifter of much-needed brandy. "I will have to speak with the High Witch to confirm some of the details. But I daresay your guess is right, St. Albans."

Now that rattle turned into an urgent pounding at the great doors. St. Albans was the closest, but he had just barely gotten to the lock when it burst open and two of the servants came in, with Mrs. Pratt, the cook at Harrow House, hanging limp between them.

"Mrs. Brightwell…" Mrs. Pratt's voice was a feeble whine.

Mrs. Brightwell rushed to her cook's side, her children close behind her. Half the party was grilling the servants, trying to decipher what had happened.

"It's all happening at the manor," breathed the cook, tears coursing down her cheeks. "The Rookwood-Nourses came by—can't say how they did it, but I saw them up at the grounds. Didn't like that. I was about to go up to the house myself when I saw Mr. Garcliffe and Basil Hode, saying that the wards had been breached. Then Mr. Brightwell, he took his crutches and went with Mr. Garcliffe up to the Hall—that's when *they* came."

Breaking through the gathered folk, Edith took Mrs. Pratt's hand. "Mrs. Pratt, do you know who I am?"

"You're the gentlewitch," said Mrs. Pratt.

"I am. And Netherford Hall is my home. You said that someone is there. Someone, presumably, who hurt you. You are compelled to tell me every truth you know."

"Don't need spells for that, my liege. *Something* came out of the woods. Strange things I've never seen in my life." She drew a shaky breath and Mrs. Brightwell squeezed her a little tighter. "Cursed creatures. Fast, with glass teeth and glowing bodies—like dogs, or cats, but worse. They herded everyone inside and then became one gigantic beast, all eyes and hair and legs like claws."

"The Boagane," whispered Poppy Brightwell.

CHAPTER FIFTEEN
IN LOVE AND WAR

No ONE HAD expected rain that night, and yet as Auden disembarked the coach in the centre of town, lightning streaked the sky and a mist fell over the village that sent his heart racing and his skin crawling.

This was the dream. His dream. Henry's dream. The one he had forgotten a thousand times. He could hear shouts on the wind—or was it just the noise of the gale swirling around him?

"I'll alert the townsfolk," said Auden, fumbling with the lantern he'd taken from the carriage. He turned to the footman: "Send word to the other houses—to the Greenstreets and Durlings, and everyone in between. Tell them to lock and bar their doors, to keep their children safe."

The footman nodded sternly and clicked at the horses, shooting off with a pair of whinnies and the driving of wet hooves on cobblestones. Basil looked grim. They had not seen a trace of Molly.

They had followed the creatures who had breached the wards—or rather, the trail of their wreckage—for miles. At least two families had been murdered and disembowelled, and two whole flocks of sheep ravaged. They left nothing but mist and shards of glass in their wake. And blood.

"Wait for me, Basil. I'll be just a moment," said Auden, half-shouting through the rain. "I'll meet you at the Holly and Sickle."

There was no time for the look of confusion on Basil's face. The one hope Auden clung to was that Edith and the Brightwells were comfortably ensconced at Burkley House, far from this nightmare.

Miss Rawlings-Vijay lived in rooms over her shop, up a narrow staircase alongside the shop front. Auden had thought, dozens of times, that he could just come for a visit, have a conversation, sit and enjoy tea. But every time he had talked himself out it.

Now, he felt a growing foreboding, and he could not leave his thoughts unsaid.

He could hear the gurgling and howling up at Netherford Hall as he rang the bell. There was not much time. As majordomo, his life was promised in defence of this land.

He was rewarded with echoing footsteps a moment later.

"Mr. Garcliffe?"

"Jamini." Her name came out a whispered plea.

Miss Rawlings-Vijay's eyes widened. "Do come out of the rain."

"Only for a moment," said Auden.

There was a small entryway behind the door, just enough space for them to stand, nearly nose to nose.

"Whatever is the matter?" Miss Rawlings-Vijay was aghast, the candlelight wavering across her dear features.

"Terrible things," said Auden, lowering his head. "And I fear I have put myself in the middle of them. And I have been blind."

Auden expected to see shock on Miss Rawlings-Vijay's face, but she looked up at him with loving understanding, and with relief—albeit a relief that came with tears in the corner of her eyes.

"Not blind," said Miss Rawlings-Vijay. "Merely preoccupied. We both were."

"Please, call me Auden. It would grant me the courage I need for this."

"Auden," said Miss Rawlings-Vijay, without hesitation.

And that was enough. In the flicker of the continual lightning strikes and mist, Auden took Miss Rawlings-Vijay in his arms and kissed her ardently, thrilled at the firm and confident response. He breathed in the smell of Jamini Rawlings-Vijay, the beeswax and brightness, and tried to remember every detail: her lips, the freckle at the edge of her mouth, the way her smooth cheek felt against his hand.

Passion could not endure, however. The whole ground rumbled.

Breathing against his neck, Miss Rawlings-Vijay asked: "Auden, what is happening in Netherford?"

"Lock your doors," said Auden, holding out the woman he loved at arm's length, trying to memorise the slope of her eyebrows, the set of her nose, the way her eyes searched his own. "If I do not return, know that I would have remained here all night in your arms had my conscience permitted it."

"I don't understand—can I help?"

"You can help by staying safe, Jamini. Stay safe for me."

And with that, Auden scooped up his lantern and burst out into the cold and chaos of the imperilled village.

"This is what we know, and it isn't a great deal."

Basil stood at the great hearth of the Holly and Sickle before a crowd of twenty or thirty townsfolk—a motley bunch, including old Salvinia the hedge witch. Molly was still nowhere to be seen.

"*Something* alerted Molly and me to its presence early this evening," continued the Warder. "It was unlike anything we had ever sensed. Initially we believed it to be a single creature, but as it meandered its way south, it fragmented into many forms. We chased them down in the early night as far as we could until we had to split up. I believe Molly is within Netherford Hall, though I cannot sense her through the pall of warped magic, along with the Rookwood-Nourses, who somehow became entangled— my guess is that they felt they were near enough to sense the wards breaking. The creatures have infiltrated the hall, now joined together again—and there are powerful witches inside who have not been able to keep them at bay."

"Where's the gentlewitch?" Someone asked from the back of the room.

"Safe," said Auden, climbing onto a chair beside Basil. "The Brightwells are with her, as are the Viscount St. Albans and family."

There was a confused muttering, and the crowd began calling for Edith to be retrieved. "It is a good thing," said Basil. "She will come when we call, but for now, before we know of the danger, we should gather what information we can.

"And we are prepared for such threats," he continued. "We have iron charms, sachets of rosemary, rue, and angelica. As Warders, we keep these things in constant supply." He gestured to where one of the barmaids was laying supplies out on a table. "But do not mistake me: you will need more worldly weapons, as well. Go to your homes and find whatever you can."

"Meanwhile," Auden said. "We have sent out a message via the portal, which has been more or less working—" Much less than more. He had no faith that it would make any difference whatsoever, considering that the old threshold had defied him more than once. "Hopefully there will be reinforcements from London soon."

The crowd broke into a dubious muttering, but to Auden's surprise, they all began lining up for sachets, and discussing tactics for surrounding the house. There were hawthorns all about the property, and some sturdy ashes as well—these should, by all accounts, provide them some protection.

"I hope there is room for one more," came a familiar voice. "I am not an expert in weapons, but I can stay here and monitor the portal."

Jamini Rawlings-Vijay had dressed in a long, wildly ostentatious kaftan over her nightgown: canary yellow, embroidered with interlacing purple thistles and green berries. She looked every inch an empress.

"Jamini," Auden half-whispered.

"Netherford is my home." She put her hand on Auden's elbow and gave him a radiant smile. "I know I am no warrior, but someone needs to stay here in case the gentlewitch arrives; I suspect she will know the danger soon." She dropped her voice and gave Auden a most wicked grin. "And I simply couldn't sleep after your all too brief visit."

Auden gave a high, half-mad giggle and then squeezed Miss Rawlings-Vijay's arm. "Well, you look stunning."

Miss Rawlings-Vijay gave a half-turn in her spectacular ensemble. "I made this for myself, but never had the right occasion. Well, dire situation as this is, I decided I would seize upon this moment. Though I think I look like a Mughal lordling half woken from a dream."

"You look enchanting," said Auden, the words falling out of him in spite of himself. "Perfection."

"Mr. Garcliffe, it's time," came Basil's voice from the front door. They were assembling. As majordomo, Auden had given his oath, swearing his life to protect the hallowed earth, and he could not go against it.

"Come back to me," said Miss Rawlings-Vijay.

In spite of himself, Auden had to take one more look as he walked away, pulling his own overcoat on to face the gathering dark.

IN THE TUMULT of leaving Burkley House, Edith asked Poppy if they could ride together to Netherford Hall. She would risk the scandal, to be near her, for the alternative was not worth considering. Edith needed to beg Poppy's forgiveness before it was too late, and to protect her as much as possible.

It was the greatest relief of the entire evening when Poppy agreed.

"I used to dream of adventures coming to our sleepy village," Poppy said as the carriage churned through the gravel driveway in the dark, lanterns swaying and guttering in the rain. "But not like this."

Edith's whole body ached with longing, with unexpressed desire, and the strain of her magic. She wondered if the growing discomfort had been caused by the wards breaking, by the peril now at their doorsteps. Or if it was a side-effect of realising how desperately, completely in love she was with Poppy Brightwell.

"You are a living adventure, Persephone Brightwell," said Edith at last, drawing her attention back to her favourite view: the woman across from her. Every detail was dearer, now, and Edith's breathlessness had very little to do with the excitement of the evening. Poppy smelled of sweat and wildflower honey, a dizzying concoction in the small space.

"I am apparently also a living Tudor manor," said Poppy, massaging the bridge of her nose. Edith could tell she was close to tears again. "That means I'm considerably older than you."

"You really snuck into Netherford Hall all those years?" Edith asked.

Poppy nodded, averting her eyes. "It was simply a part of me. A compulsion I could not ignore. Now, I know why."

"Stunning," said Edith. She did not just mean the revelation. As Edith had connected more with the land about Netherford Hall, so she had fallen more desperately in love with Poppy.

"I should have told you earlier—right away. If I knew that I could bring you to any kind of danger, I never would have—" Poppy began, fretful now.

"Do not take such blame on yourself. It is I who should beg your forgiveness, a hundred thousand times."

Poppy quirked a devastating eyebrow, straightening in her seat. "Yes, you should. You were truly wretched to me, you know, my liege."

"I was, and you did not deserve it," said Edith. "I have only known a world of clearly drawn lines, of rules and order. That was burned to the ground, buried under the rubble of Hatchney House. And then, when I met you, all I had planned fell again into chaos. I am not a powerful witch, Persephone. I worry I cannot protect you as I should, and that terrifies me."

"You are enough as you are, my liege."

"Ah, please, my darling, every time you call me that it wounds me. Can I not be your Edith?"

"It is who you are, *my liege*," countered Poppy. "You told me as much upon our last discussion, in no uncertain terms."

"No, it is who I must be; a face to wear to the world. Who I *am* is Edith. Just a middling witch in a wide world."

Poppy tilted her head, a ghost of a smile upon her lips. "You are far from middling."

Edith carefully made her way across the carriage to sit beside Poppy. She could bear the distance no longer. Their kisses had haunted her daily, how ardently Poppy had returned her own passion in the crocus field. It frightened her and enticed her.

She wanted more of it.

"Persephone," said the gentlewitch, sighing when Poppy leaned into her slightly. "Fear has consumed me—and pride. Vanity, too. I should have been governed by love, by passion, and by trust. I must beg your forgiveness again. I know it may take time, but allow me to make recompense in whatever way you desire."

Outside the carriage, the storm gathered; lightning flashed, mists rose from the triune rivers surrounding Netherford—but when Edith looked at Poppy's face, she saw naught but sunshine and felt the soft flutter of crocus petals upon her heart.

"I am not afraid, Edith," said Poppy, always the courageous one, taking Edith's hands in her own, sliding her fingers across her palm in lazy circles. "I will be brave for both of us."

Edith leaned her head forward—gently, for the carriage shook now and again—and touched her forehead to Poppy's. It felt more intimate than any kiss, both a welcome and a benediction. She drew Poppy's strong fingers up and pressed them to her mouth, taking in the scent of her, feeling the heat radiating off her soft body.

"I was a fool to rebuke you," said Edith. "Oh, my darling. I do not want to *keep* you from all that makes you wild and free. I feel so dull, so unworthy of your affections."

"You are worthy," said Poppy, her hands rising to make trails through Edith's curls. The sensation sent ribbons of shivers down Edith's spine. "You are my home."

Poppy breathed heavily, the rise and fall of her smooth shoulders crisp between flashes of light.

"Then I am forgiven?" Edith whispered the words at Poppy's ear, lips just a breath from her neck.

The answer came in a kiss: deep, knowing, and without restraint. Edith's very soul caught fire. Poppy rose, positioning herself on Edith's lap, moaning softly in between kisses, teasingly biting at her lips, her hands roaming one moment, and pulling at her clothes the next. Without hesitation, Edith tore off her gloves with her teeth, breaking their affections for the briefest of moments, and then ran her hands along Poppy's delicate stockings and up to her soft, supple thighs.

Stars and the speckled firmament, Poppy's skin was soft as velveteen, hot and yielding as Edith explored. The gentlewitch burned for this woman, this impossible creature. It was maddening, muddling. Her brain was blank save for the joy of exploring Poppy's body.

But—brimstone!—there was not enough time, nor space for her to give release to it. Edith was emboldened by Poppy's enthusiasm, her hitching breath: she had found her way under Edith's own waistcoat, fingers exploring with reckless abandon. Fumbling up over the gap in her drawers, Edith was nearly undone at the sound her lover made—a hungry, impatient moan.

"I have dreamed of loving you to ecstasy," Edith said, planting a searing kiss on Poppy's breast, feeling the flutter, the wave of passion at her very core, as she tasted her salty, smooth skin. "Dreamed as those thoughts shook me in my bed."

Poppy gave a throaty laugh. "And I have dreamed of mapping each and every freckle upon your skin, watching your body move as I mark my progress with kisses."

"You would turn my body into a journey," Edith replied, her fingers pressing against Poppy's belly, skin to skin. Their mingled scents rose, sharp with the flush of passion, and Edith's heart pounded with the anticipation of seeing her beloved blossom before her, watching as Poppy arched her back to give encouragement and access.

Close, so close. Poppy's breath shuddered in anticipation and Edith pressed her free hand against her lover's breast, delighting in the sudden vision of her nipple free from her gown and stays. She was so perfectly formed, her body soft and responsive to Edith's every touch. She would die if she could not bury her tongue between Poppy's thighs soon enough.

"Yes, Edith, please," Poppy moaned, her hands making more dizzying circles in Edith's hair.

She wanted privacy, and the coachman was so close to them. The sounds Poppy made, by God.

"I am going to give us a moment of privacy," said the gentlewitch, and closed her eyes, drawing on that well of power she now knew well, to begin weaving a liminal pocket around the coach.

The magic was subtle, but potent—silver sparks flew from Edith's fingers, vanishing as they reached the edges of the carriage. With Poppy in her arms, the spell was easy, the magic flowering and expanding—

Then the coach jolted hard, as if hit by a giant tree branch, and they were jostled apart.

Poppy said: "Oh—oh, no." Her voice was distant, confused.

Gathering herself from the tangle she had landed in on the floor of the carriage, Edith saw, with mounting horror, that Poppy had gone slack, her head leaning against the damask coach wall.

"Persephone? Did I—?"

Only through a lightning flash did Edith understand. Blood coursed from Poppy's nose, staining the front of her lavender gown; she had fallen unconscious. As she breathed out, green wisps of arcane power sparkled to life around them.

Panicking, and acting on instinct, Edith pressed her hands to Poppy's temples and tried to drop into her consciousness.

It was a murky, head-splitting descent without the belladonna, dark and meandering. What progress she made came abruptly to a stop as she was cast aside and out of Poppy's mind with a blinding green light.

A voice, strange but familiar, echoed in Edith's head: the Boagane.

Ah, gentlewitch. Thank you for showing me the way to my prize. Find your way to me, if you can, and we shall bargain for her life.

The Boagane.

Then, with a rattling in her mind, the connection between Edith and the Boagane shuttered. Desperately, Edith tried to reach out again, kissing Poppy, caressing her brow, trying to make any connection to her, but her magic only floundered.

No, no! This could not be. Not now.

Useless. She was useless!

Edith's sob began as a whimper but transformed into a scream of rage, and she hammered on the side of the coach, startling the footman. "Get us to the Holly and Sickle, as fast as you're capable!" she shouted.

As they came into view of the village, Edith could no longer see Netherford Hall where it should have been, looming in the distance. Her ancestral home was completely wreathed in an eldritch mist so thick it looked like walls of shimmering ice.

It was the modiste, Miss Rawlings-Vijay, who met her at the door to the carriage at the Holly and Sickle. She wore the most elaborate overcoat she had ever seen, its brilliance still discernible in the pouring rain and cover of night.

"Miss Brightwell needs attention now," Edith commanded. The cold rain cleansed the hot tears from her face, and she was glad of the moment's relief. "Bring Mr. Garcliffe to me immediately."

Miss Rawlings-Vijay froze. "My liege, he went up to the house."

"That *fool* has gone straight to his death," muttered Edith. "Help me with Poppy, quickly."

"My liege, what happened?"

But Edith did not answer her. "Inside."

They cleared a table within, and laid Poppy gently upon it. Miss Rawlings-Vijay, who had been Poppy's friend since childhood, immediately went to get water and clean clothes. Edith was relieved, on some level, to find that only a few others were in attendance there, for between her circumstances with the vampire and her current concerns, she looked a mess.

While they tided Poppy, Miss Rawlings-Vijay explained what had happened: strange creatures, animals that looked as if they were made of glass and mist, had come through a small break in the hawthorn hedge around Netherford Hall. Earlier that night, someone had seen the Rookwood-Nourses skulking around, and since no one knew any better—and almost everyone was otherwise involved—they assumed there was an invitation, or else another reason. At that point it had already been growing dark.

Mr. Garcliffe had arrived with Basil Hode after Molly went missing inside the hall—though it was not clear how they knew where she was—and it had been nearly an hour since they'd heard anything from the rest.

"How many were with Mr. Garcliffe?" Edith asked. She smoothed Poppy's brow, which furrowed now and again but made no indication of wakefulness. She was cold, so cold that her lips were beginning to turn blue.

"He took at least ten with him. And Mr. Brightwell's up there, too. Took his crutches and everything," said Miss Rawlings-Vijay. "I remained here, hoping for help from the London portal. Basil sent a number of messages before he went in."

Edith could not focus her mind, could not shake the voice of Old Gam that had rung in her mind. She was trembling enough that she could barely stand. But she understood what had happened.

Virginia Cawley had warned her.

Edith had woven liminal pockets all evening—and for weeks. Drunk on power, for the first time in her life. Places to hide, to breathe, ensconcing the group after Poppy's assault. And then, when she and Poppy had finally come together in that blaze of passion, together they had been a beacon for Old Gam, already growing fat at Netherford Hall from the other half of Poppy's soul among the timbers and glass. Freed of its prison, the creature had slipped in.

Miss Rawlings-Vijay looked solemnly at Poppy, taking her hand. "What do you think it is? Is it related to what is happening at the house?"

"Yes," said Edith. "Miss Rawlings-Vijay, I know this is a great deal to ask of you, but I will need you to guard me as long as you can while I do this. I think I know how to help our friends, and to help Poppy." She ventured a guess, by the pained look in the modiste's eyes. "To help Auden, too."

The modiste did not hesitate. "Of course. I will do as you command."

The front door burst open in that moment, and who should appear but Captain Evans, fresh from the party. He had not been privy to all the excitement of the evening, but he had a look of resolute fury on his face. A soldier, through and through.

"I tried hammering through that mist," he said, breath coming ragged as he made his way across the floor to them. He was limping harder than usual. "There's no way in. My liege."

"Captain. I'm glad you're here," said Edith. She took Poppy's hand. It was so cold, so stiff. "I need you to protect her while I'm gone."

"*No one* can get through that mist," said Captain Evans, confused. "Surely not even you."

"I'm not going through the mist," said Edith.

Now was the time. Old Gam wanted to feed from Poppy, yes. But a creature such as that—if Edith was correct in her research—loved bargains more. And the soul of a gentlewitch was far richer fare than that of a young country girl, no matter how wild.

ONE MOMENT, POPPY was kissing Edith, desire flooding her every sense, wrapped up in the glow of love and an intense sense of *rightness*, when she tipped forward and kept falling, inexplicably, right through the bottom of the carriage and into a void of starless silver.

Then the world shifted, and Poppy was sitting inside Netherford Hall in the extensive boudoir over the great hall. In her youth, she had only managed the trek a few times, and found it a bit melancholy, what with all the mouldering clothes and tapestries, the eccentric furniture and desiccated bird and rat corpses.

Now, though, the boudoir was revived. The low ceiling was robin's egg blue, the walls papered in toile de Jouy of deepest pink and crimson, the bed linens piled high in dizzying brocades. The light from outside was bright springtime, and as Poppy rose from the plush chair, very like the one she'd sat in just an hour before in the library at Burkley, she spied the long lawn and the border of hawthorn trees. Tulips of deepest purple and flocked red and gold tossed their heads in the breeze, and Poppy felt relief flood her.

Home. Forever home. All she needed to do was crawl up into the bed, pull the covers over her, and fall asleep forever.

Except just as she was about to go to the bed, she felt

a prickling in the back of her neck. An awareness. It was cold, here. Looking down, Poppy noticed she was wearing the same lavender gown from the dance, along with a long shawl of plush yarn with silken tassels. Yet she also saw little ice crystals gathering on her skin.

As if in response to her confusion and doubt, the fireplace roared to life, casting long amber streaks across the violet carpets.

"There you are," said someone from the doorway, an old woman in emerald green and gold, her deep wrinkles indicative of a long life of smiling and laughing, her plump cheeks flushed as if she'd come in from a crisp morning.

And there, as if she'd always been sitting beside her, was Edith. She was dressed in a lemon-yellow ensemble, more of a court style suit than anything that Poppy had seen her in before. It had interlacing crocuses embroidered all around it, and it looked familiar. Had she made it? Of course she had. She had embroidered that whole jacket, and it had taken her weeks and weeks, and Edith had been so enamoured of the final product.

Edith was smiling. Smiling and smiling until her teeth shone with ice. And now Poppy was smiling, too, even though she was very tired and very cold—but it did not matter, because now she and Edith were together at Netherford Hall forever. And she would never again lose her, or it.

HARROW HOUSE MOANED with the cold, and no one stopped Edith's progression through the house and into Poppy's room. It smelled of her, floral and bright, and Edith had to swallow her tears. Leaving Poppy behind at the Holly and Sickle had been the hardest decision of her life.

Edith *was* a middling witch, but she had learned to compensate. And even her carelessness had its advantages.

Sure enough, When Edith opened the wardrobe, there was the nautilus key. She had considered going back to get it, when she'd realised she had left it behind—but then a prickle in the back of her head that was a bit like hope and a bit like a premonition convinced her to wait. Perhaps Poppy would find it; perhaps it would turn up elsewhere.

She pulled out the silver key, weighing it in the palm of her hand, and took a long, calming breath, focusing.

This was mixed magic. Untested. She could not fail this time. Edith would need to open up a liminal pocket, using the key as a catalyst, and direct herself to the Boagane's essence. Nowhere else.

The key slid in, and immediately iced over, as Edith cast her own silver-rippling magic through the door. It smelled of lightning for a moment, and then went dark and quiet.

Hesitantly, sweat beading on her forehead, Edith opened the wardrobe and took a step in. Immediately, she could smell Netherford Hall—the beeswax, the old wood, the books and bracken—along with an alien, musky scent. All was darkness.

Another step, another still, breathing so quietly she nearly felt faint. Finally Edith felt old garments brushing past her, silky and sumptuous, and then pressed her hand against a new set of doors, green light glimmering from the edges.

Ever so carefully, Edith cracked open the doors and peered out into the boudoir of Netherford, but a boudoir revitalised—a frosted green garden.

And there, sitting on an immense ice chair by the fireplace, sat Poppy—her spirit form—with a veil draped over her sloping shoulders, poised as a winter queen. Her blue lips mouthed silent words, and more sheets of ice crept across the floor toward her like grasping fingers.

Beside Poppy sat a strange version of Edith herself, a kind of scarecrow made of clothing, fashioned around a hideous doppelgänger. It did not speak or move, rather leaned sluggishly on the chair it had been positioned into.

Before them loomed a figure so warped by corrupted magic, Edith had to bite down on her tongue and swallow back a scream.

The Boagane was a giant corpse, its skin, hair, and bones rendered in gelatinous clarity. Inside, Edith could see mummified hearts and organs, mismatched and misplaced, trapped like flies in amber. It had two heads, but one lolled to the side, with a frozen tongue protruding from its forehead. The speaking head, uttering a guttural, continuous spell, had six eyes of different colours, all whirling about, peeking beneath strings of blood red hair that covered most of its body.

Six eyes.

Henry's dream.

Edith shivered. He had tried to tell her, and she had dismissed his concerns as the nightmares of a child. And now he was lost here, among this true horror.

The Boagane was busy, its long arms—knotted and elongated beyond anything natural, ending in sharp claws that scraped upon the wood floor—drawing strange runes.

This was magic, old and profane.

But Persephone Brightwell still lived and breathed. The woman who had given Edith her heart, had called her by her own name, had made her a picnic and granted her hope. She had, in some ways, given her Netherford Hall, and with it, hope for a future.

Edith wove her two strengths together, pulling them from the very core of her: the magic of obscuring, and the liminality. Instead of a warm pool, it was a rushing, chilly river. Strewn with rocks.

And it occurred to Edith that she had been sitting on this power her whole life. She had merely been reaching it from the wrong place—she was a witch of a different design, and her abilities did not simply stem from the world of the living. She was a force beyond measure.

If she survived, Edith suspected she and Virginia Cawley had some very interesting conversations ahead of them.

Carefully, throwing aside her musings, Edith opened the door of the wardrobe. Her ears popped with pressure, but a quick glance at her hand showed her that she was, indeed, obscured. But unlike hiding in the living world, where she could see a kind of web over her very clear body, she *was* the web: iridescent, luminous, flexible. She was in the place, but not *of* the place.

Poppy shuddered on her icy throne, puffs of icy breath in the wake of her movement.

Edith didn't want to think about the strain this was causing on her. The scent of death fell heavily upon the room.

The Boagane was a creature of corruption that preyed on desperate people. It had been defeated and drowned time and again by heroic witches, but had powers to slow time and to take life, and loved to bargain. That was what had taken Poppy's soul, what had whispered to Edith in the carriage.

Even Virginia Cawley had thought she had done away with the creature, but had failed. But had she known it was a Boagane? To trap it so would have not killed it, but put into a deep hibernation, only to rise again, stronger. And unsated. Surely, such a mistake as that was unbefitting the High Witch.

Slinking out of the wardrobe, silently as she could, Edith lowered herself to all fours and waited, deathly still. The ground beneath her fingers was slick with glittering ice, but that was not all: clear, fatty slugs moved across the carpets, making a slow progress up the legs of the chairs and furniture, the walls and the tapestries. Like the Boagane, bits of particulate floated inside their bodies, like liver spots.

The trek was getting more difficult, more treacherous by the moment. Still the Boagane chanted, drawing those strange runes.

Edith finally reached the leg of Poppy's chair. The edge of Poppy's dress was within her grasp, and cold sweat broke out on her face as she reached. It would not take much, she did not think, to startle Poppy's spirit back into her body, to release her. Just a little prickle of pain—

How noble, Edith Rookwood. The flame-haired heir.

Fear, sharp and bitter, rang through Edith's body as something heavy pressed on her back. Long, draping red coils of hair brushed against her face, slick with cold, slimy water, leaving frozen droplets in their wake.

Oh, I know you. The petty witch.

Edith shuddered with fury: she was detected. Petty, indeed. Who was she to think her spells could fool a Boagane?

"I'm here for Persephone," said Edith, her hands and spine cramping from the cold and the pressure on her back. "I know who you are, Boagane."

The echoing laughter was even more painful than the insult. Edith had never imagined herself a hero, not until recently at least, but to be so diminished before this terrible creature felt particularly inauspicious end.

Such a clever little witch. Good thing, too. To make up for your many shortcomings.

The Boagane twisted its legs around with a series of sickening cracks, heads twirling on that bisected spine.

Then Edith was staring into its six rheumy eyes, each taking her in: every hair, every freckle, every bead of sweat. The Boagane shrieked at her.

Edith gasped, her own ribs creaking with the weight of the Boagane's magic. Out of the side of her vision she could see Poppy, still talking to the horrific farce that was Edith's double.

The Boagane clicked, low in its throats. *It was clever of the High Witch to keep the house and the child together. I could not see them in her circle, or through the lines of Netherford. Old lines, they are. But you can feel that now, can't you? This is your inheritance, Rookwood witch. Just like your great uncle. You are capable of channelling power, great power.*

Edith groaned as the Boagane pushed her head down onto the frozen carpet. She tasted blood in her mouth. "You don't *know* what I'm capable of," Edith bit out.

Oh, I do. I made the High Witch believe she had banished me from the mortal world—and so she had. Until someone opened the spaces again, the spaces I had shown her: The wardrobes. A lunch on the lawn. A boon for a dying man—a moment of desire in the carriage. You were a beacon to me. And once the child was far enough away from the house, it was like a trail of blood to a starving hound. I have been waiting for you. Though, I must admit, I did not expect such passion from a Rookwood.

"Release Poppy," commanded Edith. "And I offer myself in her stead." She had to fight to force the words out through chattering teeth. It was the last chance she had. "I alone, as gentlewitch, hold the key to Netherford Hall, where your prize and imprisonment lie. Show me what you offer me in return."

So be it, Rookwood witch.

Edith squeezed her eyes shut, trying to erase the vision of corruption before her, trying to reach out to Poppy, before darkness fell: *Persephone. I love you. I am so sorry.*

POPPY SHUDDERED, SHIVERED, and sat up, wiping her eyes with the back of her hands. They were stiff, frigid, almost blue—and she was covered in a sheen of ice. She was sitting in the Holly and Sickle, or rather, on one of the familiar tables.

Her head pounded, a throbbing ache down the right side of her face, as memories returned. She didn't only remember the beautiful, dreamlike spell, but also the six-eyed horror that had stalked her mind, stolen her strength, and dragged its claws down her back.

"Poppy!" It was Captain Evans, blood streaked across his face. "Oh, thank the Lord you're alive."

Miss Rawlings-Vijay was there, too, trembling like a leaf, tears coursing down her cheeks. "She found you," said the modiste, putting an arm gently around Poppy and squeezing her tight. "She really found you."

"I'm here, I'm here," Poppy said, dizzy with the effort of sitting up, and with the attention. "My head. Oh! Where is the gentlewitch now?"

Everyone fell silent.

Persephone. I love you. I am so sorry.

The only thing that monster would have wanted more than Poppy's half-soul was all the soul of a gentlewitch from the High Coven. She knew it without a doubt. And damn her, but Edith would have given it.

Grief washed over Poppy, and she let herself cry a moment, allowed the anger and fury and love to course through her, as she sobbed into her hands while her friends comforted her.

"We were to guard you, and the portal, while she went in," said Captain Evans, as Poppy dried her eyes with his handkerchief. "She went to Harrow House and did not return."

Poppy knew how, of course. She had long expected the wardrobe in her own room was a Janus garderobe. Had suspected Edith had used it at least once. It would have explained how she had broken through the dream, that dark dream, and cast her back into the light again.

"She saved me," said Poppy, drying the last of her tears. "And now I must do the same." She turned to Captain Evans. "Captain, Miss Rawlings-Vijay, I'm going to need you to stay here, to keep guard."

Captain Evans nodded and bowed at the waist. "I will protect the portal with my life, Poppy—and you, if I must. I have never promised any less."

"Love compels us," said Miss Rawlings-Vijay. "Find Mr. Garcliffe for me if you can."

"Of course," said Poppy, with growing unease.

It didn't take long to equip herself: a pair of knives, a few sachets of hawthorn berries, a heavy cloak, a belt and a pair of pantaloons. Poppy armed herself like a mismatched Valkyrie heading to battle.

She was tying back her hair with shaky fingers when the ground beneath them shook and the portal doorway sputtered to life at last. Poppy had never seen one before—they were reserved privately for witches alone—but even she could tell that it wasn't working properly. To an average mortal, it looked like a threshold in a wall with no door. But now, Poppy saw that the bricks held glyphs. Most of them now glimmered pale blue and yellow, guttering to life without any rhyme or reason.

For a brief moment, Poppy was afraid a monster was coming through the doorway, a strange conglomeration of brick and wood.

But worry evaporated to hope, and the figure who emerged was one recognisable all throughout the British Empire: Virginia Cawley, the High Witch herself, stepped into the Holly and Sickle, brushing dust from her impeccable white dress and waistcoat. Her whole person was ghostly white, all but her vibrant green eyes. She was built like a heron, all angles, accentuated by the wide lapel she wore and the long, white pins in her hair.

"Poppy Brightwell, I presume?" said Virginia Cawley, looking Poppy up and down with what might have been mild approval. "It's been some time since I saw you last."

"High Mistress," said Poppy, making as close to a curtsey as she could manage, given her current sartorial situation. Miss Rawlings-Vijay followed suit and Captain Evans bowed, blinking in wonder.

Virginia Cawley looked nothing like her sister, the Dowager Countess St. Albans, but perhaps that was her magic. They looked fifty years apart in age, but Virginia was the eldest. She had, by all accounts, inherited all the magical acumen in the family. Her capabilities were greater than any witch of the age. And her legend known far and wide.

"The Boagane has awakened," said Virginia, going to the window to look up the hill at Netherford Hall. It was still wreathed in mist, though it had started to thin. "And we don't have much time for explanations."

"Can you break through the mist?" Captain Evans' voice was firm and true. "I have tried everything within my power, but to no avail."

Virginia nodded, giving Captain Evans a kind smile. "I can. For a time. But the rest will be up to you, Poppy."

"To *me*?" Poppy had to have misheard it. "What on earth can I do that you cannot?"

"You *are* Netherford Hall, my dear," said Virginia Cawley. The High Witch came up to Poppy directly, and they were of a height. Virginia put her hands on Poppy's face: "You are a marvel. You are nothing that this world has ever seen. And there is power in that. And hope. For you. For me. And for Edith."

NETHERFORD WAS BLANKETED in a wasteland of ice, cleaving through unattended livestock and snapping boughs and branches. The hexafoil broke in two. The fountain was frozen, all the windows glazed, cartwheels affixed to the ground. The whole village was motionless, as if it was holding its breath.

"Only I could take the portal, broken as it is. Your gentlewitch and I are the only liminal witches I know of who would know how to use it—and even then, I would have to teach her," said the High Witch to Poppy, as they climbed toward Netherford Hall. "Netherford is surrounded in a kind of bell jar of time. And weather, clearly." She turned her glittering eyes to Poppy.

The High Witch had called Edith *her* gentlewitch.

"I suppose Netherford always has been, in some ways, in its own time and place, High Mistress," said Poppy, giving the High Witch a sad smile. "But it began to wake up the moment the gentlewitch returned."

This prompted a knowing nod from the High Witch as they continued forward. The trek was slippery, and the remnants of other adventurers were visible. Poppy wondered if the irregular footprints were Papa's. What on earth had convinced him to go up to the house in the first place? She did not want to know.

When they came to the shimmering wall of mist, the High Witch stopped, pressing a hand to her forehead, frowning. She flicked her long fingers, and sparks of blue light kindled in response, but then faded quickly. The air smelled of burnt pinecones.

"The Boagane is siphoning Edith's powers to fortify the walls. I had no idea she was so capable, and that is to my shame and detriment. And her peril." Blood dripped from the High Witch's nose, stark against that porcelain skin, expanding into starbursts upon her coat.

"I learned never to underestimate the gentlewitch quite early on," Poppy said, pulling a kerchief from her pocket and handing it to the High Witch, who gave her a wan smile. "She may be fighting it yet."

"The lure of the Boagane is strong, Poppy. But I hope you are right. Give me some space, I must concentrate," said Virginia Cawley, and Poppy did so. "I will get you in, and protect you from outside as I can."

The High Witch pulled out her famed staff, which she called Koivu, pale as old bones, and leaned heavy upon it. Her breath gathered in swirling clouds and mingled and vanished among the great wall of glittering mist. Poppy could barely make out the top of the house, just barely glimpsing the flickering lights within.

Virginia threw out her hand, muttering low words in an unfamiliar tongue, and cast a cascading blue ray of light onto the ground around them. The light thrummed, as if with its own heartbeat, and rose to encompass both of them. A quick look at the High Witch, and Poppy noticed she was sweating profusely.

"My lady witch?" Poppy asked, but received no reply.

Slowly at first, the blue light—now almost a kind of liquid—spread toward the mist wall, seeping into the minute spaces and expanding. Cracks began appearing in the mist wall, just a few at first—they looked like spiderwebs, they were so fine. But slowly, with Virginia Cawley's continued incantations, a space opened onto the lawn.

As soon as the space was big enough, Poppy felt herself being pulled bodily through it, without warning. Virginia Cawley could surely never have managed it with her hands—Poppy was not insubstantial—but the magic flung her forward as if she were made of straw and cork.

Poppy spun, head over heels, and came to a stop a little way up the slope. Her head almost hit the low hedge, but she was saved by her reflexes for once. Glancing over her shoulder, she had just enough time to see the gaping hole in the wall collapse and vanish, the blue light giving way to the same uniform grey mist as before.

"Well, here we are," she said to herself, climbing to her feet and gazing up at Netherford Hall. "Thank you for waiting for me."

Poppy decided to go around the house rather than take the front. The gravel driveway was iced over, smooth as glass, and there were bloodstains on the threshold. None of that made her feel right. Besides, the back entrance was closer to the boudoir, where she suspected she might find Edith.

Her progress was precarious; no matter her sturdy shoes, keeping upright was a constant struggle. She crunched through frozen flowers, clambered over fallen boughs, and picked her way as carefully as possible. Her thoughts went again and again to Edith, to her father, to the Hodes and Auden. They were counting on her, even if they didn't know it; even if, perhaps, they would never believe it.

Poppy had just reached the servants' entrance when she felt a strange breeze on her face, like old roses and too-sweet honey.

Looking up, she noticed two shapes descending upon her. With very little skill, she fumbled for her knife, but not before hearing a familiar, chilling voice:

"Hello, my darling. I really must apologise for earlier—I do hope you'll take our assistance tonight as recompense."

It was Laertes Byrne, and his sister, Ophelia, floating gently down from the sky. Their eyes glowed amber in their smooth faces, their teeth elongated in preparation for battle, silver claws extending from the tips of their fingers. They were terrible and beautiful. And *winged*, like profane angels.

"Mr. Byrne," said Poppy, backing up as carefully as she could. "You look—better." That was most certainly not the best word for it, but it would have to do.

"We found a host for Laertes, and he is as good as new. Better than new," said Ophelia. Her voice was lower, huskier, as she moved in the eerie light. "We are here to fight with you."

"How did you breach the wall?" Poppy asked, still keeping a good distance between herself and Laertes. She would not soon forget his behaviour in the library at Burkley, but if he was willing to help her find her father and save Edith, she would consider a moment's truce.

Ophelia gave a sardonic laugh. "We're undead, darling. That wretch within can't see us, can't feel us—it only hungers for the living."

"An appetite, I can assure you, we are most familiar with," Laertes finished.

"That does not mean you cannot be harmed," said Poppy.

"Netherford is our home, too," said Ophelia, steel in her voice. "And Edith Rookwood our liege."

Poppy did not want to trust the vampires, but she also felt exhaustion dragging on her every step toward the house. The Boagane may have been feeding off of Edith's power, but she was weakening, too. Going alone would be foolish.

"I got this far with the help of the High Witch," said Poppy, looking back toward where she'd come, and putting away her dagger. "I will not turn down assistance, so long as I am promised safety."

Ophelia sighed. "You have my oath that if my brother falls out of line again, I shall make him regret his name day."

The house shuddered, and Poppy felt it within her—it was calling to her, it was in pain. She shivered, gasping for air, tasting blood in the back of her throat.

"Poppy?" Ophelia went to her, steadying her, looking through her hair up to the house. "I feel it, too."

Poppy spat on the ground, then wiped her mouth. To

their credit, the vampires did not look hungry. "The house is dying," she said.

And she along with it, if they did not make haste.

HERE ARE MY terms.

I would never be a threat to you, Edith Rookwood. This is the beauty of our bargain. Our salvation approaches.

It is in your blood. Persephone, like the Queen of Death and Life, a contrarian figure, must be emptied of a soul. Then, you will have a perfect, willing vessel.

She will never know.

She will never feel it.

I will be sated, and free, and depart for a thousand years.

Never again to come to this island. Never again to come to your coven.

They will all believe you a hero; they will all believe you the greatest witch of an age.

You will never be a middling witch again.

You will burn through Persephone, and she will be your channel and worship you.

THERE WAS NO better guide through Netherford Hall than Poppy Brightwell. The house was in her bones, and her soul was in the house. The vampires would tell her, later, how they struggled to keep up with her as she meandered through the kitchens, around tables and chairs, and past frozen bodies. Poppy moved as if in a dream, hands hovering over beloved objects, lingering near doors that still opened for her without hesitation.

"They're not dead," said Laertes when Poppy came upon the prone form of Hattie just outside of her office, eyes wide in terror. "But they will be soon."

"Stars and rivers of light," muttered Poppy, trying to quiet her beating heart. Her own voice was muffled. "These poor people."

"Witches are notorious for stirring up the meanest spirits," said Ophelia, helping to move Hattie's body out of the way so they could pass without disturbing her. "And it's always the vampires that have to clean things up."

Once they made it through the kitchen and offices, they were met with a new horrific barrier to progress: thick strands of ice webbing, that could have been spun by some eldritch spider twice the size of a horse. They crisscrossed every passable space, and were so cold to the touch they burned.

"I've never wished I was a pyromancer until now," Poppy said.

"Even if we were to burn it," said Ophelia, "we can't be sure it's safe. I can feel heartbeats nearby, perhaps entangled within."

They were at an impasse. Poppy could not project herself through the ice; she could not burn it away; she could not shatter it. She was just a woman with half a soul—except, standing here, in the house, she was more than that.

"I am the house," Poppy said, turning to the vampires.

"On a technicality," said Laertes. "But I don't see how that—"

She was the house!

There was glass all around them, shards of glass in the windows in the offices and in the panes between the pantries. They were all made of fragments of her own self, and imbued with power: power from Virginia's original spells, and power from whatever Poppy herself held. Just like the glass in the powder room. Poppy only needed to concentrate.

So she closed her eyes, and envisioned the glass rising, shaping itself into delicate scissors, just like the kind she used in her embroidery.

At first nothing happened, just a fluttering sensation between Poppy's ears. And then...

"I don't believe it," murmured Ophelia.

Poppy watched as an army of scissors rose around them, sharp and incandescent. Without question, for she had the sense that if she thought about it this connection would falter, she directed the scissors at the edges of the long webs, and they followed her command.

The more the little scissors clipped away, the more Poppy understood about the structure: somehow, they were telling her about the infection before she could even see it. Each thread was made of thousands of cords, fused together for strength—but there were thicker ones twisted within, that once sundered, could no longer hold.

It was exhausting work, but she felt a sense of release when finally, the last of the webs snapped, surrounding a large mass. And within the webs was a familiar form, dear and beautiful to her.

"Papa," she said, going to him. He was so very cold, frost clinging to his cheeks in whorls, and webs in his white hair like a veil; but his eyes found hers, and they were full of relief. His hands were frozen to his crutches. "Shh—I'm here now. I'm here."

"Poppy," Papa's voice was rough, but it was still filled with the warmth he always had for her. "I should have told you. Forgive me."

"I love you, Papa," said Poppy, because she was not yet ready for forgiveness. She kissed his prickly cheek.

"I'm so tired," said Papa.

"Mr. Byrne," Poppy said, rising to her knees, and cradling Papa to her chest. "Do you think you can fly him to safety?"

Laertes nodded. "I believe I can."

"Then you are to rejoin us immediately after," commanded Poppy.

To his credit, Laertes did exactly as he was told, after shooting his sister a concerned look. He took Papa in his arms, who had fallen into a weakened sleep, and carried him toward the back door.

"There are more people here," Ophelia said softly. "And they are in pain."

Poppy knew that. She had felt them, too, through the house. The sensation made her dizzy—the more she thought about the house and her body, and their connection, the harder it was to control. Her vision swam with silvered darkness, sharp-edged blossoms at the periphery of her vision. Was someone following her? No, that was just a shadow.

"Now, now, my girl, none of that," said Ophelia. She was digging her claws into Poppy's wrist, keeping her in the present. "You cannot rest now. Not yet. I will make you a big fire and bring you the finest books to read when this is all over."

Ophelia brushed Poppy's hair from her brow, and it helped, somehow.

They continued forward, clearing away more webs, though none as complex as the first. Still, everything was freezing with greenish ice, every step precarious. And when they reached the grand staircase, the top of which divided into Edith's rooms—where Poppy had served as her lady's maid—and the boudoir, their hope dwindled to almost nothing.

What Poppy and Ophelia beheld was beyond comprehension in its grotesquerie. Icy sores grew up through the floorboards, leaking out of the walls, and obscuring the way into the boudoir. Scissors were one thing, but this would require a kind of precision that Poppy could not manage, especially not without training. She couldn't put everyone in further danger by accidentally bringing down the house around her.

And she felt weaker, just looking at the cancerous growths rising up before her. She felt a hot trickle of blood come out of her ear, and she gave Ophelia a panicked look.

"It's just a little blood," said Ophelia, but even her expression was full of dread. "Surely you can think of another way."

Poppy's mind was a gyre, her heart aching. There was no sign of anyone else—not Auden, not the Rookwood-Nourses, not Molly and Basil Hode—and she was running out of time. If only she had a wardrobe, but there was no way to get to one in time.

Poppy felt Laertes landing back on the premises and shuddered. Her senses were opening up. If she tried, she could even feel what was happening below Netherford Hall, could sense the slugs and the ants and the changes in temperature and soil.

"Poppy?"

Viola. Viola was *here*.

In a moment, they thundered through the room, arriving at the base of the grand staircase, pale faces gazing up in horror. Viola was wearing the viscount's embroidered overcoat, which looked comical over her evening gown, but she'd also put on sensible boots, because she was Viola Brightwell, and she always thought ahead.

"Viola!" In a moment the two sisters were embracing.

Viola pulled her sister away, shaking from fear and emotion, her eyes as deadly as the vampires'.

"And don't you dare tell me it's too dangerous," Viola said, kissing her sister on the cheek. "Look at you, Poppy. You're bleeding all over the place, you're shaking like a leaf, and you're surrounded by vampires."

"Excuse yourself," said Laertes. "I just took you here after you threatened to have me thrown in a lake and drowned."

"Viola," Poppy shivered, feeling faint again. She gritted her teeth and pushed against it.

Viola turned up her nose at her sister, unfazed by the horrific scene around them. "I am your big sister. I protect you."

"Heath will argue," said Poppy with a weak laugh. Speaking with Viola kept her grounded, gave her focus. She really had almost lost herself a moment ago.

"He fainted straight off when he saw Papa," said Viola. "Oliver is watching after him with Mama."

All around her, Poppy felt the pressure of the house rising, the weight of it. Had she felt this for most of her life and not known it? Now that the house was sick, infected with the Boagane's cursed magic, was it different? Or had Edith somehow mitigated the pain of the last few months? No, Poppy suspected that she was dying along with the house, that her own soul was fraying at the edges.

"We can't get upstairs safely," said Ophelia, who had spread her black wings and searched ahead while the sisters spoke. "It will take hours to make progress up the stairs, unless perhaps we can climb the side of the house. It's so slick with ice, even my talons cannot pierce it."

"Poppy, you look like you are about to faint," said Viola.

"I'm fine, Viola," said Poppy, even though it was a catastrophic lie. She felt like falling down on her hands and knees and going to sleep forever. Every step was harder than the one before.

"Did you hear Ophelia? We're stuck," said Viola.

"No," said Poppy. She reached down into her pocket, the clever little embroidered one she had sewn herself, and produced the key Edith Rookwood had given her: the silver octopus. She held it up in a trembling hand. "I just need a door."

There was a big, barred door just beneath the stairs, which led to a closet. The Byrnes dispatched with the rubble as the house rumbled again all around them. Poppy leaned heavily into Viola, listening to her breathing as if it would help her remember to keep up.

Just getting to the door felt like an eternity. If she could just get into it, she knew she could—what? Storm through? Fight the monster? She could do no such thing. She was falling apart. If she coughed again, she knew there would be blood aplenty. Her body was failing her, just as the house was failing.

Poppy felt strong arms around her as she fumbled with the lock in the door.

Her sister was arguing with Ophelia Byrne, heated and angry. Their voices were distant, and Poppy was drunk with exhaustion. Her legs felt as if they were made of sand, her heart pounding in punctuation with every step. Too slow. Too slow. No time. No time.

"We have no chance without assistance," snapped Viola. "I can help protect her, too."

"But if we don't get to you in time—if you are injured, or killed…" said Laertes. For the first time since meeting the vampire, Poppy heard a note of regret in his voice, of real hesitation.

"It is worth the risk," said Viola. "We will all perish if we do nothing."

Poppy had forgotten how to turn a key. She could see the lock, the octopus arms protruding almost comically, but she did not have the strength to turn it. The beams of the house moaned, and she cried along with it, numbing, ancient pain swirling in her stomach, down her legs.

Edith, I'm so tired. I'm sorry.

Then Poppy felt wetness on her lips, cool and sweet, and without thinking, she drank of it.

* * *

THE BOAGANE HAD taken up residence in the centre of the boudoir, its arms multiplied like a ghastly candelabra, and on each end hung one of its prized delicacies: witches, Warders, a majordomo. But Henry was conspicuously unaccounted for.

And in the middle of them all, Edith Rookwood, gentlewitch of Netherford, lost in temptation.

She saw herself a queen, powerful and feared, revered above others, with Poppy at her feet—indeed, power unimaginable. And she saw all the horror of the Boagane pushed to the edges of time, far past where she would live, or know, or care.

The Boagane had limitations. It could not undo the High Witch's magic; it could not take the other half of Poppy's soul. But Edith could.

And Poppy would never know.

And revealing that was the Boagane's greatest mistake.

Edith began to lose time again, until she felt a stirring in her soul, like her name whispered across a vast distance, shaking loose the visions. The Boagane did not seem to notice, though. It was too intent on preparing to skin Molly Hode alive, turning her over in its sharp talons, muttering to itself while she screamed soundlessly into the dark.

A rattling sound. Then a shout. Edith felt a surge of awareness, a connection, and she knew that Poppy was near. Real, *physical* Poppy. But she was changed, and she was not alone.

The wardrobe, the very same Edith had used to enter this place, burst open, hinges flying in every direction, as four figures emerged—and four sets of fangs, four sets of batlike wings, and eight taloned hands. Laertes and Ophelia, she knew, but the others—

Stars, no. No.

The Brightwell girls were fearsome and beautiful, their dark eyes aflame in the half-amber of those who have recently drunk of vampire blood. There would be time to undo it—there was no way they were fully transformed so swiftly—but it was the first step toward undeath. They would have had to be truly desperate to make such a choice.

Then, in a clarion cry, twin mists of purple light and shadow emanating from her, Poppy Brightwell came to the fore, shouting: "Hear me, Boagane. You trespass in my home, in my soul, and you malign and threaten the woman I love. Mark me, for I am your undoing."

The Boagane dropped Molly, who hit the ground and moaned.

You see, Edith. All is as I expected. She comes ready and willing.

"Now!" Poppy shouted.

"No!" Edith cried. "Poppy, stay back. Leave me!"

The two vampires at Poppy's side flew forward, carrying lengths of web between them. They were remarkable at flying, even in such close quarters, dropping the icy strands into the Boagane's face with precision. It clawed at the webbing, but Poppy had embedded some kind of glasswork in it, so the trap endured in spite of its fretting.

Poppy moved forward next, and held out her hands—magnificent woman!—and lifted the thick frosty carpets up and over the Boagane with her command, pulling them out from underneath so that the malevolent creature lost its footing. Viola, with the fierce strength gifted her by the vampires' blood, went to detangle the nearest witch, Petronilla Rookwood-Nourse, whose eyes blazed with fear and fury.

But then the Boagane had Poppy, claws around her waist, as easily as a child clutching a corn cob doll.

They will fight, but they will fail. And if they win, you will languish in mediocrity, Edith Rookwood.

Edith froze, a tingle of temptation worming its way into her consciousness. The Boagane had her in its thrall once more, showing her a vision of a future she could have: Poppy as her wife; Netherford Hall restored to gleaming perfection; a high seat on the Coven Council; unfathomable power.

Power to move time—to fold the fabric of the world. Edith could be the witch she had always wished to be, the inheritor of the family name, the pride of London. The greatest power on Earth. She need only ask, and open herself fully to the Boagane.

They would be one, eternal force.

Edith wanted it; by the rivers of the dead, she wanted it all.

She will never know. No one here will ever know. I will fade away—and you will never feel this helpless again. Give me her soul.

The Boagane squeezed Poppy, and the scream that came from her was Edith's name, and it was too much—her undoing, her doom.

"I will—" Edith began.

Then fire erupted from the corner of the room, a lance of bright red flame, and Edith staggered back to reality, the spell shattering. The Boagane reared back, dropping Poppy, who scrambled out of the way, blood coursing down her face.

Edith turned her head, clarity coming with the fire: it was Henry. He had been hiding in a cupboard the whole time, waiting.

"Cousin Edith, no!" His little voice cracked and sobbed. "You cannot do this!"

He had heard the Boagane's voice, too.

Auden had been freed, and after vomiting the contents of his stomach all over the floor—just missing the washbasin— he staggered toward Henry. "My boy! My beautiful boy!" he shouted. "Be careful!"

Henry was a pyromancer. A rare, dangerous sort of magician. The fire at Hatchney... Edith swallowed back her grief, her guilt.

Wild magefire rippled across the Boagane's skin, and it shrieked, freeing itself of the carpet, only to be stabbed in one of its eyes by Molly Hode's thrown dagger, then impaled by a floorboard courtesy of Poppy Brightwell. Giles Rookwood-Nourse stood guard over his mother's prostrate form—she had been badly poisoned—and looked on in shock as Henry continued his assault. He commanded flames with a child's wildness, but it was pushing the Boagane back and keeping Edith from its lures.

They were doing this for *her*, Edith realised. They loved her, inasmuch as they could. Even the Rookwood-Nourses. She had lost her family, but she had also gained one. Laertes and Ophelia flew arcs above the Boagane, scratching at its eyes and cursing, casting down spells that patterned its skin with runes and symbols unfamiliar even to Edith.

As if he could hear her thoughts, Henry shouted: "We're here because we believe in you, Edith. We love you!"

Still, the Boagane held Edith.

If you do not give me her soul, I will take yours, weak as it is.

The Boagane shrieked again, floundering, its agony rippling through Edith's mind, flames coursing down her own arm. But Poppy would have none of it: she pulled furniture from the walls, pelting the beast with a washbasin, impaling it with the four-poster bed. Her rage was fuelled by the vampire blood in her body, and the whole house reverberated; and not just the house, but the land itself.

Viola, unsteady on her wings, tried to attack from where Henry was still throwing magefire lances of fire toward the Boagane, when she miscalculated. One of the long arms of the Boagane came down upon her, and the older Brightwell girl went flying across the room. The sound of her neck snapping ricocheted across the room.

No mortal could survive such a blow.

Poppy made a guttural cry that blew out every window in the house and cracked the great fireplace. She was mad, in a blood-rage, a pillar of fury and incandescent grief. She would pull down the whole house onto the beast if she could. It didn't matter what the Rookwood-Nourses did; it didn't matter if the sky itself opened up, or that the room was catching fire now.

You see how fragile they are? You tie yourself to them in the face of untold power? Fool.

"I see them in ways you will never understand," Edith said to the Boagane. And then she ripped a hole in time through the creature's arm, tearing it to pieces, freeing her from its grasp at last.

Its voice went dead in her mind, and Edith was free of the Boagane's temptation as she fell to the frozen carpet, knees knocking together, jaw clicking, breathless. Her bones felt like glass, her heart a core of ash, but she was alive. Thanks to Henry. To Poppy. To everyone here.

"Keep making the wards!" Edith shouted at Molly and Basil. "Keep it back!"

Together, they pressed forward. Edith used her own knowledge of the room, and of space itself, to help direct the fire away from Petronilla Rookwood-Nourse, who had now come to Henry's side, instructing him. She was a damned powerful pyromancer, Edith thought, far more than she ever would have guessed. Her flames were not the bright orange she had seen in other witches, but a deep gold, contrasting with Henry's crimson.

And together, they amplified the flames. Never in her life had Edith worked alongside another witch, let alone a witch and an untested child. Her mother and aunt had dismissed her powers as too minimal for the effort and not worth the risk. But here, Edith could direct the flame by moving it through pockets of space, just as she could move her mind. They were unstoppable.

The Boagane did not know what to do amidst such power and pain. The wards held it down, Poppy continued her assault, and the magic fire burned away the ice, shrivelling its skin and blinding it, smothering it. Henry's fire was unquenchable.

But even when the Boagane was naught but ash, Poppy would not cease her destruction. Between the vampire blood and losing Viola, she was broken and mad, eyes hollow and unseeing. If left to her own devices, she would not just destroy Netherford Hall, but herself as well. Edith had already lost enough. They all had.

When at last Virginia Cawley, the High Witch, entered through the wardrobe behind Edith, she did not add to the destruction and devastation. Instead, understanding what she was seeing, she went to Poppy Brightwell and placed her hands upon her brow, and put her into a deep, enchanted sleep.

CHAPTER SIXTEEN
CHARMS OVERTHROWN

WITHIN HOURS OF the destruction of the Boagane, the ice melted away and the cancerous growths throughout the halls at Netherford Hall evaporated. The walls knitted themselves together, the ripped carpets mended, the glass healed and twinkled again, and the great beams shone anew in the hall.

The withdrawing room had never looked so resplendent, the ballroom never so pristine; and the boudoir had been transformed into a bower for Poppy, grown with crocuses and daffodils, striated tulips, and hyacinths.

"She is like nothing we have ever seen before," said the High Witch as she prepared to depart for London again, promising to write and bring what they had learned to the High Coven. "She will need you—and you her."

"High Mistress," Edith had tried to say. "About the Boagane—"

"There will be time," said the High Witch, and there was a weariness in her voice Edith knew meant to leave well enough alone. "But not today. Come to London in the summer, and we will speak. Of you. Of Henry. And of monsters."

The Coven Council would be calling both Poppy and Edith to court, of course, to testify. There must be an official inquest, given the situation. But they required time to heal, first.

The Boagane was truly gone, and the High Witch made certain of it.

But Viola Brightwell had died, and Poppy Brightwell slept on.

IT WAS ON a spring day, the sky streaked with long, white tufts of clouds, and the green lawn smooth and waving in the breeze, that Poppy Brightwell finally opened her eyes. Edith was reading one of Poppy's favourite novels, where the heroine finds herself the inheritor of an old country mansion and at the mercy of its ghosts, when at last she spoke.

"Edith, I've had the strangest dreams."

"Shh, now," said Edith, sitting down gently on the bed beside Poppy. "You're safe now."

"Your face," said Poppy.

Edith reached a hand to her cheek. The magefire had burned her, temple to chin, as Henry and Petronilla fought to save her from the Boagane's clutches. No healing could conceal the scar: The white streak vanished into her hairline, leaving wisps of silver in its wake.

"I'm told I look a bit roguish," said Edith.

Poppy looked fresh and vibrant, her hair in shining curls, her lips a deep flushed pink. Her vitality drew the notice of the High Witch, and it couldn't simply be accounted for by the vampire blood, though that was well out of her system now. The running theory was that Poppy and the house could both feed off of the same sources of power witches did, the ley lines deep within the earth left behind by the fae. Edith had suspected it was not so much Poppy's body that would be in need of healing these long weeks, but her mind.

Poppy blinked in the bright sunlight, shading her eyes a moment as she took in her surroundings. "Why am I in a bed of flowers?"

"You'll have to ask the house," Edith replied, brushing petals from beside Poppy's face. "It grew up around you, after…"

Watching the realisation sink into Poppy's features was like a knife to her chest, living that brutal moment again, as she had so many days over the last weeks. And her guilt, too, at what she had almost done.

"Viola." Poppy whispered her sister's name. She stretched a hand toward the wall where it had happened, but the room was now so unlike the scene a few days ago that it seemed impossible.

"Persephone—"

Poppy turned to look at Edith, dark eyes piercing. "What happened? I barely remember anything after I saw Viola and—" She swallowed, breathing faster.

"Your father is on the mend, and your mother is taking care of him," said Edith, as gently as she could. "The Rookwood-Nourses were not up to anything nefarious— they came to the house to protect it when the wards went down. And they knew something evil was afoot, but I did not listen; I took their warnings as a personal attack, and I was a fool."

She didn't know how to deliver the news about Viola.

Poppy gasped. "I remember now. And Henry. Oh, Edith." So Poppy had seen, after all, even through her rampage. "He saved us in the end, didn't he? Perhaps he was the dragon all along."

"Petronilla will be coming to Netherford Hall in a few weeks, to help instruct him," said Edith. "He will need to be closely monitored."

Poppy did not say the words, but Edith knew what she was thinking: would they be safe with Henry? She had not had the heart to ask him about Hatchney, and Auden would hear no talk of it. For now, they would be careful.

"I can feel everyone in the house," said Poppy, pressing a hand to her forehead. "What am I now?"

"The High Witch said that the house is not just strong because of you—it's strong because of both of us," said Edith. This had been the greatest revelation of them all, the one that had given Edith the hope to continue in the aftermath, a way out of her own darkness when all had seemed lost. "My magic is magic of space, and of time. Combined with your soul, in this ancient place, it has fed you, somehow, and connected us."

Poppy gave Edith a measuring glance. "Perhaps that's why I fell so desperately in love with you."

"Persephone, I do not deserve that. Especially now."

"You foolish witch."

"I almost—"

"Whatever you *almost*, you didn't." The look in Poppy's eyes was both ancient and arresting. "You are here now."

How many times would Edith need to beg Poppy's forgiveness? How many secrets would she carry with her—*from* her?

Edith summoned up a smile for her love, though her heart ached to do so. "I do not deserve you, Persephone Brightwell."

"Well, you have me. Unless you decided to settle down with one of the Greenstreet girls for a tidy sum and an overflowing bosom," said Poppy. She tilted her head at Edith like a quizzical bird.

Edith could at least share that good news. "As it stands, I am no longer in need of a wife."

"Is that so?"

"I needed a wife to secure the house, to stake my claim and prevent the Rite of Place, which inevitably I would lose." The bitter truth made her stomach lurch. "But the house is ours already."

"Is it?"

"Yes. By blood, soul, and power. And once the Rookwood-Nourses understood you were quite literally intertwined with the house itself, they could make no claim. You, therefore, are—and this is certified by none other than the High Witch herself, Virginia Cawley—my co-inheritor. Half your soul is the house, after all."

"I'm what?"

"You are legally, spiritually bound to this house, the land, and the magic. And so am I."

"And Harrow House?"

"Yes, and Harrow House."

"Oh, Edith—I didn't know. I swear on the stars, I had no idea."

"The Rookwood-Nourses will be relocating to London, where I have granted them the land on which Hatchney was built. They will create a new home for the London Rookwoods. For now, we are at a comfortable peace," explained Edith. "Of course, we have Lord St. Albans to thank for some of this, as it was his puzzling that put us to rights about the matter." Edith took a long breath, knowing she could delay no longer: "About Viola—"

"Did I miss the funeral?" Poppy's voice was flat, her gaze gone distant again. Part of Poppy was still broken, still mangled in grief. And would be for a long time.

It was easy to forget just how little Poppy still knew of the arcane. "Persephone, darling. Viola died with vampire blood in her veins."

"I don't see what that has to do with her funeral. Tell me they didn't refuse her at the vicarage—oh, I never could stand the vicar!" said Poppy, getting more agitated by the minute.

"No, nothing like that," said Edith, brushing aside the curl that had plastered itself to Poppy's forehead. "It was

Ophelia who did the deed, in the end, and it is not the best outcome, but, given the circumstances, the best we could do."

Poppy searched Edith's eyes. It was not hope there, exactly, but a kind of steely relief. "They turned her."

"They did," said Edith, expelling a long breath. She had not known how to say it.

"Oh, by the speckled firmament!"

"She is still recuperating. Her injuries were grave. For now, she is staying with Lord St. Albans—he is clearly besotted with her, regardless of the situation—but in time we will be able to see her," said Edith. "But she will be a vampire."

"I don't know how to make sense of this," said Poppy, burying her face in her hands. She did not cry, but she trembled. "I miss her so much my bones ache."

"Tell me what I can do to help, my darling," Edith whispered against Poppy's hair, as close as she would dare. "Tell me how I can take some of this burden."

Leaning in, Edith went to embrace Poppy, but she was deterred. "I need time. Let me to my flowers." Her beautiful face crumpled and she could say no more.

"Come find me when you are ready. I will be waiting."

"I know."

As Edith Rookwood shut the door to the boudoir behind her, she watched the curve of her lover's cheek turn away toward the grand windows, those refracted beehive glass panes overlooking the gardens, and knew she would never be worthy of Poppy Brightwell. But she would try. And when, and if, she let her in again, Edith would be there.

THAT NIGHT, BENEATH the covers of a simple bed in a simple loft, Auden Garcliffe rested his head on his lover's chest. That simple rising and falling, the warmth at his cheek, filled a place inside his heart he had thought lost for good when he'd seen the face of the Boagane.

Once released, he'd gone straight to the Holly and Sickle and kissed Jamini Rawlings-Vijay until she could barely breathe. They had stood there, hands roaming and tears in their eyes, in the company of half of Netherford.

"I never have nightmares when I sleep beside you," said Auden, staring up at the crackling ceiling. "And now that the Boagane is dead, I think the nightmares are gone for good. For Henry, too."

"My mother always told me I should heed my dreams. To think, if you had spent more time with me, instead of flirting awkwardly, we might have avoided some of this with Mother's good sense," Miss Rawlings-Vijay said.

Auden could not mention the real truth they had learned about Henry, and he dreaded the further conversations they would have, but for now he revelled in the simplicity of new love and the comfort of thick coverlets. The modiste may have had a humble home, but her linens were as fine as any duke's.

"So, it's settled, then," said Jamini, winding her fingers through Auden's hair. "No more pesky relatives."

"Well, the Rookwood-Nourses are a great deal less pesky than I initially surmised," said Auden. "They weren't wrong in predicting that darkness lay waiting for us. They just never expected Poppy Brightwell."

"No one ever does. She's awake now, you say?"

"Indeed. But she'll need time. And her friends," said Auden. "But meanwhile, I do think the gentlewitch will be requiring some new suits. We've been asked to visit the Regent and Queen, you know. All of us. The Hodes, included. Apparently, dispelling that creature has given us something of a reputation."

"I do know of a modiste or two, but he would need to get

more familiar with your measurements," said Jamini. She slid her hand down over Auden's chest, through the silky hairs, and down to his stomach. "And I doubt he has the same eye that I do. He might dress you in a chartreuse tie."

"As tempting as that is, I think I would like to keep you to myself, Miss Rawlings-Vijay. I could take you to London, see the grand sights," said Auden. He leaned up and kissed Jamini thoroughly, revelling in the taste of her, the nearness of her, and how his heart fluttered with every touch of her mouth, every sound she made. Breathless, he pulled away.

"So long as we can come back home and wake up like this all over again," said Jamini.

"I promise you we shall. With all my heart, I promise."

POPPY BRIGHTWELL ROSE from her bed in the boudoir of Netherford Hall and went to the wardrobe where she had emerged to destroy the Boagane and nearly lost her life, and her mind.

She was changed. Poppy felt it in every breath, in every movement of her body. There was grief, most presently, but a new awareness that left her disoriented, dizzy.

Poppy no longer needed to ask where Edith was, or anyone within the house. She knew the gentlewitch had made the master's bedroom hers, just as surely as she knew that her toes were attached to her feet. Sometimes, if she concentrated enough, she could hear the hearts beating of each and every soul within the walls. And she knew Edith's heart above all others.

As they had all fought off that pestilent beast, each of them had wordlessly pledged to protect Netherford Hall, and pledged to protect Edith Rookwood—and so they had become a part of Poppy, as well. Even the vampires.

It was nighttime when Poppy turned the silver octopus

key and entered Edith's room by way of her own boudoir, but she did not need to carry a candle. So long as she was within the confines of the manor, every outline was crisp, and clear, and certain.

The master's suite now gleamed with fresh tapestries and fur coverlets, the immense four-poster bed strewn with thick damask drapes and shiny taffeta pillows in deep purple and gold.

A low fire burned in the hearth, and the desk was a mess of papers, sketches, and diagrams. It seemed that the gentlewitch had taken to furthering her education in their time apart. No surprise there. She had a lot of work ahead of her if she was to become an accomplished liminal witch, and Virginia Cawley had taken a great interest in her studies.

Edith slept, softly snoring. She wore a long nightshirt, but it was undone to the navel, and she was splayed out in the bed as if she'd been tossing and turning. In the firelight, Poppy marvelled at how beautiful the gentlewitch was. Edith's face looked so like a Greek statue—a finer Achilles, perhaps, with flaming copper hair. She was right: the scar was roguish.

Quietly, Poppy unfastened her own yellow silk nightgown, untying each ribbon and unfastening each button, and let it slip to the floor. She had not worn stays for two weeks and she enjoyed the soft currents of cold and warm air moving over her body, unhindered by undergarments. Never had she felt so welcome within the confines of her own form, and it emboldened her.

She needed Edith's closeness. Her body. Her breath. Her absolute presence.

The covers were of finest silk, cool and sumptuous; patterns of bee orchids twirled among hawthorns. Poppy had never slept in a bed like this before—the sheets smelled of lavender, and of Edith—sweet, deep amber, and just a hint of ginger.

Still, Edith slept. And Poppy's gaze traced the lines of her love's dear face, allowing relief into her heart. There was still grief, too. She had not yet seen Viola, and did not know what the shape of her future would be without her.

Poppy banished the uncomfortable thoughts and focused on Edith alone, the strong slope of her collar bones and the proud swell of her chest.

Stirring, Edith's eyes opened, widened. She drew in a breath as Poppy edged closer to her.

"My stars, Persephone," said Edith. "Do I wake, or do I dream?"

Poppy pressed closer to the gentlewitch, feeling the distant warmth of the fire upon her bare skin. "I assure you, my liege, that you are among the living, in Netherford Hall, where you are gentlewitch, and I am yours entirely. If you are amenable."

"Entirely. Oh, Persephone, my love," said Edith, and the words sounded like a prayer, though her eyes were full of sorrow.

"Edith, my heart." There, there was joy again on Edith's face.

"Your eyes are full of wicked mischief."

"Are they?" Poppy asked.

Poppy brushed the back of her fingers against Edith's breast, feeling the rise and response against her knuckles, then cupped the skin around it, lowering her lips to plant a soft kiss on the flesh just below her collarbone. The gentlewitch let out a low gasp of surprise.

"My darling," whispered the gentlewitch. "Are you healed—are you well—are you—?"

Poppy nipped at Edith's nipple, flicking her tongue over it, and let out a throaty giggle. Then she suckled at the bud, gently raking her teeth across after a torturous moment feeling Edith writhe beneath her. She found she quite enjoyed teasing in this way, taking her time. "I woke a short time ago and was reminded of our carriage ride from Burkley House, and could not banish the thought from my mind."

"I recall that ride in vivid detail myself."

"Indeed, my liege," said Poppy. "I recall you nearly fell at my knees."

Edith laughed, a bright, rare thing, and it filled Poppy with hope.

"I have played that moment over in my mind many a night as I waited for you," the gentlewitch said, drawing lines down Poppy's back with her fingers. "Recalling how you moved with me, how your body begged to be touched."

"I do not beg now," said Poppy. She pulled the covers away for a moment, revealing her naked body, dappled in firelight. "Or did you need more proof?"

Edith stared and wiped at her eyes, blinking. "You have no right to be shaped so perfectly. My legs are weak, even in bed."

"You have a lace or two left," said Poppy, and she began untying what was left of Edith's nightshirt. Her body was so strong, so finely made—the pale skin reflected the orange glow of the fire, illuminating the tiny hairs on her like threads of silk. The muscles on her stomach and arms were defined, her hips narrow, and the slope of her sex a perfect rise. Poppy sighed in awe, heart pounding with anticipation of knowing this woman fully. "And you are the most glorious sight I've ever beheld."

Poppy writhed, her softness against Edith's hardness, wanting more closeness, needing it as she had never needed connection before. The gentlewitch grew bolder with each breath, exploring the rise and fall of her lover's body. It was what Poppy had hoped for, and as Edith's hand swept over her waist and around her buttocks, finding the crease where the back of her thighs began, she almost purred. The tickling, tingling sensation of magic sent Poppy's heart fluttering, and the growing warmth of her centre made her shiver with the anticipation of pleasure.

The scent of dark cherries and leather mingled with wildflower honey rose about them, perfuming the air.

"And this is what you want?" the gentlewitch said, looking Poppy in her eyes, piercing her to her sundered soul. Edith drew her finger down between Poppy's thighs, sucking in a breath when she discovered just how prepared her lover was.

"Yes," said Poppy, without hesitation. "Immediately."

Their kiss was no longer the sweet, delicate tease of weeks before, nor the ardent, desperate fumbling in the carriage. No, this was a kiss of hunger, need, and of sadness, too. For Poppy felt a sense of freedom intermingled with her grief, and she knew that this connection—with Edith, who could understand—was what her soul needed. Edith's power, her essence, enveloped them, a comforting blanket of dark, sweet magic.

The gentlewitch moved, lowering her to the bed and sliding her knee between Poppy's legs. Her eyes roamed over Poppy's form, drinking in the fullness of her breasts and the curve of her belly, the dimples at her thighs. Poppy felt no shame, no inhibition; how could she, when Edith looked at her with such passion, such bare desire? Her lips tingled from those bruising kisses, but she needed more.

"It is a far better view than in my coach," Edith said, sweeping her fingers across the delicate skin on the inside of Poppy's thighs, grinning. The gentlewitch's hair had fallen down over her brow, obscuring those beguiling eyes.

"I am inclined to agree," said Poppy, sliding her hands

down the taut muscular ridge of Edith's back, a giggle burbling up as she lost herself in the sensations moving through her. She wanted only to touch more, to envelop herself entirely in their collective passion, to lose sense of where her body ended and Edith's began.

"I do not need to get upon my knees now," said Edith, between deep, hot kisses down between Poppy's breasts and to her stomach. "But I plan on finishing what I began."

Every time the gentlewitch's lips touched Poppy's skin, she felt her whole being respond in kind. Little silver sparks of Edith's magic traced lines across the length of Poppy's legs, smaller reverberations of her desire, ripples of pleasure, circling and amplifying Edith's attentions.

"I had no idea you could do that," breathed Poppy.

Edith laughed huskily. "Neither did I."

And indeed, when Edith pressed her lips to Poppy's sex and tasted of her, her soul shone bright as the moon against the deep velvet darkness of the gentlewitch's magic. Edith was skilled, attentive, and knowing, the glide of her fingers punctuated the pressure of her tongue, their mingled wetness decadent and heady.

"Heavens, Edith," gasped Poppy.

The vibration of Edith's laughter nearly undid her. She paused, lifting her head to gaze at Poppy, cheeks flushed in the light of her magic. "I have dreamed of bringing you pleasure, but somehow this is so much better."

Poppy went to speak, but Edith slid three fingers into her and all thought vanished in the wake of her body filling and stretching. In silence, Edith descended again, and with each greedy stroke, that knowing tongue against her tenderest place, Poppy's world grew, fractured, and built again, the edges of her pleasure expanding beyond the bed, the room, the boudoir—out and down into the great hall, across the flowered lawn, and into the earth itself.

* * *

EDITH ROOKWOOD DID not need to create a pocket liminality when Poppy was in her arms. There were hundreds of worries in the world, some near and some far, but when they lay together at last, skin against skin, hands and tongues and bodies intertwined, time itself stood still. For a brief moment, even her own guilt was kept at bay. She loved this woman, and this woman loved her. And they loved thoroughly and well.

As Poppy breathed softly in the crook of her shoulder, Edith smiled. If there was an end to their passion, she had not discovered it. Poppy need only whisper, glance, trace a finger, and Edith was lost again. She had never known desire, nor satisfaction, of such intensity, or even thought it possible. And her *magic*. Speckled firmament, her magic could even help her along.

Just as Edith was moments away from drifting off to sleep, recalling in vivid detail how the firelight had wreathed Poppy's glorious buttocks, her lover stirred.

"Well, I think I have finally puzzled it out," said Poppy.

"I thought you were asleep," said Edith, running her hand down Poppy's back. "Perhaps I have not worn you out properly."

Poppy giggled against Edith's chest before rising up to her elbows to look her in the face. That look, that devastating look—eyes up through the lashes, brows down. Edith was never so perfectly lost.

"I believe you were the one who said you couldn't feel your legs," Poppy observed. "But you digress. I am being serious."

"Terribly serious," said Edith, swiping her hand down Poppy's cheek, smoothing the skin with her thumb.

"The dress."

"The dress?"

"The one I wore at the Greenstreets' ball."

"Yes, I recall," said Edith, who never could forget the look of Poppy in that crimson muslin gown; no one who had seen her in it could. "You thought I gave it to you."

"And you did."

Edith sighed. "I've already told you I did no such thing. Though, I admit, it is a more romantic story. I had not yet become utterly besotted with you and your honeysuckle lips."

Poppy kissed Edith's chin. "I think we both made it. Through the house. I have been excavating the boudoir, the parts that weren't overgrown with flowers, and I found all the elements needed for that dress. I think, deep down, you wanted me there. And deep down, I wanted to be there. And the house intervened on our behalf."

It was not the strangest theory Poppy had shared, but it was a magic heretofore thought gone. The makers, the petromancers—could they have accidentally resurrected this old magic between the two of them?

Stranger things had happened.

"I think I would like to believe that," said Edith, kissing Poppy on her forehead.

"Do you think it's possible?" Poppy pressed, sinking a little deeper into Edith's body, her hand playfully tracing along toward her navel.

"*You* are impossible, and yet you are here, in my arms, in this bed. So yes. I do think it's possible."

Poppy grinned brightly, then she leaned in for another kiss. "Good. Perhaps we can put my suspicion to the test. I am throwing a garden party next month."

"Are you?"

"Yes. And we shall need matching ensembles."

"I suppose I have no say in the matter."

"You may assist with the guest list. And getting me in and out of my gown. It shall be quite complex, and rather glorious."

Edith pulled Poppy to her, eliciting a little squeal, and then kissing her deeply again. "Stars and the speckled firmament, Poppy. How will I ever deserve you?"

EPILOGUE
THE VISCOUNT AND THE VAMPIRE

HER WORLD WAS ash and blood; a withered, broken simulacrum.

Where she had once felt warmth now only existed an endless cold, a dark corridor of unfeeling that plagued her night and day. The nights were starless, the days blinding in even the wan light of the sun coming from the edges of the windows in this room of torment.

She could tolerate no food, no drink, but the one brought to her by the woman, the beautiful one who was afflicted as she. She had a name, of course, and once she had known it, but now all was dust. And ash. And sorrow. And hunger.

Then there was the fire witch, the one who protected Viola from everyone else. She hated her. And needed her.

The only other visitor was a man, flesh and blood, who braved the room three times a day, a book in his hand and a candle in the other. Chained to the bed as she was, she could do little; so all she did was shriek until he departed, even as he read her stories.

THOUGH HE WAS called Viscount St. Albans, his name was Silas Drake. And after a long and bitter decade of estrangement with his own father, Silas had found himself a viscount, and master of Burkley House in Kent.

If he was rational, he would have left weeks ago. He would have turned the creature in the east wing out into the dark, or over to the care of the Byrnes, who knew far more about such things than he.

But he had been in love with Viola Brightwell as a woman; he could not give up on her as a vampire.

It was Petronilla Rookwood-Nourse of all people, a gentlewitch of recent acquaintance, who struck up a friendship with Silas and aided him in his task. She had lived abroad for decades, but now, returned with her mother and brother to England, her extensive experience with the arcane gave him new eyes into the situation. Though no more hope. Her fire was a protection, but only so far.

They sat together in the grey parlour at Burkley House in the bleak hours of the night after another one of Viola's screaming fits. She had broken free of her chains again, and it had taken its toll on them all, having to resettle her.

"I only wish that Ophelia was more help," Silas said, shivering into the pashmina he'd taken from his great aunt. She had an extensive collection.

Petronilla was a small, birdlike woman, with a crisp American accent and a penchant for flowered bonnets. But she was very clever and had a sturdiness that he appreciated immensely. Plus, she was a pyromancer, and that was one of the few ways to keep errant vampires at bay when they got out of hand.

The gentlewitch leaned forward on her chair, her black taffeta skirts ruffling. "Ophelia is not herself, and nor will she be until Viola has settled. As her maven, she is in a state of heightened protection. You're lucky she's allowing you entrance at all."

"And Laertes?"

"No one has seen him in weeks."

"I don't know what to think," said Silas, rubbing his

hands over his unshaven face—he must look atrocious, but he had not been able to summon the desire to do anything about it. If it hadn't been for Petronilla, he might not have even changed his clothing. "Perhaps I should have let her go to Howarth Castle. It is only that every time I think of it, of leaving her there, I…"

Silas could not finish the sentence. Years of schooling, etiquette classes, published novels, and a budding literary career under a nom de plume, and he could not find words to explain why he could not let Viola Brightwell go. All his love of adventure tales had vanished in the wake of her existence.

"Love defies logic," Petronilla said. She was not the kind of person who radiated empathy and kindness, so hearing such a proclamation was welcome.

"So does your loyalty. You should be in London with your family," Silas pointed out, knowing well she was missing the Season.

"Oh, I have no mind for marriage. I will leave that to Giles for the time being," said Petronilla. "And he and Mother are quite busy preparing the house for our nephew. Which reminds me, the gentlewitch herself was by earlier. She was hoping you might make some plans for your visit to the Queen. She is very keen on the goings-on here at Netherford."

Silas's stomach went cold at the mention of that, as it did every time he thought of leaving Burkley house, Queen or no. "I promise I will speak to her soon."

Fintan, Silas's valet, set a pile of letters next to him. Half were from his editor, no doubt wondering where his latest manuscript was. No one knew that D. B. Mansfield, the famed author of the Sibylle Voltairis novels, was in fact, Silas Drake, Viscount St Albans. And certainly no one but his accountant knew that those very books had brought the family fortune out of absolute ruin. Not even, and most especially, the Dowager Viscountess St Albans.

"My lord, may I speak plainly?" Petronilla asked.

"I insist on it."

Petronilla gave a tight, guarded smile. "You will need to consider your own limitations. You have a manor to run, a household to secure. I do not need to tell you how important it is for you to be seen in London, and how delicate a situation this might be."

"I don't give a fig about my reputation," said Silas, feeling aggravation rising in him again.

"No, but you should give one about Viola's existence—her 'life,' for the lack of a better term. And what will bring her as close to happiness as might be achievable given her circumstances."

He did consider it; every day he did. But until he believed the Viola he had fallen in love with—that gentle, kind soul who had seen him for who he was—was truly gone, he would not relent.

Hope still burned in him, for better or worse.

ACKNOWLEDGEMENTS

THIS BOOK BEGAN with a dream. I know, you're not supposed to start stories with dreams, but I don't like to do things how you're 'supposed to' anyway. Besides, it's the truth.

I digress.

I am a notoriously bad sleeper, and one way I cope with my brain's inability to turn off is to imagine my way through it. Sometimes, this manifests in a near lucid dreaming state. In this case, I saw Edith Rookwood standing by the large diamond-shaped window of a rather beautiful but decidedly dilapidated Tudor mansion. Somehow, I knew she was a witch. She had red hair, and was dressed in traditionally male coded Regency attire, and she was staring at a house with a moss-covered roof and a smoking chimney.

I didn't know Poppy Brightwell and her family lived there, or that the house was called Harrow House. But, quite swiftly, the story took shape and Poppy became everything to Edith. Then came the whole town: Auden, Jamini, Captain Evans, the Byrnes, and the Viscount St. Albans. And, well, Netherford was born.

This was in the midst of the pandemic, and my way of coping was by writing this story. It just spilled out almost offensively fast, defying any attempts at plotting seriously. I could hardly write fast enough to keep up.

It was not necessarily my usual fare: it was silly and joyous and sensual. Most importantly, it was unapologetically queer (okay, that part wasn't surprising). I wanted a world where queerness was just a facet of life, not the subject of bathroom bills, assault, trauma, and murder. In this England, the witches made all the difference.

When I saw an agent looking for haunted house novels, and noticed that her Twitter handle was a Regency-era painting, I took a chance and wrote to Stacey Graham that this book wasn't exactly about a haunted house, but it was something different. I can still remember her email to me after reading it: "I read *Netherford Hall* and I can't stop thinking about it."

Though it took a bit of time, eventually the story found a home with Solaris Nova, and with my amazing editor David Thomas Moore, who also understood the book's silly/sexy/moving dynamic.

This is a story about queer joy. This is a story about finding our way when we feel we were simply shaped wrong. It's also about found family, about inheritance, and who we choose to be. Writing this series—because that is what it has become—has been truly joyous, and I hope you find that reflected in these pages between the dancing and the miscommunication and the magic.

And good news: the story is just beginning. This is not the last you'll see of Edith and Poppy, and as you might imagine the love story between Viola and Silas is a bit more complicated than theirs. Lastly, we will visit a very mismatched couple in *The Game of Hearts*, but I won't spoil that for you just yet. Let's just say there's a very unforgettable werewolf.

I'd first like to acknowledge all the other disaster bisexuals out there. When I was growing up, steeped in Evangelical Christianity, I was taught there were two options: straight (good) and gay (bad). It wasn't until college that I learned there was a word for what I was, and that I hadn't just discovered another way to piss God off. It took me another ten years to come out because, erroneously, I thought marrying a man disqualified me from being part of the queer community. Listen, I had a lot to learn and those were different times.

So this story is for teen Natania, who crushed on girls and boys, and who would have absolutely fallen to pieces if she'd ever read a couple like Edith and Poppy in a book.

Immense thanks to Stacey Graham at 3 Seas Literary, who is as weird as I am (okay, maybe even a little weirder, and I love her for it), who championed this story from the beginning.

To David Thomas Moore, for utterly getting it, and then asking for even more. I can't imagine these books in better hands. For all your added Englishisms, mini history lessons, and thoughtful suggestions, I am most grateful.

To my extended family of queerfolk and friends: this is for you.

As always, thanks to Jennifer for her walks with me through the forest while I grumbled about all the near misses this book had with publishers, and for always being willing to distract me with tea and flowers and friendship.

To everyone who followed #ThreadTalk during the dark days of the pandemic—it was a chintz dress in this book that started the whole thing in the first place, and I will forever be grateful for that community and all it's given me. Like Poppy, this ADHD writer was told for so long that 'nobody cared' about my very niche interests, but that turns out to be far from the truth. Thankfully.

Of course, I must also thank my college roommate Kate Bossert, who first introduced me to Jane Austen via the 1995 BBC miniseries of *Pride and Prejudice* with Jennifer Ehle and Colin Firth, and that forever altered my DNA. I fell hopelessly in love with them both, and will be forever grateful.

I can't go without thanking my brother from another mother, John Hartness, who helped me lean into my queer/silly mode by publishing *These Marvelous Beasts* back in the day. It takes a lot for a publisher to be a real ally, and having that early on made all the difference.

To Tracy P and Lee Daly, who read the first iteration of this book and were so supportive and enthusiastic about it. I'm not sure I'd have managed to keep the momentum going.

To Dino Hicks, always.

Lastly, to my parents, who in 2000 took me to England for the first time, where I fell in love with Kent. This isn't the first time I've written about that marvelous place, but it definitely has the most ridiculous vampires in it.

Natania Barron
June 2024

ABOUT THE AUTHOR

Natania Barron is an award-winning fantasy author long preoccupied with mythology, monsters, and magic. Her often historically-inspired novels are filled with lush description and vibrant characters. Publications include her 2011 debut, *Pilgrim of the Sky*, as well as *These Marvelous Beasts*, a collection of novellas.

In 2020, Barron's *Queen of None* was hailed as "a captivating look at the intriguing figures in King Arthur's golden realm" by *Kirkus*, and won the Manly Wade Wellman award the following year.

Her shorter works have appeared in *Weird Tales*, EscapePod, and various anthologies, RPG, and game settings. In addition, she's also known for #ThreadTalk, which dives deep into the unseen, and often forgotten, world of fashion history.

Barron lives in North Carolina, USA, with her family and two dogs. When she's not writing, you can find her wandering the woods, tending her garden, and collecting rocks.

🐦 @nataniabarron
📷 @nataniabarron
♪ @nataniabooks
🌐 www.nataniabarron.com

FIND US ONLINE!

www.rebellionpublishing.com

/solarisbooks　　　/solarisbks　　　/solarisbooks

SIGN UP TO OUR NEWSLETTER!

rebellionpublishing.com/newsletter

YOUR REVIEWS MATTER!

Enjoy this book? Got something to say?

Leave a review on Amazon, GoodReads or with your
favourite bookseller and let the world know!